To Barbara,

Who with her intuitive
mind may help a mother
and father better understand
the intricacies (mysteries) of
The cottage.

And best wishes for
a super happy 1994. But do yourself
deserve a first edition!

Semper,
Jimmie Ed Bennu

Christmas

Forever

Wishing You a
Very Merry Christmas···
and a Very Blessed
New Year

Rus McAllister

1993 —

Tor anthologies edited by David G. Hartwell

The Dark Descent
Foundations of Fear
Christmas Stars

Christmas Forever

EDITED BY DAVID G. HARTWELL

TOR®

A TOM DOHERTY ASSOCIATES BOOK   NEW YORK

CHRISTMAS FOREVER

A Tor Book
Published by Tom Doherty Associates, Inc.
175 Fifth Avenue
New York, N.Y. 10010

Tor ® is a registered trademark of Tom Doherty Associates, Inc.

Library of Congress Cataloging-in-Publication Data

Christmas forever/edited by David G. Hartwell.
    p.   cm.
    "A Tom Doherty Associates book."
    ISBN 0-312-85576-1
    1. Christmas stories, American.   2. Fantastic fiction, American.
   3. Science fiction, American.   I. Hartwell, David G.
   PS648.C45C446   1993
   813'.08760833—dc20   93-26549
                                            CIP

First edition: November 1993

Printed in the United States of America

0 9 8 7 6 5 4 3 2 1

Once again, to Tom Doherty, a creative publisher,
and to Donald G. Keller and Greg Cox, for editorial assistance.
To Susan Ann Protter, agent of my dreams.
And finally, to Geoff and Kathryn, Christmas Forever.

CONTENTS

Christmas illuminates an alien mystery.

MIDNIGHT CLEAR

Jack McDevitt

The five spires stood silent against the gathering darkness.

Sylvie was stringing lights on the tree. When she was satisfied she stepped back and held out her hands. "What do you think?" she said.

Her father was hanging the greenery they'd brought in from outside. He persisted in calling it that even though it was dead-on yellow, the color of the local chlorophyll agent. He took tradition very seriously. "Let's see how it looks." He brought up the remote and squeezed it.

Nothing happened. "Doesn't seem to want to work."

She held out her hand for the instrument. "We need a new one." She opened it, bypassed the defective circuit, and gave it back to him. "Try again."

The lights blinked on. He lit up too. He was proud of her ability with electronic devices. She knew she was not all that good, but everything was a mystery to him.

She looked past the lights, through a wall-length window at the spires. They were stark and cold, gray-brown from centuries of sunlight and wind, molded like the child's polygons she'd played with years ago. She imagined them as they must have been during their great days, filled with light, towering over the city that now lay beneath the plain.

Carols filled the cottage, and pumpkin pie simmered in the back room.

Her father was watching her. "What's wrong, honey?"

There was a scattering of trees across the plain. Because there were no seasons on Capella III, they never lost their broad flat leaves, never changed color. They too were gold. They made odd Christmas trees, but you made do as best you could.

"It looks so lonely over there."

He followed her gaze to the towers, and frowned. She could see he didn't know what she meant. "Yes," he said. "It is."

Maybe it was only a mood. The calendar they were keeping bore little resemblance to the terrestrial model: it was just a count of numbers of days since the landing, bracketed into weeks. This world had an axial tilt of only a fraction of a degree; consequently, there were, in effect, *no* seasons. No December. And, no matter how long they stayed, there would be no sense of passing years. (They were celebrating the season only because someone had noticed that it was Christmas in London.) Her father and his friends were always discussing how the Capellans might have perceived time. It was a subject Sylvie didn't comprehend, but one that the adults were fond of raking over.

There is only the day-night cycle, her father had explained to her. No seasons. And no moon. *These people would be much less enslaved to time than we are. They would have no birthdays, no summer, never be twenty-one.* Sylvie understood *that.*

She also understood that there could be no Christmas. And he'd laughed, in his delicate way. "You see how lucky you are."

No Christmas. She looked out across the occasional trees and the gradual uphill slant of the plain, and watched the sunlight turn gold on the towers. *All the years since those towers were built. And this is their first Christmas.*

They had been old when the star had shone on Bethlehem.

They had stood here when the people who would become the Romans cheered the solstice, took branches and berries into their huts as reminders that spring was on its way, and celebrated by giving each other gifts.

No one knew what the inhabitants had looked like. They were a long time gone. No records remained, and no images. They must have possessed flight, because the buildings contained no means of moving from one floor to another. No stairways. No shafts. Exterior doors existed on all levels. ("Be careful," her father had cautioned on the single occasion he had taken her up into the structure they called the Aerie, "outside the door, it's a long way down.")

She had a print of Marik's *The Capellans* in her bedroom. It depicted two magnificent humanoid eagles, obviously male and female, atop a crag at sunset. Marik had known no more than anyone else, but Sylvie thought he was close to the truth. "They *must* have been like eagles, Dad," she said, imagining how it would have looked when the creatures rose into the sky.

Children of the light, Henry Harding Closs had called them in a famous poem.

Her father smiled patiently. She knew what was coming. "They could as easily have been *bats,*" he said. "Or *gasbags.* We just don't know."

He turned to examine the modest pile of presents beneath the tree. There wasn't much Christmas shopping to be done on Capella III. Consequently, if there were few gifts, they tended to compensate by being more personal. "What's this?"

She'd made a pendant for him, engraving his name, the date, and the legend *Eagles' Nest* on the polished black stone that formed its centerpiece. She'd have liked to cut it in the form of the Aerie, but that would have required a professional jeweler. The pendant was in the box he'd picked up. "You're not supposed to look," she said.

"Oh." He flashed disappointment, held the package to his ear, and shook it gently. "It tinkles."

She frowned, took it from him, and put it back beneath the tree. "Shame on you."

"I *love* presents," he said, displaying a pout.

"Christmas is the season to *give.*" She tilted her head in the coquettish manner that she had discovered. It seemed to charm males of all ages.

"Yes, it is," he said. He put his arm around her shoulder, and his voice turned serious: "But I'll tell you a secret."

"What's that?" she asked, her eyes alight.

"I don't know if there is a pleasure in this world to equal the feeling that comes with a thoughtful gift from someone you love." His eyes went far away, and she knew he was thinking of her mother, lost these six years. But the mood passed quickly, and he hugged her.

It was a good moment.

"I have an idea," she said.

Her father eased himself into a chair. "What's that?"

"I was thinking about the Christmas party this evening."

He crossed one knee over the other, and joined his hands behind his head. "What about the Christmas party?"

They had outgrown their community center, which was now reduced to serving its meals in two shifts. The structure would be doubled in size with the arrival of the *Exeter*. Meanwhile, the prospect of crowding everyone in at the same time was daunting.

"Dad, there are a couple of spaces in the towers that are pretty big. Why not move everything over there?"

He looked startled, and his smile hardened. "You mean the *party?*" He seemed scarcely to believe she could be serious.

"Sure. Why not?"

"Why? Why on earth would you want to do *that?*"

Because it's where the Capellans lived. Because it's a way of celebrating why we're here. But she only said, "Because there's a lot of room."

He softened. "It wouldn't work," he said. "It's a nice idea, but we really can't."

It was almost physically painful to think of the home of the Capellans left dark and cold tonight. *Of all nights.* "It wouldn't be hard to set up," she persisted. Heating units were already installed for the comfort of the researchers, so the cold would be no problem. As far as she could see, it would just be a matter of getting the tables and chairs, moving the alcohol over, and putting up a few quick-fix decorations. A little bit of bother, but it would be worth it.

"I think it would take a lot of work, Sylvie. And it's already late in the day."

The tops of the towers glittered in the setting sun.

"We'd help." She knew that, for such a cause, her friends would pitch in. And the prospect of light and warmth in the ancient buildings overwhelmed her. It was what the Capellans would have wanted. "Please, Dad."

He smiled that sad bad-weather smile that was intended to suggest this was a complicated issue, an adult thing, one best left alone. "We really can't do it, Sylvie. It wouldn't be right."

"Wouldn't be *right?* Why not?"

He looked uncomfortable. Her father was a slight man in his mid-thirties. He possessed a formality of manner and dress that set him apart from most of his colleagues. An older observer would have noticed that he seemed always to be speaking from a distance. His gray eyes were expressive, and tended to focus at a point over one's shoulder. Combined with a perpetual sense of distraction, as though he had something very important on his mind, they conveyed the sense that he could give a listener only a fraction of his attention. He was better with Sylvie, who was the only person in the world who could be truly said to touch him. Nevertheless, he now turned that preoccupied gaze toward her. "Because we have to have some respect for these places, Sylvie. I don't know how to explain this, I'm not sure I can put it in words that will make sense, but it would just be in bad taste to throw a *party* over there—" He gazed out at the towers. "There are some people here who would think of it as almost sacrilegious. And I'm not sure they wouldn't be right."

Sylvie could not imagine why anyone would object. And she liked the idea of celebrating her Christmas in the company of the Capellans. Or as close to their company as she could hope to get. "I don't think they would mind, Dad."

He got up, and his tone shifted to its end-of-discussion mode. "If they were around, we could ask them, Sylvie."

He went out to help with preparations for the evening party, and left her staring glumly at the tree, and at the towers.

There were five of them, named, for reasons she wasn't entirely clear about, the Queen, the Aerie, the Diamond, the Castle, and the Court. They were *round* buildings, and, when the light was right, they suggested chess pieces. The Queen was capped by a penthouse that someone must have thought resembled a crown; the walls of the Court formed a three-tiered enclosure. The Diamond was a faceted structure, a building with numerous faces and angles. The side of the Aerie that faced the town was marked by a wide, unwalled balcony. The shortest and broadest of the structures was the Castle: it was roughly three stories high, with turrets, parapets, ramps, and a crenellated roof.

By far, the greater part of the structures were underground. Her father said they went down sixty-some floors. They had once been skyscrapers, the downtown of a city that now lay buried in the plain.

She went out onto the deck.

Sylvie was entranced by Marik's vision: she would have *loved* standing with the male Eagle on its perch. *His* perch. She wouldn't tell *anyone*, not even her best friend Jaime, but it had occurred to her that boys would be far more interesting if they had wings. And the laser-blue glance of the Capellans, which penetrated right to the soul.

Her gaze fell on the balcony near the top of the Aerie. She pictured the Eagles from the print, standing casually at its lip, their wings touching, looking out across the city.

The sky had clouded over; flakes were in the air.

The five towers were stark and empty. Abandoned. Carols drifted through the night, and the town was filled with lights. A few people were already moving toward the community center. She had noticed a few years back that the memory of her mother tended, during this happiest of seasons, to acquire a spike. She was beginning to suspect there was something about Christmas that heightened *all* emotions, and not just the pleasurable ones. Something that spoke to her about more than simply an appreciation of others, but rather that seemed to penetrate to her deepest core. *Here is what you are. Here is what you need.*

She wanted, more than anything, to *give* something to the Capellans. She wanted to connect her own existence with theirs.

Behind the Aerie, low rolling hills receded into the dark.

"Sylvie? Are you going?" Evan and Lana Culpepper were in the gateway. Both were wrapped tightly in thick jackets. It was cool tonight, but not *that* cool.

"In a few minutes," she called back. "I'll see you there."

"Nice lights," Lana chirped. Her father had strung a few in a gold bush, which looked garishly purple in their glow.

"Thanks," said Sylvie.

They waved and trudged away.

Across the street, the Stuarts had found a blow-up Santa Claus, who now stood in their yard. They were getting ready for the party. Sylvie could see them moving around inside.

She felt suddenly lonely.

The Aerie stood gray and somber.

The balcony looked like a place that had been *made* for celebrations.

She stared at it. The breeze died and the night was very still. Through the front window, her tree glowed.

She reached into her pocket and withdrew the remote. There was a white star atop the tree. Little packages and reindeer and blue globes and handmade Santas and gold vine dangled from its branches. Its lights were bright and cheerful. Some were glimmers, which could be made to blink; and others were globes, which burned with a fine steady glow. They would eventually be used to mark pathways through the buried city.

She aimed the remote at the tree, and squeezed it. The lights went out.

She went inside and approached it. Without the illumination, it seemed almost forlorn. Odd that light should mean so much. She reached in through the branches, got hold of the stem, and lifted.

It came off the floor.

Not bad. It was heavy, but not so much that she couldn't manage it.

She set it back down. It scared her a little to realize that what she was thinking about *was* in fact within her power.

She retrieved forty meters of line from the depot. (Fortunately, theft was foreign to the little community, and no locks or security systems were needed.) Then she returned home, catching quizzical glances en route from the Chipaktas and the Holmans.

Her first task was to tie up the tree without damaging the decorations. She worked carefully and, when she was satisfied, laid it on its side. A reindeer fell out. She removed and collapsed the stand, and disconnected the battery. She picked up the reindeer and placed *it*, the stand, the battery, and the remote into a pouch. *What was she forgetting?* A lamp. She had to dig around a little, but she found one in the wine cabinet. She strapped it to her wrist, pulled on her jacket, and slung the pouch over one shoulder.

She wrestled the tree through the house, losing a few ornaments in the process. It was more awkward than heavy. Well, it was heavy too. She thought about getting help. This was the kind of thing Jaime would enjoy.

But if it was worth the doing, it was something to do alone. She hauled it out the rear door, and laid it on the back of the rover. The keys were in the vehicle. She started it, to allow the cab time to heat up, and went back for her pouch and the fallen decorations.

The snow had stopped, and a few stars were out. It was going to be a lovely night.

She switched on the headlamps, lifted the rover off the pad, and swung out onto the plain.

Clumps of fleshy golden plants and long irregular rows of wild hedge bent beneath the lift-fans. The plants were cactuslike. Their limbs reached out, much like persons frozen in startled attitudes.

She crossed long excavation ditches. Her lights played against lone walls and arches and a strip of ancient roadway. Dust clouds rose behind, obscuring the town.

It was a relatively still night.

The towers drew near. She passed the clutch of utility buildings atop the shaft which provided entry into the lower city, and rounded the base of the Castle.

Up close, the towers lost their ethereal quality: starlight overwhelmed by stone.

She glided past the Diamond. In the days when its polyhedral surface was polished and maintained, a multitude of stars would have glittered down at her from its thousand walls. Now, of course, it merely lay mute and dark.

Beyond it rose the Aerie.

Sylvie drifted in under the gray walls, and brought the hovercraft to earth.

The balcony looked *farther up* than she remembered.

From her living room, a few minutes ago, it had seemed easy enough to reach. She had known it was on the fifth level, but she might have overestimated her own courage.

She stepped down onto the grass, and thought it over. It would be a safe climb. All she had to do was keep her wits. And if it got too scary, she'd just quit. No big deal.

A network of ladders enclosed the building. None was more than a story high, and they were connected by ramps, which were placed to break the fall of anyone who got careless. It reminded her of Gulliver, tied down by pygmies.

Sylvie had seen drawings of the Aerie as it had looked during the days of the Capellans, when it had towered over the city. It had been a magnificent, articulated obelisk, with doors and windows opening out everywhere. Gables and cornices projected from the surviving section, and crockets and spires and arches. At its top, the building narrowed to a broken shaft. The missing piece had not been recovered. Her father believed it had been an antenna, although Sylvie knew there were some who thought it had also functioned as an airship mooring. She liked that idea.

She picked out the route she would follow. Up the ladder that was directly in front of her to the second level ramp, left a few paces, and up to the third floor. Then left again. At the fourth level, she would have to go around the corner of the building. This was because the balcony that was her objective ran completely across the front (assuming this *was* the front; nobody really knew, and it was so named simply because it faced the town) and projected too far out. A ladder would have angled climbers over a very long drop.

She placed the tree carefully at the foot of the ladder, and tied her cable to it, securing it at top and bottom. Satisfied, she laid out about six meters and coiled the rest over her shoulder. Then she started up.

After the first few rungs she paused. The going was slow and awkward. She needed one hand to prevent the pouch from slipping off her shoulder, another to push the trailing cable away so she did not get tangled with it, and two to climb the ladder. She had expected to be on the balcony within ten minutes. But it wasn't going to work out that way.

At the second floor, she was above the tree line. The town, not quite a kilometer away, looked warm and inviting. Even at this distance, the wind carried bits and pieces of Christmas music to her. She suspected her father would be wondering where she was.

The ramps were roughly two meters wide, enough to allow the passage of the handtrucks that the researchers used to move artifacts. Handrails were constructed along their edges, but you wouldn't want to lean on one.

There was an open doorway. The door itself had long since fallen from its hinges. Like most of the building, it was constructed of a plastic polymer, and was almost indestructible. Someone had picked it up and leaned it against a wall. She extended her wrist and flashed a beam down the passageway.

Despite the heaviness of the overall structure, and the fact that few decorations or pieces of furniture had survived, there was still an ethereal quality about the corridor. It was much wider than high, quite unlike the relative squareness of passageways in terrestrial buildings. Had it been so designed to allow its occupants to stretch their wings? The thought brought a smile, and a tremor of excitement. The floors had been carpeted, although no one could reconstruct the pattern or the weave. They were also curved, rising in the middle, which made for hard walking. Not designed for humans. She wondered whether these halls had *ever* echoed to footsteps.

Sylvie peeked over the side at her tree, and uncoiled enough cable to get her to the next floor. Then she started up again. The outside wall was rough, corroded, scored. Daddy had told her that the buildings would stand as long again as they had already stood. Had the people who erected this structure expected to be here so long? Had they wanted to leave something behind?

Yes, she thought. It would be terrible to have lived and died, and to leave no sign of your passing. It seemed to her that someone among the Capellans, at some point, would have contemplated the ages and known that *she* would come.

Greetings, young lady from London.

She was getting quite high. And the ramp looked hopelessly narrow.

The wind played in her hair, blew it in her eyes. At the ramp on the third level, she tied it back.

Darkness poured out of windows and doorways. This time she did not cast her light into the building. The place felt like a church. Maybe her father was right: it would not have been a good setting for a Christmas party.

At the fourth floor, she stood beneath the balcony. It was gently curved, relatively narrow near the sides of the building, broader toward the center. It was wide enough to play tennis on, if one didn't mind a precipitous drop along the fault line. A network of struts supported the structure. Some were almost low enough to touch.

She walked to the corner, turned, and climbed the final ladder.

Her hands and shoulders were beginning to ache. She puzzled about it as she ascended, grateful for any kind of distraction from the void over which she clung. Her breathing had become somewhat uneven, and she gripped the rungs tightly. *Maybe that was the reason she was hurting.*

The fifth-level ramp did not have direct access to the balcony. It ended only a couple of meters away, and there was nothing to prevent her from jumping across. The only obstacle was the narrow rail around her own perch. It was a jump she could easily have made. *On the ground.* But up here . . . no thanks.

There was an entrance to the building just a few meters away. She intended to use it, and come out onto the balcony. Safe and sane. Then she would haul up her tree.

But it occurred to her that there was a problem: she could not take the cable through the building.

She considered lifting the tree to the ramp where she now stood. But it was around the corner and in the wrong position. It would get dragged about thirty meters.

No: she had to get her remaining cable, about ten meters of it, across the open space.

She could try *throwing* it. She took the loop from her shoulder and placed it on the ramp. It began to slide over the edge. Too heavy.

She could *jump*.

She could use her head. There had to be something around that would serve as a weight. Maybe some loose rubble.

She inspected the ramp, all the rooms that opened out on this side of the building, and a couple of passageways. The only movable object was another door laid against a wall. She couldn't very well heave *that* across the space.

What else?

Her *pouch*. She took out its contents, and removed her jacket and shoes and stuffed them in. When she'd finished she wound several lengths of cable around it, and set it down. It didn't move. Satisfied, she walked to the railing, looked across at the graceful sweep of the alien balcony, and made one or two practice motions with her right hand. Then she launched the pouch.

It sailed across the abyss, trailing silver line, bounced, and skewed toward the edge (while her heart fluttered). And rolled to a stop.

Pleased with herself, Sylvie hurried into the passageway. It was cold. The air was cold, and the ground over which she moved chilled her stockinged feet. When the corridor turned away, she entered a suite of rooms, and spotted the balcony through a window.

She had seen photos of it before. But now it spread before her, an esplanade, a courtyard without walls. The fine dust that had accumulated on it sparkled in the starlight. She could see no footprints, but there was enough wind during the day to erase any marks left by researchers.

Fluted columns were scattered randomly through the area. The columns were not whole, but only fractions, mere slices, like pieces of pie, which appeared to have had their tops lopped off. Some were cut flat across, others were sharply angled. Only one was taller than Sylvie, and that by not much more than a hand's breadth. They supported nothing.

She swung a foot over the sill.

The edge of the ramp on which she'd stood was off to her right. The pouch, and the cable, lay where it had fallen. Thank heaven: if it had gone over the side, that would have been *it*.

She climbed out through the window, and retrieved them.

Then she turned to face the Aerie.

A high triple doorway anchored the balcony, but, in the unsymmetrical style of the Capellans, it was well to the right of center. The doors and windows all gaped at her now, black and exposed. There had once been glass.

And light.

And music? Had these people known music? What would it have sounded like? How sad to think that, whatever it might have been, it was gone now, quite beyond recovery.

Yet the Aerie did not feel like a dead place. The way cemeteries felt, for example. Or the *Antiqua*, the alien starship orbiting Deneb, its origin unknown, its mummified crew still at their stations. No: maybe the Capellans were so long gone that no part of them remained, and so this was only a pile of rock and plastic. Or maybe this place had thoroughly served its purpose, and its builders had lived their lives and passed on and nothing more could be expected.

She shivered. It was a little spooky up here. Hard not to keep her eyes on the silent openings, not to think that, the moment she turned away, there would be movement inside.

The half-column she wanted was located ten paces from the edge. Its top was angled at about thirty degrees, and it was waist-high. She took in the slack, drew the line around it, walked it over to a second shaft, which was little more than a quarter of a pie piece, and secured the cable.

Now she returned to the half-column, and began to reel in the tree. It was not as heavy as she had feared, and she knew when it was clear of the ground. She drew in her line, hand over hand, and simultaneously drew back toward the shaft that she had begun to think of as her quarter-post. She looped it around the quarter-post, and then went back to the half-column, and repeated the process. In this way, she was able to rest at intervals. And if she lost her grip on the line, the tree would not fall more than a few meters.

As if that would not be enough—

It was gustier up here than it had been on the plain. But it felt good: it surrounded her and lifted her spirits, and she pulled on the tree and stopped occasionally to look down at the town, which seemed much farther away than it should have.

The wind brought occasional snatches of song to her. And she could see movement in the streets.

What had it been like when the Capellan city was spread across the plain? And this was the top of a skyscraper? Rivers of light flowed through the nightscape, and the stars were cold and bright. And they had stood on (or floated across) this balcony. This balcony with no protecting wall. Whose floor in fact dipped slightly as it approached the edge, as if to provide a running start into the void.

Launch pad.

Her periods of rest grew longer. But that was okay: the tree was going to get here, and that was all she cared about.

Her adrenaline ran and she pulled and the line came in and she looped it around the quarter-post until there was a substantial quantity of it stretched across the dust-covered plastic surface. *It had to be getting close.*

She crept out to the lip of the balcony and peered down. It was about halfway.

After that, she looked regularly, and when it drew near, she lay at the edge and pulled it the last few meters, leaning out farther than prudence would have dictated, to haul it safely up with a minimum of breakage.

She did snap off a limb, and she heard a few ornaments go. But when she released the restraining cords, the big yellow branches spread out, and the reindeer and blue globes looked reasonably intact. She straightened its star, and set it into its stand.

A burst of wind almost took it out of her hand. Okay: she picked a spot where it would be visible from town, but which allowed her to secure it among three columns. She tied it carefully in place, fluffed out the branches, adjusted the ornaments. When she was satisfied, she attached the battery, and picked up the remote.

Sylvie looked again at the dark face of the building.

If anyone is watching, merry Christmas.

She squeezed the unit, and the lights blazed on.

The tree was magnificent: its soft glow spilled across the balcony.

She clapped her hands and closed her eyes and felt the plain fall away, and saw the alien city, incandescent in the moonless night, spread to the horizon. And she felt the wind suck at her, draw her forward. It whispered through her feathers, and lifted her toward the stars.

She felt herself gliding into the night, riding a gust of cool air, curving round the Queen.

There was a way to celebrate Christmas.

Halfway to town, she met her father. He had Jerry Haskin with him, and Millie Michel, and Wolf Sangmeister, and two or three others. They were loaded down with cable and medical kits and spotlights, and they all looked very sternly at her.

Daddy assured everyone she would be dealt with properly, and they all tried to keep straight faces. But Daddy was too relieved to be angry for long. Nevertheless, he was clearly annoyed that she had disobeyed his wishes.

"You'll be grounded, young lady," he said in his severest tone. "Indefinitely."

"I'm sorry, Daddy," she said.

He peered disapprovingly at her. "But you would do it again."

She hesitated. "Yes."

"Why?"

"I'm not sure," she said. "I thought they needed a tree." She giggled at the absurdity of the proposition.

"I see." He frowned. "You could have been killed."

"I was careful." Here, at least, her conscience was clear. "I took no chances."

"Well, I hope you're satisfied." He delivered a long, deep sigh. *I don't know what I'm going to do with you.* "Did you get anything back?"

"Daddy?" She didn't understand.

"There should be a return. Do *you* have anything to show for your effort?"

She looked out the window toward the Aerie. The tree glittered. "Yes." She was silent for a long time. "We might not know what they looked like," she said, "but they *were* Eagles."

Only adults, who generally lack a sense of magic and imagination, are able to sleep easily on *this* night. Silvie tossed restlessly, listening to her father moving around downstairs, listening to the wind push against the side of the house. Outside, occasional voices drifted by. Late revelers headed home.

And it occurred to her that Christmas was coming at last to Capella III.

At a few minutes before midnight, she sat up against her pillows so she could see the top of the Aerie.

Wonder certainly is subjective.

NOT A CREATURE

Damon Knight

It was the night before Christmas, and Ebenezer Scofield was sitting in front of the fireplace with a shotgun across his thighs. Under the shotgun was a plaid lap robe that he had inherited from his father, along with this house and about half the land in the township. He had a shawl over his shoulders, too, and a nightcap on his bald head, because the fire was banked for the night like always and he was sitting well back from it in case he had to shoot anything.

This happened about thirty years ago, and Scofield's name really was Ebenezer. It was not a funny name when he was born in 1899, but later on he was kidded about it every Christmas, and it was one of the things that made him sour. Even in school, the kids had never called him Ben, or Eben, but always Scrooge or Skinflint.

In his sixties, he lived alone as he always had in the house he was born in, high on the slope below Parker's Knob, north of a town called Charlesburg in a depressed part of Vermont. His nearest neighbor was three miles away, Bill Louderbuck, and they didn't even nod when they met. That was an old story; Scofield and Louderbuck had fallen out in the late thirties over a scheme that would have built a ski resort on Parker's Knob and made the whole town rich, so they said.

Louderbuck and his friends owned about half the acreage the promoter wanted; Scofield owned the other half, but they couldn't agree on terms and the deal fell through. The promoter built his resort elsewhere. The town blamed Scofield, and many people went to bed at night cursing his name. He knew all about that; he had had enough phone calls and unsigned letters, never mind the rocks thrown at his house and the spitting on the sidewalk when he went by. Long ago when he saw things were never going to change, he could have picked up and left—he was rich enough—but he wouldn't let them say they had driven him out.

It was along about four o'clock in the morning now, and there wasn't a sound. Nothing crunching in the snow outside, no creaks in the floorboards, not even a mouse.

Twice before, about a week apart, there had been little wood-ashy blurred footprints on the floors, and things missing. Food mainly, but some gold jewelry of his mother's too, and a spool of copper wire, some silver spoons and a Mason jar of pennies. Other small things were gone, probably, but he couldn't call to mind what they were.

The sheriff had laughed at him on the phone. "Goblins coming down your chimley, Scrooge? Sorry to hear about that. Ho, ho, ho!"

Kids from town, it must be, climbing over his fence, putting a ladder up in the middle of the night, hauling the booty out, and running away. How they kept the dogs from barking he didn't know; their parents must be in on it.

The fire popped a little, and a spark fell on the apron. Scofield had been dozing, but the sound brought him up broad awake. There was nothing in the fireplace but the banked logs and the golden glow. Then, as suddenly as that, there was something there, a little bronze and greeny-gold thing, child-sized but not a child. It hopped out of the fire and stood looking at him.

Scofield brought the gun up and let go with both barrels. There was a screech and a flurry, and by the time he could see straight, the thing was gone and the back wall of the fireplace was pockmarked with buckshot. He thought he heard a scrabbling in the chimney, then the dogs set up an unholy racket outside.

Scofield threw off his lap robe and ran to get his coat and boots. He reloaded the shotgun in haste, picked up a flashlight, and put another box of shells in his pocket. By the time he got out the back door, the dogs were silent. There was a funny smell in the air, not just the prickly-cold snow smell but something different. Singed wool, he thought, but that wasn't right either.

There was a clear line of pawprints in the snow where the two dogs had run uphill. Scofield followed them with his flashlight and came to a place where the dogs had stopped to sniff around a depression in the snow.

He called, but the dogs didn't answer. He picked up the tracks again and went on crunching up the hillside behind the dim yellow fan of light, feeling how big and dark the world was around him. It might be better to go on back to the house and wait till morning, but then he would feel worse, not knowing what was out there and what it might be up to.

Fifty yards up the slope he came to another place where the dogs' tracks huddled around a depression in the snow, and then about twenty yards farther, another one. There weren't any tracks that he could see, except the dogs', between one depression and another. Could the thing jump that far—or fly?

Ten yards more, and there were the two dogs lying side by side. There wasn't a mark on them, but they were dead.

Scofield aimed his light up the hill. There was another depression up there, and he went to see it, because the others had been partly covered up by dogprints. It looked like one of the patterns kids made in the snow, falling on their backs and then waving their arms to make angel wings.

Scofield was beginning to feel more scared than he had ever been in his life, but he wouldn't turn his back on it now, and he went on up to the next depression a yard or two away. Above it a trail of wavering footprints kept on going, as if something that had been injured couldn't fly any more, and was walking now up into the trees.

Scofield followed the prints, lost them in the bare earth under the pines and maples, found them again in patches of snow. A little farther on there was a place where the thing had fallen and got up again.

Then he had caught up to it, under a maple tree near the top of the Knob. It was about the size of a six-year-old child, but it was metallic-looking and had skinny arms and legs like a bug, and yellow-brown insect wings. There were straps and buckles around it, and some kind of mesh bag under the wings. It had crawled the last two or three feet before it died.

Scofield sat down there in the snow and looked at it until the sky began to lighten gradually. Up in the bare limbs of the maple there was something that looked like a little platform, and above that a round shape as big as a dinner table that glittered against the sky.

He leaned his shotgun against the tree, turned off the flashlight and laid it on the ground, and with some difficulty hauled himself up as far as the platform. It was woven of willow branches, looked like, and tied together with strips of bark. On it were some things he couldn't recognize, along with his silver spoons, the gold jewelry, a wedge of cheese, a half-empty bottle of milk, and somebody's ragged teddy bear. Over his head, the big round thing was dented and had black smoke-stains running up from a hole in the side.

Scofield took the spoons and necklaces and stuffed them into his pockets. He climbed back down again and walked to the edge of the woods, where he could look out over pretty much the whole township. There was Bill Louderbuck's house, there was Wall's house and dairy barn, and there were the distant rooftops and smoking chimneys of Charlesburg.

As soon as he called the newspapers, there would be scientists here from all over the world. He'd be famous, Charlesburg would become a tourist town, with a museum and gift shop and a new hotel and restaurant, just like Bill Louderbuck had wanted it to be thirty years ago. Bill would come up to him on the street with his greasy smile and say, "Well, Ebenezer, you're not so bad after all."

Scofield thought it over for a while. Then he went back to the maple tree and put two shots through the platform. It sagged, and things rained down through the branches. He reloaded and fired at the dead creature on the ground. Point-blank, the buckshot scattered it into bits. He reloaded again and fired at the round thing higher up. He reloaded and fired, reloaded and fired, until the branches gave way and the thing came crashing down. He kept on firing until he was out of shells, and the thing was just a ragged pile of junk. Then he walked back down the hill.

There was a heavy snowfall later that week, and the snow lay deep on the Knob until spring. When Scofield went up there in May to look around, there was nothing to be seen except a few strips of rusted metal that could have come from anywhere.

Christmas offers a strange reunion.

MY FAVORITE CHRISTMAS

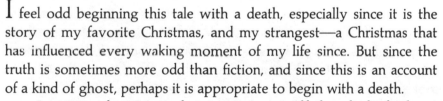

Dave Wolverton

I feel odd beginning this tale with a death, especially since it is the story of my favorite Christmas, and my strangest—a Christmas that has influenced every waking moment of my life since. But since the truth is sometimes more odd than fiction, and since this is an account of a kind of ghost, perhaps it is appropriate to begin with a death.

In 1974, when I turned sixteen, my grandfather died of a heart attack in Wheeling, West Virginia. My dad had run away from home to Oregon at the age of fourteen and seldom spoke to my grandfather, so my grandfather's landlord mailed our family the old man's few possessions. Among them was a shoe box that contained a yellowed picture of my great-great-grandfather Benjamin Franklin Fawkes, and everyone who saw it thought it was a picture of me.

Ben's brown hair was combed strait down to his shoulders, making it longer than mine, and his face was a tad narrower, but his eyes were mine—clear, penetrating—and somehow I knew that if I saw them in color, they'd be the same hazel that seems to change to green or gray or blue with the weather. A note scrawled on the bottom of the photo showed that it had been taken in the mountains of West Virginia in September 1863, when Ben was fifteen. He wore denim jeans, a checkered wool shirt. Slung low on his hip was a gun belt with rows of bullets. His right hand held a long-barreled Calvary pistol. My dad knew a little family lore and said the photo had been taken only six months after Ben watched a band of Union soldiers loot his home and gun down his mother. Ben later became a Rebel soldier and lost his right leg to gangrene in 1865, so we suspected that the photo was taken on the day that Ben left to fight for the South, hoping to get some vengeance.

We kept the photo on the television beside a picture of me. It served as my only link to my father's family. My father had no brothers or sisters, and his mother died young, so I'd never met another Fawkes. Then that very winter, ten days before Christmas, Edward came.

My mom, dad, and I had gone to Eugene to shop, and we came back to the farm just before sunset. My dad owned four hundred acres which he leased to a Christmas tree farmer, and our house was right in the middle. We snaked up the long gravel driveway through the young Douglas fir and blue spruce, and as we topped the hill we spotted a red Ford pickup down in the valley by the house. Some brute sat on the front porch swing, patting the head of our normally cautious cocker spaniel, and as we drove up, the man stood. I looked into his eyes and recognized him immediately as family. His eyes were like mine, like Grandpa Ben's, and I would have known him anywhere in spite of his oddities. He was tall, at about six-three, but also very heavy. He had silver hair, and the cold cloudy skies made his eyes look grayer than they were, but his most noticeable features were the scars. His right ear was mangled into the shape of a cauliflower, and the right side of his face was a horror of half-rate plastic surgery, with skin stretched taut over the knotted cords of his facial muscles. His right hand curled into a gnarled little fist.

We hopped out of the car, and he muttered through a twisted mouth, "By Golly, I sure have found the right place! You're Fawkeses, all right!"

"May I help you?" my dad asked, uncertainly.

"How ya doing, Little Jackie?" he smiled. "Don't you recognize me? I'm Ed."

"Uncle Ed?" My dad said with his normal lack of tact, "God, I heard you had gotten blown apart in World War II, and Uncle Charley keeps expecting you to die, but I never imagined you would look so bad!"

Ed just grinned and hugged my dad, then extended his right hand to me. "This one looks like old Benjamin." I shook his hand reluctantly, afraid I might hurt him. He was missing two fingers, and the hand felt icy, colder than any living tissue should feel. I wondered how long he'd been sitting out here in the wind.

"This is your grandpa's brother," my dad said. "He and I were good friends when I was a kid. Uncle Ed and I used to do everything together." Then my dad turned to Ed and said, "How long are you visiting? Where are you staying?"

"Well," Ed drawled, "I thought I'd like to stay a week or so." He looked out over the fields of Christmas trees around the house with a gleam of desperation in his eye. "I didn't know you lived so far out in the sticks. I saw a motel back in Junction City. I guess I could stay there, unless there's something closer."

"Oh, that's too far to drive——" my dad said, just as I knew he would. We were country folk, and perhaps not as cautious as we should have been. "We have a guest room. Why don't you stay with us?"

And that is how the hulking invalid moved in. We grabbed his suitcases from the cab of the truck, took them in as my mom began cooking up chicken-fried steak for dinner. I headed out back to feed my pigs, then stayed in the pig shed thinking till after sunset. The two red, mule-footed hogs ate and grunted, often anxiously looking up from their troughs to see if I'd dump in something tastier than rolled oats.

I could tell this would be a rough week. Christmas break was coming up, and I'd planned on spending time with Constance Hunter. Now, with Ed here and my parents both working, my folks would want me to entertain Ed during the days, and I wouldn't be able to see her unless my monstrous uncle tagged along. I felt cheated, embarrassed.

A chill ran down my spine: If he'd had a hunch, Ed would have looked like Quasimodo, the Hunchback of Notre Dame. What would Constance think? I wanted to forgive Ed his looks, since they weren't his fault, but I wasn't sure I could ignore those looks.

I resolved to be polite to Ed, but avoid him. I still had one day of school before Christmas break, and after that I figured I could spend most days hunting ducks or visiting Constance at her house. Nights would be easy—dad got off work from the sawmill at five, so he'd entertain Ed at night. I would hardly have to see Ed at all.

My mom called from the back door, and I returned to the house. We sat at our little table, and I sat next to Ed, watching him eat. Ed had a pale complexion, and the skin on his forehead around the wounds had begun to peel. He gave off a faint, chemical odor, as if he'd lived in a hospital. Dad asked questions of Uncle Ed, such as, "Whatever happened to that old hermit who used to preach in the cave?" and, "Remember that traveling salesman who tried to buy the neighbor's two-headed calf?"

Ed gobbled down the food. I've never liked people who are immoderate—those who eat or breed or spend too much—and the scarred red cords on Ed's face stretched so taut as he chewed and swallowed that it almost looked alien. I could hardly stomach eating, so I averted my eyes and listened to the conversation.

Halfway through the meal, headlights blazing on high beam shone through the dining room window, announcing that a car was coming down the driveway.

"My, we're getting a lot of visitors," my mom said. Dad and I walked to the front door. It was Kaman Porter, the fellow who leased my dad's land. Kaman was dark with close-set eyes, a pulpy face, and a thin beak of a nose. If you've seen *The Good, the Bad, and the Ugly*, just imagine the Ugly with a Bad nose. He didn't even wait till he got out of the car before he began shouting, "What the hell is going on here, Jack?"

"What do you mean?" Dad asked. My dad was short, easily intimidated, and I could hear the fear in his voice.

"I just caught a bunch of Mexicans coming down your driveway with a truckload of trees. They say you sold them the trees! What the hell is going on?"

"Now, Kaman, you know I wouldn't do anything like that!" Dad said, but Mr. Porter just glared. "If they'd come over the hill, I would have seen them. But no one has come over the hill tonight that I'm aware of!"

"They had six trees, at thirty dollars a tree," Porter said. "I'll give you the same deal I gave them. Either pay me for the trees, or I'm calling the police. They said you have all their money, so I'm calling the police on them."

"I'm not paying for any damned trees!" my dad shouted, suddenly angry.

"Then I'll just take the price of the trees off our lease. And if I find any more stumps out in those fields, I'll charge you for those trees, too."

My dad's jaw quivered, a sign that he was really mad. Christmas tree thieves are about as common in Oregon as athlete's foot, and there was no way we could hope to stop them all. "If you withhold payments," Dad said, "you'll be breaking our lease, and I'll take your whole damned crop!"

Kaman Porter had been leasing the land for seven years, and some trees were finally ready to harvest, but most of the crop would come in over the next two years. His face got hard. In the faint light from the porch you could see him fuming. "This may be your land, and you may think you're cute by selling off my trees, but, by god, if you make trouble for me, I'll make trouble for you!" Porter shouted, and he threw himself into the car and the tires spit gravel as he drove off.

I glanced at my watch. It was almost six-thirty, and our high school football team would be playing Harrisburg in an hour. It was one of our biggest games of the season. I needed to hurry to get Constance before suiting up. I ran upstairs for my coat and an extra blanket for Constance. The phone rang, but I let my parents pick up.

As I pulled a blanket from the shelf in the upstairs linen closet, my mom came up. "Your dad just got called back to the mill. One of the saws broke, and they need him to fix it. Can you take Uncle Ed to the game?"

"Does Ed like football?" I said, hoping that he'd told her he liked football about as much as he liked sauerkraut smothered in Tabasco sauce.

"Oh, Ed loves football!" Mom said. "He played in school." Her voice took on a commanding undertone. "It would mean so much to him if you'd take him."

When she used that tone of voice, you just couldn't argue. "Yeah, I'll take him," I said, imagining Uncle Ed swinging from the goal posts and laughing like Quasimodo capering on the ropes in the bell tower. Ed grabbed his coat, an umbrella and a second blanket, and we drove on over to Constance's, picked her up.

Now, I have to tell you about Constance. Her dad made a small fortune designing automated packaging tools for the food service industry, her mother was gorgeous, and both of them just lounged around the house all day being good parents between exotic vacations. Somehow the best of both parents came out in Constance. She was beautiful—sparkling blue eyes, perfect teeth, sandy blond hair, nice figure. Beyond that, she had her father's brains. When my high school economics professor nearly persuaded me to become a communist, Constance sat down with me for five minutes and, just sort of thinking about it, talked about Russia's problems with black market profiteering and how the communist farmers and factory workers engaged in subtle protest through inactivity and, with just a little bit of common sense, explained why all the communist countries were doomed to collapse under the weight of their own bureaucracy as their gross national products continued to spiral downward. Then she likened it all to the failure of the local hippie communes over the last five years. By the time she finished, I was more than a born-again capitalist—I was a Republican. I'd never heard that kind of talk from a girl, and I thought she was pretty amazing.

And as she and Ed watched the football game that night, I resented my misshapen uncle. An Oregon storm broke, pelting us with great droplets of sleet, and Ed had the umbrella. I played nose guard, and every time that I glanced over to the bleachers, Ed would be leaning close to Constance, showing the unblemished half of his face, and as he protected her with the umbrella, he often touched her hand.

It made me sick. It had taken me six months to build the courage to hold her hand.

We'd never beaten Harrisburg, since their school was three times as large as ours. Nearly every player on their front line outweighed ours by fifty pounds. Since I was the biggest man on our defensive team, no matter which side I lined up on they would run or pass the other direction, and from my point of view, the whole damned game got discouraging pretty quick. At halftime they led 24 to 3, and with our offense I figured the game was over.

At the start of the third quarter, I went over to the sidelines as Harrisburg kicked off. Uncle Ed was joking about the game. He pointed out that our team was playing in the slush without thermal undershirts beneath their uniforms, and he laughed. "It's no big deal," he said. "Back in West Virginia, our school was so small that we didn't have uniforms—our coach would send us to play in the snow with nothing but jock straps and a bad attitude. We couldn't afford helmets, so we'd tie a Sunday newspaper over our heads. We only had one cheerleader, and she was so ugly that when she cheered, the hounds would howl and wag their tails, thinking she was in heat." He kept up a steady barrage, but I didn't hear any more, because suddenly he touched Constance's knee, and she giggled, and all the sound just seemed to go away. I'd never touched her knee.

Our scrawny offensive players got bounced around, run over, and stomped on during the next three plays, and I was almost happy when we punted and I got to go back in. We lined up, and I could hear Uncle Ed laughing up in the stands, and couldn't help thinking he was laughing at me. I glanced at him, and his hand hovered near Constance's knee again, and he smiled at her, undressing her with his eyes. I went crazy.

Harrisburg's right tackle was a monster named McMurty, and when the center snapped the ball, McMurty lunged for me. Usually he would fade back a step to protect his quarterback, but since he lunged I knew they were going to try to run past me. I reared back and slammed his helmet with my head, knocking him down, and when their halfback tried to charge by, I stuck out one arm and caught him by the throat, lifted him and slammed him on his back. The halfback sort of whined, "You don't have to be so rough."

I bent over and shouted in his face, "Stay in the backfield, damn ya, or I'll kill you!"

McMurty roused enough to stagger back to the huddle, and I looked up in the stands. Constance was looking at me and cheering, and Uncle Ed was just watching her face, totally absorbed, admiring her.

Next thing I remember, the ball had been snapped. I jumped past McMurty, slamming his face with my elbow as I went. Their quarterback was fading back to pass, and he saw me coming for the blitz and opened his mouth in terror. He tried to throw the ball over me, so I leapt up, grabbed it in one hand, and slapped it back in his face. I came down nearly on top of him, and planned to tackle him and make it hurt, but I was so mad I just lifted him over my head and then gave him a body slam into the wet grass.

When I got done, the zebras were dancing around me, blowing their whistles in my face. I sort of looked at one of them, astonished. I'd never intentionally fouled anyone before, and somehow I hoped he had missed it. He blew his whistle an inch from my nose and growled, "You're out of the game!" just like that, not even a warning.

When I got back to the bench, I took off my helmet and our

coach grunted, "I don't know what the hell got into you, but I wish it would happen more often." I could feel every eye in those bleachers boring into the numbers on my back, and Uncle Ed shouted, "Hey, Dale, why don't you use those moves come wrestling season?" McMurty had to be helped off the field, and their quarterback had pulled a muscle in his shoulder. Our team rallied a little, so we didn't lose too bad.

After the game I dumped Ed at the house quicker than a sack of wet garbage, then drove Constance to her parents' modest mansion in the hills. When we pulled into her driveway she said, "You've been awfully quiet tonight. Are you all right?"

"Yeah," I said.

"I never saw you foul a quarterback like that. Did he say something to make you mad?"

I turned away, shaking. "Yeah."

She must have seen how it aggravated me, so she changed the subject. "I thought your Uncle Ed was cool, really nice. I like him," Constance said. I don't know whether she was telling the truth—whether she was really able to overlook his appearance and see something in him that I couldn't—or if she was just trying to make the best of a bad situation.

I really didn't want to think about him. I knew Ed was innocent, that he didn't really mean anything by touching her hand, her leg. Could I blame him for admiring her? Obviously she'd never want anything to do with some old, deformed man. Still, I couldn't talk about it.

"He's okay," I said, then we began kissing. Kissing with me and Constance was fairly new. When it came to women, glaciers normally moved faster than I did. With Constance it took me six months to ask her on a date, six months to hold her hand, six months to kiss her—but that night something changed.

They say that most men reach their sexual peak at age nineteen. I was ahead of schedule, and I figure I hit my sexual peak that morning. I was kissing her and hugging her and sweating pure testosterone down her blouse, and Constance kept breathing deeply and perspiring and sometimes moaning softly as she kissed me back. After fifteen minutes we broke off in frustration, and she sighed.

"What do you want for Christmas?" she asked, and I said I didn't know. "I know what I want for Christmas," she said. "I already asked my dad."

I was a little let down that she would ask her dad before she would ask me, but it was obviously a leading question, so I said, "What do you want?"

"My parents like to move a lot," Constance answered. "We've never lived in one place for more than two years, and we've already been here that long. My dad wants to move to Tonga."

"Oh," I said, trying to hide how much that news hurt and frightened me.

"So for Christmas, I asked if we could stay here for two more years—until I turn eighteen." She didn't say it, but we both knew what she meant. If you were raised in the sticks in Oregon, and you had a boyfriend, you tended to get married on your eighteenth birthday. That was the closest she'd ever come to telling me she loved me.

"What did your dad say?"

"He's thinking about it. I'm sure if I press, he'll give in. My mom and dad both like you an awful lot. So what do you want for Christmas?"

I didn't know how to answer. I wanted to tell her I loved her, but I was too shy. I wanted to say that when I kissed her, sometimes I would inhale the taste of her, and that later I would lie in bed at night savoring those kisses. I wanted to tell her that when we kissed, the blood pounded in my ears like thunder, and something inside of me seemed to soar up like a hawk through black storm clouds. Or that when I touched her, it was almost as if her slightest pressure left sweet bruises that ached for hours afterward. I wanted to hold her forever, but I was afraid that if I told her how I hungered for her, even if she loved me, it would frighten her.

I kissed her passionately for a moment, wondering if I should try to seduce her. But I wanted to make love to her, and I wanted her to consent without feeling pressured, so I whispered, trying to keep my voice from going husky with desire, "For Christmas, I want to unwrap you."

She sat back startled, looking like a deer frozen in my headlights. She fumbled for the door handle, then stopped, stared into my eyes and held my hand a second. She was shaking, face pale. She nodded yes, just a little, but not so much that I could be sure, then we both got out and I walked her to the house. At the doorstep, I whispered, "I think I love you."

As I drove home through blinding snow, the perspiration on my brow cooled, and I felt scared, and I cursed myself for saying "I think," fearing that Constance might see it as a lack of commitment.

Some people claim that farmboys have some advantage over city kids when it comes time to copulate. For me, that wasn't true. The prospect scared the hell out of me. When I was fifteen, a neighbor had to butcher one of his boars. The boar had gotten so huge that when he tried to breed with his sows, he would break their backs. I'd asked my dad if things like that ever happened to humans, and he assured me that it did. "If you get a big enough man," he said, "and a small enough woman, he can crush her pelvis bones." I thought about that as I drove. I'm pretty big, and Constance just average. I was taking Constance into unknown territory, and I wanted her desperately. Half the time I fantasized about what it might be like to sleep with her, and the other half I feared losing her, or worse, sending her to the hospital.

When I got home, the electricity was off, the house dark. I figured someone had hit a power pole in the snow. I climbed upstairs and lay down in bed and had nearly forgotten about Uncle Ed, when he began to whine.

He was in the guest bedroom next to mine, muttering and raging in his sleep. I listened through the walls. "Colonel Zharnov, tell men . . . power down. Motion in quadrant three. Don't sleep. Don't sleep!" He kept muttering and tossing. Just when I thought he had dropped off, he shouted, "Son of a bitch—grenade!" then he screamed, a long agonized cry that I thought would surely awaken my parents in their bedroom on the far side of the house. If I hadn't heard him talking first, I would have thought someone was slicing him open. As it was, he kept muttering and crying, and I imagined I could almost hear the shrill sounds of war planes echoing from his skull, the cries of wounded and dying, till at last I got my electric hunting lantern and went into his bedroom. The small bulb in the lantern gave just enough light to see Uncle Ed, covered with sweat. He shook and his face was pale. He stared up at the ceiling and didn't seem to see me at all.

I touched his forehead and asked, "Are you all right?" His skin was cold, colder than anyone's I'd ever felt. He was shaking and had all the blankets twisted around him. I ran to the linen closet and got several more. It hadn't seemed that cold to me at the football game, but now I realized that someone old and sickly, like Uncle Ed, shouldn't have stayed out in that cold. I got the blankets and covered him, and was about to run and get my mom, when Uncle Ed sighed and grabbed my hand.

His hand was warm now. It was as if he'd had ice running through his veins one moment, then someone had pumped warm water through him. He quit shaking, and his eyes focused on me. I touched his forehead to be sure, and it was warm too.

"I think you're sick," I told him. "I'll go get Mom."

He held my hand to keep me from going, his grip like a vise. "No," he said. "I feel better." He began breathing heavily, almost panting, but his skin was much warmer, as if he might be getting a fever.

"Are you sure?" I asked. "You don't look good."

He laughed weakly and turned his face to me, the scars showing horribly in the yellow lamplight, like long fibers of burned plastic. "It's been a long time since I've looked good to anyone." He coughed. "I came a long way to see you all, a long way. Your Uncle Charlie keeps thinking I'm going to die," his breathing rasped, "and I guess I probably will. I can feel it coming. Death, stalking me. Turn out the light. Let me rest."

His hands went limp, and my mangled uncle lay unmoving, staring at nothing. I stood a moment, scared, watched him until his chest rose a little. I stumbled back to my bed.

Now I knew why he'd come—to see us once before he died. My dad had always mentioned Ed with fondness, but Ed had never called, never visited. I remembered a Christmas card he'd sent, but that was it. Perhaps, like me, he felt an emptiness at not having an extended family. I lay for a long time and finally heard him cough lightly. I went to sleep.

When I rose in the morning, my mom was frying eggs and bacon on the old cast-iron woodstove instead of the electric. The power was still off, and the kitchen was the only warm room in the house, so Ed and I sat at the little table in the kitchen. My dad had worked all night, so he still slept. Ed whispered to me, "I hope I didn't give you too much of a scare last night," then winked.

"You feeling better?" I asked.

"Dale," he said, "I'm a tough old bull, all gristle and bone. People have been expecting me to up and die for most of my life, but I'm still here."

We tried calling the power company to see when the electricity would come back on, but the phone was dead. Ed looked at me and suggested that we go into town to make some calls. We hopped in the pickup, but just as we reached the end of our driveway, Ed said, "Look up there!"

Our power lines and phone lines had snapped at the junction box by the road. We hopped out of the pickup and Ed studied the dead wires. "See this?" he asked, pointing to the frayed ends of the wires. "Here's some shrapnel. Someone shot the lines down." He dug at the dead wire with a fingernail, and sure enough a piece of lead fell into his palm. "I'll bet you know the cockroach who did this," Ed said, eyes sparkling, almost happy.

"Kaman Porter?" I asked.

"Well, he does think your dad is a tree thief, and he did promise to make trouble. I've seen plenty of mean-spirited punks like him in my time."

My mom had taught me to never think evil of anyone. "It was probably kids," I said, "shooting at a bird on the wires."

"Shooting down both wires, in the dark?" Uncle Ed said. "Get a clue!"

We drove to a neighbor's house, reported the downed wires to the power company and Bell Telephone. When we got home, Uncle Ed told me to keep quiet about what we'd found, and he only told my dad that the power company had promised to fix the lines soon.

Constance and her parents always spent Sundays in Eugene visiting friends, so I drove up to Fern Ridge to go duck hunting and bagged a pair of mallards. Just as I pulled back into our driveway, Sheriff Carnaghan drove in behind me. Jerry Carnaghan had lived down the road from us for twelve years, and though he and my dad were friends, I could tell this wasn't a social visit. He had two Mexicans in the back of his car.

Sheriff Carnaghan got out of his tan patrol car, left the Mexicans inside. Our cocker spaniel barked at him. "Dad home?" he asked, taking off his Smokey hat and trying to sound casual. He was a tall fellow with a mustache, gray hair, and an air of authority. I invited him in.

We found Mom, Dad, and Ed all sitting in the living room, swapping stories. The sheriff said, "Jack, I've got to tell you, it sounds to me like you're in trouble. These two Mexicans say you sold them some trees last Wednesday but told them not to pick them up until yesterday because you had men working out in the fields."

"You know I wouldn't do that!" my dad said too loud.

Jerry Carnaghan raised his hand and said mildly, "Well, I don't believe it either. Kaman pays his Mexican workers dirt cheap, and I figure they probably just decided it wouldn't hurt nothing if they gave away a couple of trees to help out some friends at Christmas. But Kaman wants to press charges against you, Jack, and I've got to take you out there and see if those men can identify you as the one who sold the trees." I couldn't tell if Jerry believed my dad or not. Jerry had a real poker face. I guess it comes from being a cop in a small town where you almost always have to arrest people you know.

Uncle Ed leaned forward. "Sir," he says. "I've got a hotel receipt out in the cab of my pickup that proves I was in Denver on Wednesday. Would you care to try a little experiment?"

Jerry smiled slyly, and Uncle Ed raised himself from the couch with a grunt. I followed them, and Uncle Ed put on a big old scowl as we walked out the door. He glared into the back of the squad car at the Mexicans, and both of them began shaking.

"Is this the man who sold you the trees?" Jerry asked, and the Mexicans looked at each other.

"Yes, that's the one!" the littlest Mexican said. "The ugly one— he sold us trees. How could I forget such a horrible face!" They both nodded enthusiastically.

Jerry went to Uncle Ed's pickup and looked at his hotel and gas receipts. I heard him mumble under his breath, "It's pretty amazing how well they *comprende* English all of a sudden, now that they're accusing *you* of a crime." Jerry went back to the police car and drove off, his face passive. Those two Mexicans were in a whole lot of trouble, but they didn't seem to sense it. Like I say, unless Jerry told you, you could never tell what he was thinking.

We stayed up late that night, talking by the fire. For a while we watched a made-for-TV movie about someone struggling to overcome the rare malady of the week, but Mom turned it off so Dad and Uncle Ed could tell stories from when they were young. Ed seemed withdrawn, and every time my dad mentioned some incident, Ed would say, "I almost forgot about that, Jackie." At one point, my dad said, "You sure seem to have forgotten an awful lot."

Ed nodded, pointed to the scarred mass of tissue on his face. "I have, Jackie, I've forgotten most of what I knew. A grenade took it all. You know, I remember you as a kid, but it's all kind of hazy, like a dream. You've probably wondered why I quit writing after the war. It's not that I didn't want to know you anymore, it's just that . . . all of my memories seemed to have wandered off, the way our family has wandered, spread all across the country."

"Jesus," Dad whispered.

"Anyway," Ed said, patting Dad on the leg, "I'm glad I came all this way. It's good to get to know you, again." He paused, gazing into the fireplace. He looked feeble, wrung out. "I think I'd best get to bed."

I escorted him upstairs to his room, remembering how he'd just patted my dad on the leg, the way he'd patted Constance on the leg the night before. So it was a habit that meant nothing. All the anger I'd felt earlier just seemed to wring itself out of me.

When we reached the top of the stairs, he stood a moment, swaying, and I took his arm and half dragged him to his room. I asked if I should get a doctor, and he whispered, "Not yet, not yet." He didn't seem to be talking to me, but to someone else. His eyes were focused forward, watching something I couldn't see.

I helped him lie back on the bed, studied him. I touched his hand, and it was icy cold again, so I piled the blankets on. He mumbled, "Tell the emperor to get his skinny ass back in the bunker and let me win this war for him!" It was such an intriguing comment that I waited to hear more. Uncle Edward began sobbing, then stopped short, becoming deathly silent. I touched the scarred part of his face, took his little claw of a hand. He felt colder than before, and his face was getting pale, almost blue. His eyes were open a slit, and he didn't seem to be breathing. I got scared.

"Uncle Ed?" I said, shaking him. "Uncle Ed?" He roused, looked at me dully, as if I were far away.

"It's all right," he said. "I . . . It's just been a long trip. It takes so much energy. No one has ever come this far before. I don't have that much energy."

"Are you all right?" I said, trying to make sense of the ranting.

"It's worth the pain, Dale, to see family again. Even if I die, it's worth it." He squeezed my hand with his little claw, and I wondered what it would be like to be so scarred. He was ugly as hell. Ed had never married, never had a family. Lots of men give their lives for their country, but it seemed to me that Ed had given far more than anyone should be asked. I let him hold my hand until he drifted to sleep, then slipped out quietly.

As I closed the door to his bedroom, the phone rang and I grabbed it quickly, hoping it was Constance. "Hello?" I said.

Kaman Porter began shouting on the other end. "You tell your dad that I don't care if he is buddies with Sheriff Carnaghan, I'm going to watch him and catch him and have his butt tossed in jail! Do you hear me! I'm going to have someone watching your house every minute! You won't get away with nothing! I-"

"Screw you," I said, and slammed the phone down. It was the most courageous thing I'd ever said to an adult. Filled with righteous anger, I clenched my fists and wished to hell that Kaman Porter would dare come to the house so I could beat the crap out of him. I went down to the living room and told Dad what had happened, and he laughed at me. I don't think he'd ever seen me so mad before.

"Well," Mom said, resigned, "I guess Kaman just believes we're tree thieves, and there's nothing to do about it." She was sitting on her end of the couch, underneath Dad's trophy elk head, knitting a red bow to put on a wreath.

My dad sighed, rocked in his chair, scratched his head. "That reminds me, it's a week till Christmas. We ought to get a tree tomorrow. Where should we get one?"

I knew where a perfect tree was, about fifty yards from the house. Before this whole thing started I'd kind of wanted to sneak up there and cut it down some night, but of course my parents would never allow me. Now, I don't think they could have stopped me. "I know where I can get a good one."

My dad gazed at me with a mischievous sparkle in his eye, rocked a little faster. My mom stopped knitting, stared at me hard. "You better not be thinking what I think you're thinking!"

"There's a lot of trees up on the flats, by Alsea Falls," I added quickly. "They logged that area off about ten years ago, and there's a lot of nice trees." My mom went back to her knitting. She never thought evil of anyone.

Dad nodded, "Yeah," he said, eyes boring into me, giving me permission. "We'll leave it to Dale to pick a tree this year."

In the morning my parents both left for work at seven, Dad to the mill, Mom to the grocery store. I didn't have to be to school till nine. The grinding of chainsaws from Porter's tree harvesters woke me at eight, and I fixed breakfast for Ed. He wandered down from the bedroom at eight forty.

"I loaned your parents my pickup," he said. "One of your cars got a couple of flats. Your mom asked me to tell you that you'll have to catch the bus."

I looked up at him in horror. "The school bus passed here fifteen minutes ago," I said. I'd never missed school before, not without being sick.

"Ah, well, you'll just have to be late, then. Do you have a tire pump?" he asked. I nodded. "We can probably pump up the flats long enough to get into town," Ed said, then sat down to eat. When we finished breakfast, we tried to pump up the tires, but both tires had leaks the width of a half-inch knife blade.

I was mad enough to curse, but Uncle Ed didn't seem to take it hard. I looked up on the hillside. Old Man Porter had his migrant workers cutting trees near the top. One of them turned off his chainsaw and watched me. Uncle Ed calmly walked into the house. When I found him, he was in the kitchen, paging through the phone book. I thought he'd call Old Man Porter and give him a good verbal thrashing, but instead he phoned the power company.

"Hi," he says without flinching. "This is Kaman Porter, out in Alpine. I'm moving tomorrow and I'd like to have my power disconnected." He read off Kaman's address and phone number from the book, then called the phone company with the same story. He called the post office and asked them to forward Kaman's mail to a motel in Eugene that he picked from the Yellow Pages. Then he called the motel and told them he would be having his mail forwarded, and asked them to hold it indefinitely.

Just when I started to get amazed at how easily Uncle Ed was sabotaging Kaman Porter's life, Ed called up the *Corvallis Gazette Times* and asked to buy a full-page, three-color advertisement offering free Christmas trees for senior citizens. He was willing to pay plenty extra if they would place the ad in the afternoon edition. The type would be overlaid on a picture of a red and green Christmas wreath, and it boasted, *Bring a Grandparent, and you can cut a tree, free!* He had them print our farm address on the advertisement, but had the bill for the ad sent to Kaman. I could hear the saleswoman talking excitedly, and Ed saying sweetly, "Of course you can bring your grandmother and get a tree! This is just our way to help out our senior citizens. Heck, you can even get one for yourself. Thank you, bye." Then he called the IRS and left an anonymous tip, saying that his employer, Kaman Porter, evaded income tax by not accurately reporting tree sales made to local lots.

When he finished, Uncle Ed sat there calmly thinking, stroking his chin. He glanced at me, and must have seen the shock on my face. "Don't look so surprised," Ed said. "The purpose of any military engagement is to demoralize the enemy. This is only the start. Kaman Porter will rue the day he crossed paths with this old mutant."

"I . . . Is this legal?" I asked.

"Not exactly," Uncle Ed said, "but Porter could never make the charges stick. Just remember, Dale, when you commit a crime, make sure the benefits outweigh the risks. This kind of crime carries minimal penalties, but offers great satisfaction."

My mouth must have dropped open. Ed raised a brow over his good eye. "Don't be so surprised. One thing you're going to find out about us Fawkeses is that we're all assholes. Why do you think your dad ran away from home when he was fourteen?"

"I don't know," I answered.

"'Cause your grandpa was an asshole. So was his dad before him, and your great-great-grandfather Ben." He smiled at me. "I can see there's a lot of things your dad hasn't taught you about the family. Did your dad tell you about his twelve great-uncles—the legislator, the judges, the sheriff?"

"Yeah," I said proudly. My dad had often told me about my prestigious uncles, pointing out how easy it was to make something of your life.

"They were all moonshiners and gangsters back in the thirties, every one of them," Uncle Ed said, "and they bought their way into office to cover their illegal activities. They didn't just live in the mountains of West Virginia, they *ruled* those mountains. Your ancestors were all big men—and every one of them was tougher than a Marine's butt and meaner than a truckload of escaped convicts.

"But, you know," he said softer, "your dad isn't one of us. He doesn't look like a Fawkes—too short, too dark. It's all that Cherokee blood in him. Maybe the family curse skipped a generation. But you, you got it. When you get mad, you get old Ben's fire in your eye—even though you're too damned tame to know what to do with it. Now Ben, he was a hell of a man—meanest man you would ever want to meet. Even at sixty, wearing his wooden leg, he'd walk into a bar, pick half a dozen loggers, and start a brawl with them just for fun. He put a steel toe on that wooden leg of his, and when he kicked you, he could break a kneecap or put out an eye. On the day he died, every church congregation in the county offered a prayer of thanks."

I must have looked astonished, and Uncle Ed said. "You didn't know that? What do you know about your family? What do you know about me?"

"I just thought you were a cripple, working in the steel mill, waiting to die."

"A steel mill? Is that what Uncle Charlie said?" Ed ran a hand through his white hair. "Hell, kid, I joined the Marines fresh out of high school, and when they kicked me out of the service with a purple heart and a medal of valor, I took a job in Africa helping advise Kikuyu headmen in the proper conduct of a tribal war. I've been a mercenary for over twenty-five years. I could get this face fixed up a bit, but out in the Third World, the dictators want to see proof that you're tough. Hell, I got shot nine times down in Latin America." He rattled off something in Spanish, and said, "Remember the Bay of Pigs? Do you really think an incompetent like Castro could have fended off the US without a few men like me?"

Uncle Ed held my eye. Suddenly things that I'd only half known about the family made sense—the reason my dad had run away from home, why one of my great-uncles had gone to prison for shooting an FBI agent. Moonshiners. I'd known that my grandfather had run a "gentleman's hunting lodge" in West Virginia back in the thirties, but now I understood what kind of establishment it had been. Once, in a letter, grandpa had referred to my dead grandmother as "that Indian whore," but until that moment I'd always thought he had spoken figuratively.

So this was what it was like to have a family. I wandered upstairs, looked in the bathroom mirror, and thought about what Uncle Ed had revealed. It seemed to explain a lot about me: Why I got so mad sometimes and wanted to tear the limbs off people like Kaman Porter, why I could love Constance and still consider using her. I pulled off my shirt and flexed my muscles in front of the mirror. I was pretty big, with twenty-inch biceps. Tougher than a Marine's butt and meaner than a truckload of escaped convicts. Now I knew why it was so easy for me to break the high school weight-lifting records.

Still, something bothered me: Uncle Ed's admission that he had worked for Cuba. There had been a smile in his eye as he said it, a jarring unevenness to his voice. He'd been having too much fun. I suspected he was exaggerating, stretching things. Still, there were his nightmares, and the scars. I didn't doubt that he had lived for years at war.

I waited until lunchtime, went out and looked at the hills around the house. The tree cutters were gone, the chainsaws silent. Porter sent his trees south to California by rail, and with only a week till Christmas, I was surprised he had kept cutting this long. I went into the tool shed, got a saw, climbed the hill.

The tree I wanted was still standing—a luscious blue spruce about six feet tall with nice thick foliage. I studied the valley, looking for sign of Porter's men, but didn't spot anyone. I cut the tree quick and nearly ran as I pulled it downhill.

On the ridge behind me, Kaman Porter shouted. "Hey, you dirty bastard—drop that tree!" I turned and looked. Even though I knew the area where he hid, he was hard to spot. He stood in the trees, wearing camouflage hunting gear, a pair of binoculars dangling from his neck. He didn't have a gun.

"Up yours!" I screamed, and I dragged the tree to the house.

"I'm calling the cops!" Kaman shouted as I pulled the spruce in the front door. I slammed the door closed, sagged against it, and knew I couldn't keep the tree. I knew Jerry might come to arrest me, and I would tell him about our slashed tires and cut power lines, and Jerry would get mad and tell both me and Kaman to grow up or go to jail. It didn't matter. I wanted that tree, in my house, just for a while.

Uncle Ed stood by the window in the living room, looking uphill. "Porter's gone to call the police, I reckon," Ed said. "Do me a favor, and call me a taxi."

"The nearest taxi service is twenty-five miles away," I argued.

Ed nodded. "Have it meet me at the bottom of the driveway. Meanwhile, I want you to disappear until dinner. Give me a couple of hours."

"What are you going to do?" I asked.

"Demoralize the enemy." Ed dragged my tree into the kitchen, began pulling off branches. I phoned a taxi, then headed into the hills with my shotgun, up to some beaver ponds where mallards nested. Mr. Porter must have called the police from the CB in his car, because he stood on the hilltop and watched me leave.

I returned at dusk. My mom and dad were home. New tires had replaced the flats on Mom's old Ford. Through the kitchen window I could see Mom fixing dinner. As I walked up to the house, Ed met me at the door.

I asked, "Has Sheriff Carnaghan been here yet?"

Ed shook his head. "I called his number and got his wife. She says he took his bear dogs out to run for the afternoon and won't be back till tonight."

I put my gun up, fed the pigs, then went in to eat. A tall, scraggly Douglas fir sat in the front room, all decorated with lights. The branches were thin, and the tree had two pretty equal tops. It wasn't bad for a wild tree, but not near as nice as one of Mr. Porter's cultivated trees.

As we ate, Sheriff Carnaghan pulled up the driveway and Mr. Porter came running downhill, still dressed in his camouflage. I figure he had been waiting up there all day, watching the house. We all went out to the front door, and as soon as Sheriff Carnaghan pulled himself out of the car, Kaman Porter began shouting, "That's the one! He stole my tree!" He pointed at me. "I can show you right where he cut the tree! He's got it in the house."

"I don't know what he's talking about, sir," Uncle Ed said. "Dale and I have been together all day. We went up to a place called Alsea Falls and cut down a tree, and when we got back, this fellow came running down to the house, swearing at Dale and threatening to slug him. I had to push Dale in the house to protect him from Mr. Porter. Isn't there a law against beating up minors?"

Kaman Porter stood frozen in shock. He stuttered. "Tha . . . that's a lie! I've never seen this guy before." Jerry studied us calmly, reached into the glove compartment of his patrol car, and pulled out a tape measure and a flashlight.

"Can you show me the stump where this tree was cut down?" he asked, and Kaman Porter nodded, led us uphill in the dark. The stump measured seven inches across. Sheriff Carnaghan pulled some spruce needles from a branch that still stuck out from the trunk. "Now how tall was this tree of yours—six, seven feet?" Kaman nodded. Jerry turned to my dad. "You mind if I have a peek at your tree?"

"Go ahead," my dad said.

We went downhill, into the house. Jerry Carnaghan just looked at the tall Douglas fir and wrinkled his face in disgust. That tree Uncle Ed had gotten took up every inch of the ten-foot span between our floor and ceiling in the living room. "This doesn't look much like a farm-grown tree to me," Jerry said. He got down on his knees and made a show of measuring the base of the tree. He had to push aside the little yellow tag they gave you when you bought the $1.00 permit to cut trees on public lands. Uncle Ed had tied it around the trunk, all nice and legal. "Eight inches," Jerry said. "Not even close."

"Well, well, that's not the tree!" Kaman said. "There's got to be another one here in the house."

"You're welcome to search," Ed offered.

Jerry looked at him sideways. "I think I'll do that," he said suspiciously. He walked upstairs, checked the bedrooms and bathroom. He wasn't just looking, he was sniffing, trying to catch the scent of that tree. I thought about that blue spruce, with all its fresh pitch, and started feeling kind of nervous. If Uncle Ed had put it in a closet, Jerry was sure to sniff it out. I looked at Uncle Ed, and he was sweating.

Jerry finished searching upstairs, then went through the downstairs. Ed wiped the sweat from his forehead just as Jerry came out of the kitchen.

Jerry told Kaman. "Look Porter, I can't find any other trees in this house. I suspect you've been watching the house all day. Has anyone taken a tree out?" Kaman hung his head, shook it. "Did you see any smoke from the chimneys?" Kaman shook his head no. "Well then, I think you owe these folks an apology."

"You know, officer," Uncle Ed said. "We've had a regular crime spree around here the last two days. Mr. Porter threatened to make trouble for us a couple of days ago, and he nearly battered poor Dale here earlier this afternoon. Someone shot down our power lines, knifed a couple of tires last night. Would you mind keeping an eye on things here, stick close by? I'm an old man, and I feel threatened."

Sheriff Carnaghan gave Porter a sidelong look. "Would you like to pay these folks for their tires, or shall I go up to your car and search for the knife?"

Porter glared and kind of hissed, pulled out his wallet. Mr. Porter's wallet was so full of bills, I suspect he probably *was* selling a few trees on the side, and wondered if the IRS would nail him.

"Uh, they were very expensive tires," Ed added. "I have the receipt right here in my pocket." I felt kind of sorry for Mr. Porter. Tomorrow promised to be one of the worst days of his life.

After they left, we stood admiring our Christmas tree and listened to Sheriff Carnaghan drive off down the gravel road. Uncle Ed put his arm around me, and I put my arm around him, and for the first time, I was glad to have met my uncle. I hugged him and, well, just felt really close. It seemed a miracle, never having had a family beyond my mom and dad, to feel such a warm glowing feeling for someone.

My dad put his arm around Uncle Ed's shoulders. Not turning his head, he asked, "Where did you stash the tree, Ed?"

My mom hurried into the kitchen, saying, "I don't think I want to hear this." She clasped her hands over her ears.

"Well, that chest freezer of yours out back was looking kind of empty," Ed whispered. "So I filled it up."

Dad grunted, "Clean it out in the morning." Then he sort of leaned back his head and sighed pleasantly. "You know, this kind of reminds me of our Christmases back home when I was a kid in West Virginia. The screaming, the fights, the cops."

"Yup," Ed whispered.

My dad sighed again. "I never missed it."

Later that night, Constance drove over in her mom's Cadillac and we went up to my room to sit on the bed and talk. She seemed nervous, excited, and after a bit she said, "I bought you your Christmas present yesterday. You want to open it?"

I nodded, and she unbuttoned her blouse just a bit, flashed her chest. She was wearing a blue silk teddy under the blouse, and she grinned at me. The blood pounded like oceans in my ears, and my throat and my crotch got tight at the same time. She giggled and said, "You have to wait until Christmas to open it," and scooted to her side of the bed. She seemed breathless. "Here's the plan. On Christmas night, I'm going to ask your parents if you can come to my house for dinner, and then you can ask my parents if I can come to your house for dinner. Then, you can come pick me up and take me to Eugene. I rented the honeymoon suite at the Hilton for us."

I nodded dumbly, surprised that she'd concocted such a scheme, wondering how she'd gotten so much money to do it. She bit her fingernail, then pulled her hand away quickly and looked at it, not me. Her voice got quiet, nervous. "I . . . I want this to be special. I want it to be romantic. Do you understand? Not quick and then over."

I leaned forward, took her hand, not sure how to make it romantic. "I'll be gentle," I promised. We kissed, and my hand strayed to her breast for the very first time. She pushed my hand away but kissed me harder. When I walked Constance down to her car, something had changed between us. I could sense it—as if there were an invisible bond between us, a hidden cord connecting us, and I didn't want to let her go. I held her hand, kissed her good night. Her confidence seemed to falter then, and she turned away. I could tell she was still uncomfortable with the idea of making love. I watched for a long time after the taillights of her car disappeared over the hill.

I went upstairs and lay on my bed, then got scared again. Before, when thinking about having sex, I'd mainly been afraid that it would destroy our relationship, afraid I might lose Constance. Now, I was just afraid to have sex. I think that everyone is selectively stupid about some things. For example, I know a chemist who could tell you all about how emulsifiers in detergent whiten your clothes by forming covalent bonds with ionized dirt particles in the washer, but he's so butt-stupid about how to wash his own clothes that he's always wearing pink underwear.

I was selectively stupid about sex. I started thinking about it when I was thirteen. My dad and I had gone to Ron Holloway's to buy a calf, and when we got out by the barn we caught some stray terrier copulating with his prize Brittany spaniel retriever. We each put a boot up on the bottom rail of the corral and watched the two go at it. Ron Holloway yelled at the terrier, trying halfheartedly to separate the dogs, but the stupid terrier couldn't get his penis unstuck, so he just looked at us mournfully.

I asked dad if anything like that ever happened to people. He gave me a sidelong glance. "Sure—especially with teenagers, the first couple of times they try it."

I wrinkled my nose, looked at the dogs. "What do you do when it happens?"

Dad kind of shrugged. "Well, when your mom and I got married, we had to call the ambulance to get us separated. That's what most folks do. But if you're smart, you'll just give it a couple of hours, and you'll find a way to work it out."

One of the cowboys at school had the hook-shaped penis bone of a raccoon that he wore in his hat, so I asked, "But, how do people get hooked together like that? I mean, we don't have penis bones like a coon, do we?"

"Sure we do," Ron cut in. "It's right up behind your anus. You just never see it pop out until you get real excited, like when you make love to a woman. That's why when your penis gets all erect, it's called an 'erection,' but when the penis bone drops down, people call it a 'boner'—'cause there's a bone in there." Ron yelled at the little terrier to get off, but the terrier just started humping harder and harder.

Dad said, "Aw, Ron, just let them have their fun. A couple of years ago, I tried to scare a stray off my bitch, and he ran off so quick he pulled off his penis."

Ron got a sour look on his face and said, "Ew, I hate it when that happens."

So you can imagine why I was frightened about making love to Constance. I was worried that I'd crush her pelvis, or we'd get stuck and have to call an ambulance and they'd tell our parents, or maybe I might even rip off my whole danged set of paraphernalia in the act. If that wasn't enough to worry about, there were all the sexually transmitted diseases on the periphery of my awareness—crabs and genital warts and jock itch.

Remarkably, the only thing I wasn't much concerned about was getting Constance pregnant. I mean, down the street, for the past *eight years* Greg and Julie Helm had been asking folks in the Baptist church to help pray for them to produce a child. I figured that if some people couldn't get pregnant after eight years even with the help of God, then maybe it just wasn't as risky as your parents wanted you to believe. So, I lay in my bed, relishing the lingering scent of Constance's perfume and wondering how I could make it romantic for her.

Ed stopped at my bedroom door, inhaled deeply. "Now that," he said with satisfaction, "is the smell of Constance Hunter." I looked at him, not sure if I liked the idea of him savoring her smell as much as I did. "She's a pretty one. Smart, too. You're a lucky guy. So what are you doing tomorrow?" he asked.

I sort of shrugged. "I'm going duck hunting in the morning, I guess."

Ed nodded slowly. "It's been a long time since I've gone duck hunting."

"You want to come?" I offered, and he nodded.

I got up the next morning, put the cocker spaniel in the pickup, and drove Ed down to the river. We walked along the levy, climbed up Redrock Hill to a little blind between some fir trees. It was my favorite place to hunt—quiet, secluded. It looked out over a bend in the river, and at sixty feet in the air, the ducks would often fly right at eye level.

Uncle Ed had my dad's shotgun, but didn't even bother to load it up. Instead, he blew the duck call while I waited for a duck to fly by. After a few minutes, a big old Canadian goose flew down the river channel, honking. I raised my shotgun to shoot, but Uncle Ed put his hand on my barrel. "Just look at that," he whispered with awe in his voice. I stopped and gazed out over the Willamette Valley, emerald green even in the dead of winter, and the fog was hanging low over the valley, turning to golden mist as the sun rose, and that goose flew past, never even seeing us, and kept honking. "Just look at that"—Ed whispered as it left—"So beautiful and perfect. It won't last forever. Just hold it in your mind forever."

I lowered my gun, and Uncle Ed kept blowing the call. The goose circled back toward us, flew up the river two more times, looking for the source of the call, and a flock of mallards skated into the water in front of us. I didn't take a shot all day, and our poor spaniel never could figure out what was wrong. I looked at Ed's twisted face and realized he wasn't really a mercenary. He had too much respect for life in him.

As we were walking back to the car, picking our way through the brush along the riverside, Ed got all quiet, solemn, and I could tell something was on his mind. "That's quite a girlfriend you've got," he said at last.

"She's pretty nice." I admitted.

"Pretty nice?" Ed said. "I'd say she's more than that. I'd say a woman like her only comes around once in a lifetime—if you're lucky. If you're even luckier, a woman like that would fall in love with you."

I nodded thoughtfully.

Ed said, "I guess I ought to tell you that when I was on my way up to bed last night, I heard you two talking, making your plans."

"What do you mean?" I asked, suddenly terrified. I hadn't heard him come upstairs or open the door, but then I had been preoccupied.

He stopped, looked me in the eye, and said nervously, forcefully, "I mean only this. If you make love to that girl, for you it would be a release. But from her point of view, it's bondage. If you make love to her, you'll want to have her over and over again. Even if you get lucky, even if she doesn't get pregnant, she'll have that lingering fear every time. For a young man like you it gets easier and easier to make love out of wedlock, but for a smart young woman like her it gets harder and harder. It won't take long for her to figure out that you're putting her in a tough situation. Part of her will resent the way you use her. In time it will sour your relationship, as sure as heat sours milk."

Ed's voice got softer. "When I was young, I was a lot like you. I wanted all the wrong things out of a relationship. Then this happened," he pointed at his face, "and I never had another chance. If I were you, I'd be careful. Look at me. I'm a lonely old man. Don't make the same mistake I made."

"I ... I ..." I couldn't say anything. We reached the car, and my mind kept racing, wondering if it were true. I thought about the couples at school who were having sex—the way the light seemed to go out of their eyes after a while. I didn't want that light ever to go out of Constance's eyes. But I'd reached my sexual peak that week, and I couldn't bear the thought of not making love to her, at least once, maybe once in a while.

Porter had a big white sign with red letters out on our property that read "Porter's Tree Farm." When we topped the hill, a dozen cars were parked in front of the sign, all filled with old folks and their grandchildren. Kaman Porter was pacing by the roadside, watching them cut down his trees, his face red as a poker.

Uncle Ed slowed the car, rolled down the window and shouted real neighborly, "That's a nice thing you're doing, Mr. Porter. And it's also a good tax write-off." Porter didn't know yet that his power and phone had been disconnected. It might take him a week to figure out that his mail had been forwarded elsewhere. And who knew when the IRS would audit. But Porter looked at Uncle Ed and his face got all purple and screwy. "I'm going to nail you for this!" Porter shouted, shaking a fist. "You did this! I don't know how, but I'm going to nail you!"

Ed punched the gas and said to me, "Stick a fork in him, he's done."

For the next few days, Ed and I went out to look at ducks every morning, and I spent the evenings with Constance. At nights Ed was still tormented by nightmares of war and his sick spells, but I didn't worry about it so much. Somehow, Ed seemed immortal to me, someone who wouldn't ever quite put up with death. Maybe it was his own confidence shining through. Constance seemed to have taken a liking to him, and on Wednesday night when she pointed out that Ed and I looked a lot alike, old Ed turned his profile to the good side. Though he was overweight, I could see some resemblance and said so, not at all ashamed to look like him.

On the morning before Christmas Eve, Ed went out and bought us all presents, set them beneath the tree. Ed seemed like a fairly poor man to me—old worn clothes in faded blue, nothing that looked nice, so Constance and I bought him a new outfit, and I sure hoped he liked it.

And then on Christmas Eve, the strange thing happened. It was late in the afternoon, and I was planning to go Christmas caroling with Constance and her family later that night. The house was all cozy and decorated, and it looked like we might have the most perfect Christmas ever. Tony Bennett sang "Have Yourself a Merry Little Christmas" on the radio, while we talked in the living room by the tree. My dad had gone into the kitchen to get us all some hot apple cider to drink, and the phone rang. Since he was by the phone, he picked it up and talked loud and happy to someone for a moment. I thought maybe it was one of my mom's sisters out in Nebraska, but my dad's voice quickly became worried and low. I glanced into the kitchen, but my dad had moved out of my line of sight. A moment later he hung up the phone and walked quietly upstairs.

My mom called, "Jack, what's wrong?" but my dad didn't

answer. He went into his room and my mom said, "What's wrong, what's going on?" more loud, frightened.

My dad came out of the room with a rifle, came down to the landing, and pointed the rifle at Ed's belly. "That was Uncle Charley on the phone. He just called to tell me that Ed has died. Charley tried to call him up to invite him over for Christmas dinner, and Ed never answered, so Charley drove over to Ed's house. They found Ed's body. He's been dead for over a week."

I turned to the man I thought was Uncle Ed. He had a vague flickering smile, and he slowly got up from the couch, raised his hands. He licked his lips. "I'm not dead, Jackie," he said. "Look at me! Look in my eyes! I'm your family. I'm not dead. I came all this way!"

My dad stared at him hard for several seconds, but then his eyes got cold, angry. "I don't know who the hell you are!" Dad shouted. "But if you don't walk out of here right now, I'll blow you to hell!"

My dad was trembling, his face a mask of rage, and I knew he'd shoot.

The man who claimed to be Ed grinned faintly. "Why Jackie," he said, "maybe you have some of the family spirit after all." He backed up, real slow, headed for the door. When he reached it, he opened it gently, closed it behind.

"Jack?" my mom said, pleading, and I knew what she meant. Whoever had just left the house, he was a Fawkes. Yet my dad had no living uncles but Charley and Edward.

A chill ran through me as I realized that Ed had died a week ago, about the time that this man showed up. I ran to the door, opened it. Ed's red pickup still sat in the driveway with its West Virginia license plates. Ed wasn't around. I looked down the road, scanned the hills full of Christmas trees. He hadn't closed the door thirty seconds ago, yet he was gone. I circled the house, but couldn't spot him or any fresh tracks heading up the mud embankment into the trees.

So we were left wondering who Ed was, what he was.

I got up the next morning, opened my presents like usual. Dad had given me a Winchester Model 100 twelve-gauge goose gun with a full choke. I'd wanted that gun for a long time. I inhaled the scent of the fresh bluing on the barrel, ran my hands up and down the glossy stock, pumped it a few times. She was a beauty—solid, smooth action. Dad had also given me a box of $3\frac{1}{4}$-inch shells and a goose call. Ed's present was there, so I unwrapped it. It was a book called *Sex and Dating*. I hid it in my room.

I went outside, looked in the driveway. Ed hadn't taken the red pickup, and he wasn't sleeping in it. I had the odd feeling it would stay there forever, if we let it, abandoned. I felt a great sense of unease.

I put on my hunting jacket, boots, and stocking cap, then drove down to the river. I walked along the river up to my favorite spot on Redrock Hill. The morning was quiet, dark, with heavy gray clouds that smelled like snow. The geese must have all realized that it was Christmas, for they seemed to have taken the day off. A couple of little blue-winged teal flew by, but I didn't bother shooting them. Instead, I wondered about Ed, and sometimes I fantasized about Constance, thought of how good it would feel to make love to her that night.

After a couple of hours I headed home, back along the river. At one bend in the river was a spot hard to negotiate. A barbed-wire fence ran through the fields, into the brush along the river's edge, and out into the water. At this spot the brush was heavy, with lots of small alders along the river. In summer the cattle tended to come down to drink where the fence met the water, so the ground there was always churned and muddy, slippery. Just around the bend was a secluded spot where mallards liked to lie, so I flipped the safety off on my shotgun just in case I needed to pull off a quick shot.

I got to the fence and tried to squeeze between the wires. If I'd had my old shotgun, I'd have set it down in the mud till I got through, but I didn't want to get my new gun muddy. The top wire caught in my hunting jacket, and I tried to pry it up.

Nearby, Ed said, "Do you need some help?" He stepped out from behind a tree not ten feet away, and I stared hard at him. He wore the new outfit I'd bought him, except that he still had on his old, ratty belt. I knew that he couldn't have gotten the package unless he'd sneaked into the house while we slept. "I wanted to say goodbye. I thought I might find you here," he said, then stopped, and across the river a dozen canvasbacks wheeled along up the channel, their wings whistling. "They're beautiful, aren't they?" he said, gazing at them.

I lifted the wire above me, started to pull my foot through, and slipped in the mud. The trigger of the shotgun got caught in the barbed wire, and the gun discharged. For a moment I was relieved that I hadn't been hit, but then Ed grunted and fell. I twisted around, and Uncle Ed was lying on the ground twenty feet away. I dropped the shotgun and ran to him. He lay in the short grass, moaning.

I'd shot him in the leg, right near the crotch. Blood was pouring everywhere, and Uncle Ed tossed his head in pain. 'Oh shit. Oh shit!" he said, looking at the wound. "You hit the femoral artery. Go get a doctor! Run!"

I stopped, unsure what to do. It was a bad wound, in a dangerous place. Ed needed an ambulance, but if I didn't get the bleeding stopped before I left, he would die long before I could retrieve help.

I sat on my knees, looked at the wound. Those magnum shells had made hamburger out of his thigh, and blood poured out. I pulled off my coat, took off the new flannel shirt I'd gotten for Christmas, and used it to staunch the wound.

"Go on, Dale, get out of here!" Ed said, his teeth gritted. He tried to get up on one elbow. "You aren't helping me!"

"Shut up and don't move!" I shouted, pushing him onto his back. His face was colorless, and I reached into his thigh, felt the blood pumping there. I pinched off the artery with two fingers, the blood slippery.

"Oh God! Oh God!" Ed moaned. His face was pale, and I think he fainted a moment. I sat there for five minutes, trying to get the blood to stop, and during that time he began to grow cold to the touch. Sweat pooled on his brow.

He grew quiet, quit moving. Then I very distinctly heard a click, right by my bloody hand, and the whining noise of a small motor. Something hot began running over my hand, something like warm oil, and I forced myself to look down into the shattered horror of Ed's leg. There was a clear plastic tube in it, like a pipe, and some kind of hot blue oil was running through the pipe, dripping onto the wound. Something small and clear, like a water insect, plopped onto the wound and crawled over it. Seconds later dozens of others rushed out, began spreading the blue liquid everywhere with tiny, paddle-like legs.

I fell back, lunged away. Whatever Ed was, he wasn't human. The warm fluid pumping through his body seemed to rouse him a bit, and he muttered in delirium, "So far, I came so far."

"Who are you?" I shouted. "What . . . what did you come here for?"

"Just . . . I just wanted to relive my favorite Christmas," Ed panted, and then he began shaking his head no. "Son of a bitch, shot me." He began panting faster, trying to raise up.

I ran then. I ran because I was afraid that Ed would die, but I was also too afraid to help him. I got a hundred yards, stopped and looked back. Ed had rolled to his side, was trying to pull off his belt. He fumbled with it, fell back.

A tourniquet! I realized, and I rushed back to help him put it on. Ed pushed himself up on one arm, fumbled with the belt buckle. I had seen the belt buckle before. It seemed an ordinary brass buckle, small. But he did something to it, for when he held it at arm's length, large red numbers and letters shimmered in the air.

I stopped again, frozen. Ed lay panting, grunting, only twenty feet away. The little plastic insects had spread the blue oil all over his wound, sealing it. But my attention focused on the letters shimmering in the air. Some letters marked buttons in the air, outlined in blue, while numbers seemed to be only senseless strings in long columns. It was like a shimmering television screen, just floating. He pushed one button in the air. *Reset.* Whole columns of numbers disappeared, and he quickly jabbed a second button beneath the first. *Coordinates.* Strings of red numbers appeared in the air in columns. He punched the top number string, and the red numbers turned green. Then he pushed a button in the lower left quadrant of the fiery window: *Date.* A new column of numbers appeared, and he selected the top date. *AD 6/6/ 2274.*

A red flashing question appeared at the top of the screen: *Return to Home coordinates?* Beneath the question were two boxes. He pressed *yes.*

The fiery screen faded, and a strong wind began blowing at my back. I was watching Uncle Ed, but he seemed to be moving away— or maybe not moving away precisely, more like shrinking. I tried to watch him, but something baffled my vision. A black rainbow formed around his body. He blurred and bent, as if his whole body turned into hot taffy, and though I was watching right where he lay, I can only say that he seemed to *twist* away—as if he were a ship on the horizon that suddenly goes too far and drops out of view. I was looking into some sort of dark tunnel, and at the other end I could see light—a glimpse of a clear sunny sky.

The wind at my back got stronger, blowing hard toward the tunnel, and I suddenly felt dizzy, found it hard to breathe with all the wind rushing away. I dropped to the ground, holding on for fear that the wind might carry me, and heard a loud snap. My ears popped.

The wind stilled. Everything got still. No birds peeped. The very clouds seemed to have stopped in the sky. I looked up, and Ed was gone.

I went to the grass where Ed had fallen. No bloodstains splattered the ground, yet the grass was crushed flat, and I still had blood on my hands.

I stood looking at the place for a long time, berating myself. I should have known what Ed was right from the start, from the moment I looked into his face and saw my own eyes staring out at me.

As a child I had often wondered what it would be like to see Santa Claus, to touch an elf, to watch reindeer fly. To touch magic. As I looked at the ground, my whole body ached with a sense of wonder, and I knew.

Until then, I had never thought much about the future. Now, I cannot stop thinking about it. My grandfather lived from the era of steam engines to watch men walk on the moon. And the pace of change is growing exponentially. In the seventies, scientists did not believe we could travel back in time. Today, they have discovered new equations, new theories, and everywhere I turn I meet physicists who expect to see time travel within their own lifetimes. I hear them talk at symposiums, not always understanding the equations myself, and I nod my agreement, for I have seen the clear blue skies of the future.

Around the world, physicians recognize that we are on the brink of a medical revolution, and some doctors say that children born today may not die in a hundred or even a thousand years— children born today might, with the aid of technology, become immortal.

I think about the numbers on Edward's screen. Three hundred years. If things go as I believe, I will live for three hundred years. And in that time, much will happen.

Sometimes it scares me. I don't know what kind of life the man who claimed to be Edward lived, but I believe he lived with war, countless ages of war. And I wonder: Was longevity a gift freely given to all, or did he win it as a prize from some petty dictator?

Already I have deviated from the path that Edward showed me, altering my course forever, and I wonder if I will survive as long as Ed.

I went to college and studied genetic engineering after high school, resisting the lure of easy money that the government was forced to offer when they abandoned the draft. I put away all of my guns long ago, though I still go down to the river on quiet mornings to watch the ducks fly against the sunrise.

And I've changed my future in other ways. Edward seemed a lonely old man, perhaps bitter, willing to risk death in order to relive his favorite Christmas. Perhaps if I were old and maimed, perhaps if I looked back with solitary eyes to the only Christmas that I had ever made love to a girl, I would have shared his sense of nostalgia. Yet, in the end, he had warned me against that path.

So on that Christmas night, when Constance and I got to the motel, she timidly removed her coat and hung it by the bed, keeping her face down. I took her face in my hands and kissed her. I was trembling, sweating testosterone again, but I couldn't do it. I don't know, maybe I'd already passed my sexual peak by a few hours.

I held her hand and whispered, "I really want to make love to you, but right now, I want something more. Has your father agreed to stay here for two more years?" She shook her head, eyes downcast, then looked up at me. That clear light was still in her blue eyes, and I said, "Then let's go ask him together, for both of us." And we did.

That was eighteen years and three kids ago. Now, every year for Christmas, Constance buys a new teddy and giggles when I unwrap her. I've had a dozen Christmases far more thrilling than that one ever could have been. And each time I take Constance in my arms, I feel grateful to have met the ghost of my Christmas future, and I wonder and look ahead with awe, and sometimes even with a little dread, anticipating miracles.

A familiar story of birth, gone awry.

PRINCE OF THE POWERS OF THIS WORLD

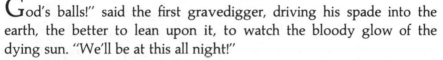

Roger Zelazny

God's balls!" said the first gravedigger, driving his spade into the earth, the better to lean upon it, to watch the bloody glow of the dying sun. "We'll be at this all night!"

"God damned ground's harder nor a stone," said the second. "Just like the old bastard to die midwinter and us to have the buryin' of 'im."

The third paused to blow upon his hands.

"Sooner the damned better he's underground. Out of sight, out of mind," he observed. "'Twas good watchin' his church burn. By the Old One's split feet! We could use some of that warm now, sure!"

The others chuckled.

"Aye!"

"True!"

They watched the sun slip away, the shadows rush to fill its place.

"Hark! What star is that, on high?" asked the first, pointing.

The others looked in the direction of his gesture.

"He's a right bright ruddy bastard," said the second. "But he ain't big-balled Mars. I don't know. . . . Never seen his like afore."

"Son of a bitch seems to be movin'," said the third, "off to the north."

"Aye," said the first.

"What's this?" asked the second. "Music? D'you hear it?"

"Music? Yer daft," said the third. "Y'd too much ale a' Mistress Doll's."

"Yer bloody deaf! Get the shit outen yer ears and give a listen!"

"He's right," said the first. "It seems to be comin' up outen the ground." With that, he pushed upon his spade with his foot and removed a clod of earth. He leaned then. "Pay heed," he said after a moment. "'Tis down there."

The others bent forward, listening.

"By Holy Joe's holy horns!" said the second. "'Tis pipes and some stringy thing and a drum, risin' like a fart outen the bowels of the earth—"

"Lads," said the third, dropping his spade and climbing out of the hole, "I've a mind not to be about when that wind breaks."

The others quickly retreated, also.

As they drew back from the half-dug grave the music came louder and the earth began to vibrate beneath their feet. Then, a dozen paces from their work, they were cast to the ground by a spasm that rippled through it like a wave through water. They shaded their eyes against the sudden illumination of flames which burst from the grave.

"Lords of the year! We're undone!" cried the first. "Behold what elevates from the Pit!"

Like a statue carved from old night, the horned, bat-winged figure rose amid the flames to tower above them. Its great yellow eyes moved from side to side then fixed upon them where they lay quivering. The music throbbed and skirled about it as it raised a leg to place a hoof the size of a bread loaf upon the grave's edge. Suddenly, its voice sounded, flute-like, above the tune from the earth:

"Rejoice, you miserable motherfuckers, for tonight is the night of your lord's birth!"

"Glad to hear that," said the first,

"I'm rejoicin' a'ready," said the second.

"Me, too," said the third, eyes darting toward the cover of a nearby thicket.

"This night he is born to a former virgin tupped screamin' by the Lord of Darkness in the convent where she dwelled," the dark creature went on. "Cast out by the nuns, refused shelter by the fearful country folk, she wandered, half-mad, till this night when she gives birth in a cave occasionally used for the quartering of animals. Her son is the Messiah of Hell, and I, Asmodeus, proclaim his reign to you! Now get your asses over to the cave and pay him homage!"

The music had risen as he spoke, retreated now as he concluded.

"Aye, Lord Asmodeus," said the first. "But—uh—where shall we find this cave with the babe in it?"

Asmodeus raised his right hand, pointing a talon on high.

"Follow the damned star," he said, "'Tis really a demon in a fiery chariot. He'll halt it above the cave so there can be no mistake."

"Yes, sir!" said the second.

"We're on our way!" said the third.

Asmodeus leapt from the grave and began to dance. The earth shook again, and from somewhere a chorus of childlike voices accompanied him as he sang:

> What child is this that is brought to birth
> With eyes like coals a-blazing?
> This, this is the Prince of Earth,
> Who'll take it to its ending.

When the first gravedigger looked back he saw that the other two were not far behind him.

Coming at length to a cave from which a faint glow emerged, the gravediggers halted, then advanced slowly, to peer within.

They beheld a mother and child, reclining on a bed of straw, huddled amid pigs, rats, ravens, and a pair of strange furry creatures.

"What are the two big 'uns?" whispered the second gravedigger.

"Jackals," said the first. "I saw their like one time in a book at the castle. The lord was readin' on the eve of a hunt, and he'd a mind to show us pictures of animals from other lands. Don't know what these two might be doin' here, though."

"P'raps they're someone's pets as got free."

"P'raps."

The third gravedigger cleared his throat.

"We'd best be payin' our respects," he said. "Wouldn't want to have Asmodeus mad at us."

"You're right," said the first.

Simultaneously then, all three of them cleared their throats.

The woman, almost a child herself, turned her head in their direction.

"Who's there?" she asked.

"Just—just some gravediggers," said the first, entering. "We were told to follow a star and we'd find this place. We came to pay our respects—to your child." The others followed him into the cave. The jackals raised their heads and regarded the men with yellow, unblinking eyes. It was difficult to tell where the light—a pale red glow—came from. Perhaps from the child himself. Silently, the mother began to weep.

"Well, here he is," she finally said, indicating the small black figure at her side. "He's sleeping just now."

The men dropped to their knees.

"'Tis good you'd a warm furry robe to wrap 'im in," said the second.

She laughed, though her tears continued to flow.

"'Tis not a robe. 'Tis his own hairy hide," she said.

"Oh," said the third. "Seein' as you're not so fortunate, let me give you my cloak."

"I can't take your cloak. It's cold out there."

"I've another at home. Take it," he said. "Even with your animal friends you'll be needin' it."

He extended it, let it fall upon her.

"I hope he brings you some kind of joy," said the second.

She bit her lip.

"Who knows? He might take more after me than after his da. 'Tis possible, you know."

"Of course," said the first, turning away. "I wish you good fortune—and that the young 'un will love you and honor you and care for you."

"Why should I?" came a tiny voice.

He looked back, and the child's strange eyes (he could never recall their color) were open and fixed upon him.

"He has been able to speak since the moment of his birth," the mother stated.

"Why should I?" the child repeated.

"Because she loves you and tends to you and has suffered for you and will suffer for you," the first replied.

The child turned his gaze upward.

"Mother, is this true?" he asked.

"Yes," she answered.

"I do not want you to suffer," he said.

"There is little you can do about it," she told him.

"We shall see," he stated."

"I guess we'd best be going now," said the first gravedigger.

She nodded.

"Thank you for the cloak," she said to the third.

"Bide a moment," said the child. "Who told you to follow the star to this place?"

"A demon named Asmodeus," said the second. "He came up out of the ground and so bade us."

"And why did you do as he told you?"

"Why, we feared him, sir," said the first.

"I see. Thank you. Good night to you."

The gravediggers backed out of the cave, were gone into the night.

"Those men," the child said then, "do not love me or tend to me as you do. They came because they feared that they would suffer if they did not obey my uncle. Is that not correct?"

"Yes," his mother said. "That is correct."

"Then which is stronger, love or fear?"

"I do not know," she said. "But the one did not give me his cloak out of fear, and he will suffer from the cold because of it."

"Does that mean that he loves you?"

"It is a kind of love to tend to another when you do not have to. But it is more a friendly thing than a lovely thing. With fear, you do things because you must or you will be hurt."

"I see," said the furry child, snuggling against her. "The man is a friend."

Later, as they dozed, three more figures approached the cave and begged permission to enter. They were three kings who had traveled far and over the sea out of the East and the South, bearing gifts of opium, strychnine, and silver, each of which gave power over people by different means. They desired that their kingdoms be spared when the days of the conflagration arrived—and that, as future allies, they might benefit from the destruction of their neighbors who resisted.

"I begin to understand," the child said after they had left. "They do not love me, they fear me."

"That is right," she said.

"They are not even friends."

"No, they are not."

At midnight a great rush of fire occurred beyond the cave mouth, filling the entire enclosure with baleful brilliance. The mother gasped and shielded her eyes, but the child stared into the flames, where a dark, brooding, masculine form took shape. With a laugh, the figure strode forward, to regard them. Then he stooped, snatched the gravedigger's cloak away from the woman and cast it back over his shoulder, where it burst into flames. Then he threw an ermine robe atop her and the child.

"You!" she gasped.

"Yes," he replied. "My son and my mare deserve the best of garments." Reaching behind him, he produced a stack of shirts, skirts, and swaddling clothes which he laid nearby. "And good meats, fresh fruits, bread, vegetables, herbs, wine." He placed a massive basket upon the floor. Then he leaned to examine the opium, the strychnine, the thirty pieces of silver. "Ah, the kings have been by to plead for their pathetic realms," he said. "Well, do with them as you would, when your time comes."

"I shall," said the child.

"Do you know who you are, boy?" the dark one asked.

"I am her son, and yours."

"That is right, and you can summon a legion of demons to do your bidding simply by naming them. If you think about it, you will see that you know all of their names."

"It seems that I do."

"Do you know what it is that I want of you?"

"Something involving blood and fire and destruction, I believe. Someone may have referred to it as the final conflagration."

"That is close enough. The details will become clearer to you as you grow older. And you can always call upon me for a consultation if you are in doubt."

"Thank you."

"The means will be a young man who would be king. You will meet him one day, make him your slave, help him to his kingship, see him unite this realm, then have him cross the Channel to kick down the remaining holdings of the Roman Empire, take it for his own, and forge it into a new power under his command. Then you will be in position to execute the next phase of my plan—"

"Father, what will his name be, this young king?"

"I cannot see that deeply into things that are yet to be. There is always a cloud about major events."

"Will this man love me, or will he fear me?"

"Neither, if you use your powers properly. Think upon the lessons of your gifts. The silver teaches that people will betray others, and that everything has a price. The strychnine teaches that those who are too troublesome can be eliminated. The opium teaches that people may be placed in thrall, may be led as you choose, by a dulling of their senses and a laying on of glamour. That may be the easiest route with your king. You will know what is best when the time comes."

"I understand you," said the child. "How am I to know this man?"

"A fair question, my son. Behold!" With that, the dark one turned to his rear. When he turned back, he held a blade in his hand. He brandished it on high and it took fire with a roaring sound. Then, with a single step, he crossed the cave and plunged the weapon into a stone. "There," he answered. "He will be the only man capable of drawing that sword from that stone."

"I see," said the child. "Yes, I, too, see these things that are yet to be, through a cloud, dimly. I understand how I may use it."

"Very well, lad. If you need anything, call upon my minions. They will obey you as they would me."

"I shall, father."

The dark one turned, retreated into the flames beyond the cave mouth, and was gone. Moments later, the flames died.

The child yawned and snuggled against his mother once again. "Tell me, son," she asked. "Can you really see the future, like your father?"

"Better," he replied, yawning again. "Arthur shall be my friend."

A Christmas journey through Wonderland.

THE COCKATRICE BOYS

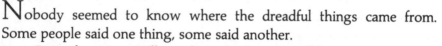

Joan Aiken

Nobody seemed to know where the dreadful things came from. Some people said one thing, some said another.

But at least I can tell you how the business all began.

It was on a wretched, rainy Sunday in the month of September. Recently the winters had all been bitterly cold and snowy, while the summers were shorter and windier and wetter. On this September Sunday, people were coming home from their holidays, flying in on planes from Sardinia and Spain and Sicily, but, for most of them, wherever they had been, the weather was so nasty that they hardly felt they had been away.

Tired, disgruntled passengers disembarked from their planes at the big airport outside Midchester. They scurried through streaming rain to the airport building, then filed slowly through Passport Control, and began waiting in the Baggage Claim Hall for their luggage to arrive. Soon they hoped to see it come sliding up a moving ramp, tip over the top, and come slithering down on to a travelling circular platform. All the passengers squeezed as close to this platform as possible, hoping to be the first to grab their own bags and hurry off to Customs.

But a whole lot of time passed by. People waited and waited and waited. They grumbled more and more loudly as they gazed at the rubber belt, which kept sliding by with nothing on it.

"Only twenty yards' walk from our plane," said one woman. "A one-legged rheumatic snail with athlete's foot could have fetched the luggage faster than those handlers are doing."

"Snails don't have legs *or* rheumatism," snarled her husband. "And I *told* you, Brenda, only to bring carry-on luggage for a weekend in Brittany."

"It wasn't a weekend; it was five days."

"I can see something coming," said a pigtailed girl who was with her aunt. She had red hair and looked thin and sad. Oddly enough, from where she stood, it wouldn't have been possible to see anything coming up the ramp. Yet she was quite right; in a moment something did come rolling over the summit of the ramp, and toppled down the other side.

"*That's* not proper luggage," said the woman called Brenda.

It certainly wasn't. It was an enormously large, lumpy, shapeless sack, tied at the neck with thick rope. It seemed to have some object inside about the size of a sofa, but not at all the *shape* of a sofa; this thing, whatever it was, must have had as many corners, dimples, bulges, dents, bilges, swellings, creases, convexities, and gibbosities as a seven-ended pineapple. The sack which contained it was uncommonly thick and stout, rather grimy, as if it had travelled half across the world, covered with tags and labels and scribbles, and coloured in wide stripes of orange and purple.

Almost at once it was followed by another sack, of a similar kind, and quite as large, but a different shape; this one was long, about the length of two beds put end to end, but lumpy, with a fitted bit of the sack covering a kind of prong that stuck up at one end.

"Maybe there's a camel inside it, lying down," guessed the pigtailed girl.

"Don't be silly, Sauna," said her aunt. "People don't send *camels* in parcels. Oh my stars, I wish our luggage would come. I want to get home. I want my tea."

Everybody wanted to get home and have their tea. Still the

luggage did not come. Instead, more and more and more of the large mysterious sacks came trundling up the ramp and tumbling out on to the moving circular beltway, until the whole circle was covered with them, gliding along, one after the other, like a lot of purple-and-orange ghosts.

"What the *dickens* can they be?" people were saying. "Who do they *belong* to? Why doesn't somebody claim them? It's not right! There's no room for *our* luggage with all those things on there."

"Maybe they are musical instruments," said the woman called Brenda. "Maybe they belong to one of those pop groups."

"Oh, sure!" snarled her husband, whose name was Ron Glomax. "And what stage in the whole *world* do you think is big enough to hold all those objects? And what do you think they are? Superpianos? Alphorns?"

"Matterhorns, more likely," someone said. "Anyway, if they are instruments, where's the group they belong to?"

"P'r'aps they come from Mars, and are stuck at Immigration."

"I'm going to complain," said Ron Glomax.

The moving belt was now completely packed with the big shapeless bags, wedged tight as dominoes in a box, and all shiny with wet.

"One of them moved," said the pigtailed girl.

"Nonsense," said her aunt. "Stop fidgeting about, Sauna. You stay close by me."

At the end of its track the moving belt travelled through a hole in the wall, beyond which was the outside area where the handlers stacked on the baggage. This hole was screened by a curtain of swinging leather strips. Beside it was a door marked NO EXIT FOR PASSENGERS. Ron Glomax opened this door and put his head out. But the rain outside was coming down in blinding sheets, so he pulled his head back in again, grumbling that it was all disgraceful.

But now, mysteriously, the number of sacks began to grow less. Gaps appeared between them. Then the gaps became wider. Nobody was seen to take a bag off the belt, yet there were many fewer. At last there were hardly any left.

"They go out, under the curtain, and then they don't come in again," said the girl called Sauna. Then she gave a gasp of horror, her eyes grew enormous, and she cried, "Oh, I can see something *huge* . . ."

"Quiet, dear," said her aunt. "Thank goodness, there comes our blue case at last. You hold my handbag while I reach for it—"

People were so happy to see their own luggage that they soon forgot about the big lumpy bags; nobody wasted any more time wondering who had sent them, or who picked them up, or where they had gone on that streaming wet Sunday in late September.

Several months went by before the first of the Cockatrices—for that was what they came to be called—made its appearance.

On a dark freezing December evening a truck driver called Sam Dwindle burst into his foreman's office looking very upset. He was white and sweating, and he shivered badly, despite the thick jacket he wore.

"Yeah, yeah, I just *know* what you're going to say," he told the boss, "but listen to this: an hour ago when I was coming up the A3 on that new bit of bypass, I see this *Thing*, with big three-cornered flaps along its back, and a tail the length of a tennis court, and round ears that swivelled about like radar shields, and it was running along beside the motorway on its four fat legs. Running as fast as I was driving! And *I* was doing seventy."

"Then you didn't ought to of been," said his boss, "not with a load of wine-glasses. I suppose you'd put in a couple of hours at the *George* in Milford?"

"No I hadn't, then," said the driver, injured. "I knew you wouldn't believe me. And if you don't, I'm sure I don't care! But I'm telling you, if that Thing had taken a fancy to cross the A3, instead of going off Dorking way, your truck would have been as flat as a Brillo pad, and me with it.

"It had a tassel on its tail," he added. "And flaps there, too."

"And a bow of pink ribbon on its head, I suppose," said his boss.

"Okay, okay! You can give me my cards. If there's going to be things like that around, I'm going back to window-cleaning."

The next of the Cockatrices was sighted by a school botany class, who were out on the town moor near Appleby-under-Scar, hunting for rabbit and deer tracks in the snow.

Two boys, Fred and Colin, had run on ahead of the rest, but they came racing back to the main group, as fast as their legs would carry them.

"Miss! Come and see! There's a dinosaur in Hawes Dell."

"Now what moonshine have you got in your heads?" remarked the teacher, Miss Frobisher. But the whole class hurried up to the lip of the dell, and looked down inside it.

"Gracious me! Somebody must be making a film," said Miss Frobisher. "But that's not an *ordinary* dinosaur, Colin. It's a, it's, um, Tyrannosaurus rex. You can tell that from its teeth and claws. The claws are at least eight inches long and the teeth—"

"Will it bite us?" nervously asked a girl called Lily.

"No, dear. It's only a model, a very clever one, indeed. I wonder where the cameramen are, and the film technicians. Dear me, what a lot it must have cost to make a model that size."

"It's coming this way," said Fred.

"Coo, it doesn't half stink," said Colin. "Like a whole truckload of rotting seaweed. Are you *sure* it's only a model, Miss?"

"Now, Colin! Use your intelligence! You know there aren't dinosaurs about any more. They lived millions of years ago."

"Look at its tracks in the snow," said Lily. "Aren't they huge? Listen to it pant. Miss, I'm scared. I want to go home."

"Don't be a baby, Lily," said the teacher. "Just when you've got a chance to study this very clever model, which must be radio-controlled. Now you can see what it would have been like to live millions of years ago—"

Those were her last words.

The newspapers carried the mysterious disappearance of Miss Frobisher and her class. "Their tracks were traced as far as the top of Hawes Dell," reported the Appleby *Herald*, "but heavy snow, falling soon after, prevented the police from discovering where they had gone next. A local farmer, James Robson, claimed to have seen what he described as a 'mammoth footprint' in the snow, but there has been no confirmation of his suggestion that some large beast was responsible for the strange fatality. Mr. Adrian Mardle, Chief Constable of West Humberland, is in charge of the case."

The next sighting was by an old lady, Mrs. Ada Backit, who lived in a high-rise apartment tower in Glasgow. "Eh, Hannah," she said to her daughter who had come in to cook her supper, "there's a face at the window, looking in!"

"Och, come on, Ma, be your age," said Hannah, who was in the kitchenette frying fish fingers. "How can there be a face at the window when we're thirty floors up? Unless it's an angel wanting to watch *Stalky & Co.?*"

"There's a face," said the old lady obstinately. "I can see its two big sad eyes, the size o' porridge plates. I'm going to—"

Then there was a silence. Hannah, walking in next minute with the dish of fish fingers, found nobody in the room.

"It was quite a shock to me," she reported that evening on local television, "because there is no other way out of the room. So where could Mum have gone? The window was shut and locked, and the flat is thirty stories up."

QUEER DISAPPEARANCE OF GREAT-GRANDMOTHER, the newspapers called it.

Then there was the business of the Christmas tree at Chiddinglea.

The residents had, as usual, erected a sixty-foot tree in the middle of the village green, and decorated it with lights, tinsel, and coloured fruit. On Christmas Eve a party was always held on the green, organised by the chairman of the Tree Committee, Colonel Clandon. Carols were sung, the lights were lit, and the whole village danced hand-in-hand round the tree.

"Hey!" called a boy called Michael, pausing to stare up at the starry sky.

"Look, there's something up there!"

Three or four people heard him and gazed up likewise. They saw that the stars were being blotted out by what seemed like a huge inky cloud. From this cloud, something hung down which swept in circles with a faint whistling sound. And, from the very centre of the blackness, two great pale luminous eyes glared down at the revellers. Suddenly, with a loud sucking snap, the Christmas tree was uprooted from its fastenings; it flew upwards like a pin raised by a magnet.

Gasps and yells of indignation and fright rose among the dancers.

"Hey! What's going on? Put back our tree! What kind of joke is this?"

"If it's that aerial club from Wormfleet with their helicopter—" began Colonel Clandon, but he said no more.

The carol singers of Chiddinglea, like the schoolchildren of Appleby, vanished for ever, sucked upwards into the dark like spilt sugar into a vacuum cleaner.

Very soon the population of the British Isles had become noticeably smaller.

Cars stood around without drivers. Houses appeared to be empty. Bus queues were very much shorter. Prams had no occupants. High Streets of towns were silent at midday.

In five years, half the country had become a desert. Buildings had fallen, or been knocked flat. The whole of London had gone underground. People didn't dare venture out in daylight anymore. Shops were hidden in cellars. Parliament sat in a dungeon under the Tower of London. Schools were held in crypts. Even the Royal Family lived in the basement which was all that remained of Buckingham Palace.

"Things can't go on like this much longer, Harold," said Lord Ealing, the Prime Minister, to General Grugg-Pennington, the Minister of Defence.

"No, they won't," agreed the Defence Minister. "Soon there won't be anybody left at all."

The two men were sitting in deckchairs on the Piccadilly Line, westbound, of Leicester Square tube station. Nobody else was there.

"I wonder where the monsters came from, in the first place?" mused Lord Ealing.

"Who cares *where* they came from? The point is that soon they'll have the whole place to themselves. The Snarks are the worst," said General Grugg-Pennington with a shiver.

"How can you tell? You've never seen a Snark."

"Of course I haven't! Everybody knows that if you see a Snark you vanish."

"I'd rather vanish than be munched up by a Flying Hammerhead."

"Remember that football match between Ipswich and Nottingham Forest?"

"Hammerhead got the goalie just as he was going to make a beautiful save," sighed the Prime Minister. "That was the last match played above ground."

The two men sat in silence for a while. Then Lord Ealing said,

"Harold, I want you to set up a Cockatrice Corps."

People had fallen into the habit of calling *all* the creatures Cockatrices. There were too many kinds to remember all their individual names: Kelpies, Telepods, Bycorns and Gorgons, Footmonsters, Brontotheres, Shovel-tuskers, Glyptodonts, Bonnacons, Cocodrills, Peridexions, Basilisks, Manticores (which some people called Mantigers), Hydras, Sphynxes, and Chichivaches. And, worst of all, the deadly Mirkindole.

The country was completely infested with monsters. They had grown and multiplied as fast as tadpoles in a pond.

"A Cockatrice Corps?" repeated the Defence Minister doubtfully. "But what about transport? How would they get around?"

"By rail."

"Underground? Hardly feasible."

"No, we shall construct a special armour-plated train to run above ground."

"But what fuel will it use?"

Stocks of oil, coal, and gas had long ago been exhausted. People had to manage without.

"The train will run on wind power. Or maybe solar energy."

"There won't be a lot of that," said the General. "The monsters raise too much dust."

This was true. Monsters flying over the dry, bare ground raised such clouds of dust that the sun was hardly ever seen, and, even before fuel ran out, aircraft had had to stop flying; the dust got into their compressor blades and the engines caught fire.

"Well, wind power, then," said Lord Ealing. "Plenty of that."

"Hm, a wind-powered, armour-plated train. That *might* be a possibility . . ."

"All the old tracks are there, so far as we know," said Lord Ealing.

"Gregory Clipspeak would be a good man to put in charge of the Corps. But it would be a most dangerous mission. We'd have to call for volunteers."

"You'd get plenty. People are fed up with living underground."

"Very well," said the Defence Minister. "I'll set up an Operations Room at once."

And that was how the Cockatrice Corps came into being.

The very last recruit was a drummer-boy called Dakin Prestwich.

When he told his mother that he had been accepted for the anti-monster corps, she burst into floods of tears.

"Oh, Dakin, you never! What d'you want to go and do *that* for? You must be out of your finitical *mind!*"

"I'm sick of living in the strongroom of Barclay's Bank Shepherds Bush," said Dakin. "I want to see some daylight."

"You'll be killed for sure! You'll be crunched up by a Flying Hammerhead. Or stamped on by a Footmonster. Or the deadly Mirkindole will get you. And I shall be left all alone," wept Mrs. Prestwich.

"Except for Mrs. Monk, Mrs. Prateman, Miss Jeppardy, Mr. Teal, and Mrs. Widsey," pointed out Dakin. These were the other people with whom Dakin and his mother shared the strongroom of the bank.

"You just don't *care* about your poor old mother."

"Yes, I do, Ma. And I'll be all right. They're going to give us Snark Glasses, and there'll be radio advance warning on the train, and a ballista for firing red-hot missiles at the Mirkindole. I'll come back safe and sound—you'll see—and maybe I'll be able to bring you a few dandelion leaves or a bit of wild spinach."

People were absolutely starved for greenery because they never dared go into the open country. All the food came from tins.

"Those Snark glasses are no use," wailed Mrs. Prestwich. "They say you can only use them six times. After that you see the Snark through them and vanish away."

"I'll be all right," repeated Dakin. Then he hugged his mother and left, because he could see that no amount of argument would ever convince her.

The troop train was waiting for its crew in a huge pillared hall underneath King's Cross station.

The Cockatrice Belle, as it came to be called, had been constructed with tremendous care and enthusiasm. People were so happy to do anything that might rid the land of monsters that they had been prepared to work all hours. Hundreds of willing helpers had worked for weeks in relays; the train had been built from all the bits and pieces left over from buildings that had been smashed by the devouring invaders. Everybody brought something. Fishermen brought hooks, old ladies brought scissors and needles, children brought paintboxes.

The train was armour-plated in bronze, inlaid with gold stripes, and the windows were triple bulletproof glass, with Snark-proof shades that could be automatically lowered at the touch of a button in the operations coach. On the roof were the wind-vanes and a row of solar energy panels, in case the sun ever shone. The wheels were steel, with rubber suction-tyres.

Dakin Prestwich ran up to the uniformed sergeant who kept guard at the ticket gate and saluted smartly.

"Drummer-boy Prestwich reporting for duty, sir," he said.

"Ho!" snorted the sergeant, who was tall and stringy and red-faced. "I wonder why Colonel Clipspeak saw fit to recruit a little chitty-faced object like *you*, when there was plenty others to choose from?"

"It's because I play the drum real psychedelic," said Dakin.

"Speak when you're spoke to! And you address me as Sergeant. Sergeant Bellswinger, I am, but Sergeant's enough for you."

"Yes, Sergeant."

"You get along to the boot-car, that's your station. Corporal Dwindle will issue you with uniform, and tell you your duties. And don't let me hear that drum," added the sergeant, scowling with great disfavour at Dakin's enormous instrument, "don't let me hear that drum *ever*, unless orders comes as it's to be sounded."

"How can I practise, then?"

"None of your lip. Double along to the boot-car."

Sergeant Bellswinger turned to bark at a new group of recruits, or rookies, and Dakin went along to the far end of the train.

Corporal Dwindle, a sad, scoop-faced man, issued Dakin with his uniform, which was dark brown, the colour of plain chocolate, with gold buttons.

"And here's a pair of Snark glasses, which have to be greased every day with Vaseline, and a compass, a walkie-talkie, and a liquid-air pistol," said the corporal, handing Dakin these items. "Sign the receipt form here, please. I'll be giving you instruction how to use the pistol; meantime don't go fooling about with it. You can stack your drum up there in the rack. Your duties are as follows: at seven ack emma every morning you take the colonel his early-morning tea from the galley—"

"Where do I find the colonel?"

"In his private coach, that's past the table-tennis car and before you get to the video-van. After the colonel's had his tea, polish the boots of all officers and NCOs. Then you gets your breakfast in the men's mess car. Then you cleans the windows," said the corporal, his eye lighting with enthusiasm, because he had once been a window-cleaner himself.

"What? *All* of them?"

"Every one. And I want to see 'em glitter."

"Every day, I have to do that?"

"Every blessed day. Visibility has to be kept at a maximum. When that's done you takes the colonel and officers their mid-morning coffee."

"I reckon they won't get their coffee till tea-time," said Dakin, looking along the length of the train at the rows of glass panes.

There were sixteen coaches in the Cockatrice Belle. During the two weeks' training period that followed, before the Monster Brigade were allowed out on active service, Dakin learned the order of the cars by heart, backwards and forwards; every morning while he cleaned the windows he had to recite them to Corporal Dwindle.

"Engine cab—arsenal—broom cupboard—ops room—men's mess —Galley—officers' mess—officers' parlour—video room—colonel's cabin—table-tennis car—four privates' barracks—boot-car."

To help himself remember the order, Dakin took the initial letters, E, A, B, O, M, G, O, O, V, C, T, P, P, P, P, B, and made a sentence from them: "Every agile boy outwits monsters. Grapple off, on very cold Tuesdays, Pythons, Peridexions, Pookas, Porcupines, and Basilisks."

The Colonel's car and officers rooms were handsomely furnished, with Turkish carpets, mahogany couches, brass fittings, and potted palms. The men's carriages were much plainer, with slatted bunks that had to be folded back in the daytime, and the men were crowded ten to a compartment, whereas the colonel had a whole bedsitter coach to himself, with armchairs, bookshelves, and a grand piano. The officers slept on folding beds in their spacious parlour, but there were only four of them—two captains, two lieutenants—so at least they were better off than the privates.

"It doesn't seem fair," said Dakin to Corporal Dwindle, as he polished windows.

"Nobody asked your opinion," said Corporal Dwindle. But then he added, "Life ain't fair, take it or leave it. Why should my missus have got swallowed by a Hammerhead? She never did nothing wrong her whole life—only watched telly and knitted four hundred and seventy-two pairs of socks. Life ain't fair. You might as well get used to that."

Dakin went on polishing windows.

On the first morning, as soon as Ensign Driver Catchpole blew the reveille on his engine whistle, Dakin shot out of his bunk in the boot-car, flung on his uniform, and dashed along the corridor to the galley, where he boiled a kettle on the brass hotplate and made a pot of tea for the colonel. He knew how, since he had often made tea for his mother, Mrs. Prateman, Miss Jeppardy, and the other people who lived in the Barclay's Bank strongroom. Then he carried the tea, on a tray, to the colonel's cabin, tapped on the door, opened it, and went smartly in.

A brown face glared at him from under the royal-blue velvet counterpane—a face with glittering grey eyes, bristly white eyebrows, and long sweeping white moustaches.

"And what in the name of the Pink Panjandrum brought *you* in?" snarled the colonel.

"Morning, sir, Drummer Dakin, sir, brought your tea, sir," said Dakin, and set the cup on the mahogany bed-pedestal.

After one sip, the colonel's eyebrows almost glided over the top of his bald head.

"You call this gnats' bathwater *tea*? What did you make it with?"

"Stewed dried grass, sir, like always."

Real tea had long since vanished from the British Isles.

"Well, you can take it and tell the mess orderly to wash dishes in it. Or his feet. From now on I'll make my own tea."

And the colonel pointed to an automatic tea-maker at the other side of his bed. It had a radio-controlled kettle which, just at this moment, blew out a puff of steam and then shot a neat jet of water into a small pot, while a bugle recording played "It's great to get up in the morning." From the pot floated a smell of brandy.

"Blow me!" said Dakin, greatly impressed.

"Neat, eh?" The colonel poured himself a cup of tar-coloured liquid. "Ahhhh! That's better. Now run along, boy, and take my boots, and polish them till you can see your teeth in them. And don't bring me any more of that hogwash tea."

"No, sir, thank you, sir."

After two weeks of training, it was announced that the Cockatrice Belle would go out on a trial run the next day.

"Where are we going?" Dakin asked Corporal Dwindle, who was giving him instructions in how to clean his liquid-air pistol.

"Manchester."

"Coo. My auntie Floss lives there. I went once, when I was a kid, before the Cockatrices came. It's a big place, ain't it? I remember high buildings, and a lot of buses."

"No buses now, I don't suppose. And the people are all starving. That's why we're going—to take them food. There's a big colony of Snarks all round Manchester—got the town surrounded. The people built a town wall and dug a moat, but they're trapped inside. Been radioing for help."

"What grub are we taking them?"

"Tinned carrots."

"I think I'd just as soon starve," said Dakin.

"I'd as soon starve as eat the muck they serve us in the mess," muttered Private Quillroy, stropping away at his Kelpie knife.

Everybody was grumbling about the food served in the mess.

"How are we supposed to fight Hammerheads and Shovel-tuskers on watery mashed and goat soup?"

"The bangers taste of minced mud."

"The tapioca's nobbut ground-up fibreglass."

"The wads are made of plasterboard."

Still, despite complaints about the food, the whole troop were in high spirits when, for the first time, on the first of December, the Cockatrice Belle huffed and chuffed slowly backwards up the long ramp that led from the pillared chamber under King's Cross. A military band on the platform played Tosti's *Goodbye.* The Prime Minister, the Minister of Defence, the Royal Family, and a large tearful crowd were left behind, waving flags made of old tea-cloths. Ensign Driver Catchpole joyously tooted his whistle, and the great glittering train crept gingerly into real daylight at last. It was all garlanded in tinsel and hung with small red and green glass bells, because Christmas was only a few weeks away.

"Coo!" breathed Dakin, blinking against the dazzle as he gazed out, but Sergeant Bellswinger roared over the intercom: "Snark Glasses—at the double—in *position!*" and they all clapped their protective spectacles on their noses. Behind the train the defensive gate clanged down over the mouth of the tunnel, the engine unhitched and rolled up a side track to the front of the train. Then it rehitched itself, and the Cockatrice Belle was on her way.

At first the landscape north of King's Cross was a bit of a disappointment to Dakin. For sixty miles, nothing could be seen but pink and yellow rubble, great dusty piles of smashed houses. Gradually these were replaced by snow-scattered country—very *wild* country, with clumps of scrubby trees and bramble thickets, and tangly ten-foot hedges, and huge ragged weeds on the railway embankments. It was all quite silent, except for the mild regular noise of the train, chunketa-chunketa-chunk, chunk, manunka-chunk, as it ambled its way along the rusty rails.

Occasionally the shriek of a monster could be heard. And among the bushes monsters of every kind could be seen, lurking, prowling, flapping, fighting each other, or just staring at the train with huge glassy eyes as it slipped by.

"What about *bridges?*" General Grugg-Pennington had said to Lord Ealing, who replied peevishly, "How can we tell? Who knows what condition the bridges are in? The men will have to survey and repair bridges when they come to them, if necessary, under covering fire from the train."

Luckily the bridges during the first part of the journey, as far as Oxford, were found to be in a fair condition; the Cockatrice Belle passed over them safely, gliding at a cautious twenty miles per hour.

Meanwhile the men of the troop had their hands full. Many monsters attacked the train. Flying Hammerheads swooped down from above, their ugly jaws snapping and scooping, and were fought off with flame-throwers and crossbows; great herds of Griffins, Footmonsters, Cocodrills, and Shovel-tuskers roamed beside the permanent way, often crossing the rails, snapping and clawing at the men as they battled to clear the track. Progress was often exasperatingly slow.

"Still," as Corporal Dwindle said to Sergeant Bellswinger towards the evening of the first day, "every little helps, and we must have done in a good few of the brutes. The men are getting used to 'em."

"Pity Private Quillroy had to go and get swallowed by that Shovel-tusker. If only he'd studied his drill and remembered to hold his crossbow sideways on—"

"Ah well," said Corporal Dwindle, "at least it's a lesson to others. Now do you see," he told Dakin, "why you got to keep them windows crystal clear? We need all the view we can get."

"Beg parding, Sergeant!" exclaimed Private Bundly, coming into the men's mess, where Dakin was cleaning the windows and the two NCOs were taking a cup of tea, "beg parding, but we've found a stowaway in the Arsenal. Hid away at the back, behind a stack of December guns, she was."

"She?" demanded Bellswinger. "And who the blazes may she be?"

"Here she be, Ser'nt," said Private Bundly, and he pushed into the mess cabin a rather strange figure, at first sight hardly recognisable as a person, for it was all tied up in sacks. However, when these were removed they saw a lanky melancholy-looking grey-haired woman wearing a homespun skirt and leather kneeboots and a man's jacket.

"Why the pize was she wearing all those sacks?"

"To look like a bundle of hammunition, I reckon."

"The colonel will have to see her. Come along, you!" Bellswinger snapped at the woman, who seemed too alarmed to speak, and he led her to the cabin of the colonel, who was playing waltzes on his grand piano.

Dakin followed inquisitively. Dusk had fallen by now, and he didn't see the point of cleaning windows if you couldn't see out anyway.

"A stowaway? A female stowaway? In my train?" The colonel was scandalised. "What's your name, woman? What d'you mean by it? Why in the name of blue ruin did you *do* it?"

The stowaway seemed to pick up a bit of courage in the colonel's presence.

"Oh, please, sir, my name's Mrs. Churt, and I hid under all those pepper-grinders, or whatever they are, because I *did* so long to get a glimpse of anything green. I used to have a little garden, sir, before all these horrible Griffins and Footmonsters and Bonnycons come along, we lived out Blackheath way, and I grew lettuce and Canterbury bells and radishes, and I can't *abide* living all my life in the dark like a blessed earwig, sir! That was why I done it."

"Well, but, my good woman, other people have to put up with living underground; and so must you. There's no *room* for you on this train. We'll be obliged to stop, you know, and put you off."

"Beg pardon, sir," muttered Lieutenant Uphold in an undertone. "Know it ain't my place to speak, but the old lady wouldn't last ten minutes if you put her out here. There's a deuce of a lot of Basilisks about. You can *smell* 'em—like wet washing, don't you know."

"I don't need *you* to teach me my business, thank you, Uphold," snapped the colonel, but Mrs. Churt fell on her knees and clasped her hands and cried, "Oh, please, please, sir, don't put me off! I can cook!—my old Churt, what was took by a Telepod, used to say I was a real Grade-A-one cook—and I can make drinks for the lads, and cakes, and that, and give 'em little treats, like those Vivandeers used in the Foreign Legion!"

"Humph! Well; that's as may be. I'll think about it. Overnight. In the meantime," Colonel Clipspeak said to the sergeant, "you had best lock the woman in the broom cupboard.—Is it true, Sergeant, that the men have been grumbling about the catering?"

"Can't say as to that, sir," said the sergeant stiffly.

"That in the officers' mess leaves *everything* to be desired," murmured Lieutenant Uphold.

Sergeant Bellswinger hustled Mrs. Churt away, but Dakin, lingering, whispered urgently, "Sir, the food's horrible! Soup made of melted bootpolish. And the spuds is like summat that's been dug up."

"Potatoes *are* dug up, you idiotic boy."

"No, sir, I knows better than that. They comes out of tins."

In two days Mrs. Churt was cooking for the entire troop, both officers and men. Her vegetable stews were mouth-watering; so were her steamed puddings: rich, crumbly, and wreathed in strawberry jam. Her doughnuts were light as thistledown, her raisin cake was satisfyingly stodgy.

Mess Orderly Widgery, who had been doing the cooking, was sent back to greasing December guns in the Arsenal, and Mrs. Churt presided over the galley. She had green fingers, too: she grew little slips of parsley and chives in jam jars, she polished the colonel's potted palm with salad oil, and she rescued the drooping geraniums in the officers' parlour from an early death.

Dakin became very fond of Mrs. Churt. He used to sit in the galley, sometimes of an evening, practising his drum-taps on a teacloth stretched over a sieve, while she made sassafras drink for the men, and talked about the happy times before the monsters came.

"We used to go to Broadstairs in the summer. You ever been to the seaside, Dakin?" He shook his head. "Eh, poor boy, fancy that! Deary me! Sometimes I wonder what we ever done to deserve having those monsters sent here."

"You reckon they was sent, Mrs. Churt?"

"Oh, they were sent all right, boy! Only, very like somebody didn't realise what a peck o' trouble they was pushing our way. See what I mean? I did hear, in the old days, factories used to dump all their rubbish out to sea; or, later on, up in the high sky, where they reckoned it'd blow away. Maybe somebody did the same with that little lot; just dumped them on us, like kittens in a rain barrel."

Corporal Bigtoe and a couple of privates came in, asking if there was any chance of a hot drink. While Mrs. Churt served them, Dakin pondered over what she had said.

Could somebody have wanted to get rid of the monsters, and just thought that this was the best place to tip them?

He decided that Mrs. Churt was probably right.

On the eighteenth day of travel they approached the outskirts of Manchester. Progress had been extra slow for the last forty-eight hours. Several bridges had needed a lot of repair; and two of the men engaged on this work had been lost: Private Goodwillie carried off by a Manticore, while Private Skulk had the misfortune to look at a Basilisk, and of course died instantly.

"Didn't keep his Snark glasses properly greased," grumbled Sergeant Bellswinger.

"Snark glasses won't help, not against a Basilisk," said Corporal

Enticknap. "In fact if you ask me, Snark glasses aren't much good at all. What we need is Snark *masks*, like what Driver Catchpole got issued."

"If you know so much, why don't you go to the colonel and say so?"

"I've a good mind to do just that."

"You go billocking to the Colonel, I'll put you on wind-vane duty," growled the sergeant.

Wind-vane duty was very risky. It meant crawling along the top of the train, often through driving snow, clearing out the vanes, which soon became choked with dust, and wiping the solar energy panels. The worst danger was from flying sharks, but also the train rolled from side to side as it travelled, so there was a fair chance of being flung off.

Enticknap scowled, but remained silent. But when Dakin took in the colonel's beautifully polished boots next morning, the latter demanded,

"What's all this about Snark masks?"

"They're saying as how the men ought to be issued with them, sir."

"Do you know how much a Snark mask costs, boy?" snapped the colonel.

"No, sir."

"Lord Ealing told me I was only to use them in the last resort."

"Where would the last resort be, sir?"

"Oh, go away!"

"Sir," said Dakin.

"Well? Now what?"

"Sir, I never gets a chance to play my drum. Ser'nt Bellswinger won't let me. He says it makes too much finical row, that it would rouse up all the finical monsters between here and Gretna Green. Sir, when *can* I play it?"

"Don't you worry," said the colonel, rolling over under the velvet spread to help himself to another cup of tea. "You'll get to play it soon enough."

At that moment, both Dakin and Colonel Clipspeak were astonished to hear a voice coming, apparently, out of the Colonel's early-morning tea-kettle. It said, "Hey, we gotta bloke here wants to get to Hempfields. What's it like out that way?"

"No go," said another voice. "It's a regular breeding-ground for

Snarks. Tell 'im if 'e goes, it's at 'is own risk. The corporation won't admit liability."

"Oke, I'll tell him that."

"You got Snarks your way too?"

"*Have* we got Snarks? Warrens full of 'em."

"They do say the young ones are harmless. You look at 'em, you don't die."

"You ever tried?"

"No, but my cousin Albert did. His kid brought one in for a pet. Cuddly little thing, it was."

"What happened?"

"It grew a bit older and looked at them and they all died."

"Well, then."

"What I mean is, if we could go after 'em when they're young . . ."

The two voices died away in a forest of crackle.

"Well I'm blessed," said the colonel. "My kettle seems to have picked up a radio frequency."

"Yes, sir," said Dakin. "Hempfields is a place in Manchester, sir. My auntie Floss used to live there. Do you think I'll get to see my auntie Floss by Christmas, sir?"

"Never mind that. You send Captain Slipper to me, right away."

"Yessir."

The outskirts of Manchester were more devastated than those of London, in a different way. There were great greasy frozen swamps, with derelict factories, twisted metal girders, ruined concrete overpasses, and piles of snowy black coal dust grown over with bindweed. But the town had not been flattened; far away in the distance, high-rise buildings could still be seen. The problem here had been Snarks, not the Shovel-tuskers which had knocked London flat.

Before it reached the city, the rail track sank down out of sight into a greenish peaty bog, puddled all over with ice and rainbow patches of oil. A party of ten sappers was sent out to make good the track, layering it underneath with rapid-setting filler and plastic ties. The men wore well-greased Snark glasses and carried Kelpie knives for close combat; they were protected by another party in the driver's cab armed with flame-throwers and also December guns, which fired explosive missiles of ice cooled to $-60°$ Centigrade.

But despite this they suffered badly. Dakin, dashing about in the cab, feverishly cleaning the big glass windows, wiping off Snark scales, Telepod fur, powder burns, and men's sweat, keeping the vision clear for the marksmen, was horrified to see how, man by man, the brave sappers were picked off. Six of them just vanished when Snarks came too close; one was dragged away by a Telepod, one chopped in two by a Manticore; and two were pulled into the swamp by Cocodrills. Just the same, in five days they had managed to finish their task. The track had been made usable, and the Cockatrice Belle clanked slowly and cautiously over the doubtful stretch, and then very much faster up the slope beyond, Engineer Catchpole switching in half-a-dozen of his wind-generators.

But the colonel was cursing long and bitterly, as he paced about his cabin, with Captain Slipper and Captain Twilight taking turns to look through the periscope that allowed a view of the track ahead.

"Some of my very best men! Those butterheads at Supply just don't know the first thing about Snarks."

"How many real Snark masks were we given, sir?" asked Captain Twilight.

"Only enough for half the troop! And it's plain we're going to have a pitched battle on our hands before we can get into Manchester. The men will *have* to wear masks for that. —Ensign Catchpole!" he barked over the intercom.

"Sir!"

"Cut your engine. We'll stop here for the night and recharge. Sergeant Bellswinger!"

"Yessir."

"We'll have a sally at first light tomorrow. A hundred men with full battle equipment—masks, Griffin capes, the lot. Meanwhile, tell the lads to take it easy and turn in early. And—harrumph—tell Mrs. Churt to give them something extra-tasty for their evening meal. And, Bellswinger, send Drummer-boy Prestwich along here, will you?"

"Yessir."

Dakin was in very low spirits. He had seen ten people he knew, men who had been kind to him, cracked jokes, given him butter-tokens, shown him a fast way to load his pistol, told him tales of Cockatrices, and how to deal with Bonnacons—he had seen these men vanish like drops of water on a hotplate, and it had upset him badly. His expression was very dejected as he knocked and entered the colonel's cabin.

"Now, Prestwich," said the colonel, taking no notice of this, "there's a kind of monster in these parts that's hypersensitive to loud rhythmic noise."

"Sir?"

"The monsters can't stand a regular row. All the ones in the Apocarpus family are like it."

"I don't know no Apocarpuses, sir."

"We don't have many round London. But here there are whole schools of them. Hydra, Cocodrill, Glyptodont, Telepod, Kelpies, Griffins—they all belong to the Apocarpus family."

"Quite a big family, sir."

"If they hear a loud, sustained regular noise, they tend to fall in half."

"Coo, sir."

"So you'll be out there, tomorrow, with those hundred men, Prestwich, and I want you playing your drum really loud, so long as the battle lasts. D'you understand? I won't want you to stop for a single moment. Can you do that?"

"Coo, sir! Yes, sir," said Dakin joyfully.

"Ask Mrs. Churt to give you a mug of hot milk with malt and molasses and rum flavouring in it, last thing tonight and first thing tomorrow. Tell her I said so."

"Yes, sir. Goodnight, sir!"

"Goodnight, Dakin."

"That ain't a bad boy," said Captain Slipper, as the silver-handled door closed behind Dakin. "He's got some sand in him."

When Dakin went along to Mrs. Churt for his bedtime drink, he found her with a melancholy, distant look in her eye. She, too, had been grieved by the loss of the ten men.

"That Corporal Bigtoe, he was a real one for a laugh. Come to that, they was all nice boys. Lively. I'd like to set up some kind of memorial to 'em."

"What kind, Mrs. Churt?" asked Dakin sipping his hot molasses-and-milk.

"I'll have to think. Now, you hop it off to bed. You got to keep busy tomorrow."

Next day at dawn, Dakin, reporting in the galley for his molasses-and-milk, was surprised not to find Mrs. Churt presiding over the big copper cooking-plates that were heated by power from the engine. Instead, Orderly Widgery was back in charge, stirring the cauldrons of porridge and toasting raisin buns for the men's breakfast.

"Where's Mrs. Churt?"

"Having a lie-in, I daresay, after that beanfeast she cooked last night."

Dakin thought this unlike Mrs. Churt, but he had no time for more talk; the call for assembly was sounding on Catchpole's whistle; men were tumbling out of the big doors at the rear of the train, and forming into squares of twenty. Dakin, who had been polishing his drum since three A.M., tumbled out himself, and took his place at the side of the troop, who all looked like unicorns in their pronged Snark masks. They carried long, wicked December guns, squat wide flame-throwers, and had Kelpie knives slotted all over their equipment, wherever there was room.

"Now then—you little smitchy-faced article!" roared Sergeant Bellswinger to Dakin. "You keep your eye on Captain Twilight there, and follow wherever he goes. When I say the word *march*, you begins to play, and you doesn't stop till you hears Catchpole play the recall. Understand? Comprenny? Troop! Shun! Verse—arms! Eyes—front! Left—turrn! At the double—*marrch!*"

"Titherump, titherump, titherump, rat-a-tat-tat-tat-tat-tat *tum*," sang Dakin's drum under his rattling drumsticks, as he panted along in Captain Twilight's rear beside the division of men, who were hurrying, grimly and gaily, up towards the top of a long rough slope of moorland. When they reached the summit they could see, down on the other side, though morning mist, the battered tower-blocks of Manchester.

Between the troop and the town swarmed a wild medley of monsters, hopping, swooping, galloping on nine legs, gliding on slimy suckers, prancing on claw-fringed hoofs, floating on bat-wings.

"Croopus," said Private Mollisk. "It's the Teddy Bears' Picnic."

"'Tis as good as a panto," said Private Reilly. "All we need's the Fairy Queen."

"Rumpa-tumpa-tump!" beat Dakin's drumsticks.

"Squad—load!" bawled Sergeant Bellswinger. "On the word—*fire!*"

A sheet of flame swept across the open space, and a black hail of missiles.

It was a ferocious battle. Out of the mists to the south, a dim red sun presently mounted, and cast patches of crimson light on the frosty slope, on the grisly, many-shaped monsters, and the men, who looked almost as wild, in their Griffin capes, Gorgon shields, and Snark masks.

Dakin, too, had been issued with a Snark mask. It was much too

g for him, and kept slipping; every few minutes he had to hitch his
ead back to shake it into position. He was often tempted to take it
ɔff and sling it over his shoulder, but he did not, for three reasons:
first, Sergeant Bellswinger had threatened to cut his tripes out if he
did so; second, he observed Ensign Crisworthy take *his* mask off to
blow his nose, and, a second later, vanish like a burnt tissue as a Snark
winged down on him; third, rattling away at the big drum like a mad
woodpecker, Dakin simply hadn't time to do anything but keep drumming.

Sometimes the fight roared and seethed all around him,
sometimes it swept away; sometimes he had the satisfaction of seeing
some beast pause, hesitate, catching the sound of his desperate tattoo,
and then suddenly fall in half, like a tree struck by lightning. On the
whole, he received very little notion as to how the general trend of
the battle was going, whether the Cockatrice Corps were winning or
losing. There seemed an unlimited supply of monsters; they kept
pouring out of the sky, and from the towers of Manchester, like
swarming starlings or hungry locusts. Dakin thumped away, often
ducking a whistling wing or leaping aside to dodge a raking talon;
once he was wrapped in slimy tentacles and had to slash himself loose
at frantic speed with his Kelpie knife, transferring both drumsticks to
his left hand; but not once did he stop drumming; not even when he
thought he saw Mrs. Churt hurry across the hillside, through the men
in their dark-brown uniforms and the cream-coloured, salmon-pink,
yellow, grey, and leopard-spotted monsters.

"I must have imagined that I saw Mrs. Churt," Dakin thought.
"What would she be doing in a battle like this? Maybe I'm getting
feverish. I've got cramp in my arms and feet, and I can't feel my hands
at all."

Then, all of a sudden, the battle was over. Not because one side or the
other had gained a definite victory; but simply because of the weather.
Sharp, slashing javelins of snow hissed down out of the low grey
clouds, now purpling towards the sunset of Christmas Eve; the snow
cut and stung and blinded men and monsters alike. In five minutes,
hardly a living creature was to be seen on the rough hillside. Bodies
lay scattered here and there—men, Manticores, Hydras, Cocodrills,
tossed higgledy-piggledy. Dakin recognised the bodies of two men
and an officer, Captain Twilight, but he was too dead tired to feel
anything but a kind of puzzled sadness. His one wish was to find his

way back to the train, fall on his bunk, and sleep for a hundred hours. Had the recall been sounded? And which *was* the way back? During the battle he had been pushed farther and farther along the slope; now he found himself at the foot of a shallow gully, but it was hard to see more than a few yards through the slicing, stinging snow.

It must be right if I go downhill, he thought, and ran, stumbling, as fast as he could over the tussocky ground, his drum banging awkwardly on his hip. A layer of snow caked over his Snark mask, blinding him, so he took off the mask. Snarks can't like this weather any more than I do, he decided. And if I keep it on I shall only walk into a river or something.

Looking everywhere for the troop train, he was dismayed to see, instead, a high wall ahead. It was so high that its top was veiled in cloud and snow. Oh, crumbs, I must have gone wrong; that must be Manchester town wall. I'll just have to turn and go back—

Before he could turn he was halted by a shout. "Who goes there? Man or monster? Stop or I shoot!"

"I'm a m-m-m-man," called Dakin through chattering teeth. His uniform was soaked through and his boots were full of snow; he felt like an icicle.

"Man? You don't look like it," said the voice. "Well: come forward—slowly—for if either of us makes a mistake you'll end up with a stomach full of red-hot sand."

Dakin scrunched slowly over the snow towards a narrow gate which he now saw in the wall ahead of him.

"Holy smoke!" said the voice. "It *is* a nipper! Wait till the Warden of the Gate hears this. Come along in, you poor little sausage—you must be half perished!"

Five minutes later, Dakin found himself in a warm, bright, noisy place—the barrack-room of the Manchester town wall guard squad—where he was given a cup of hot herb tea, rubbed with towels, and questioned eagerly by the warden, the mayor, the guards officers, and half the citizens of Manchester, about the battle, his part in it, and the cargo of the Cockatrice Belle.

"We lost radio contact, you see, with all that cloud of monsters," the mayor explained. "And the visibility was so bad, and the Snark glass in our windows is so thick, that we couldn't see what was happening. Sometimes the monsters have battles among themselves; we thought it might be that."

You could have sent out a party to make sure, Dakin thought, but he was too tactful to say so.

"We're all a bit weak here, you see," the Mayor apologised. "Half a cup of thin gruel each a day for the last six weeks."

Dakin realised that the Manchester men did look desperately thin, and he forgave them for not dashing out to help their rescuers.

"There's a big load of tinned carrots on the train," he said.

"Carrots! I'll see if I can make radio contact with the train now that dark has fallen."

Radio contact was presently made with Colonel Clipspeak's tea-kettle, and Dakin learned that the men of the sally party had fought their way back to the train, having inflicted heavy casualties on the monsters, and not suffered too badly themselves. Colonel Clipspeak was delighted to hear that his drummer-boy was safe in Manchester, and promised to bring in the carrot supply at first light, as a Christmas present for the population of Manchester.

"The boy had better stay with you; we'll pick him up in the morning."

Dozens of people then offered Dakin a bed for the night. He had never felt so popular. But he said, "My auntie Floss used to live in Manchester. Mrs. Florence Monsoon. I'd like to see her if she's still here."

Somebody knew where Mrs. Monsoon lived, in a high-rise block called Brilcreme Court, and Dakin was taken there in the Mayor's rickshaw, pulled by a dozen weak but grateful citizens.

Brilcreme Court was a gaunt concrete high-rise at the end of a cul-de-sac.

"The stairs are through that door," pointed the Mayor's son. "You won't mind if we don't come up? Weeks of gruel don't leave your legs much use for stairs. Your auntie's at number fifteen."

Dakin said he could find his way, thanked them all, and started up the steps. After weeks on the flat, and the long day's battle, his own legs did not feel too strong.

As he toiled slowly up the concrete flights, a queer feeling took hold of him. What was it? In the battle he had had no time to feel frightened; the monsters did not scare him. But now he realised that the hungry, shadowy feeling inside him was fear. He was afraid, and yet he did not know why.

As he neared the door of no. 15 he was walking more and more slowly.

The door, which was old, dirty, and battered, had a little spy-hole in it. When Dakin stood outside, his heart went pit-a-pat. He heard people talking in the flat.

"I can see Cousin Dakin," said a soft voice, and a louder, annoyed voice said, "Oh, don't be so tiresome, Sauna. You put me out of patience, that you do!"

Then there came the sound of a sharp slap, and a low cry.

Dakin tapped on the door. Immediately there was complete silence inside. Then a pale-grey eye surveyed him through the spy-hole.

"Who's that?" snapped a voice—the same that had said, "You put me out of patience."

"Drummer Dakin Prestwich, looking for his auntie, Mrs. Monsoon."

The door opened slowly. A skinny woman stood regarding him with suspicion. Then her face cleared.

"Well, upon my word. It *is* Dakin. Whatever are *you* doing here?"

"Come to give you Mum's best wishes," said Dakin. "I was on the troop train what brought the carrots to Manchester."

"Oh! Carrots!" breathed the girl who stood behind Mrs. Monsoon. She was Dakin's size, red-haired, and would have been nice-looking if she were not so thin and sad.

"Cousin Sauna!" Dakin exclaimed. "Remember how you used to play my mouth-organ?"

He would have shaken hands with her, but, strangely enough, Sauna's hands were tied behind her with a trip of bandage.

"We have to do that," hastily explained her aunt. "Sauna's too active for this flat. She'd have everything topsy-turvy in no time."

There was not an inch of spare space in Mrs. Monsoon's tiny apartment. Hundreds of little china pots covered every surface.

"I used to collect 'em. Brought 'em back as souvenirs from holidays," said Aunt Floss, noticing Dakin's eyes on the pots. "Then Sauna's parents died abroad, and I had to bring *her* back. And then we had to stop travelling." It was plain that she blamed her niece for this. Dakin began to feel very sorry for Sauna, shut up in such a small flat with all those pots, and Mrs. Monsoon, who looked like a short-tempered woman.

"Well, Dakin," she said sharply, confirming his impression, "you can't stop the night *here*, for we've no room. Maybe Mrs. Beadle next door could take you; I'll just step round and ask her. Don't you touch nothing while I'm gone!"

The moment she was out of the door, Dakin, with his Kelpie knife, cut through the bandage fastening Sauna's wrists.

"How *can* she tie you up like that?" he said. "It's dreadful!"

"Oh, no, it's really best," Sauna told him earnestly. "Otherwise I'm sure to knock something over. She only ties my hands between tea-time and breakfast, because——" Then her eyes grew as large as saucers, and she gazed at Dakin in fright.

"Oh! I can see a woman who knows you! She's being chased by a Manticore!"

"Where?"

"In the street out there. Her name's Mrs. Churt."

"But *how* can you see her?" demanded Dakin, for the windows had blinds nailed over them.

"Oh, I can see through walls. Quick, quick, let's go and help her!"

As they dashed down the narrow concrete stairs Dakin panted, "Will Aunt Floss be very angry when she finds you've gone out?"

"No. She'd like to be rid of me altogether. She often says she wishes I'd been left with *your* family. Look—look—"

Sauna had dragged Dakin round a couple of corners, running through dark empty streets. Now they came to a bit of waste land covered with lavender bushes, and saw Mrs. Churt, who was being chased by a huge Manticore. She was running clumsily, weighed down by the two heavy baskets she carried. The Manticore gained on her at every bound. It was just about to pounce—

"Stop it, stop it!" screamed Sauna.

Dakin dragged out his liquid-air pistol, aimed it as best he could with shaking hands, and pressed down the plunger. A fierce narrow jet, unbelievably much colder than ice, melted the Manticore into dark-blue jelly when it was only two leaps behind Mrs. Churt.

"Well, my gracious!" exclaimed that lady. "I *am* pleased to see you, young Dakin. I thought I was a goner that time! Wish we could make him into blackberry tart," she added, looking critically at the dissolved monster. "And who's this little beauty, eh?"

"This is my cousin Sauna," said Dakin, thinking how much better his cousin looked when her cheeks were pink with excitement.

"Pleased to meet you, dear! Now we'd best be getting back to the train. I'd have been back long ago, making sorrel soup for the boys, if that monster hadn't chased me out of my way." And Mrs. Churt indicated her baskets of salads and greenery. "I got a little bit of heather, too, to grow in a pot as a memorial for Corporal Bigtoe and those others what got killed."

"But how can we get back to the train, Mrs. Churt? We're inside the town wall."

"Yes, dear, but there's a way through here no one seems to have noticed, prob'ly because it's all covered by them lavender bushes."

And, sure enough, in ten minutes, Mrs. Churt had led them along a narrow gully, back to where the Cockatrice Belle was parked, lit from end to end, as the combatants sang and drank sassafras tea with rum in it, and played table tennis, and discussed the battle, and planned next day's manoeuvres. All the red-and-green Christmas bells were being rung by an invention of Corporal Widgery, from heat generated by the men as they played Ping-Pong.

Colonel Clipspeak was pleased to see Dakin back, and even happier to welcome Mrs. Churt, who had been given up for lost.

"Never, *ever* leave the train again without an escort," he scolded her. "We can't spare you, Mrs. Churt!"

"No, but you'll be glad of all those lovely greens I got," she replied placidly. "A *beautiful* mess o' salad I'll be able to make for the boys now. And this young lady's going to come and be my helper, aren't you, dear?"

"*That* young person? Certainly not!" exclaimed the Colonel. "*One* female on this train is quite enough. Two would be out of the question."

"Oh, now, sir, just you wait! Don't you go for to be so hasty! This young lady's got a real talent—haven't you, dearie," said Mrs. Churt comfortably. "She can see things as hasn't happened yet—through walls and all, she can see 'em."

It took quite a long time to convince the colonel that Sauna could be really useful on the Cockatrice Belle. She had to demonstrate, again and again, that she really *could* see things—Hammerheads, Cockarices, and people—not only through walls, but sometimes ten minutes before they arrived, or even more.

At last the Colonel said, "Oh, very well. She may come for a trial trip. Just on the run back to London. I don't promise more than that! Should a message be sent to her family?"

So, next morning, Christmas Day, while the carrots were being delivered under guard, a note was despatched to Aunt Floss requesting the services of Miss Sauna Batwing as Assistant Mess Orderly Female Supernumerary Second Grade. But—strangely enough—Aunt Floss was not to be found among her thousands of small china souvenirs. Nor, indeed, was she ever seen again.

And it was not until the Cockatrice Belle, scented from end to end with lavender posies donated by the grateful citizens of

Manchester, had started her journey back to London, that Sauna, stirring soup in the Galley, suddenly exclaimed,

"Oh! My goodness!"

"What, dear?" inquired Mrs. Churt, chopping raisins. "Don't let that soup boil over, love; shift it to one side."

"I just remembered that baby Snark I found last night sheltering by the dustbins, when I threw out the tea leaves. Poor little thing, it looked so miserable and floppy, I brought it in for a warm-up. I put it in the airing cupboard and was going to let it out in the morning before Aunt Floss saw it—"

"Well—let that be a lesson to you, dearie," said Mrs. Churt. "Your aunt's no great loss, from all I heard. But there's some things as oughtn't to be brought inside. And we don't want no baby Snarks on *this* train."

In dark times, the importance of Christmas.

AND WHEN THEY APPEAR

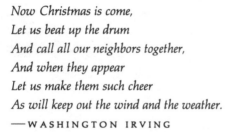

Gene Wolfe

Now Christmas is come,
Let us beat up the drum
And call all our neighbors together,
And when they appear
Let us make them such cheer
As will keep out the wind and the weather.
—WASHINGTON IRVING

Concerned about Sherby, and himself as well, House sent forth both Kite and Mouse.

If you had seen Mouse, you would have seen nothing. That is to say, you would have told yourself, and quickly convinced yourself, that you had seen nothing; so swift did Mouse scurry over the snow. You were not present, but an owl saw Mouse and swooped down upon her, huge-winged and silent as death, for owls are too wise ever to tell themselves that their eyes did not see what they eyes have seen. Its talons closed about Mouse, and a thin blade shot out. The blade was intended for fingers, but it worked well on talons. The owl shrieked, and flapped away upon wings that were silent still, leaving a claw-tipped fraction of itself bleeding on the snow.

Mouse squeaked (a sound too faint for human ears) as the blade retracted; this was the first time that it had been used since Mouse had been made, and the self-lubricating bearings it pivoted on were dry.

Kite soared higher than the owl ever had, so high that he saw Lonely Mountain whole. He saw the tracks of cars and people in the snow where a bridge crossed the Whitewater, and directed Mouse toward the great, domed doughnut that was the Jefferson house. That was how Mouse found Kieran Jefferson III (Principal Operating Officer of The Beauharnais Group) dead next to his Christmas tree with his brand-new Chapuis express rifle still in his hands. Mouse told House about it right away.

"I have decided to have a Christmas party," House told Sherby. "I've thought the whole thing over, and decided it is the right thing to do."

"I'd like to see my mom and dad," Sherby told House. Not because it had anything to do with the party, but simply because the thought, filling his mind, had popped from his mouth as soon as he opened it. Sherby was still in his yellow pajamas, having worn them all day.

"And so you shall," House assured him, knowing full well that what it meant had nothing to do with what he meant.

"Not holos." Sherby could not read House's mind, but he had known House all his life; if he had been able to read House's mind, it would have made no difference.

Nor could House read Sherby's. (*The big steep steps down and down into the basement, the heavy door of the cold storage locker that Sherby could not open without House's help.*)

"You must write the invitations," House told Sherby. "I can't manage that. I think we should invite Santa Claus first of all. That will get things off to a fine start."

"I didn't see Santa Claus last night," Sherby objected. "I don't think he's real."

"You fell asleep," House explained gently, "and since he's very busy on Christmas Eve, and had dropped in without an invitation, he didn't awaken you. His busiest day is over now. He always relaxes on Christmas Day. He sleeps until dark, then eats a big dinner. He will be in a relaxed mood, and may very well come."

"All right." Enthusiasm comes easily at Sherby's age, and often arrives unbidden; Sherby's showed plainly on his face.

"You mustn't expect more presents," cautioned House, who had no more. "Santa gave away all the toys he had yesterday."

"That's okay," Sherby said. "I like real things better than toys anyway."

Then he went into the Learning Center, where House showed him how to make the letters, sometimes projecting hard ones (like *M* and *Q*) right onto the drawboard where Sherby could trace them. Sherby wrote:

DEAR SANTA

PEOPLE   MUST   ASK   YOU   LOTS   AND   LOTS   OF

QUESTIONS   MINE IS WILL YOU COME TO OUR HOUSE ON

LONELY MOUNTAIN FOR A PARTY TONIGHT   BRING THE ELFS

IF YOU WANT TO

SHERBY

"That's a good one," House told him, "and while you were writing it I had another good idea. Let's invite all the rest of the Christmas people, too. There are a great many of them, live toy soldiers, the Nutcracker, and countless others."

Sherby looked down sadly at the light-pen, which felt very heavy in his fingers. "I don't want to write a whole bunch more of these," he said.

"You won't have to," House promised. "Only one."

So Sherby wrote:

ALL XMAS PEOPLE ESPCIALLY CHILDREN

ARE INVITED TOO   EVEN THE GRINCH

SHERBY

He had no sooner laid down the light-pen than House's doorbell rang. Sherby ran to answer it, knowing that House was quite capable of doing it himself — and would, too, if the visitor were left standing outside for what House (who as a rule did not have a great deal of patience) considered an excessive length of time.

This visitor was not Santa Claus at all, and did not even look as though he might be much fun. He was an old man with granny glasses and wisps of white hair sticking out from under his tall beaver hat. But he wore a green greatcoat and a red cravat, and cried, "Hallo!" so cheerfully, and smiled with so many twinkles that Sherby got out of the way at once, saying, "Would you like to come in?"

"What's to-day, my fine fellow?" inquired the old man as he stepped into House, beating the snow from his greatcoat in blizzards. (It melted as it reached the floor, but left no puddles there.)

"Christmas," Sherby told him.

"Not Christmas Eve!" For a moment, the old man appeared quite frightened.

"No, Christmas Day. The night of it." House groaned as even the very best houses do on cold nights, and Sherby added tardily, "Sir."

"Ebenezer," said the old man, and offered Sherby his hand in the most friendly fashion possible.

"No, sir, my name's Sherby," Sherby told him. And was about to shut the door (since he was getting cold and House had not yet done it) when he caught sight of a man in foreign garments, wonderfully real and distinct to look at, with an axe in his belt, leading a little black donkey laden with wood up the moonlit drive.

"It's Ali Baba," the old man explained. "Dear old honest Ali Baba! He *did* come to see me one Christmas, my boy, just like this. Now it's your turn, and I've brought him to you, not only for his entertainment and yours, Sherby, but in order that you may know a great secret."

He twinkled more than ever when he said this, and Sherby, who liked secrets more than almost anything else, asked, "What is it?"

The old man crouched until their eyes were nearly at a level. "You think that I am House," the old man whispered. "And so I am."

"You're a holo," Sherby told him.

"Light projected upon air, Sherby?" The old man leaned closer. "Light's wondrous stuff, but it cannot speak. Or think."

"That's House," Sherby acknowledged.

"And that," the old man pointed through the doorway and out into the moonlit night, "is Ali Baba. I brought him with me so that you could learn that there is a vagrant magic in Christmas still, after all these years. You have not as long to learn it as I had, perhaps." He straightened up. "May he bring his donkey in? I know it isn't regular, but the poor donkey would be uncommonly cold, I'm afraid, standing out all evening in the snow."

Ali Baba, who was close enough to overhear them by this time, grinned at Sherby in such a way as to guarantee that the donkey was housebroken.

"Okay," Sherby said, so Ali Baba brought his donkey in with him; and the donkey, a little bareheaded man in sandals and a brown habit like a lady's dress, with a rope around his waist.

As they left the vestibule and went down the hall to the family room, Sherby tried to touch the little man's back, but his hand went right through like he knew it would.

A fat man in livery came in with a tray of drinks that Sherby could not drink, hors d'oeuvres that he could not eat, and a carrot for the donkey. Ali Baba had begun to unload it and build a big fire in the fireplace when the doorbell rang again.

This time it was twelve stout young men with clubs, and a thirteenth who wore a fox skin hanging down his back, with the fox's face for a cap, so that it looked as though the fox were peering over his head. All thirteen shouted, "Hail, Squire!" to Sherby; then they performed a dance to the rapping of their own clubs, coming together by sixes and striking their clubs together, while the fox (so Sherby thought of him) leaped and whirled among them.

When they were finished, the twelve with clubs ran past Sherby into House, each wishing him a merry Christmas. The fox seemed to have vanished, until Sherby closed the door and discovered that the fox was watching over his shoulder. "A glorious Yuletide to you, Young Squire," the fox said.

Sherby turned very quickly and backed away from him, and although he knew the fox was fake, the door that stopped him from backing farther was very solid indeed.

"I'm Loki," the fox told him, "the Norse personification of fire. I seek to steal the sun, and you've just seen me driven forth in order that the sun may return. I creep back in, however, as you also see. It's my nature—I am forever creeping back in. Will you not wish me good Yule in return?"

"It's not Yule," Sherby said. "It's Christmas."

"Christmas for some, but Yule for all. Yule means tide, and tide means time," the fox told him. "This is the time of winter solstice, when day begins to lengthen, and ancestral spirits must be placated. Did you know you had ancestral spirits?"

Sherby shook his head.

"We are they," the fox told him, and as he spoke, someone seemed to pound the door so violently that the blows shook House.

Two young men stood on House's porch, and five more were hauling an enormous stump across the snow. Six young women and three dogs followed them, and a seventh young woman rode the stump sidesaddle, one leg hooked about an upthrust root. She cried, "Faster! Faster!" when she saw Sherby standing in the doorway, and there was a great deal of laughter, barking, and shouting.

"House would like you to get to know all of us," the fox explained, "but Kite says there isn't time for more than a glimpse. Even so, you'll remember this Christmas as long as you live."

The seven young men pushed and pulled their Yule log into the vestibule, where the young woman dismounted. "Merriment all through the house," she told Sherby, "as long as the log burns. But you've got to save a brand to light the next one. Roast pig and peacock pie." She hurried away in the direction of the kitchen.

"The boar's for Frey," the fox whispered. "Frey rides a boar with golden bristles, a dwarfgift. When he left Asgard to dwell amongst men as Fridleef, King of Denmark, his folk served him a boar at Yule to show they knew him. The apple in its mouth was the sun he had brought back to them. Finding himself discovered, he mounted the roasted boar and rode back into the sky." He pointed through the open doorway. "Now look yonder, and see the type of your holly wreath."

There was a wheel of fire rolling down the mountain.

"House's holos can't reach that far," Sherby said, but the fox had vanished.

A young man came in with a spray of mistletoe, which he hung from the arch between the vestibule and the hall. "Do you see the white berries?" the young man asked. "Each time a girl gets kissed under the mistletoe, she's supposed to pull off one berry. When the last berry is gone, the mistletoe comes down."

Everybody explains, Sherby thought, but nobody explains anything I want explained. House doesn't know.

He went out into the snow. It was cold, and tickled his bare feet in a very chilly way, but it was real, and he liked that about it. He walked clear around House and his five-car garage, until the ground fell away in icy rocks and he could look down into the shadowed valley of the Whitewater at the foot of Lonely Mountain. He could have seen the same things by looking out of the big picture window in the family room, but looking like this, with no glass between himself and the night and the cold, made it real.

He shivered, wishing that he had worn his blue bathrobe, and wiped his nose on his sleeve.

Down in the valley there was a little dot of red light where something was burning, and House was flying Kite over it, a speck of black against the bright stars. The fire was probably a bonfire or a campfire, Sherby decided, and there would be people around it cooking hotdogs and marshmallows. He shivered again; house might fix real food if he asked. He looked up at the picture window, then went a little farther down the slope where he could see it better. It was dark, and there was no smoke rising from the chimney.

Climbing back up was harder than going down had been, and once he slipped and hurt his knee. When he got back to the front door, a small black-and-white horse with no one to ride him was coming up the drive. He stopped and turned his head to look at Sherby through one wide, frightened eye.

"Here, pony!" Sherby called. "Here, pony!"

The little horse took a hesitant step forward.

"Here, pony!" Sherby recalled the donkey's hors d'oeuvre and dashed into the vestibule, down the hall past the roaring family room, and into the kitchen.

The fat man in livery was there, talking to a plump woman in an apron as both put deviled oysters wrapped in bacon into little cups of paper lace. "Yes, Master Sherbourne," the fat man said, "what can we do for you?"

"I just wanted a carrot," Sherby told him. "A real one."

The big vegetable drawer rolled forward, and a neat white compartment was elevated twenty-six centimeters to display two fresh carrots. Sherby snatched one and sprinted back to the porch, certain that the little horse would have gone.

He had not, and he cocked his ears in a promising fashion when Sherby showed him the carrot.

"You will require a halter of some sort, I am afraid," a heavily accented voice behind Sherby said.

Sherby turned to find a very tall man, wearing a very tall hat of starched gauze, standing in House's front doorway.

"That is good, what you do now," the tall man said. "You do not look at him." The tall man fingered his small, round beard. "We men —even boys—there is *exousia* in the eyes. He is afraid of that, poor little fellow."

Sherby put his other hand in front of his eyes and peeped through his fingers. Sure enough, the little horse was closer now. "My bathrobe's got a long belt. Usually I step on it."

The tall man nodded sagely. "That might do. Go and get it, and I will watch him for you."

When Sherby returned, the tall man was standing beside the little horse's head. "You are very young yet," he told Sherby. "Can you tie a knot?"

"I think so," Sherby said.

"Then give him that carrot, and tie your belt about his head while he eats it."

Sherby was afraid of the little horse's big teeth at first, but the little horse took the carrot without biting him and munched away, seeming quite content to let Sherby tie the blue terrycloth belt of his bathrobe around his neck, though it took three tries to get the knot right. "He smells like smoke," Sherby said. "I'm going to call him Smoky."

"His stable burned, poor little fellow, so it is a good name for him. My own is Saint Nicholas, now. It used to be Bishop Nicholas. I was bishop of Myra, in Lycia; and though I am not Santa Claus, Santa Claus is me."

Sherby was looking at Smoky. "Do you think I can lead him?"

"I am sure you can, my son."

Sherby tugged at the blue terrycloth belt; and the little horse backed away, his eyes wide, with Sherby stumbling and sliding after him. "I want him to come in," Sherby said. "My feet are cold."

"You are learning now what I learned as a parish priest," Saint Nicholas told him.

Sherby braced his feet and tugged again; this time the little horse seemed ready to bolt. "You said I could lead him!"

"I did, my son. And I do. You can lead him wherever you wish him to go. But you cannot pull him anywhere. He is eager to follow you, but he is a great deal stronger than you are."

"I want him to go in House!"

Saint Nicholas nodded patiently. "Yet you yourself were not going into House. You were faced away from him, matching your strength against his. Now you are facing in the correct direction. Hold your rope in one hand, as though you expected him to follow you. Walk toward me, and if he does not follow at once, jerk the rope, not too hard. Say *erchou!*"

Sherby tried it, making the word almost as guttural and rasping as Saint Nicholas had, and the little horse followed him readily, almost trotting.

When all three were in the vestibule and House had shut the big front door behind them, Sherby looked up at the tall, grave saint with new respect. "You know a lot about ponies."

"My charioteer knew much more," the saint told him, "but I know something about leading."

"Do you know if there are any other kids like me at the party?"

The saint, who had been solemn the whole time, smiled. His smile made Sherby like him very much. "There is one, at least, my son. He was speaking with Father Eddi when last I saw him. Perhaps Father Eddi can help you."

Sherby, still leading Smoky, had entered the family room before it occurred to him—much too late—that he ought to have asked Saint Nicholas what Father Eddi looked like. There were a great many people there, both men and ladies, and it seemed to Sherby that the men were all plenty old enough to be fathers, for many were older than his own father. He caught at the wide sleeve of a tall figure in black; but his fingers grasped nothing, and when the tall figure looked down at him it had the face of a skull and curling horns. Hastily, Sherby turned away.

A small blond lady in a green dress that seemed (apart from its flaring collar of white petals) made of dark leaves appeared safer. "Please," Sherby said, recalling his manners after the scare he had gotten. "Do you know Father Eddi?"

The blond lady nodded and smiled, offering her hand. "I'm Christmas Rose. And you are . . . ?"

"Sherby."

She smiled again; she was lovely when she smiled, and hardly taller than he. "Yes, I know Father Eddi, Sherby. He is Saint Wilfred's chaplain, and he'd like this little horse of yours very much. Did my friend Knecht Rupprecht startle you?"

"Is he your friend?" Sherby considered. "I'd like him better if he wasn't so big."

"But he wouldn't frighten demons and bad children half so much if he were no bigger than I, Sherby. He must run through the streets, you see, on Advent Thursday, so that the demons will think that a demon worse than themselves holds the town. For a few coins he will dance in your fields, and frighten the demons from them, too."

Quite suddenly, Knecht Rupprecht was bending over Sherby, the skeletal bone of his jaw swinging and snapping. "Und den vor Christmas, vith Veihnachtsmann I come. You see here dese svitches?" He held a bundle of apple and cherry twigs under Sherby's nose. "You petter pe gud, Sherpy."

Surprising himself by his own boldness, Sherby passed his free hand through the bundle. "You're all just holos. House makes you."

He was sorry as soon as he did it, because Christmas Rose was so clearly disappointed in him. "It's true that what you see now are holograms, Sherby. But we are real, nonetheless. I am a real flower, and Knecht Rupprecht a real custom. You will learn more, believe me, if you treat us as real. And since Carker's Army is coming, you may not have much time in which to learn. Kite says they're at the McKays' already, and Mouse is going to see whether they left anyone alive."

"Will they come here?" Sherby asked.

"We have no way of knowing that, Sherby. Let's hope not."

Knecht Rupprecht said, "If dey do, I vill schare dem avay, Sherpy. I dry, und dot's a promise."

"I didn't like you at first," Sherby told him. "But really I like you better than anybody. You and Christmas Rose."

She made him a formal curtsy.

"Only I don't understand how you can scare them away if they're bad, when you look like you're bad, too."

"Der same vay I schare der demons, Sherpy, und der pad kinder. Gut ist nod schared of vot's gut, put pad's schared py vorse. See dese?"

He held out his switches again, and Sherby nodded.

"I tell you now a secret, put you must nod tell der pad kinder. Vunce I gome vith dese to make der fruits grow. Id ist der dead manns, der dead animals vot does dat, zo I gome vor dem. Schtill I do, but der volk, dey don' know."

Christmas Rose said, "We are comrades, Knecht Rupprecht and I, because of my other name. The botanists call me Black Hellebore. Not very pretty, is it?"

Sherby shook his head sympathetically.

"It's because my roots are black. See?" She lifted her skirt to show black snakeskin shoes and black panty hose. "Of course, I *am* poisonous, but I can't help it. I'm very pretty, I bloom in winter, and if you don't eat me, I'll never harm you."

"Did my mom and dad eat you?" Sherby asked.

"No, that was something else." Christmas Rose moved out of the way of a tall black man with a crown on his turban. "I could tell you its name, but that would convey no meaning to you. It's an industrial chemical; your father brought it home from one of his factories."

"They shouldn't have eaten any." A spasm of recollected sorrow crossed Sherby's face and was gone.

"Der Mamma nefer meaned it," Knecht Rupprecht told him kindly. "Do nod vorget dot, howefer old you lif."

"You should have stopped them!"

Smoky stirred uneasily at the rage behind Sherby's words.

"We couldn't," Christmas Rose told him; there was a catch in her voice that Sherby was too young yet to recognize. "We were not there, neither Knecht Rupprecht nor I."

"You could because you're House!"

"Who I say I am, I am." Red lights glowed in the eye sockets of Knecht Rupprecht's bleached skull. "Did I say I vas House?"

The fat man in livery, who had been passing with a tray of empty glasses, halted. "May I be of service, sir? I am House, the butler."

Christmas Rose said, "This little boy is looking for Father Eddi, House. If you happen to see him . . . ?"

"Of course, madame."

Sherby tried to grasp the skirt of House's blue-striped waistcoat, but no resistance met his fingers. "You should've stopped them! You know you should!"

"I could not, Master Sherbourne, as long as your father was alive. And as your mother was, ah," the butler cleared his throat, "the first to leave us, I was helpless until your father's, hmm, demise. Had you not dawdled over your dinner, I should have been unable to preserve your life. As I did, Master Sherbourne." He returned his attention to Christmas Rose. "Father Eddi, madame. I shall endeavor to locate him, madame. There should be no great difficulty."

Sherby shouted, "You can make them go away! Make them all go away!" but the fat butler had already disappeared into the crowd.

As Sherby spoke, there was a stir on the other side of the big room. Knecht Rupprecht, who was tall enough to see over the heads of most of those present, announced, "Id ist der Mamma und der Poppa, Sherpy. So priddy she ist lookin'!" He began to applaud, and everyone present except Sherby and Smoky joined in. Under the storm of sound, Sherby heard the *snick, snick, snick* of a hundred bolts shot home. A moment later the moonlit valley of the Whitewater slowly disappeared, blotted out by the descent of the picture window's security shutter.

A thin and reedy voice at his ear said, "A very merry Christmas to you, my son! You wished to speak with me?"

Sherby turned; it was the little man in sandals.

"I'm Father Eddi, my son. Are you Master Sherbourne? That big fellow in the striped waistcoat said you wished to speak with me, and I'll be glad to help if I can." Seeing Sherby's expression, Father Eddi's own face grew troubled. "You certainly look unhappy enough."

Sherby gulped, knowing that his mother and father, dead, were talking and laughing with their guests. "I—I sort of hoped some other kids would come."

"Some have," Father Eddi assured him. "Tiny Tim's over there with Mr. and Mrs. Cratchit, and Greg—the doctor's son, you know, who helped to make the pasteboard star—is about somewhere, and Louisa, the girl who felt sorry for the Little Guest." Father Eddi paused expectantly; when Sherby said nothing, he added, "I can introduce you to them, if you like."

"A man . . ." Sherby had forgotten the tall saint's name already. "A man said you were talking to some other kid. I thought that if I could find you, I could find him."

"So you can! Father Eddi's smile was radiant. "Follow me. He's behind the tree at this very moment, I believe." He started away, then stopped so abruptly that Sherby and Smoky ran into him, burying their faces in his insubstantial, brown-clad back. "He's behind the tree, just as I told you. Every Christmas he's behind the tree. Before it, too, of course."

Christmas Rose called, "Good-bye, Sherby! Good luck!"

It was a most magnificent tree, as yellow and shiny as real gold, alive with lights and hung with ornaments that were like little toys, although Sherby was forbidden to play with them. Santa Clauses rode sleighs and airplanes and even space ships, stepped into red-brick chimneys, swung gaily from the clappers of bells, and carried tiny trees of their own, mostly green. There were jumping jacks and jack-in-the-boxes, rag dolls and snowmen and tiny boys with drums, and lovely silver deer that might have been of almost any kind except reindeer. It smelled marvelous, too; Sherby inhaled deeply.

A dark-eyed, rather swarthy boy with curling black hair stepped out from behind the tree. "Hello, Sherby," he said. "Were you looking for me?"

Sherby nodded. "You know my name."

"I was at your christening." The swarthy boy held out his hand. "I'm Yeshua bar-Yoseph. Welcome to my birthday party."

"This is my House." Sherby wiped his nose on his sleeve.

"I know," Yeshua said. "Thanks for letting us celebrate it here, Sherby."

Behind him, his mother exclaimed, "Oh, you've found the baby Jesus!" She knelt next to Sherby, lifting the skirt of her beautiful gown so as not to kneel on it, and reached for the little blond ceramic doll in the miniature manger under the tree. Sherby knew she wanted to pick it up, but couldn't because she was a holo and it was real.

"Never mind her," he told Yeshua.

"Oh, it's all right." Yeshua grinned, his teeth flashing in his dark face.

"Did you get real nice presents?" Sherby wanted to ask a favor, but he felt that it might be a good idea to talk a little more first and make friends.

"Lots. I haven't opened all of them yet."

Sherby nodded; he knew how that was. "What did you like the best?"

"My favorite present?"

Sherby nodded again.

"I'll tell you what mine was if you'll promise to tell me what yours was, after."

"Okay," Sherby said.

"Mine was what I said—you and your mother and father giving me this party," Yeshua told him. "It's really great, something I'll never forget. Now what was yours?"

Sherby patted the little horse's nose. "He is. I call him Smoky. I got a Distracto, and a copter that really flies and you can steer around, and a bunch of other stuff. But I like Smoky the best." He took a deep breath. "Will you do me a favor?"

"Sure."

"I want to go downstairs and open the big locker and—and—"

"Just look at them for a while," Yeshua supplemented.

"Uh-huh. An' I want you to come. I know you can't help work the door or anything, but I'd like you to come anyway. Okay?"

From noplace and everyplace, all over the room, House said, "This is most unwise, Sherby."

Sherby ignored him. "Will you?"

Yeshua nodded, and Father Eddi said, "I'll go with you too, Sherby, if you don't mind."

Remembering the tall man with the tall hat, Sherby said, "That's good. Come on," and turned and hurried away, walking right through several people who failed to notice him and get out of his way, the little horse trotting after him, its hoofs loud upon the carpeted floor.

A wide door in the kitchen opened upon a flight of wooden steps. It was hard to persuade Smoky to go down them, but Sherby led to the best of his ability, saying *"Erchou!"* half a dozen times, and praising Smoky each time he put a hoof onto a lower step. "Where's Yeshua?" he asked Father Eddi.

"Here with us." Father Eddi had been walking up and down the steps energetically to show Smoky how easily it could be done, and was rather out of breath.

"I don't see him."

"What you saw—the hologram—isn't here," Father Eddi explained.

"I'd like to see him."

"You don't think much of them." Father Eddi sat down on a step to wipe his forehead with the ragged hem of his brown habit. "So House did away with it. He's here just the same."

"Well, I'd like to see."

"Then you shouldn't have walked through the holograms upstairs, and should've wished your mother Merry Christmas."

"Are you a Christmas person? Like Knecht Rupprecht and Christmas Rose?" Sherby turned around to look back at Father Eddi, which surprised Smoky so much that he went down another step without urging.

"I certainly am."

"What makes you one?"

"One Christmas, I said a mass nobody came to except a donkey and an ox."

"Is that all?"

"I'm afraid it is." Father Eddi looked crestfallen. "I didn't put myself forward to House as a Christmas person, you understand, my son. But donkeys have been my friends ever since that night; so when you said that Ali Baba could bring in Kawi I came too, remembering my midnight service for the Saxons and hoping that I might be of some use here.

> 'The altar-lamps were lighted,—
>   An old marsh-donkey came,
> Bold as a guest invited,
>   And stared at the guttering flame.'

"No doubt he forgot me and my service long ago, but I haven't forgotten him, my son—no more than you've forgotten your father and mother in the frozen food locker down here. How did you get their bodies down these steps, anyway? You can't have carried them yourself."

"Mariah and Jeremy were here then. House had them do it. *Erchou!*" This last was for Smoky, who (gaining confidence as he neared the cellar floor) actually went down four more steps without further urging before he halted again.

"Then they went away and left you here with House? That wasn't very wise, I'm afraid."

"House made them," Sherby explained. "He's supposed to take care of me when there's nobody else to do it, and Mariah and Jeremy weren't supposed to take me anywhere unless my mom said it was okay. House wouldn't let them open the door as long as I was with them. They said they'd send somebody."

"Somebody else will get here sooner, I'm afraid," Father Eddi told him. "I will have some advice for you, if you can get the big stainless door open."

"You could ask House to open it for me. He can do that. You could pretend like you're doing it. You could put your hand on the handle and House would pull it and open the door and you could go inside and tell me to come in." It was a lot of talking for Sherby, and made him glad that Father Eddi was not much bigger than he was.

"He won't do it, my son," Father Eddi said gently. "He doesn't think it good for you to come down here and look at them. Neither do I. But if you get the freezer door open, I'll have some advice to offer, as I told you."

"*Erchou!*" Sherby said, and Smoky clattered down the last two steps to stand beside him. "Watch me."

He untied the blue terrycloth bathrobe belt, then tied its ends together in a new knot, pulling hard to make sure it would hold. That done, he looped it around the handle of the big freezer door, and put the other loop over Smoky's head. Returning to the foot of the steps, he shouted, "*Erchou!*"

Smoky eyed him nervously.

"I think you'd better go back upstairs, my son," Father Eddi said.

"I was looking that time. That's not the right way to do it." Sherby started up the steps. "*Erchou!*"

Smoky pulled the big handle forward by perhaps half an inch.

"There's another carrot up there," Sherby said. "I *know* that'll work, only I want to try something else first. Watch me!"

He carried Mariah's empty scrub bucket to Smoky's side, inverted it, and mounted. "Now come on! *Erchou!*" Sherby kicked Smoky with his bare heels, and Smoky took a hesitant step or two forward.

The big stainless steel door swung open.

"I'm going in to look at them," Sherby told Father Eddi. "You don't have to come in with me."

"I wish that I could."

Even to stand in front of the door was to enter a second winter, colder even than the snow and the night wind on Lonely Mountain.

Sherby stepped inside.

Father Eddi called, "I can't go any farther with you, my son. There are no hologram projectors in there."

"That's all right," Sherby told him. He was looking at his mother. There was a fine powdering of ice crystals on her cheek, and one hand was lifted as if she had died gesturing. Telling his father not to eat what she had, Sherby decided. Only his father had meant to, and had done it anyway.

"It might be a good thing for you to take Smoky in with you and shut the door, my son."

Sherby shook his head, shivering. He was still looking at his mother, and absentmindedly stroking Smoky's nose.

"You can't be locked in. There's a push bar on the inside that makes the door very easy to open."

"I'm coming out in a minute," Sherby said. His father's face was twisted. Because he knew what was happening, Sherby thought. It had been wrong, wrong of his father particularly, to go away and leave him alone with House.

"You see, my son, Carker's Army is looting and burning all the homes along East Mountain Road, and they've left the McKays'. They will probably burn this house as well. If they do, that freezer is the part of House most likely to survive. If you snuggle up with Smoky, you might stay alive until they leave."

"No," Sherby said. He wanted his mother to pat his head the way she always had when she put him into bed, and thought of bending down and touching her hand with his head. He knew it would not be the same, but he did it anyway; then turned away, shivering worse than ever, and led Smoky out into the cellar again, where Father Eddi waited.

"This is your best chance, my son. You know that House can open this door. He'll open it for you when it's safe."

Sherby did not bother to reply. He pushed hard against the big door, swinging it shut.

"Are we going back upstairs? Santa Claus is about to appear. It will be the high point of the party."

"I don't care about Santa," Sherby declared.

Smoky, who had been so reluctant to go down the stairs, trotted up them quite readily. "House!" Sherby called when they were back in the kitchen. "House, say something! Answer me!"

"What is it, Sherby?" The big voice seemed to come from all around him, as it always had, but there was a tension in it that Sherby had never heard before.

"I want to see out front. Is it okay to open the front door?"

"No," House told him. "There is a screen in the study—"

"Not that. You let me open it before."

"They were not here then, Sherby. Now they are."

Sherby considered the problem. Behind him, Father Eddi said, "House would like to show you Santa Claus, and this may be the last chance you'll ever have to see him with a child's eyes. Won't you please go into the family room and look?"

House said, "I will make an agreement with you, Sherby. If you'll see Santa, I'll open the security shutter on one of the windows in the living room a little and let you look out there, I promise."

"All the way. And look for as long as I want."

House hesitated. Smoky stamped in the silence; faintly, Sherby could hear voices outside, and the loud bangs of people pounding on things. At last House said, "All right."

There seemed to be fewer guests in the family room than Sherby remembered. Christmas Rose was talking to the tall, turbaned king and an older king with a long, white beard; but Knecht Rupprecht was nowhere to be seen. As Sherby and Smoky advanced toward the fireplace, in which the immense Yule log was blazing, Santa Claus stepped out of the fire, a fat little man no taller than Sherby himself, his red-and-white clothing all tarnished with soot and an enormous bundle of toys on his back.

"Look, my son!" Father Eddi exclaimed from behind Sherby, "There's Santa Claus! He came!"

Sherby nodded. A sort of aisle had opened between Santa Claus and himself. His mother was standing on Santa Claus's right, his father on left, and an elf was peeping from between his father's legs. As Sherby advanced, leading Smoky, Santa Claus roared with laughter. "Here I am again, Sherby! Second time today!"

"Are you really Santa Claus?" Sherby's voice wanted to shake. It was as if he had been crying.

"I certainly am!" Santa Claus laughed again, louder than ever: "Ho, ho, ho, ho!"

"Then you're nothing," Sherby told him. Sherby could not talk as loudly as Santa Claus, but he talked as loudly as he could. "You're a big nothing, and I never, never want to see you any more. House! Are you listening to me, House?"

Sherby waited for House's reply, and all the guests were silent, too. His mother and his father looked at each other, but neither spoke. Smoky nuzzled his hand.

"I'm the only one here, House! You've got to do what I tell you! You know you do!" Sherby looked for the butler in the crowd of guests, but could not find him. "Make them all go away. I mean it! No more promises. Make them all go away *right now!*"

He and Smoky stood alone in the big, dark, empty family room; the fireplace that had blazed an instant before was cold and dark.

Gradually the lights came up, so that by the time Sherby and Smoky had taken a few steps toward the door, the room was lit almost normally, though nowhere near as bright as it had been during the party.

"House, I'm hungry. I'm going to the study now, to look out. When I'm finished I want a bowl of Fruit Loops. Get out the stuff."

House's big voice, coming from a dozen speakers in that part of the house, said, "There is no milk left, Sherby. I told you so at noon, remember?"

"What is there?"

House considered, and Sherby knew there was no point in interrupting.

"There are sardines and two slices of bread. You could make a sardine sandwich?"

"Peanut butter?"

"Yes, a little."

"I'll have toast and peanut butter," Sherby decided. "Get out the peanut butter. Toast the bread and have it waiting for me when I'm through looking."

"I will, Sherby."

The hall was nearly dark, the study as black as pitch. House said, "If I turn on the lights, they will see you at once when I raise the security shutter, Sherby."

"Turn on the lights now so I can get over to the window," Sherby instructed him. "Then turn them off again. Then pull up the shutter."

His father's desk was still there, and the big computer console, its screen dark. Save for one large and equally dark window, books lined the walls—his grandfather's lawbooks, mostly; Sherby remembered his mother opening one for him to show him his grandfather's bookplate.

"I wish that you would go back to the frozen food locker, Sherby. That would be the safest place for you and Smoky."

"What's that banging the front door?"

"A log."

The light above the desk dimmed, then winked out. Sherby flattened his nose against the chill, black thermopane of the window, and the security shutter glided smoothly up.

There were too many people to count outside, some of them so close they were nearly touching the glass. Among them were policemen and firemen, but no one paid any attention to them; when he had been looking out for perhaps half a minute, Sherby recognized one of the firemen as the fox. A man holding a big iron bar ran right through the fox toward the window, but two women stopped him and pulled him out of the way.

The window exploded inward.

Sherby found himself on the floor. The light was bright and the shutter closed again, and he lay in a litter of broken glass; his right hand was bleeding, and his head bleeding from somewhere up in his hair. He cried then for what felt to him like a very long time, listening to the *bang, bang, bang* from the big front door.

When he got up, he took off his pajama shirt, wiped the blood away with it, blew his nose in it, and let it fall to the floor. "Where's Smoky?" he asked.

"In the dining room, Sherby. He is all right."

"Is my toast ready?"

"It will be by the time that you reach the kitchen. I would not try to catch Smoky again right now, Sherby. The shots frightened him very much. He might hurt you."

"Okay," Sherby said.

Kneeling on a kitchen chair, he spread the last of the peanut butter on his toast. He found that he was no longer hungry, but he ate one piece anyway. Somebody banged on the security shutter of one of the kitchen windows and went away. Climbing the stairs to get to his bedroom, Sherby thought that he had seen Yeshua on the landing. Yeshua had smiled, his white teeth flashing. Then he was gone, and it seemed he had never been there at all. "Don't do that," Sherby told House.

House did not answer.

In his bedroom, Sherby slipped out of his pajama bottoms and pulled on underwear and long stockings, jeans, and his red sweater. He was not skillful at tying shoes, but that morning there had been green Wellingtons under the tree. Now, for the first time ever, he tugged them on; they were only a little bit too large, and they did not have laces to tie. His green knit cap kept the blood from trickling into his eyes.

"You are not to go out, Sherby."

"Yes, I am," Sherby announced firmly. "I'm going to get on Smoky and go someplace else." He paused, thinking. "Down the mountain." Smoky had been very unwilling to go down the cellar stair, but Sherby felt pretty sure he would run faster down Lonely Mountain than up.

House said nothing more, but Sherby could hear people running and shouting downstairs. It sounded as if House was showing the party again, and Sherby told himself that if it sounded like the party it couldn't really be as bad as House had been pretending.

It was hard to decide which toys and books to take; in the end he settled on the yo-yo with the blinky lights in its side and the copter, telling himself that he could make the copter fly after him when he didn't want to carry it. He put on his big puffy down-filled coat, buttoned the easy buttons, slipped the yo-yo into one side pocket and the copter control into the other, and went out onto the landing again.

Knecht Rupprecht was there, standing at the head of the stairs—but a new Knecht Rupprecht, hideously transformed. Shreds of decaying flesh dangled from his skull face now, his eyes were spheres of fire, and he was taller than ever; in place of his bundle of switches he held a sword with a blade longer than Sherby and wider than Sherby's whole body.

People were clustered at the foot of the stairs staring up at him, arguing and urging each other forward. After a second or two, Sherby decided it might be better to go down the back stairs to the kitchen; but as he was about to turn away, something very strange happened to Knecht Rupprecht: he vanished, reappeared, roared so wildly that Sherby took three steps backward, dimmed, and dropped his sword.

The lights went out.

Something knocked Sherby down, and something else stepped on his fingers.

A flashlight beam danced on the ceiling before it, too, winked out.

Sherby tried to crawl on his hands and knees. Somebody tripped over him and said, "Shit! Oh, shit!"

Something was burning in the hall downstairs; from where he lay, Sherby could not see the flames, but he saw the red light of them and smelled smoke.

Thick, soft, warm arms scooped him up. "Little boy," the owner of the arms said in a voice like a girl's. "Little cute boy. Don't cry."

Outside the moon was up, and some of House's security shutters were lying on the snow-covered flower beds. Behind them, their windows glowed with orange light. Thick black smoke was coming through the shutters over his mother's and father's bedroom windows.

Smoky galloped through a milling crowd of people. One threw a bottle at him, and there were popping noises. Smoky stumbled and fell, tried to get up, and fell again. Someone hit him with a snowball, and someone else with a big stick.

"You want to hit him, little boy?" the man holding Sherby asked. Sherby could feel the man's whiskers scraping his ear. "You can hit him if you want to."

Sherby said nothing, but the man set him down anyway. "You can hit him if you want to," the man said again in his girl's voice. "Go ahead."

It would be better, Sherby thought, to do what they said. To be one. He got closer, not looking at the man behind him, stooped, and tried to scrape up enough of the trampled snow for a snowball. It stung his fingers and there wasn't enough, so he found a rock and threw that instead.

The fat man picked him up again. "I'm going to call you Chris," he told Sherby, "'cause you're my Christmas present. You can call me Corporal Charlie, Chris." He was bigger than anybody Sherby had ever seen before, not as tall as Knecht Rupprecht but wider than Sherby's bed. "You come along with me, Chris. We'll go on back to my van. You got cut, didn't you?"

Sherby said, "Uh-huh."

"I'll put a little splash of iodine on that when we get back home. We—"

House's roof fell in with a crash as he spoke. A great cloud of swirling sparks rose into the sky, and Sherby said, *"Oooh!"*

"Yeah, that's somethin', ain't it? I seen it before. All these soldiers here are meaning to do some more, but you and me are going home." Corporal Charlie chuckled. "We'll take off our clothes and have some fun, Chris. Then we'll go to bed."

Corporal Charlie took up the whole front seat of the van, so Sherby rode in back with furniture and some dresses and a lot of other things. There was a thing there lying on some coats that Sherby recognized, and when he was sure that it was what he thought it was, he traded the copter control for it.

That night at Corporal Charlie's house, when Corporal Charlie was asleep and Sherby was supposed to be asleep on Corporal Charlie's smelly old sofa, Sherby got the thing he had found in the van out again. "Merry Christmas, Mouse," he said to the shiny round lens in front. "It's me, Sherby."

But Mouse was quiet, still, and cold.

Sherby put her under the sofa cushion.

Christmas was funny, Sherby thought, snuggling underneath the coats. Christmas was happy and sad, green and red, real and fake, all mixed together. "I don't like it," he muttered to himself; but as soon as he had said it, he knew it was not true. He wished—somehow—that he had been nicer to Santa Claus, even if Santa Claus was not real.

The Christmas spirit yields renewal.

WE TRAVERSE AFAR

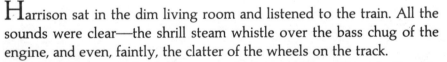

James P. Blaylock and Tim Powers

Harrison sat in the dim living room and listened to the train. All the sounds were clear—the shrill steam whistle over the bass chug of the engine, and even, faintly, the clatter of the wheels on the track.

It never rained anymore on Christmas Eve. The plastic rain gauge was probably still out on the shed roof; he used to lean over the balcony railing outside the master bedroom to check the level of the water in the thing. There had been something reassuring about the idea of rainwater rising in the gauge—nature measurably doing its work, the seasons going around, the drought held at bay. . . .

But he couldn't recall any rain since last winter. He hadn't checked, because the master bedroom was closed up now. And anyway the widow next door, Mrs. Kemp, had hung some strings of Christmas lights over her back porch, and even if he *did* get through to the balcony, he wouldn't be able to help seeing the blinking colors, and probably even something like a Christmas wreath on her back door.

Too many cooks spoil the broth, he thought, a good wine needs no bush, a friend in need is one friend too many, leave me alone.

She'd even knocked on his door today, the widow had; with a paper plate of Christmas cookies! The plate was covered in red and green foil and the whole bundle was wrapped in a Santa Claus napkin. He had taken the plate, out of politeness; but the whole kit and caboodle, cookies and all, had gone straight into the dumpster.

To hell with rain anyway. He was sitting in the old leather chair by the cold fireplace, watching snow. In the glass globe in his hand a little painted man and woman sat in a sleigh that was being pulled by a little frozen horse.

He took a sip of vodka and turned the globe upside down and back again, and a contained flurry of snow swirled around the figures. He and his wife had bought the thing a long time ago. The couple in the sleigh had been on their cold ride for decades now. Better to travel than to arrive, he thought, peering through the glass at their tiny blue-eyed faces; they didn't look a day older than when they'd started out. And still together, too, after all these years.

The sound of the train engine changed, was more echoing and booming now—maybe it had gone into a tunnel.

He put the globe down on the magazine stand and had another sip of vodka. With his nose stuffed full of Vick's Vapo-Rub, as it was tonight, his taste-buds wouldn't have known the difference if he'd been drinking V.S.O.P. brandy or paint thinner, but he could feel the warm glow in his stomach.

It was an old LP record on the turntable, one from the days when the real hi-fi enthusiasts cared more about sound quality than any kind of actual music. This one was two whole sides of locomotive racket, booming out through his monaural Klipshorn speaker. He also had old disks that were of surf sounds, downtown traffic, ocean waves, birds shouting in tropical forests . . .

Better a train. Booming across those nighttime miles.

He was just getting well relaxed when he began to hear faint music behind the barreling train. It was a Christmas song, and before he could stop himself he recognized it—Bing Crosby singing "We Three Kings," one of her favorites.

He'd been ready for it. He pulled two balls of cotton out of the plastic bag beside the vodka bottle and twisted them into his ears. That made it better—all he could hear now was a distant hiss that might have been rain against the windows.

Ghost rain, he thought. I should have put out a ghost gauge.

As if in response to his thought, the next sip of vodka had a taste—the full-orchestra, peaches-and-bourbon chord of Southern Comfort. He tilted his head forward and let the liquor run out of his mouth back into the glass, and then he stood up and crossed to the phonograph, lifted the arm off the record and laid it in its rest, off to the side.

When he pulled the cotton out of his ears, the house was silent. There was no creaking of floorboards, no sound of breathing or rustling. He was staring at the empty fireplace, pretty sure that if he looked around he would see that flickering rainbow glow from the dining room; the glow of lights, and the star on the top of the tree, and those weird little glass columns with bubbles wobbling up through the liquid inside. Somehow the stuff never boiled away. Some kind of perpetual motion, like those glass birds with the top hats, that bobbed back and forth, dipping their beaks into a glass of water, forever. At least with the Vick's he wouldn't smell pine sap.

The pages of the wall calendar had been rearranged sometime last night. He'd noticed it right away this morning when he'd come out of what used to be the guest bedroom, where he slept now on the single bed. The pink cloud of tuberous begonias above the thirty-one empty days of March was gone, replaced by the blooming poinsettia of the December page. Had he done it himself, shifted the calendar while walking in his sleep? He wasn't normally a sleepwalker. And sometime during the night, around midnight probably, he'd thought he heard a stirring in the closed-up bedroom across the hall, the door whispering open, what sounded like bedroom slippers shuffling on the living room carpet.

Before even making coffee he had folded the calendar back to March. She'd died on St. Patrick's day evening, and in fact the green dress she'd laid out on the queen-size bed still lay there, gathering whatever kind of dust inhabited a closed-up room. Around the dress, on the bedspread, were still scattered the green felt shamrocks she had intended to sew onto it. She'd never even had a chance to iron the dress, and, after the paramedics had taken her away on that long-ago evening, he'd had to unplug the iron himself, at the same time that he unplugged the bedside clock.

The following day, after moving out most of his clothes, he had shut the bedroom door for the last time. This business with the calendar made him wonder if maybe the clock was plugged in again, too, but he was not going to venture in there to find out.

Through the back door, from across the yard, he heard the familiar scrape of the widow's screen door opening, and then the sound of it slapping shut. Quickly he reached up and flipped off the lamp, then sat still in the darkened living room. Maybe she wasn't paying him another visit, but he wasn't taking any chances.

In a couple of minutes there came the clumping of her shoes on the front steps, and he hunkered down in the chair, glad that he'd turned off the train noise.

He watched her shadow in the porch light. He shouldn't leave it on all the time. It probably looked like an invitation, especially at this time of year. She knocked at the door, waited a moment and then knocked again. She couldn't take a hint if it stepped out of the bushes and bit her on the leg.

Abruptly he felt sheepish, hiding out like this, like a kid. But he was a *married man*, for God's sake. He'd taken a *vow*. And a vow wasn't worth taking if it wasn't *binding. She will do him good and not evil all the days of her life*, said Proverbs 31 about a good wife; *her lamp does not go out at night.*

Does not go out.

His thoughts trailed off into nothing when he realized that the woman outside was leaving, shuffling back down the steps. He caught himself wondering if she'd brought him something else to eat, maybe left a casserole outside the door. Once she'd brought around half a corned beef and a mess of potatoes and cabbage, and like the Christmas cookies, all of it had gone straight into the garbage. But the canned chili he'd microwaved earlier this evening wasn't sitting too well with him, and the thought of corned beef . . .

He could definitely hear something now from the closed-up bedroom—a low whirring noise like bees in a hive—the sewing machine? He couldn't recall if he had unplugged it too, that night. Still, it had no excuse. . . .

He grabbed the cotton balls, twisting them up tight and jamming them into his ears again. Had the bedroom door moved? He groped wildly for the lamp, switched it on, and with one last backward glance he went out the front door, nearly slamming it behind him in his haste.

Shakily, he sat down in one of the white plastic chairs on the porch and buttoned up his cardigan sweater. If the widow returned, she'd find him, and there was damn-all he could do about it. He looked around in case she might have left him something, but apparently she hadn't. The chilly night air calmed him down a little bit, and he listened for a moment to the sound of crickets, wondering what he would do now. Sooner or later he'd have to go back inside. He hadn't even brought out the vodka bottle.

Tomorrow, Christmas day, would be worse.

What would he say to her if the bedroom door should *open*, and she were to step out? If he were actually to *confront* her. . . . A good marriage was made in heaven, as the scriptures said, and you didn't let a thing like that go. No matter what. Hang on with chains.

After a while he became aware that someone up the street was yelling about something, and he stood up in relief, grateful for an excuse to get off the porch, away from the house. He shuffled down the two concrete steps, breathing the cold air that was scented with jasmine even in December.

Some distance up the block, half a dozen people in robes were walking down the sidewalk toward his house, carrying one of those real estate signs that looked like a miniature hangman's gallows. No, only one of them was carrying it, and at the bottom end of it was a metal wheel that was skirling along the dry pavement.

Then he saw that it wasn't a real estate sign, but a cross. The guy carrying it was apparently supposed to be Jesus, and two of the men behind him wore slatted skirts like Roman soldiers, and they had rope whips that they were snapping in the chilly air.

"Get along, King of the Jews!" one of the soldiers called, obviously not for the first time, and not very angrily. Behind the soldiers three women in togas trotted along, shaking their heads and waving their hands. Harrison supposed they must be Mary or somebody. The wheel at the bottom of the cross definitely needed a squirt of oil.

Harrison took a deep breath, and then forced jocularity into his voice as he called, "You guys missed the Golgotha off-ramp. Only thing south of here is the YMCA."

A black couple was pushing a shopping cart up the sidewalk from the opposite direction, their shadows stark under the streetlight. They were slowing down to watch Jesus. All kinds of unoiled wheels were turning tonight.

The biblical procession stopped in front of his house, and Harrison walked down the path to the sidewalk. Jesus grinned at him, clearly glad for the chance to pause amid his travail and catch his breath.

One of the women handed Harrison a folded flier. "I'm Mary Magdalene," she told him. "This is about a meeting we're having at our church next week. We're on Seventeenth, just past the 5 Freeway."

The shopping cart had stopped too, and Harrison carried the flier over to the black man and woman. "Here," he said, holding out the piece of paper. "Mary Magdalene wants you to check out her church. Take a right at the light, it's just past the freeway."

The black man had a bushy beard but didn't seem to be older than thirty, and the woman was fairly fat, wearing a sweatsuit. The shopping cart was full of empty bottles and cans sitting on top of a trash bag half full of clothes.

The black man grinned. "We're homeless, and we'd sure like to get the dollar-ninety-nine breakfast at Norm's. Could you help us out? We only need a little more."

"Ask Jesus," said Harrison nervously, waving at the robed people. "Hey Jesus, here's a chance to do some actual *thing* tonight, not just march around the streets. This here is a genuine homeless couple, give 'em a couple of bucks."

Jesus patted his robes with the hand that wasn't holding the cross. "I don't have anything on me," he said apologetically.

Harrison turned to the Roman soldiers. "You guys got any money?"

"Just change would do," put in the black man.

"Nah," said one of the soldiers, "I left my money in my pants."

"Girls?" said Harrison.

Mary Magdalene glanced at her companions, then turned back to Harrison and shook her head.

"Really?" said Harrison. "Out in this kind of neighborhood at night, and you don't even have quarters for phone calls?"

"We weren't going to go far," explained Jesus.

"Weren't going to go far." Harrison nodded, then looked back to Mary Magdalene. "Can your church help these people out? Food, shelter, that kind of thing?"

The black woman had walked over to Jesus and was admiring his cross. She liked the wheel.

"They'd have to be married," Mary Magdalene told Harrison. "In the church. If they're just . . . living together, we can't do anything for them."

That's great, thought Harrison, coming from Mary Magdalene. "So that's it, I guess, huh?"

Apparently it was. "Drop by the church!" said Jesus cheerfully, resuming his burden and starting forward again.

"Get along, King of the Jews!" called one of the soldiers, snapping his length of rope in the air. The procession moved on down the sidewalk, the wheel at the bottom of the cross squeaking.

The black man looked at Harrison. "Sir, could we borrow a couple of bucks? You live here? We'll pay you back."

Harrison was staring after the robed procession. "Oh," he said absently, "sure. Here." He dug a wad of bills out of his pants pocket and peeled two ones away from the five and held them out.

The man took the bills. "God bless you. Could we have the five too? It's Christmas Eve."

Harrison found that he was insulted by the *God bless you*. The implication was that these two were devout Christians, and would assuredly spend the money on wholesome food, or medicine, and not go buy dope or wine.

"No," he said sharply. "And I don't care what you buy with the two bucks." Once I've given it away, he thought, it shouldn't be my business. Gone is gone.

The black man scowled at him and muttered something obviously offensive under his breath as the two of them turned away, not toward Norm's and the dollar-ninety-nine breakfast, but down a side street toward the mini-mart.

Obscurely defeated, Harrison trudged back up to his porch and collapsed back into the chair.

He wished the train record was still playing inside—but even if it had been, it would still be a train that, realistically, had probably stopped rolling a long time ago. Listening to it over and over again wouldn't make it move again.

He opened the door and walked back into the dim living room. Just as he closed the door he heard thunder boom across the night sky, and then he heard the hiss of sudden rain on the pavement outside. In a moment it was tapping at the windows.

He wondered if the rain gauge was still on the roof, maybe measuring what was happening to Jesus and the black couple out there. And he was glad that he had had the roof redone a year ago. He was okay in here—no wet carpets in store for him.

The vodka bottle was still on the table, but he could see tiny reflected flickers of light in the glassy depths of it—red and green and yellow and blue; and, though he knew that the arm of the phonograph was lifted and in its holder, he heard again, clearly now, Bing Crosby singing "We Three Kings."

To hell with the vodka. He sat down in the leather chair and picked up the snow globe with trembling fingers. "What," he said softly, "too far? Too long? I thought it was supposed to be forever."

But rainy gusts boomed at the windows, and he realized that he had stood up. He pried at the base of the snow globe, and managed to free the plug.

Water and white plastic flecks bubbled and trickled out of it, onto the floor. In only a minute the globe had emptied out, and the two figures in the sleigh were exposed to the air of tonight, stopped. Without the refraction of the surrounding water the man and the woman looked smaller, and lifeless.

"Field and fountain, moor and mountain," he whispered. "Journey's done—finally. Sorry."

He was alone in the dark living room. No lights gleamed in the vodka bottle, and there was no sound but his own breath and heartbeat.

Tomorrow he would open the door to anyone who might knock.

Merry multicultural Christmas. Better duck.

JOYFUL ALL YE NATIONS RISE

Margaret Ball

We were only trying to plan a little party to raise the spirits of those still alive in the camp. But like most multiethnic committee meetings on Novi Gritska, this one got out of hand. Every festival that one group celebrated offended some other group. Right now it was the Visoks against the Gritiks. Professor Hrkati, a skeleton in a tattered yellow Gritik shirt, threw himself bodily at Professor Nezhenjo and nearly pulled off his baggy gray Visok trousers. "Visok child-raper," he screeched, "how dare you suggest polluting the Festival of the Sacred Prothios with your filthy rites?"

"Stuff your rites of the Sacred Prothios up his own arse, where you Gritiks keep your brains!" Nezhenjo shouted. "You don't even recognize the Sacrifice of the Seven Pallikaroi—"

"Blaspheming thief!"

"Gritik cow-brain!"

They rolled over and over what had, just six months ago, been a grassy quadrangle in the center of the loveliest university campus this side of the galaxy. Now the graffiti covered the buildings, makeshift tents filled the passages between them, and latrine ditches bordered the open quadrangle. Dull from cold and six months of slow starvation, I wondered whether a mere graduate student should stop two full professors from rolling in their own shit. The Bursar solved that problem.

"Professor Hrkati! Distinguished Professor Nezhenjo!" She strode across one of the few strips of solid ground and poked Hrkati in the ribs with her cane. "What will those shit-stinking Mamurluk guards think of us?"

She'd hit on the one argument that could possibly have stopped this brawl over nothing. The scarecrow professors stopped their fight within inches of the latrine ditch and got up, straightening the remains of their garments and apologizing to the Bursar. If there was one thing a Visok, a Gritik, and a Juznak (the Bursar) could agree upon, it was the despicable nature of all Mamurluks. Especially since their conquest of Ciselo Vrnje had been announced six months ago. There was a serious flaw in the argument, of course, but none of the participants knew about it, and I wasn't willing to take the risk of telling them.

This sort of interethnic wrangling had been going on for over three hours Galactic Standard (five hours Novi Gritskan). By now I was bored enough to stick my neck out.

"It looks as though there isn't any currently practiced winter festival that all ethnic groups here can agree on," I said. "Perhaps we should look a little further back in history. After all, we did start as a conference on the common roots of Novi Gritskan folklore."

"That," said the Bursar, "was some time ago." She straightened the tattered remnants of her black cloak of office and nodded at me. "What exactly did you have in mind?"

"Novi Gritskans emigrated from a part of OldTerra called Europe, which also suffers a prolonged winter. The Europeans had a number of winter solstice festivals: the Roman Saturnalia, the Medieval Christmas, and the Wiccan Fire-Lighting."

"Christmas," the Bursar said slowly. "I saw a history tri-d on that once. Looked rather jolly. Lots of food—well, we can't do much about *that*. Singing, sparkling decorations, and of course a fire—all solstice celebrations have a fire."

"Never mind the fire," Professor Hrkati interrupted, "does

anybody remember what this Christmas was *about?* I seem to remember it was more than just the standard death-of-the-sun solstice festivity."

I looked back at my notes. "Well, I think they were celebrating the birth of a baby."

"Oh, how *nice*," the Bursar said. "Let's do that one, shall we?"

"I remember that sect!" burst in Nezhenjo. "Read a paper somewhere. Sure, they celebrated the baby's birth, but then they killed it!"

"Dear me," said the Bursar, frowning, "that doesn't sound so nice. . . ."

"Yes, and then they ate it!" chimed in Professor Hrkati. "I read that paper too. There's a fragment of an ancient text that makes it perfectly clear. 'Corpus tuum, Domine, quod sumpsi, et sanguis, quem potavi, adhaereat visceribus meis,'" he intoned, and then translated for us. "May thy body, Lord, which I have eaten, and thy blood, which I have drunk, adhere to my viscera."

"I really do *not* think—" the Bursar began.

"Oh, that's all right," Professor Hrkati assured her. "The baby's birth is all they celebrate at the solstice. They didn't kill it until the spring equinox."

"Oh. Fattening it up, I suppose. Well that makes sense, even if it is rather nasty. Still, we needn't go into that part of it." The Bursar looked at me. "All right; you're in charge of a subcomittee to reconstruct the rites and plan the festivities."

Just like academia. Speak up, and you get stuck with the work. Most of the committee members scurried for their bunks before I could nab them. I slumped back against the oversized statue of Katsiano and scowled at the latrine ditches. I'd never have come here of my own free will, not with the endemic wars breaking out between all combinations of ethnic groups: Visoks and Juznaks on the west, Juznaks and Gritiks on the coast, and Gritiks and Visoks in the mountains. I don't like wars. But the boss pointed out that the Gritik-controlled city of Ciselo Vrnje and the land around it had been under a truce for almost five years. And since this conference was held between school sessions, I should even be safe from the usual undergraduate riots.

Not, however, safe from intense boredom. On the first day I was already close to brain death from the keynote speech. Since the academic goals of the symposium had no relation to my real business here, I had no reason to listen to this crashing bore. Come to think of it, neither had any of the genuine professors and students trapped in here. It was faintly possible that a study of the common roots of Novi Gritskan folklore might lead us to some way of bringing together the ethnic groups that had been feuding with enthusiasm ever since Novi Gritska was settled, but I doubted it. Judging from the audience around me, so did the rest of the civilized world. Nearly all the attendees were obviously Novi Gritskan professors from this very university, proudly wearing their national costumes under their black academic sashes. On the far side of the auditorium there were a few Galactics and the only nonhuman attendees: the professor from Pahtl and his entourage. There'd always be a Pahtl at any open Novi Gritskan conference; they coveted Novi Gritska's heavy mineral deposits and were always looking for a way to get control of the planet.

I should have been sitting over there with the other Galactics, where I'd have a chance to eavesdrop; but I'd screwed up when everybody poured into the lecture hall, trying to keep a good distance from any Galactics who might recognize me. Now I could see that I hadn't needed to be so cautious; they were all total strangers who'd have no reason to question my academic credentials.

Oh, well, Distinguished Professor Nezhenjo was winding up his peroration now. He made some glancing references to the mountain drum code which all Novi Gritskans had used during the Decade of Unity, when they joined together to wipe out the mountain bandits. Apparently these had been equal-opportunity bandits, willing to rape and murder Gritiks, Visoks, Juznaks, and even Mamurluks who tried to use the passes; between control of the mountains and pirate ships on the one navigable sea, they'd immobilized the continent and wrecked the economy for a generation before the legendary Katsiano organized an amalgamated army of all ethnic groups and destroyed the bandits' strongholds one by one.

So far, so good, and even rather interesting. It was probably only a legend, of course—I couldn't imagine these people cooperating for any purpose so sensible as saving their own economy. But it was a good note to start the conference on.

Unfortunately, Professor Nezhenjo decided to quote some lines from the Song of Katsiano as his rousing conclusion.

The opening refrain sent shivers down my spine. Every Novi Gritskan in the audience knew it, whatever their ethnic affiliation, and the chant of those deep rolling voices echoed through the auditorium until the walls quivered.

> *'The falcon's talons are bloody,*
> *Red are the wolf's fangs,*
> *Give us blood for blood against our enemies!'*

This legend was to unite Novi Gritska?

Then Nezhenjo intoned the first verse, and all hell—or perhaps I should say all Novi Gritska—broke loose.

> *'Katsiano on the hills, high on the mountain ridges,*
> *Gathered with him his brave men, first Visoks like himself.'*

There was a rumbling disturbance in the back of the hall. A ponderously fat man wearing the Gritik pleated yellow shirt under his black sash rose and bellowed, "A minor correction, my distinguished colleague! The earliest known manuscript of the Song of Katsiano clearly reads, 'Gathered with him his brave men, *Gritiks* like himself!'"

"Gritik shit-eater!" howled a mere graduate student in a slashed black robe that plainly showed his red plaid kilt underneath. "Forgers! Everybody knows Katsiano was a Juznak!"

The Visok contingent surged to the front of the assembly hall, forming a wedge of black sashes and baggy gray pants around Nezhenjo while he chanted the second verse of the Song of Katsiano, Visok style.

> *'Katsiano brought Gritiks and Juznaks,*
> *Even Mamurluks he brought to his stronghold.'*

"There you go, dumping on the Mamurluks again!" shrilled a lean girl just in front of me. She jumped atop the back of her seat and hurled something at the massed Visoks. One of the Juznaks wrenched his seat out of the floor bolts and threw it at her. Losing her Mamurluk blue veil, she toppled into the lap of the man beside me.

"You're outnumbered, better stay out of it," he advised her, but she wriggled loose and charged back into the fray. Me, I took his advice. Nobody noticed my departure; they were too busy fighting and singing.

> *'The falcon's talons are bloody,*
> *Red are the wolf's fangs,*
> *Give us blood for blood against our enemies!'*

Once outside, I set off briskly towards the Galactics' dormitory. I was nearly there when some interfering jerk yelled, "Hey, lady, that's the wrong door! You can't—"

The swish of the closing door cut him off, and the brilliant clashing reds and oranges of Pahtl silk hangings assaulted my eyes. I sank down on one of the squashy couches the Pahtls favored and wiped my forehead. With any luck, the Pahtls would all be caught in that assembly brawl for five or ten minutes at least, by which time—

Well, some days you don't get lucky. One of them oozed out from behind the quivering silk hanging on the far side of the suite and demanded in Pahtlian, "What are *you* doing here?"

I smiled sweetly at him and answered in Standard, "I'm sorry, I don't speak Pahtlian. Got lost on the way to my room, felt dizzy— Could I just sit quietly and rest for a moment?"

The Pahtl didn't speak Galactic Standard, or didn't choose to understand. As it approached me, waving its fore-tentacles, I added, "Actually, I'm feeling quite faint," and collapsed among the squishy cushions. The billowing silks engulfed both arms to the elbow and stuck to my nose and mouth, choking me with the musky-garlic scent favored by wealthy Pahtls. Much more of this, and I probably *would* be feeling faint.

I didn't have time to test the theory. The Pahtl picked me up— one scaly tentacle under my breasts, the other around both ankles— opened the door, presumably with a mid-tentacle, and deposited me outside as though I were an unwanted package, not marked *Fragile*.

"Ouf!" I sat up and dusted myself off. It was no good; take a shower, or two or three, to get rid of the musk-and-garlic scent.

"I must say you take being kicked out rather well," said the man who'd shouted at me before. This time I looked him over: intense blue eyes, square shoulders, broad misshapen hands. Not bad. If I hadn't had my own reasons for dropping in on the Pahtls, I might have listened to him before.

"Oh, well." I got to my feet, surprised at how annoyed I felt at having been caught at a disadvantage. Goodness knows it's happened enough times in what I laughingly refer to as my career. "It was an interesting excursion, anyway."

"Not half as interesting as what I could show you."

"What makes you think that?" It had occurred to me, actually, considering the shoulders and the eyes, but it was scarcely a good move in the game to admit it this early.

"I," he said, "am neither a Novi Gritskan nor a professor. Who else are you going to find who'll buy you a *pivo* without refighting the Mamurluk-Gritik war or correcting your footnotes?"

"Good point," I admitted. "But if you're not with the conference, what *is* a nice boy like you doing here? And what's a *pivo?*"

I got lengthy answers to both questions, in a dingy one-roomed bar full of *kjrill* smoke and grinning men in hard hats. *Pivo* tasted rather like OldTerran beer mixed with ginger ale and lemon juice. Somewhere around the bottom of the second pitcher I was prepared to admit that it didn't taste nearly as bad as that description makes it sound, though I still wasn't sure about Leroy's assertion that you could drink pitchers of the stuff without getting bombed. After all, he had more than twice my body mass. Better let him finish the third pitcher, I decided, pouring myself one last tumbler while he launched on another of his horror stories about the things under the old science lab buildings.

Leroy was an expert in demolitions, toxic waste removal, and bomb defusing. He'd been trained "on the job" during the Capellan Wars, and in the process had lost two fingers of his right hand and had his left thumb relocated by field surgeons. He didn't seem to resent this. "Taught me to be careful, didn't it?" he remarked, draining the third pitcher of *pivo*. "Slow and careful, that's what you want when you're cleaning up a mess like this. Those Gritiks been chucking all their leftover experimental materials down into the cellars since the University was founded. Never a thought about not putting your volatiles next to your oxidizers, or building up a dangerous mass of radio isotopes. *Not* to mention that the main lab was a weapons dump during the Gritik-Mamurluk war, and nobody cleaned up after they expelled all the Mamurluks from Ciselo Vrnje."

"Not all, surely?" The map I'd been given in the conference info packet showed a small "Mamurluk quarter" as well as Juznak and Visok enclaves. Ciselo Vrnje might be mainly a Gritik city, but there were plenty of the other ethnic groups around.

"Oh, there's a few Mamurluk moved back in the last couple of years," Leroy admitted, "but nothing like what it was before the war." And he returned to his main interest, the polluted basements under Ciselo Vrnje's science labs. "You wouldn't believe it. Looks like an Old Terran toxic waste dump!"

It wasn't difficult to look horrified. OldTerra's self-pollution was a classical case in freshman ecochemistry texts; that they'd pretty much cleaned up their act now didn't discount the tales of scarred mountains, black dead rivers, babies born without brains or hands.

Leroy was a good raconteur, though I did notice that most of the stories showed him in a good light: look at me, he was saying, how brave and clever and desirable I am. They also showed some things he probably didn't intend to reveal: he was almost certainly selling some of the war surplus on the black market. I mentally shrugged. Stopping a minor part of the Novi Gritskan arms trade wasn't my job. Anyway I didn't plan to be here long enough to be affected by any of the little ethnic wars.

So much for plans.

"Okay, anybody have some data on the Christmas Solstice rites?" My subcommittee consisted of Professor Hrkati and Distinguished Professor Nezhenjo, because they had been too exhausted from their previous fight to escape when I was hunting for "volunteers," and the Bursar, probably because she felt guilty for saddling me with the task. Great. One Gritik, one Visok, and one Juznak: we'd never have more than two votes in favor of anything. All we needed to complete the happy circle was a Mamurluk.

The trouble was, there weren't any Mamurluks left in Ciselo Vrnje, except for the one who made daily announcements of such exciting camp rules as a cut in the ration bars or a new site for latrine ditches. My fellow committee members thought they knew why there weren't any Mamurluks in the camp, but they were wrong. I really did know why, but I didn't dare tell them.

"I found an Old Ameringlish hymn in this text," Professor Hrkati announced. "So far I've only translated the first line into Galactic Standard. It appears to read, 'Garnish the auditoriums with shoots of *hali*,' and then there's a plainsong interpolation, 'Fa la la la la la la la la.'"

"Is that all you've translated?" grumbled Distinguished Professor Nezhenjo. "Doesn't tell us much, does it? What's this *hali*, anyway?"

"It could be a version of *hoelle*, the Christian Underworld," Professor Hrkati hazarded.

Nezhenjo snorted. "Not very likely in a sacred hymn. Probably it's an alternative version of *Kali*, Goddess of Death. After all, these people *were* baby-killers."

"The death part is at the spring solstice," Hrkati reiterated. "This is a celebration of a *birth*, and—"

"I know what *hali* is!" the Bursar interrupted, looking very pleased with herself. "The history tri-d had a tree with shiny things decorating it. You must have mistranslated the text, Hrkati; it should read, 'Garnish the *hali* in the auditoriums,' not 'Garnish the auditorium with the *hali*'"

"These things would be a lot easier if I had access to the library and my research notes," Hrkati muttered, while on the other side Nezhenjo mumbled "'La la la . . . '" Call that a translation? Scholarship's not what it was in my day, by the Seven Pallikaroi, that it isn't!"

Since the only trees on campus had long since been cut down for firewood, we agreed to wreath vines of a prickly evergreen called bitterweed around the statue of Katsiano. I peered glumly up the forty-foot height of the statue, having a premonition of who was going to do the actual garnishing. Still, anything for peace, and I was beginning to have an idea how this Christmas decoration could be useful . . .

By now you've probably figured out why we were all sitting around freezing our infrastructures off in the snow instead of discussing Novi Gritskan folklore in a nice warm auditorium. Ciselo Vrnje had been caught up in another of those damn ethnic wars. At least, that's what we were meant to believe.

The announcement interrupted the very first session on the day after the keynote address fight. The speaker's gravelly voice was replaced first by sputters and crackles, then by a young, shaky voice saying something in one of the Novi Gritskan dialects—which one I couldn't tell, because my implant was only for Standard, and I got a buzzing sound in my head whenever a dialect word was used. Context and the reactions of the audience made the missing bits easy enough to understand, though.

The girl speaking through the sound system announced that Ciselo Vrnje had been retaken by the exiled Mamurluks, and we were all to be interned here until civil order was restored.

I looked around the assembly hall. No blue veils; no Mamurluks. It might be true. When we got outside, I could see that the rest was true enough. A shimmering force field distorted our view of the city of Ciselo Vrnje and the mountains around it. The campus was isolated within the bubble of the force field. Armed soldiers, looking like upright turtles in their complete protective gear, had taken up stations at all four points of the quadrangle. They gestured silently with their weapons and we let them herd us back into the auditorium. I managed to be one of the last ones pushed back in, so I got to see the force field flicker a couple of times, heard the sobs and screams as people from the city were shoved into the campus area.

By the next morning they evidently felt confident enough to let us out. Overnight the campus had been divided like the city. All of us from the conference, Novi Gritskans and Galactics alike, had the auditorium as our quarters. I suppose they trusted us, being intellectuals, not to get caught up in ethnic rivalries like the common citizens. That should have warned everybody; Mamurluks wouldn't have been that naive about their compatriots.

The dorms where conference visitors had been staying were closed, no explanation given. I never saw my sequined black dress or my iridium pearl drops again. The other dorms became the Gritik quarter. The Juznaks and the Visoks from the city had to camp in the Humanities and Sciences complexes respectively.

There wasn't any decent way to be alone in such a crowd of miserable people, but I did the best I could, wandering over to the Katsiano statue and slumping down at its base, trying to look anonymous and so unhappy nobody would want to come near me. Everybody else was milling around, wondering when we would get something to eat and explaining to each other why there weren't any Mamurluks interned. They believed the coup story, all right; getting killed or interned by their next-door neighbors was the sort of thing they expected on Novi Gritska.

I rested my head against the wristband of my watch and listened to another explanation. Useful thing, that wristband. Right now the com unit was linked to the spyder I'd left between two cushions in the Pahtl suite, and the Pahtls were having a very interesting conversation indeed. Every once in a while my Pahtlian implant buzzed in frustration at a slang term or a military abbreviation, but I could fill in the blanks well enough.

I listened so intently that I hardly remembered the people milling around me until a pair of scuffed boots nudged my own toes and a loud, gravelly voice interrupted me.

"Say, what's a nice girl like you doing in a place like this?"

"Shut up," I snarled before remembering where I was and who I was supposed to be. I lifted my head. "Leroy? What are *you* doing with the academics?"

"Workin' under the labs when they closed off the U," he said. "Guess they just assumed everybody on campus was part of your conference. Anyway, where else would I go? Your good luck, sweets."

Leroy explained how lucky I was to have him to look after me. None of us academics would know how to steal enough food and blankets to keep alive, or how to treat boils with hot leaf poultices and a penknife, or how to trade back to our captors the things we'd stolen from them the night before.

He was right, too. During the months that followed I profited from the skills Leroy had gained as a POW on Capella IV. We all lost weight, but Leroy showed me how to stave off scurvy by adding bitterweed leaves and stems to the daily mush. We all shivered in the unheated auditorium as winter came on, but Leroy picked the lock on a cellar door and made the two of us a secret nest lined with insulating foam from the inactive heat pipes. He traded the rest of the foam to Gritiks for spare dormitory blankets, to the faceless camp guards for medicines from Outside that alleviated Professor Nezhenjo's heart palpitations, for a hundred other things that made life in camp just a little bit more bearable for many of us. By the time the days began closing in towards the dark winter solstice, many of the others had become accomplished thieves and traders and scroungers. But in the beginning, Leroy was our single greatest asset. Our private hidey-hole saved my sanity when I needed to get away from the ceaseless academic chatter.

Which made it very difficult for me when it seemed I might have to kill him.

I'd been listening in on the Pahtl conversations whenever I could, but I seldom got more than tantalizing fragments. They never showed themselves where anybody in camp could see them—unless those masked and suited guards were Pahtls, and *they* never talked. So the only use I got out of my Pahtlian language implant was when they happened to talk in the room where I'd hidden the spyder, just when I was listening to my wristband. What I did pick up that way, though, was disturbing enough.

The Mamurluks weren't free in the city, as my colleagues supposed. They had been BZZZZZ for ZZZZT, according to my implant, and context made the meaning all too clear. The Pahtls didn't mind forcing all the Mamurluks into unvented transport canisters, and disposing of the bodies afterwards, but they never said in plain Pahtlian that they had killed them all. No. They simply congratulated themselves on having arranged a completely empty city that left them free to search for—ZZZZBFRZZZZ. Fucking cheap language implant.

What little I knew about conditions outside Ciselo Vrnje came by way of such Pahtl comments. Since they were talking to each other, I assumed most of it was true. I put in a fair amount of time drifting through our quarter of the camp, starting rumors to counteract the official camp announcements made by the Pahtl's Mamurluk puppet. As winter closed in on us, most of our quarter knew that the announced Mamurluk takeover of Ciselo Vrnje had set off another half-dozen minor wars all over Novi Gritska. (The Mamurluks had, apparently, taken credit for Ciselo Vrnje, even though they could have had no more idea than anyone else what had actually happened.)

The flickering lights we saw on the mountains around Ciselo Vrnje represented three separate armed camps of Gritiks, Visoks, and Juznaks, all hoping to retake Ciselo Vrnje for themselves. Occasionally one of them would aim a cutter beam at the secondary force field surrounding the whole city. We knew because we saw the beams spatter on the invisible boundary of the field.

Some of the Pahtls worried about those outlying camps. Their field generator was strained to its limits, keeping one force field around the university campus and another around the outer city. A single beam, or even a half dozen, could be repelled by the outer field. But if all three camps joined at once to bombard the city with everything they had, the field might fail.

That was information I would have loved to pass to the camps on the mountainside. Unfortunately, I could think of no way to do it. The force field was impervious to sound and to physical bodies; only light could come through. Once a day it flickered when our inadequate rations were shoved through, but never for long enough to do any good. Even if I could have got through then, I'd only be trapped between the inner and outer fields, in the deserted city where Pahtls ranged in search of ZZZZBFRZZZZ.

I toyed with the idea of spelling out a gigantic message in Novi Gritskan, telling the Gritiks and Visoks and Juznaks on the mountain to get it together and bombard us all at once with all their ammunition, but somehow I felt the Pahtls would notice if I began painting sheets and blankets with foot-high letters and spreading them out over the latrine trenches in the quad.

And I certainly didn't want to spread the information that the Pahtls occasionally considered simplifying their task. If all of us in the camp were BZZZZZ for ZZZZT like the Mamurluks, they wouldn't need to use generator energy on isolating the camp from the rest of the city, and the outer force field would be that much stronger against a combined attack.

Assuming Novi Gritskan guerrilla armies ever could combine. Hmmph. Sometimes, contemplating the prospect of being BZZZZZ for ZZZZT like the unfortunate Mamurluks, I was just as glad the Gritiks and Visoks and Juznaks couldn't get it together. Safer to wait until GalFed got their act together and came to rescue us.

But *would* they come? The Pahtls never worried aloud about that. Perhaps the entire galaxy believed that the capture of Ciselo Vrnje was just one more move in the endless interethnic wars of Novi Gritska. In which case, they had no excuse to intervene. GalInt knew the Pahtls coveted Novi Gritska, of course, and suspected they were planning a coup of some sort: that was why they'd sent me in, with my background as a xenology grad student, to find out what I could. They might even suspect the Pahtls of taking Ciselo Vrnje, but they couldn't prove it. I had no way to get the evidence to them—and I knew better than to think they'd risk the political future of GalInt to pull out one minor agent who was very likely, as far as they knew, dead by now.

There were deaths every week after the first hard freeze; starvation and exposure took some, and more succumbed to depression as the long dark nights set in. The Bursar decided we'd better do something to raise morale in the camp. Couldn't we, as unbiased scholars, combine Novi Gritska's ethnic rites into one solstice festival for everybody?

The answer, as you've seen, was no. Which was how we came to be reconstructing the rites of a religion so long dead that none of us knew enough about it to fight; and how I came to be wasting so much time in committee meetings that my listening hours dwindled to almost nothing and Leroy began to complain of neglect.

I should have been spending less time arguing over whether the winged things called "angels" were the same as the winged birds called "turkey" that Christians roasted on the solstice day, and more time listening to the Pahtls and to Leroy.

I did, however, figure out from random conversations what sort of thing ZZZZBFRZZZZ must be. It was something the Novi Gritskans already had, were known to have, were known to have somewhere right here in Ciselo Vrnje, so that its release could be plausibly explained as an unfortunate accident of war and nothing to do with the unfortunate Pahtls who'd been "trapped" here during the coup. It could wipe out the Novi Gritskan population without harming the Pahtls; what's more, it would scare any other humans away from ever approaching Novi Gritska again, leaving the planet for the Pahtls.

The only thing was, I couldn't figure out what could have such properties. Maybe Leroy would know; he considered himself an expert, after all.

"Leroy," I asked, as we snuggled together in our nest of foam insulation and shredded blankets, "there are bombs that kill people but leave buildings intact, right?"

"Of course there are," he said. "Haven't you taken *any* science courses? Ever hear of neutron bombs? Or do you Xeno types spend all your time collecting quaint folklore stories instead of learning about the real world?"

He needn't have been snide. Of course I knew about neutron bombs; but those were outdated and not suitable for the Pahtls' purposes. I didn't argue, though. Once Leroy got started on the subject, he kept going along tracks that turned out to lead just where I needed to go. "Novi Gritskans don't go in for stuff like that," he told me. "Some kind of point of honor with them to stick with old-fashioned weapons. You should know that too, being a specialist in Novi Gritskan folklore and all. The more enemies a man kills one at a time, the more honor he gains—even if he's using a laser-tracer sniper from a nice safe position two mountains away. Look what they did to that biowar sales tech a few years back."

"Biowar's against the GalFed Conventions," I pointed out.

"Yeah, but Novi Gritska never paid much attention to GalFed," Leroy said absently. "Only reason they never used the GeneX virus—"

"They *had* a biowar virus?"

"Some jerk from the Capellan System developed one a few years back, thought the Novi Gritskans were natural customers. Showed up here with a sample case during the last war," Leroy told me. "Right here in Ciselo Vrnje. Gritiks thought he was dishonorable; besides, he couldn't guarantee that the virus would be able to tell Gritiks from Visoks or Juznaks or even Mamurluks, come to that. See, genetically they're all the same; it's just the dialects and customs and history that split 'em apart. His mistake."

"So the GeneX operates on DNA?"

Leroy nodded. "Screws up the proteins real, real good. You don't see any effect in this generation, but the next generation's shot to hell—stillbirths, muties, lots and lots of brain and spinal cord damage."

"That's—"

"Yep." Something in Leroy's tone stopped me. "Gritiks thought so too. They impaled him. Standard execution for traitors. Took him five days to die."

I decided it would definitely not be a good idea to let anybody in the camp find out I had a Pahtlian language implant.

"Couldn't think of any safe way to dispose of his sealed samples, though," Leroy went on, "so they stashed 'em under the science labs with the rest of the toxics and radioactives. Stupid bastards." He yawned and wrapped his arms around me. "Snuggle up, girlie. You're shivering. Old Leroy's got a cure for that. Of course," he added reflectively while his left hand wandered down my body, "I haven't been able to figure out a safe disposal method either. Gonna have to call in a biochem expert when this little war's over— Hey," he broke off with an aggrieved tone, "what's the matter? You always liked that before!"

I had gone stiff without thinking. Now I put my arms around Leroy until the fingertips of my right hand just touched the watchband on my left wrist. "You know where the GeneX samples are?"

"Sure, I know, and I ain't clearing anything *near* that end of the basement until I get a biochem to deal with the cases."

"This stuff is keyed to human DNA?" I had to make absolutely sure.

"Yep."

"So it wouldn't have any effect on nonhumans?"

"Cows, horses? Dunno. Might hit any Earth-origin mammals; told you, that's not my field."

"I was thinking more of . . . aliens." *Like Pahtls.*

"Oh, they'd be all right."

Just one more question, and then I'd have to do it.

"Have you told anybody else about the virus?"

"Uh-uh. No use scaring people before we can get somebody in to deal with the stuff. But there must be plenty of Gritiks around who remember that guy and his little sample case."

I relaxed. Of course, that meant we were in worse danger than ever before; all the Pahtls had to do was stop searching the Old City and start interrogating a few of the Gritiks in this camp. But at least it relieved me of one duty I'd been dreading, ever since the need for it occurred to me a few minutes earlier. I kissed Leroy.

"You," he told me, "are one weird female. Talking about biowar turns you on?"

"No," I told him, "knowing I don't have to kill you. You see, if you'd been the only one who knew where the GeneX was stored—"

Leroy started laughing. "Little bitty thing like you? Girlie, why on earth would you *want* to kill your favorite hunk, let alone think you could?"

That irritated me. I touched the recessed button on the inside of my watchband and felt the sliversteel slide into my hand. A slight turn of the wrist was all it took to make Leroy feel the prick of the needle in his neck.

He stopped laughing.

"I still would kill you," I told him, "except I think you can be of some use. Now— As a registered agent of Galactic Intelligence, I hereby request and command your cooperation in a matter affecting the survival of the civilized races." I rattled off the key legal words, but Leroy hardly seemed to hear them. "You're good at stealing things and wiring things up to do stuff," I went on.

After I explained exactly what it was I had in mind, Leroy agreed. But he seemed to have lost any desire to snuggle in our nest; he pulled on his pants and got out of there as if I'd threatened something more valuable than his life.

Next stop was Professor Nezhenjo. He was so flattered by my interest in his work that he gave me a complete transcription of Katsiano's drumcode. And at the next committee meeting he was still feeling so positive about me that he voted with the Bursar and me to put a star on top of the vine-wreathed Katsiano statue instead of a turkey. (Or an angel. Whatever.) I think it was my promise to get the star wired up to flash light that really clinched the matter. In the end even Professor Hrkati voted for the star (He had held out for an angel. Or turkey. Whatever.), making us possibly the first multiethnic Novi Gritskan committee to bring in a unanimous vote on anything.

Leroy came through in style, "liberating" not only lights and wiring but also enough "spare parts" to set up a sound system so that we could play carols during the rites. He told me this while we were on opposite sides of Katsiano's head, forty feet from the ground, connecting the last terminals to set up the flasher sequence.

It was a grand Christmas Solstice Winter Festival Rite, if I do say so myself. Katsiano's statue looked like a gigantic *hali* tree, wreathed around and around with thorny bitterweed vines. The sound system blared out Professor Hrkati's version of his ancient hymn over and over again, pleasing him no end. And when the entire population of the camp was gathered in the quadrangle before the statue, the light show began.

It started modestly enough, with a switch from the *hali* hymn to the one song every Novi Gritskan knew, the ballad of Katsiano. Instrumentals only; words would have been divisive. At the first chorus, five thousand voices—all that was left of Ciselo Vrnje— roared out the words in unison while the star blinked out its message to all of us, to the deserted city of Ciselo Vrnje, and to the distant camps of Gritiks and Visoks and Juznaks on their separate mountainsides.

> *'The falcon's talons are bloody,*
> *Red are the wolf's fangs,*
> *Give us blood for blood against our enemies!'*

It took three choruses to flash out the entire drumcode message, but Leroy's star was nice and bright; all the mountainside camps must have seen it perfectly.

Then, give Novi Gritskans credit for quick reactions: they didn't waste any time conferring or holding committee meetings. All three camps opened fire on the outer shield with everything they had. The force field quivered, broke into a rainbow dazzle of fractured light, and disappeared. A moment later, a stray beam must have taken out the field generator, because the shimmering veil of the second force field died away. The separate ethnic camps combined forces in the center of Ciselo Vrnje, hunted down the Pahtls and finished the solstice rites in style.

For a while I hoped that we had celebrated the birth of an infant peace, but in traditional Novi Gritskan fashion, they killed it before the spring equinox.

A story of salvation and loss.

PAL O' MINE

Charles de Lint

1

Gina always believed there was magic in the world. "But it doesn't work the way it does in fairy tales," she told me. "It doesn't save us. We have to save ourselves."

2

One of the things I keep coming back to when I think of Gina is walking down Yoors Street on a cold, snowy Christmas Eve during our last year of high school. We were out Christmas shopping. I'd been finished and had my presents all wrapped during the first week of December, but Gina had waited for the last minute as usual, which was why we were out braving the storm that afternoon.

I was wrapped in as many layers of clothes as I could fit under my overcoat and looked about twice my size, but Gina was just scuffling along beside me in her usual cowboy boots and jeans, a floppy felt hat pressing down her dark curls, and her hands thrust deep into the pockets of her pea jacket. She simply didn't pay any attention to the cold. Gina was good at that: ignoring inconveniences, or things she wasn't particularly interested in dealing with, much the way—I was eventually forced to admit—that I'd taught myself to ignore the dark current that was always present, running just under the surface of her exuberantly good moods.

"You know what I like best about the city?" she asked as we waited for the light to change where Yoors crosses Bunnett.

I shook my head.

"Looking up. There's a whole other world living up there."

I followed her gaze and at first I didn't know what she was on about. I looked through breaks in the gusts of snow that billowed around us, but couldn't detect anything out of the ordinary. I saw only rooftops and chimneys, multicolored Christmas decorations and the black strands of cable that ran in sagging geometric lines from the power poles to the buildings.

"What're you talking about?" I asked.

"The 'goyles," Gina said.

I gave her a blank look, no closer to understanding what she was talking about than I'd been before.

"The gargoyles, Sue," she repeated patiently. "Almost every building in this part of the city has got them, perched up there by the rooflines, looking down on us."

Once she'd pointed them out to me, I found it hard to believe that I'd never noticed them before. On that corner alone there were at least a half-dozen grotesque examples. I saw one in the archway keystone of the Annaheim Building directly across the street—a leering monstrous face, part lion, part bat, part man. Higher up, and all around, other nightmare faces peered down at us, from the corners of buildings, hidden in the frieze and cornice designs, cunningly nestled in corner brackets and the stone roof cresting. Every building had them. *Every* building.

Their presence shocked me. It's not that I was unaware of their existence—after all, I was planning on architecture as a major in college. It's just that if someone had mentioned gargoyles to me before that day, I would have automatically thought of the cathedrals and castles of Europe—not ordinary office buildings in Newford.

"I can't believe I never noticed them before," I told her.

"There are people who live their whole lives here and never see them," Gina said.

"How's that possible?"

Gina smiled. "It's because of where they are—looking down at us from just above our normal sightline. People in the city hardly ever look up."

"But still . . ."

"I know. It's something, isn't it? It really is a whole different world. Imagine being able to live your entire life in the middle of the city and never be noticed by anybody."

"Like a bag lady," I said.

Gina nodded. "Sort of. Except people wouldn't ignore you because you're some pathetic street person that they want to avoid. They'd ignore you because they simply couldn't *see* you."

That thought gave me a creepy feeling and I couldn't suppress a shiver, but I could tell that Gina was intrigued with the idea. She was staring at that one gargoyle, above the entrance to the Annaheim Building.

"You really like those things, don't you?" I said.

Gina turned to look at me, an expression I couldn't read sitting in the back of her eyes.

"I wish I lived in their world," she told me.

She held my gaze with that strange look in her eyes for a long heartbeat. Then the light changed and she laughed, breaking the mood. Slipping her arm in mine, she started us off across the street to finish her Christmas shopping.

When we stood on the pavement in front of the Annaheim Building, she stopped and looked up at the gargoyle. I craned my neck and tried to give it a good look myself, but it was hard to see because of all the blowing snow.

Gina laughed suddenly. "It knows we were talking about it."

"What do you mean?"

"It just winked at us."

I hadn't seen anything, but then I always seemed to be looking exactly the wrong way, or perhaps *in* the wrong way, whenever Gina tried to point out some magical thing to me. She was so serious about it.

"Did you see?" Gina asked.

"I'm not sure," I told her. "I think I saw something . . ."

Falling snow. The side of a building. And stone statuary that was pretty amazing in and of itself without the need to be animated as well. I looked up at the gargoyle again, trying to see what Gina had seen.

I wish I lived in their world.

It wasn't until years later that I finally understood what she'd meant by that.

3

Christmas wasn't the same for me as for most people—not even when I was a kid: my dad was born on Christmas day; Granny Ashworth, his mother, died on Christmas day when I was nine; and my own birthday was December 27th. It made for a strange brew come the holiday season, part celebration, part mourning, liberally mixed with all the paraphernalia that means Christmas: eggnog and glittering lights, caroling, ornaments, and, of course, presents.

Christmas wasn't centered around presents for me. Easy to say, I suppose, seeing how I grew up in the Beaches, wanting for nothing, but it's true. What enamored me the most about the season, once I got beyond the confusion of birthdays and mourning, was the idea of what it was supposed to be: peace and goodwill to all. The traditions. The idea of the miracle birth the way it was told in the Bible and more secular legends like the one about how for one hour after midnight on Christmas Eve, animals were given human voices so that they could praise the baby Jesus.

I remember staying up late the year I turned eleven, sitting up in bed with my cat on my lap and watching the clock, determined to hear Chelsea speak, except I fell asleep sometime after eleven and never did find out if she could or not. By the time Christmas came around the next year I was too old to believe in that sort of thing anymore.

Gina never got too old. I remember years later when she got her dog Fritzie, she told me, "You know what I like the best about him? The stories he tells me."

"Your dog tells you stories," I said slowly.

"Everything's got a voice," Gina told me. "You just have to learn how to hear it."

4

The best present I ever got was the Christmas that Gina decided to be my friend. I'd been going to a private school and hated it. Everything about it was so stiff and proper. Even though we were only children, it was still all about money and social standing and it drove me mad. I'd see the public school kids and they seemed so free compared to all the boundaries I perceived to be compartmentalizing my own life.

I pestered my mother for the entire summer I was nine until she finally relented and let me take the public transport into Ferryside where I attended Cairnmount Public School. By noon of my first day, I realized that I hated public school more.

There's nothing worse than being the new kid—especially when you were busing in from the Beaches. Nobody wanted anything to do with the slumming rich kid and her airs. I didn't have airs; I was just too scared. But first impressions are everything and I ended up feeling more left out and alone than I'd ever been at my old school. I couldn't even talk about it at home—my pride wouldn't let me. After the way I'd carried on about it all summer, I couldn't find the courage to admit that I'd been wrong.

So I did the best I could. At recess, I'd stand miserably on the sidelines, trying to look as though I was a part of the linked fence, or whatever I was standing beside at the time, because I soon learned it was better to be ignored than to be noticed and ridiculed. I stuck it out until just before Christmas break. I don't know if I would have been able to force myself to return after the holidays, but that day a bunch of boys were teasing me and my eyes were already welling with tears when Gina walked up out of nowhere and chased them off.

"Why don't you ever play with anybody?" she asked me.

"Nobody wants me to play with them," I said.

"Well, I do," she said and then she smiled at me, a smile so bright that it dried up all my tears.

After that, we were best friends forever.

5

Gina was the most outrageous, talented, wonderful person I had ever met. I was the sort of child who usually reacted to stimuli; Gina created them. She made up games, she made up stories, she made up songs. It was impossible to be bored in her company and we became inseparable, in school and out.

I don't think a day went by that we didn't spend some part of it together. We had sleepovers. We took art and music and dance classes together and if she won the prizes, I didn't mind, because she was my friend and I could only be proud of her. There was no limit to her imagination, but that was fine by me, too. I was happy to have been welcomed into her world and I was more than willing to take up whatever enterprise she might propose.

I remember one afternoon we sat up in her room and made little people out of found objects: acorn heads, seed eyes, twig bodies. We made clothes for them, and furniture, and concocted long extravagant family histories so that we ended up knowing more about them than we did our classmates.

"They're real now," I remember her telling me. "We've given them lives, so they'll always be real."

"What kind of real?" I asked, feeling a little confused because I was at that age when I was starting to understand the difference between what was make-believe and what was real.

"There's only one kind of real," Gina told me. "The trouble is, not everybody can see it and they make fun of those who can."

Though I couldn't know the world through the same perspective as Gina had, there was one thing I did know. "I would never make fun of you," I said.

"I know, Sue. That's why we're friends."

I still have the little twig people I made, wrapped up in tissue and stored away in a box of childhood treasures; I don't know what ever happened to Gina's.

We had five years together, but then her parents moved out of town—not impossibly far, but far enough to make our getting together a major effort—and we rarely saw each other more than a few times a year after that. It was mainly Gina's doing that we didn't entirely lose touch with each other. She wrote me two or three times a week, long chatty letters about what she'd been reading, films she'd seen, people she'd met, her hopes of becoming a professional musician after she finished high school. The letters were decorated with fanciful illustrations of their contents and sometimes included miniature envelopes in which I would find letters from her twig people to mine.

Although I tried to keep up my side, I wasn't much of a correspondent. Usually I'd phone her, but my calls grew further and further apart as the months went by. I never stopped considering her as a friend—the occasions when we did get together were among my best memories of being a teenager—but my own life had changed and I didn't have as much time for her anymore. It was hard to maintain a long-distance relationship when there was so much going on around me at home. I was no longer the new kid at school and I'd made other friends. I worked on the school paper and then I got a boyfriend.

Gina never wanted to talk about him. I suppose she thought of it as a kind of betrayal; she never again had a friend that she was as close to as she'd been with me.

I remember her mother calling me once, worried because Gina seemed to be sinking into a reclusive depression. I did my best to be there for her. I called her almost every night for a month and went out to visit her on the weekends, but somehow I just couldn't relate to her pain. Gina had always seemed so self-contained, so perfect, that it was hard to imagine her being as withdrawn and unhappy as her mother seemed to think she was. She put on such a good face to me that eventually the worries I'd had faded and the demands of my own life pulled me away again.

6

Gina never liked Christmas.

The year she introduced me to Newford's gargoyles we saw each other twice over the holidays: once so that she could do her Christmas shopping and then again between Christmas and New Year's when I came over to her place and stayed the night. She introduced me to her dog—Fritzie, a gangly, wire-haired, long-legged mutt that she'd found abandoned on one of the country roads near her parents' place—and played some of her new songs for me, accompanying herself on guitar.

The music had a dronal quality that seemed at odds with her clear high voice and the strange Middle Eastern decorations she used. The lyrics were strange and dark, leaving me with a sensation that was not so much unpleasant as uncomfortable, and I could understand why she'd been having so much trouble getting gigs. It wasn't just that she was so young and since most clubs served alcohol, their owners couldn't hire an underage performer; Gina's music simply wasn't what most people would think of as entertainment. Her songs went beyond introspection. They took the listener to that dark place that sits inside each and every one of us, that place we don't want to visit, that we don't even want to admit is there.

But the songs aside, there didn't seem to be any trace of the depression that had worried her mother so much the previous autumn. She appeared to be her old self, the Gina I remembered: opinionated and witty, full of life and laughter even while explaining to me what bothered her so much about the holiday season.

"I love the *idea* of Christmas," she said. "It's the hypocrisy of the season that I dislike. One time out of the year, people do what they can for the homeless, help stock the food banks, contribute to snowsuit funds and give toys to poor children. But where are they the rest of the year when their help is just as necessary? It makes me a little sick to think of all the money that gets spent on Christmas lights and parties and presents that people don't even really want in the first place. If we took all that money and gave it to the people who need it simply to survive, instead of throwing it away on ourselves, we could probably solve most of the problems of poverty and homelessness over one Christmas season."

"I suppose," I said. "But at least Christmas brings people closer together. I guess what we have to do is build on that."

Gina gave me a sad smile. "Who does it bring closer together?"

"Well . . . families, friends . . ."

"But what about those who don't have either? They look at all this closeness you're talking about and it just makes their own situation seem all the more desperate. It's hardly surprising that the holiday season has the highest suicide rate of any time of the year."

"But what can we do?" I said. "We can't just turn our backs and pretend there's no such thing as Christmas."

Gina shrugged, then gave me a sudden grin. "We could become Christmas commandos. You know," she added at my blank look. "We'd strike from within. First we'd convince our own families to give it up and then . . ."

With that she launched into a plan of action that would be as improbable in its execution as it was entertaining in its explanation. She never did get her family to give up Christmas, and I have to admit I didn't try very hard with mine, but the next year I did go visit the residents of places like St. Vincent's Home for the Aged and I worked in the Grasso Street soup kitchen with Gina on Christmas Day. I came away with a better experience of what Christmas was all about than I'd ever had at home.

But I just couldn't maintain that commitment all year round. I kept going to St. Vincent's when I could, but the sheer despair of the soup kitchens and food banks was more than I could bear.

7

Gina dropped out of college during her second year to concentrate on her music. She sent me a copy of the demo tape she was shopping

around to the record companies in hopes of getting a contract. I didn't
like it at first. Neither her guitar-playing nor her vocal style had
changed much, and the inner landscape the songs revealed was too
bleak, the shadows they painted upon the listener seemed too unrelent-
ingly dark, but out of loyalty I played it a few times more and
subsequent listenings changed that first impression.

Her songs were still bleak, but I realized that they helped create
a healing process in the listener. If I let them take me into the heart of
their darkness, they took me out again as well. It was the kind of
music that while it appeared to wallow in despair, in actuality it left its
audience stronger, more able to face the pain and heartache that
awaited them beyond the music.

She was playing at a club near the campus one weekend and I
went to see her. Sitting in front were a handful of hardcore fans, all
pale-faced and dressed in black, but most of the audience didn't
understand what she was offering them any more than I had the first
time I sat through the demo tape. Obviously her music was an
acquired taste—which didn't bode well for her career in a world
where, more and more, most information was conveyed in thirty-
second soundbites and audiences in the entertainment industry
demanded instant gratification, rather than taking the time to explore
the deeper resonances of a work.

She had Fritzie waiting for her in the claustrophobic dressing room
behind the stage, so the three of us went walking in between her sets.
That was the night she first told me about her bouts with depression.

"I don't know what it is that brings them on," she said. "I know I
find it frustrating that I keep running into a wall with my music, but I
also know that's not the cause of them either. As long as I can
remember I've carried this feeling of alienation around with me; I wake
up in the morning, in the middle of the night, and I'm paralyzed with
all this emotional pain. The only people that have ever really helped
to keep it at bay were first you, and now Fritzie."

It was such a shock to hear that her only lifelines were a friend
who was hardly ever there for her and a dog. The guilt that lodged
inside me then has never really gone away. I wanted to ask what had
happened to that brashly confident girl who had turned my whole life
around as much by the example of her own strength and resourceful-
ness as by her friendship, but then I realized that the answer lay in her
music, in her songs that spoke of masks and what lay behind them, of
puddles on muddy roads that sometimes hid deep, bottomless wells.

"I feel so . . . so stupid," she said.

This time I was the one who took charge. I steered her towards the closest bus stop and we sat down on its bench. I put my arm around her shoulders and Fritzie laid his mournful head upon her knee and looked up into her face.

"Don't feel stupid," I said. "You can't help the bad feelings."

"But why do I have to have them? Nobody else does."

"Everybody has them."

She toyed with the wiry fur between Fritzie's ears and leaned against me.

"Not like mine," she said.

"No," I agreed. "Everybody's got their own."

That got me a small smile. We sat there for a while, watching the traffic go past until it was time for her last set of the night.

"What do you think of the show?" she asked as we returned to the club.

"I like it," I told her, "but I think it's the kind of music that people have to take their time to appreciate."

Gina nodded glumly. "And who's got the time?"

"I do."

"Well, I wish you ran one of the record companies," she said. "I get the same answer from all of them. They like my voice, they like my playing, but they want me to sexy up my image and write songs that are more upbeat."

She paused. We'd reached the back door of the club by then. She put her back against the brick wall of the alley and looked up. Fritzie was pressed up against the side of her leg as though he was glued there.

"I tried, you know," Gina said. "I really tried to give them what they wanted, but it just wasn't there. I just don't have that kind of song inside me."

She disappeared inside then to retune her guitar before she went back on stage. I stayed for a moment longer, my gaze drawn up as hers had been while she'd been talking to me. There was a gargoyle there, spout-mouth open wide, a rather benevolent look about its grotesque features. I looked at it for a long time, wondering for a moment if I would see it blink or move the way Gina probably had, but it was just a stone sculpture, set high up in the wall. Finally I went back inside and found my seat.

8

I was in the middle of studying for exams the following week, but I made a point of it to call Gina at least every day. I tried getting her to let me take her out for dinner on the weekend, but she and Fritzie were pretty much inseparable and she didn't want to leave him tied up outside the restaurant while we sat inside to eat. So I ended up having them over to the little apartment I was renting in Crowsea instead. She told me that night that she was going out west to try to shop her tape around to the big companies in L.A., and I didn't see her again for three months.

I'd been worried about her going off on her own, feeling as she was. I even offered to go with her, if she'd just wait until the semester was finished, but she assured me she'd be fine, and a series of cheerful cards and short letters—signed either by her or by just a big paw print—arrived in my letterbox to prove the point. When she finally did get back, she called me up and we got together for a picnic lunch in Fitzhenry Park.

Going out to the West Coast seemed to have done her good. She came back looking radiant and tanned, full of amusing stories concerning the ups and downs of her and Fritzie's adventures out there. She'd even got some fairly serious interest from an independent record label, but they were still making up their minds when her money ran out. Instead of trying to make do in a place where she felt even more like a stranger than she did in Newford, she decided to come home to wait for their response, driving back across the country in her old station wagon, Fritzie sitting up on the passenger seat beside her, her guitar in its battered case lying across the backseat.

"By the time we rolled into Newford," she said, "the car was just running on fumes. But we made it."

"If you need some money, or a place to stay . . ." I offered.

"I can just see the three of us squeezed into that tiny place of yours."

"We'd make do."

Gina smiled. "It's okay. My dad fronted me some money until the advance from the record company comes through. But thanks all the same. Fritzie and I appreciate the offer."

I was really happy for her. Her spirits were so high now that things had finally turned around and she could see that she was going somewhere with her music. She knew there was a lot of hard work still to come, but it was the sort of work she thrived on.

"I feel like I've lived my whole life on the edge of an abyss," she told me, "just waiting for the moment when it'd finally drag me down for good, but now everything's changed. It's like I finally figured out a way to live some place else—away from the edge. *Far* away."

I was going on to my third year at Butler U. in the fall, but we made plans to drive back to L.A. together in July, once she got the okay from the record company. We'd spend the summer together in La La Land, taking in the sights while Gina worked on her album. It's something I knew we were both looking forward to.

9

Gina was looking after the cottage of a friend of her parents when she fell back into the abyss. She never told me how she was feeling, probably because she knew I'd have gone to any length to stop her from hurting herself. All she'd told me before she went was that she needed the solitude to work on some new songs and I'd believed her. I had no reason to worry about her. In the two weeks she was living out there I must have gotten a half-dozen cheerful cards, telling me what to add to my packing list for our trip out west and what to leave off.

Her mother told me that she'd gotten a letter from the record company, turning down her demo. She said Gina had seemed to take the rejection well when she called to give her daughter the bad news. They'd ended their conversation with Gina already making plans to start the rounds of the records companies again with the new material she'd been working on. Then she'd burned her guitar and all of her music and poetry in a firepit down by the shore, and simply walked out into the lake. Her body was found after a neighbor was drawn to the lot by Fritzie's howling. The poor dog was shivering and wet, matted with mud from having tried to rescue her. They know it wasn't an accident because of the note she left behind in the cottage.

I never read the note. I couldn't.

I miss her terribly, but most of all I'm angry. Not at Gina, but at this society of ours that tries to make everybody fit into the same mold. Gina was unique, but she didn't want to be. All she wanted to do was fit in, but her spirit and her muse wouldn't let her. That dichotomy between who she was and who she thought she should be was what really killed her.

All that survives of her music is that demo tape. When I listen to it, I can't understand how she could create a healing process for others through that dark music, but she couldn't use it to heal herself.

10

Tomorrow is Christmas Day and I'm going down to the soup kitchen to help serve the Christmas dinners. It'll be my first Christmas without Gina. My parents wanted me to come home, but I put them off until tomorrow night. I just want to sit here tonight with Fritzie and remember. He lives with me because Gina asked me to take care of him, but he's not the same dog he was when Gina was alive. He misses her too much.

I'm sitting by the window, watching the snow fall. On the table in front of me I've spread out the contents of a box of memories: The casing for Gina's demo tape. My twig people and the other things we made. All those letters and cards that Gina sent me over the years. I haven't been able to reread them yet, but I've looked at the drawings and I've held them in my hands, turning them over and over, one by one. The demo tape is playing softly on my stereo. It's the first time I've been able to listen to it since Gina died.

Through the snow I can see the gargoyle on the building across the street. I know now what Gina meant about wanting to live in their world and be invisible. When you're invisible, no one can see that you're different.

Thinking about Gina hurts so much, but there's good things to remember, too. I don't know what would have become of me if she hadn't rescued me in that playground all those years ago and welcomed me into her life. It's so sad that the uniqueness about her that made me love her so much was what caused her so much pain.

The bells of St. Paul's Cathedral strike midnight. They remind me of the child I was, trying to stay up late enough to hear my cat talk. I guess that's what Gina meant to me. While everybody else grew up, Gina retained all the best things about childhood: goodness and innocence and an endless wonder. But she carried the downside of being a child inside her as well. She always lived in the present moment, the way we do when we're young, and that must be why her despair was so overwhelming for her.

"I tried to save her," a voice says in the room behind me as the last echo of St. Paul's bells fades away. "But she wouldn't let me. She was too strong for me."

I don't move. I don't dare move at all. On the demo tape, Gina's guitar starts to strum the intro to another song. Against the drone of the guitar's strings, the voice goes on.

"I know she'll always live on so long as we keep her memory

alive," it says, "but sometimes that's just not enough. Sometimes I miss her so much I don't think *I* can go on."

I turn slowly then, but there's only me in the room. Me and Fritzie, and one small Christmas miracle to remind me that everything magic didn't die when Gina walked into the lake.

"Me, too," I tell Fritzie.

I get up from my chair and cross the room to where he's sitting up, looking at me with those sad eyes of his. I put my arms around his neck. I bury my face in his rough fur and we stay there like that for a long time, listening to Gina sing.

A Christmas story with a moral.

HOW THE COHML LEECHED
OUT CHRISTMAS

Alexis A. Gilliland

At the far edge of the Solar System, a fleet of Cohml space ships dropped out of i-space, emitting, as always, an intense burst of radiation at right angles to their line of flight. Circular they were, those ships, and highly elliptical in cross section, rather like pancakes. In i-space, they traveled flat, in a stack, but in n-space they traveled individually and edgewise, extending a little drive spike behind them. Matte white in color, the Cohml ships were marked with vivid green symbols on the bottom or trailing (in i-space) side, and running lights of amber and turquoise on the top. In operation the matte black drive spike glowed dull red.

The local time was the late thirteenth century A.D., a few days before the winter solstice. The time cannot be placed closer than that because our human sources do not agree on the year, and the Cohml logs, like those of any FTL vessel, reconcile with the Cohml calendar only upon their dates of arrival and departure. The mission of that fleet was exploration for colonization. Sensors collected the sunlight reflected from the local planets, studying, tweaking, and manipulating it to determine whether there was life worth investigating.

Suddenly there was a joyous shout. "Life, ho. There is life, there is chlorophyll-based life, there is chlorophyll-based life on the third planet. Let us proceed at once to make a fuller determination."

The fleet of eight ships accelerated at a comfortable 1,109 cm/sec/sec towards the third planet, a beautiful blue world with a large, airless moon. Swiftly they reached it, driven (as they would tell you) by the Cohml hunger for knowledge, and also (as they would never admit) by the Cohml thirst for blood, and the Cohml lust for sex. Four of them swung into a low polar orbit over the target planet, dragging the sensors that would sniff out the secrets of the place, tasting its riches and its perils. The other four posted themselves at one of the Lagrange points, analyzing the rich data stream that came pulsing in like fresh, warm blood.

Listen, these Cohml crewing the ships were not even vertebrate. They consisted of colonies of hive-mind leechoids nurtured and cosseted inside large stainless-steel drums. These drums were traditional, studded with false rivets in memory of old days long forgotten. However, they were also functional, being hung with all sorts of attachments, rather like metallic spiders with jeweled and gleaming eyes, metallic antennae, and pincers-like claws. Sessile by nature, most of the crew was immobile, fixed to their duty stations by life-support plumbing. Nevertheless, those long-legged steel drums were ambulatory, capable of extended activity before returning to the umbilicals that supported the leechoid colony inside.

"This planet looks very promising," said the commander of Low Polar Orbit ship #1.

"Yes," agreed LPO–4. "The smells of the local megafauna are truly delicious. With luck our senescenti shall feast like hell to die engorged with fertile eggs."

"Not so good, not so good, after all," came the distant mutter of the commander of Lagrange Point ship #5. "There are tool users here, megafaunal tool users."

"No feasts on sentients?" queried LPO–1, recalling a similar incident many years before. "Rocks to break bones aren't *really* tools, are they?"

"So sorry," muttered LGP–5 apologetically. "These megafaunoids work iron and copper, wood and stone. They are most of the way to full technological competence, and could already be unexpectedly dangerous."

"How sad, how very sad, how very, very sad," twittered LGP–7 wistfully. "Our megafaunoids appear to be edible to the uttermost limits of digestibility, and their puny weapons will pose no threat to our ships for many years to come."

"We could feast and feed and breed and leave," said LPO–1. "It is against the rules, but no enforcement of the rules should be made in such a case as this, where the megafauna are so edible and so delicious."

"They sail the waters of their world in wooden vessels," came the mutter of LGP–5. "Taking out thousands of vertebrate gill-breathers with nets of string."

"Most gill-breathers appear to be edible," said LGP–8, "but boring, boring and bland to the taste. Some, at least, are poisonous."

"So always with oceans," came the hitherto silent voice of LPO–2. "And with rainforests. We find a few edible, a few non-poisonous species, but most of them are bland and grievously boring after only the barest acquaintance. The delicious smells, the wonderful tastes, the interesting flavors, the arresting flavoroids, all these are invariably associated with the most appalling poisons, poisons that catch us in the most terrible ways. Maybe also with these too-delicious and too-edible megafaunoids?"

"The target megafauna use fire and congregate in dense clusters," pointed out LGP–5, the voice of reason, the voice of duty. "They are sentients, so therefore they are not food."

"Ah, what a pity," murmured LPO–4. "For although their flavors are indescribably delicious, they seem to be, a rare thing in any species, edible to the limit of classification."

"We should leave this place," said LGP–8. "We should honor our commitments, honor the formation of intelligent life, honor sentience wherever it is found and in whatever shape."

Honor: It deserves a word of explanation. In their remote past the Cohml had fed upon more than one sentient race, invariably with unfortunate and often with catastrophic results. Long study convinced the learned among them that feeding upon sentients was to be avoided, but the most lively controversies swirled around the issue of why such feeding produced an evil outcome, and whether that outcome was necessarily evil. For the less learned Cohml, the commanders of their starships among them, it was simply a matter of indoctrination, a command to be honored because it had been issued by the proper authorities.

"It is the honorable choice," LGP–8 concluded. "Finish the survey here, and let us proceed to the next star system."

"Incorrect," asserted LPO–1. "We cannot decline to taste such truly delectable, such marvelously delicious blood as is flowing on the planet below. It is a chance that will come only once in a lifetime of lifetimes. We should feast and feed and breed and leave to let our senescenti die fulfilled."

"Once we breed, it is our offspring that must choose to leave the sentient food that fed their senescenti," LGP–5 declared. "We know they will not, even though feeding upon a sentient race is dishonorable."

The response was as hotly passionate as leechoids can ever manage. "These megafaunoids are food to die for. We cannot leave them uneaten, untasted, so grossly unappreciated within their own food chain."

"Then let the fleet have a vote to decide," said LGP–5, who were only too well aware of how delicious the megafaunoid flavors promised to be. "Let us vote for appetite or honor."

"Not just the captains, though," declared LPO–1, who was himself not totally indifferent to the claims of honor, and rather suspected that his fellow captains might vote against appetite. "On such a momentous issue as this, the crews must vote as well."

"Very well, then. The crews vote to decide their ships. A majority of ships decides the issue."

"Done, done, done, and done." Around the fleet went the acclamation of plan to decide the issue, and a vote was ordered.

When the vote was taken, the fleet split 4–4 by ships. Since no tie-breaking procedure had been agreed upon in advance, LGP–5 wanted the tie broken by the vote of the captains, who were 5–3 in favor of honor. LPO–1, on the other hand, wanted to use the total vote of the crews, which was 52–48 in favor of eating, as the tie breaker. The issue remained deadlocked.

"How is this difficulty to be resolved?" asked LPO–1, who had emerged as the leader of the eat-and-run party.

"What about if we have a contest?" The thought was murky and unamplified—one of the crew on LGP–6—but LPO–1 picked it up.

"What sort of contest?"

"Yes," thought the commander of LGP–5. "What sort of contest could we have?"

"A precision drill competition," explained the crewcohml. "We have four ships that want to feed, and four ships that wish to honor sentience. Select an area, and select a time, and place a token for each team at one of the sites."

"What sites?" asked several voices together.

"The target megafauna use fire," said the crewcohml. "At night, these fireplaces are well characterized. Each ship can use tractor beams to place a single token beside as many fireplaces as possible. We then count the tokens. The winner of the precision competition decides which of the two choices we take."

"What sort of tokens?" asked several voices again.

"The usual for competition," said LGP–5. "They should mark a radius of 2.5 meters to secure each fireplace for the team placing it there, and be available for polling to determine the winner."

"Wait, wait," said LPO–3. "These are very sophisticated markers we are placing. And we are placing them among sentients, who will surely find them, who may save some of them, and who might thus eventually puzzle them out. These markers need to be disguised."

"Agreed, agreed, agreed, and agreed. What sort of disguise should we be using?"

After consultation each ship selected its own disguise. Three of the four ships in favor of eating those delicious albeit sentient megafaunoids hid their markers in lumps of coal on the theory that burning the coal would destroy the marker. The remaining ship put its marker in the handle of a willow switch. Of the four ships in favor of honoring sentience, two hid their marker in the orange rind of a tropical fruit, while the other two put their markers in wooden children's toys, one in a wooden top called a dreidl, the other in a painted wooden soldier.

After days of intense preparation, all ships were ready, and the time was announced: Two hours before the antemeridian at the midpoint of the site. The site selected was the coastal region, 100 kilometers deep, around a landlocked arm of the ocean known locally as the Baltic Sea.

The timers of the Cohml fleet were synchronized and set, and the eight flying saucers started within a single millisecond of each other. For two hours there was a frenzy of activity around the fireplaces along the Baltic coast, and then, as suddenly as it had begun, it stopped and all was quiet. Polling the devices took longer, but it was evident by the time the sun rose that the better discipline and training aboard the saucers choosing to honor sentience had given them a decisive edge, and by early morning the tally was complete. Their survey finished, the eight flying saucers left for the next star system.

That is all that the Cohml did; how, then, were they instrumental in leeching the meaning from Christmas? The Blessed Olaf, the Venerable Stanislaus, Waldemar the Pious, and other authorities affirm it: Until the advent of the mass to celebrate the birthday of Christ our Lord, the time of the winter solstice went unnoticed and unremarked save for a few obscure pagan ceremonies best forgotten by all decent folk. Once the True and Only Church pointed out to the people that the birth of Christ coincided with the rebirth of the sun after its annual death, the people were happy to celebrate, with prayers and fasting as is only proper, the birth of Our Lord at Christ's mass.

Nevertheless, the Cohml left behind a puzzle for those sentient megafaunoids of delicious taste and unparalleled digestibility. In shtetl, hamlet, village, and town, the story was the same. Someone had been there, and whoever it was, they had left something behind. Here a wooden soldier, there a dreidl, across the street a lump of coal (conspicuous in places that burned wood) or a willow switch. The incurious grownups ate the oranges, threw the coals on the fire, beat their children with the willow switches, and forgot about the whole silly business.

The children, however, played with the dreidl or the toy soldier that had mysteriously appeared in the night, and wondered who had brought them. The children remembered, and they remembered, too, that some houses got switches and lumps of coal, and they wondered why. They grew old wondering, and because they wondered, they made up their own explanations.

It was not a big, important event compared to the wars and rumors of wars that teased the kings and princes of the world. But still . . . To while away the long winter evenings in the Scandihuvian states, the German principalities, in Poland, Finnmark, and the cities of the Hanseatic League, those children, who had grown into old folks, would tell tales to the children of their children.

Popular among them was the story of an elf or sprite or saint, who in the name of justice, gave rewards and punishments to children, depending on whether they had been good or bad that past year.

Since the incident had taken place near the winter solstice, it became associated with Christmas, and at first the pagan elf had to yield pride of place to Saint Nicholas, as pagan had always yielded to Christian.

In time the stories rubbed together, variations and thousands of variations polishing themselves like pebbles being tumbled in a drum. Being child-centered—for in memory the elderkins telling the tale drew on the events of their childhood—none of stories were more true. Nevertheless, some were more interesting, some were more morally instructive, and some of them were simply more satisfying.

In the end, the perennially youthful audience decided that being happy was more important than being just, and the switches and lumps of coal simply vanished into the footnotes of the folkloricists. Saint Nicholas fused with the elf, taking on the benign and cheerful aspect of Santa Claus, a secular sprite habitually seen in low polar orbit. To commemorate the now ancient tale, children were first given a secular gift, an orange or a sugar plum, on Christmas Day. Eventually, as times grew increasingly prosperous, and despite the protests of priest and pastor, who objected to a fable made up by the ignorant detracting from the true and necessary devotions of the faithful, the children were given a whole stocking full of presents, as well. Thus was the meaning leeched from Christmas by the Cohml, evil beings from outer space. The alternative explanation, that those best-forgotten pagan customs had reasserted themselves over the True Faith, is simply unthinkable.

Ignoring the legalistic admonitions that speculation is not admissible as evidence, and that eyewitnesses are not always to be trusted, there is a moral to this tale. The moral is that even a colony of hive-mind leechoids is likely to do better in competitive events if it stays away from fatty foods and sex while upholding the high ideals handed down by the proper authorities.

A Christmas mystery in a mansion.

DANCE IN BLUE

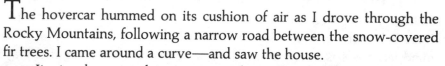

Catherine Asaro

The hovercar hummed on its cushion of air as I drove through the Rocky Mountains, following a narrow road between the snow-covered fir trees. I came around a curve—and saw the house.

It stood on a plateau across the valley I was just entering. Mountains sheered up behind it, on its north side, the peaks scantily dressed in scraps of cloud. On the east and west sides, cliffs dropped down until they disappeared into the lower peaks. The house was three stories high, with arched windows on its upper levels. At first I thought the peaked roof was blue, but as I drew nearer I realized it was covered with panels of glass that reflected the sky and the drifting clouds.

I smiled. Soon I would see Sadji again. *Come to the mountains*, he had said. *Come spend Christmas with me*. It would be my first visit to his private retreat. I wasn't performing in the New York Ballet Theater's production of the *Nutcracker* this year, so they let me have the holiday.

Sadji Parker had been a multimedia magnate when I was in kindergarten. When we first met last year, I had been so intimidated I could hardly talk to him. But I soon relaxed. He was like me. He also had grown up on a farm, also loved walks in the country and quiet nights in front of a fire. He too had found unexpected success in an unexpected talent. For him it was holography; he built his fascination with lasers and computers into a financial empire, earning with it an unwanted fame that he sought refuge from in the privacy of his holidays.

There was only one difficult part. Sadji had invited his son to spend Christmas with us, and I had a feeling if the son didn't approve of me I would lose the father.

As I pulled into a courtyard in front of the house, the wall of a small building on my right rolled up into its roof. I looked inside and saw an unfamiliar hovercar parked there, a black Ferrari that made my rental car look like a junk heap.

I drove into the garage and pulled in next to the Ferrari. When I turned off the ignition, my car settled into the parking pad so gently I hardly felt it touch down. Then I slung my ballet bag over my shoulder, got out, and headed for the house.

It would be good to see Sadji. I had missed him these past weeks. He had been traveling, something to do with his business rival Victor Marck, the man who owned the Marcksman Corporation. Sadji's preoccupation with the war he and Marck were fighting had spilled past the usually inviolate barrier between his private and professional lives. Before he left on his trip he had told me how much he needed the respite of our holiday together.

I stopped in front of the house, faced by two imposing doors made from mahogany. The mirrors of a solar collector were set discreetly into the wall above the door frame, their surfaces tilted to catch the sun. When I rang the doorbell, chimes inside played a Mozart sonata.

No one answered. After a while I knocked. Still no answer. I looked around, but there was no other entrance. Nor was there any way around the house. A rough stone wall bordered both the east and west sides of the courtyard, and on the other side of each wall, cliffs dropped down in sheer faces. Beyond that, the spectacular panorama of the Rocky Mountains spread out for miles.

"Hello?" My breath came out in white puffs. I rang the bell again, then pulled on the door handles.

"Bridget Fjelstad?" the doors asked.

I jumped back. "Yes?"

They swung open. "Please come in."

I blinked at them. Then I walked into a wonderland.

Tiles covered the walls, the floor, even the ceiling of the entrance foyer. Shimmering globes hung in the air in front of each square. The spheres weren't solid; when I stretched out my hand, it passed right through them. If I moved my head from side to side, they shifted relative to each other as if they were solid. When I moved my head up and down, their relative positions stayed fixed but they changed color. Rainbows also filled the foyer, probably made from sunlight caught by the solar collector and refracted through prisms. It was like being in a sea of sparkling light.

I smiled. "Sadji? Are you here? This is beautiful."

No one answered. Across the foyer, a doorway showed like a magical portal. I walked through it, coming out into an empty room shaped like a ten-pointed star. The doorway made one side of a point on the star, with the hinges of the door in the tip of the point. The three points on the east side of the room were windows, six floor-to-ceiling panes of glass. Pine tiles covered the other walls, each a palm-sized square of wood enameled with delicate birds and flowers in colors of the sunrise. Light from the foyer spilled out here, giving the air a sparkling quality. It made faint rainbows on the wood and the white carpet.

But there was no Sadji. I felt strange, alone in his oddly beautiful house. I went to the windows and stood in a point of the star. Outside, the wall of the house fell away from my feet, dropping down into clouds. All that stood between me and the sky was a pane of glass.

Something about the window bothered me. Looking closer, I realized a faint glimmer of rainbows showed around its edges. Was it spillover from the foyer? Or was that breathtaking view only a holo? It wouldn't surprise me if this place had the best holographic equipment the twenty-first century had to offer. If anyone had the resources to create a mountain-sized holo it was my absent host, Sadji Parker. Why he would do it, I had no idea.

Then I had an unwelcome thought: what if the view was real but not the glass? Although there were no sounds to make me think I stood in front of an open window, there wasn't really anything to hear out in that chasm of sky. And I had been in stores with exits protected by moving screens of air that kept heat in and wind out better than a door. The newer ones were so sophisticated you couldn't detect them even if you were right next to them.

But if this was a holo, where was the hologram? My only knowledge of holography came from a class I had taken in school. This much I remembered, though, to make a holo you needed a hologram, a recording of how light bouncing off an object interfered with laser light.

I shook my head and my reflection in the glass did the same, showing me a slender woman with yellow hair spilling over her wool coat down to her hips.

Then I smiled. Of course. This couldn't be a holo. There was no way my reflection could show up in it unless I had been there when the hologram was made.

I reached out and pressed glass on both sides. It wasn't until my shoulders relaxed that I realized how much I had tensed.

There's no reason to get rattled, I thought. Then I went to look for Sadji.

Footsteps. I was sure of it.

I peered through the glittering shadows. Coming in here had been a mistake. I couldn't see anything. It was dark except for sparkles from a chandelier on the ceiling. The chandelier itself wasn't lit, but its crystals spun around and around, throwing out sparks of light. There had to be laser beams hitting them, but the scintillating lights made it impossible to see anything clearly.

More footsteps.

"Who's there?" I asked. "Who is that?"

The footsteps stopped.

"Sadji?" So far I had found no trace of my host in the entire house. But I had made other, much less welcome discoveries. The front doors had locked themselves. There was no way out of the mansion, no food, no usable holophones, not even a working faucet.

A man's accusing voice came through the glittering darkness. "You're Bridget Fjelslad, aren't you? The ballet dancer."

I tensed. "Who are you?"

He walked out of the shadows, a tall man with dark hair and big eyes who was a few years my junior. I recognized him immediately. Sadji kept his picture on the mantel in the New York penthouse.

"Allen?" I exhaled. "Thank goodness. I thought I was trapped in here."

"You are," Sadji's son said. "I've searched the house twice since I got here this morning. There's no way out. Nothing even works except these damn crazy lights."

"You don't have a key?"

"Don't you?" The shifting light made his face hard to read, but there was no mistaking the hostility in his voice. "You are his girlfriend, aren't you?"

The last hour had made me wonder. I couldn't figure out what was going on. "I don't know." I regarded him. "Did you turn on these lights?"

"Don't flatter yourself." Although he spoke curtly, he almost sounded hurt rather than angry. "I have better things to do than make light shows for my father's money-grubbing mistress."

I stared at him. If anything, Sadji's intimidating wealth had almost scared me off. I stepped back, as if distance could soften Allen's words, and bumped into a horizontal bar at waist level. It felt like a ballet bar, what we held on to during exercises.

I ran my hand along the wood. Brackets fastened it to the wall. But how could a wall be here? More sparkles glittered beyond the surface than on this side. The glitters went back a long way. A *long* way.

It was a mirror. Of course. When I looked closer, I could make out my reflection. I knelt and laid my palms on the floor. It felt like wood too.

"What are you doing?" Allen asked.

I stood up. "We're in a dance studio."

He stared at me. "So Dad built his new love a new dance studio in his new house." He swallowed. "Nothing like throwing away the old and replacing it with the new."

I would have had to be a cement block not to hear the pain in his voice. I doubted it was easy being Sadji's son, the child of a woman who had divorced Sadji over ten years ago.

I spoke gently. "Allen, let's try again, okay? I don't want to be your enemy."

He regarded me. "And I don't want to be your son." Then he turned and walked away into the glittering shadows.

I was afraid to call him back, sure that my clumsiness with words would only make it worse.

Blue. Blue tights, blue leotard, blue skirt. Dance in blue, dance to heal.

Chassé, pas de bourrée, chaînés, whirling through the glitters that sparkled even now, after I had found the regular lights. In defiance of being trapped here, I had left my hair free instead of winding it on top of my head. It flew in swirls around my body.

When I first joined the Ballet Theater ten years ago, I dieted obsessively, terrified they would decide they had made a mistake and throw me out. I ended up in a hospital. Anorexia nervosa; by giving my fear a name, the doctors showed me how to fight it. Three months later my hair started to fall out. A dermatologist told me that when I quit eating, my body let the hair die to conserve protein. There was no logic in my reaction, yet when I started to lose my hair I felt like I was losing my womanhood.

But hair grows back. It danced now as I danced, full and thick, whirling, whirling—

"Hey," Allen said. "You found the light."

I stopped in mid-spin, the stiff boxes of my pointe shoes letting me stand on my toes. Allen stood watching from the doorway.

"Doesn't that hurt your feet?" he asked.

I came down and walked over to him. "Not really. The shoes are reinforced to support my toes."

"Where did you get the dance clothes?"

I motioned to my ballet bag in the corner. "I carry that instead of a purse." Sadji had once asked me the same question in the same perplexed voice. I think he understood better when he realized that with performances, rehearsals, and technique classes, I often spent more time dancing even than sleeping.

Allen spoke awkwardly. "You . . . dance well."

The unexpected compliment made me blush. "Thanks." After a moment I added, "It helps me relax when I'm worried."

He grimaced. "Then you better get ready to do it again."

"What do you mean?"

"I'll show you."

We followed wide halls with blue rugs, climbed a marble stairway that curved up from the living room to the second story, and went down another hall. He finally stopped in a circular room. There was a computer console in one corner and hologram screens curving around the walls.

"Dad left a message here." Allen turned to the wall. "Replay six."

The holoscreens glowed, speckled swirls moving on their surfaces as the room lights dimmed.

Then, in the middle of the room, Sadji appeared.

The holo was perfect. From every angle it showed Sadji walking towards us, a handsome man in gray slacks and a white sweater, tall and muscular, his dark curls streaked with gray. If I hadn't known better, I would have sworn he was real.

And that was what had made Sadji Parker rich. He didn't invent the holomovie, he did the inventors one better. Twenty years ago, using genius, hard work and luck, he had figured out who would first find practical ways to make holomovies that could be seen by a lot of people at once. Then he bought huge amounts of stock in certain companies at a time when they were barely surviving. In some he became the major shareholder. People said he was an idiot.

Now, two decades later, when those same companies dominated the trillion-dollar entertainment industry, no one called Sadji Parker an idiot.

Sadji stopped in front of us. "Hello. There is a holophone in the garage. Call me when you get there."

Then the image faded.

I stared at Allen. "That's it?"

"That's it."

"We can't get to the garage. We're locked in here."

He gritted his teeth. "I know that."

There has to be an explanation, I thought. "His business must have held him up."

Allen shook his head. "I talked to him yesterday. He was just getting ready to come up here."

I voiced the fear that had been building in me since I realized Sadji wasn't here. "Maybe he had a car accident."

Allen regarded me uneasily. "We should have seen something— broken trees, marks in the snow. That road is the only way here. If it happened off the mountain, *someone* would have seen. There's always traffic down there. We would know by now."

"The phones don't work."

"A helicopter would come for us."

I exhaled. Of course. If Sadji had been hurt, people would swarm all over this place looking for Allen. He was the heir, prince to the kingdom. Actually, glue and tape was a better description. His father was training him to run Parker Industries, protection against a stockholder panic if anything ever happened to Sadji.

But if Sadji hadn't been in an accident, where was he? I couldn't believe he had locked us up on purpose. Yes, he could be ruthless. But that was in business. I had also seen what he hid under that hardened facade, the gentle inventor who wanted to curl up with his girlfriend and drink mulled wine.

"None of this makes sense," I said.

Allen pushed his hand through his hair. "It's like one of his holoscapes, but gone crazy."

"Holoscapes?"

"They're role-playing games." He smiled, and for the first time I realized how much he looked like his father. "It's fun. He makes up whole worlds, life-sized puzzles. Last week he sent me a mysterious note about how I should be prepared for adventure and intrigue on New Year's Eve." His smile faded. "But it's all haywire. He never messes with people's minds like this."

I motioned towards the door. "Let's try to get to the garage."

We went back to the rainbow foyer, but the front doors still refused to open. I clenched my teeth and threw my body against them, my ballet skirt whirling around my thighs as I thudded into the unyielding portals. Allen rammed them with me, again and again.

I wasn't sure how long we pounded the doors, but finally we gave up and sagged against them, looking at each other. I didn't know whether to be frightened for Sadji or angry. Was he in trouble? Or was this some perverse game he was playing at our expense?

We went back to the star room and stood looking out at the mountains. Our reflections watched us from the glass, breathing as we breathed. I sighed, leaned against the window—

And fell.

No! I felt a jet of air and heard Allen lunge. My skirt jerked as he grabbed it, but then it yanked out of his grip. My thoughts froze, refusing to believe I fell and fell—and hit a padded surface. A weight slammed into me. Struggling to breathe, I looked out at a blue void. Blue. Everywhere. I closed my eyes but the sky stayed like an afterimage on my inner lids.

The weight shifted off of me. "You okay?"

Allen? He must have fallen when he tried to catch me. I opened my eyes again, looking to where I knew, or fervently hoped, I would find the cliff.

It was still there. Emboldened, I looked around. We had landed on a ledge several yards below the window. Allen sat watching me with a face as pale as the clouds. Behind him the sky vibrated like a chasm of blue ready to swallow us if we so much as slipped in the wrong direction.

Then the ledge jerked, the sound of rock grating against rock shattering the dreamlike silence.

I sat bolt upright. "It's breaking."

Allen grabbed my arm. "Don't move."

Breathe, I told myself. Again. The ledge was holding. All we had to do was climb up to the window. Except that the wall was sheer rock. There was no way we could climb it.

Allen looked up at the window. "If you stand on my shoulders, I think you can reach it."

I nodded, knowing we had to try now. It was freezing out here. Soon we would be too stiff to climb anywhere. "If—when I get up there, I'll get a rope. So you can get up."

He pulled a medallion out of his pocket, a gold disk on a chain. "My Dad sent this with his note about New Year's Eve. It must do something. If I don't make it and you do, you might need it."

I stared at him, absorbing the horrible realization that he would die if the ledge broke before I got him help. Then I took the medallion and put the chain around my neck.

Suddenly the ledge lurched again, groaning as if it were in pain. I held my breath while it shifted. Finally, mercifully, it stopped.

Allen took a deep breath, then turned to the wall and braced himself on one knee like a runner ready to sprint. "Okay. Go."

Struggling not to think of what would happen if I fell, I got up and put my hands on his shoulders. But when I knelt on his back, I couldn't keep my balance well enough to stand up. I finally found a tiny fingerhold on the wall. It wasn't much to hang on to, but it let me hold myself steady while I maneuvered my feet on his shoulders. Then I stood slowly, my cheek and palms sliding against the wall.

"Ready," I said.

Allen grunted, and began to stand. The wall slid by, slid by— and then I was at the window. When he reached his full height, my chest was level with the opening. I could see the glass retracted inside the wall like a car window rolled down into its door.

I clutched a handful of carpet and tried to climb in. My feet slipped off his shoulders, leaving me balanced on my abdomen with only the top third of my torso inside the tower. My legs kicked wildly in the air outside as I started to slide out the window.

Clenching my hands in the carpet, I heaved as hard as I could—and scrambled into the room. Then I jumped up and *ran*.

The only place I had seen a rope was in the kitchen. Running there seemed to take forever. What was Allen doing? What if he died because I didn't run fast enough?

Finally I reached the kitchen. I yanked the rope off its hook on the wall and took off again, running through the house. Halls, stairs, rooms. I reached the star room and skidded to a stop at the window.

Allen was still there.

I lowered an end of the rope out to him. As soon as he grabbed it, I sped to the doorway to the foyer. I looped the rope around both knobs on the door that opened into a point of the star—

The screech of breaking stone shrieked through the room, and the rope jerked through my hands so fast it burned off my skin. I clenched it tighter and it yanked me forward, slamming me into the door and slamming the door against the wall. Braced against the door, I struggled to keep my hold while the rope strained to snap out the window.

Then it went limp.

"Allen, *NO*. Don't let go!" I spun around—and saw him sprawled on the floor. I ran over and dropped down next to him. "Are you alive?"

He actually smiled. "I think so."

I laughed, then started to shake. He sat up and laid his hand on my arm. "It's okay, Bridget. I'm fine."

I took a breath. "The ledge broke?"

He nodded. "Come on. Let's get out of this whacked-out room."

We headed for the dance studio, the nearest place with no windows. I wanted to believe that open window had been an accident, some computer glitch. But then why had there been a holo of it? I hadn't even known you could create an instantaneous holomovie of reflections. It couldn't have happened by accident any more than the air jets had "accidentally" kept us from feeling the cold.

When we walked into the dance studio, an army of reflections faced us. Most studios had mirrors on one wall, so dancers could see to correct their steps. But this one had them on all four. The Bridget and Allen watching us in the front mirror also reflected in the one behind us, and that image reflected to the front again, and on and on. The image of our backs also reflected back and forth, so looking in the mirror was like peering down an infinite hall of alternatively forward and backward-facing Bridgets and Allens. It was strange, especially with the chandelier's light show reflecting everywhere too.

Allen stood staring at the images. "He's gone nuts."

I knew he meant Sadji. "Maybe he's angry. Maybe he thinks what you said before, that I just want his money."

Allen glanced at me. "Do you?"

"Of course not."

"Everyone wants his money."

"Including you?"

"No." He hesitated. "There's only one thing I've ever wanted from my father. But it's a lot harder for him to give than money."

I touched his arm. "You mean everything to Sadji."

Allen regarded me warily. "A part of me still wants to believe he feels that way about mother too." After a moment he exhaled. "I don't think she ever believed it, though. He was so absorbed in his work, day and night. It made her feel like she didn't exist for him."

That hit home. More than one man had said the same to me. It wasn't only that dance demanded such a huge part of my life. I also felt awkward and stupid with men, lost without the social education most people absorbed as they grew up. Ballet was all I had ever known. But as much as I loved dancing, I couldn't bear the loneliness. It was the only thing that had ever made me consider quitting. My success felt empty without someone to share it with.

Then I had met Sadji, who understood.

Allen was watching me. "Dad never used to much like Tchaikovsky's ballets. But after he saw you dance Aurora in *Sleeping Beauty* it was all he could talk about."

I had only done the part of Aurora once, as a stand-in for a dancer who was sick. "That was months before I met him."

He smirked. "It took him that long to get up the guts to introduce himself."

Sadji, afraid of me? I still remembered the night he sent me flowers backstage and then showed up at my dressing room, tall and broad-shouldered, his tousled hair curling on his forehead. He was about the sexiest man I had ever seen. "But he's always so sure of himself."

"Are you kidding? You scared the hell out of him. Bridget Fjelstad, the living work of art. What was it *Time* said about you? 'A phenomenon of grace and beauty.'"

I reddened. "They got carried away." I looked around the room, trying to find a less personal subject. "I guess Sadji didn't understand about dance studios. There shouldn't be mirrors on all four walls."

Allen shrugged. "My father never makes mistakes. Those other rooms had a purpose."

Something about his reflections bothered me. I pulled my attention back to him. "Purpose?"

"The display in the foyer distracted us when we came in so we didn't notice the doors locking." He thought for a moment. "The light it spilled into the star room must have hidden the lasers making holomovies of our reflections in the window."

"I didn't think it was possible to make realtime movies like that."

"The hard part would be the holograms." Suddenly he snapped his fingers. "The window, the one next to where we fell. I'll bet it's a thermoplastic."

His reflections kept distracting me. "Thermowhat?"

He grinned. "You can make holograms with it. The stuff deforms when you heat it up. And it erases! All you have to do is heat it up again. Last year Dad showed me a holomovie he made by hooking a sheet of it up to a thermal unit and a computer."

His enthusiasm reminded me of Sadji. "But wouldn't it have to change millions of times a second to make a movie?"

Allen laughed. "Not millions. Just thirty or so. The newer thermoplastics can do it easy."

I nodded, still trying to ignore his reflections. But they were driving me nuts.

"What's wrong?" Allen asked.

"I'm not sure. The mirrors." I gave him back the medallion, then tucked my hair down the back of my leotard. Then I did a series of *pirouettes,* turns where I lifted one foot to my knee and spun on my toe. I spotted my reflection, looking at it as long as possible for each turn, then whipping my head around at the end. It was how I kept my balance. Normally I could easily do double, even triple turns. But today I stumbled on almost every one.

Spin. Again. Something was wrong, something at the end of the turn. Spin. Again. Again—

"It's delayed!" I turned to Allen. "That's what's throwing me off. The reflection of my eyes comes back an instant later than my real eyes."

He whistled. "Another holomovie? Maybe whatever is making it can't keep up with you."

"Then where's the holoscreen?"

"It must be the mirror itself." He pulled me over to the doorway.

But at the edge where it met the mirror, we could see the silvered glass.

"This looks normal," I said.

He motioned at the far wall. "Maybe the screen is behind that. A holo there would reflect here just like a real object."

We went over to the other mirror. I reached out—and my hand went through the "glass," vanishing into its own image. "Hah! You're right."

Then I walked through the holo.

I had one instant to register the screen across the room before I heard the whirring noise. Spinning around, I saw a metal wall shooting up from the floor. It hit the ceiling with a thud.

"Hey!" I pounded on the metal. "Allen? Can you hear me?"

A faint voice answered. "Just barely. Hang on. I'll find a way to get you out."

I looked around, wondering how many other traps Sadji had set for us. The room was small, with pine walls and a parquetry floor. Light came from two fluorescent bulbs covered by glass panels on the ceiling. A table and a chair stood in the center of the room. Actually, "table" was the wrong word. It was really a large metal box.

I scowled. If this was Sadji's idea of a "warm holiday" I hoped I never saw his vision of a cold one. Lights glittering like demented fireflies in an otherwise darkened room, mirrors to make the studio look huge—it was an ingeniously weird way to trick us into this prison. And when I had found the studio's normal lights instead of stumbling in here, the chandelier's display gave perfect cover for the laser beams that had to be crisscrossing the studio.

I went and sat in the chair, too disheartened to stand anymore.

"Hello," the table said. "I am Marley."

I blinked. Marley? "Can you let Allen and me out of the house?"

"Yes."

That sounded too easy. "Okay, do it."

"You must use your key."

"I don't have a key."

"Then I can't let you out."

That wasn't much of a surprise. "So why are you here?"

A panel slid open on top of the table, revealing a hole the shape of Allen's medallion. "I am the lock."

I put my thumb in the lock. "Here's the key."

A red laser beam swept over my hand. "No it's not."

Oh well. I hadn't really expected it to work. "How do you know what the key looks like?"

"I have a digitized hologram of it. By using lasers to create an interference pattern for whatever appears in the lock, I correlate how well it matches my internal record."

Could it really be this easy? A holo made from Marley's own hologram would correlate one hundred percent with its record. I grinned. "Good. Make a holo of the key inside the lock."

"I can't do that."

"Why not?"

"I have nothing to print a hologram on."

I motioned at the ceiling. "What about the light panels?"

"I have no way to print or etch glass."

"Oh." So much for my bright idea. "I don't suppose there's anything else here you could use."

Marley's laser scanned the walls, floor, ceiling, and me, avoiding my eyes. "Appropriate materials are available."

"You're kidding."

"I am incapable of kidding."

"What materials?"

"Your hair."

I tensed. "What do you mean, my hair?"

"It is of an appropriate thickness and flexibility to use in making a diffraction grating that can serve as a hologram."

"You want me to cut my hair?"

"This would be necessary."

"No." I couldn't.

Why not? I could almost hear the voice of the therapist who had treated my anorexia. *You're the same person with or without your hair.* She had also said a lot of things I hadn't wanted to hear: *You've spent your life looking in mirrors to find flaws with yourself, striving for an impossible ideal of perfection. It's no wonder you've come to fear you're nothing without the beauty of form, of motion, of body that your profession demands.*

"Pah," I muttered. Then I got up and hefted the chair onto the table. By clambering up onto it I was able to reach the light panels. Both came off easily. I climbed down, put one panel on Marley, and smashed the other against the table.

Just do it, I thought.

So I did it. I used a glass shard and my hair fell on the floor in huge gold swirls. While I mucked up my hair, Marley's laser played over me. When I finished, a panel slid open on the table to reveal a cavity full of optical gizmos.

"Put the materials inside," Marley said.

As soon as I had stuffed the hair inside with the glass, Marley closed up the cavity again. Then I waited.

After what felt like forever Marley spoke. "The hologram is complete."

"Use it to make a holo inside the lock."

The glass slid up out of the table, looking like it had been melted and re-formed with my hair inside. The glossy gold swirls were so intricate it was hard to believe they came from hair. Marley shone its laser on it, using a wide beam, and a red medallion appeared in the lock. I moved my head and saw a reversed image of the medallion floating on the other side of the glass.

"Will you let us go now?" I asked.

"Yes. Mr. Parker is in the hallway north of this room. He appears to be looking for an entrance into here."

So Marley could see the rest of the mansion. It had probably monitored our actions all day. "Can you talk to him?"

"Yes."

"Good. Tell him I'm free, that I'll meet him in the garage. Then let me out of here and unlock the front door to the house."

Marley paused. "Done."

I heard the wall behind me move, and I turned in time to see it vanish into the floor. When I walked into the studio an infinity of shorn Bridgets stared back at me from the mirrors. I looked like I had stuck my finger in a light socket.

I surprised myself and laughed. Then I set off running.

The front door was wide open. I sped out into a freezing night, heading for the garage. It was also open, spilling light out into the darkness. I could see Allen inside seated in front of a computer console on the garage's north wall. There was a holophone next to the console, a dais about six inches high and three yards in diameter. Fiber optic cables connected it to the console and a holoscreen about ten feet high curved around the back of it.

Allen looked up as I ran over to him. "How did you—God, what happened to your hair?"

"I'll tell you about it later." I motioned at the holophone. "Did you reach your father?"

He shook his head. "There's no answer at his house. I'm trying his office."

A dour-sounding computer interrupted. "I have a connection." Then the booth lit up and Sadji appeared on the dais, sitting at the desk in his office. The curtains were open on the window behind him, showing a starlit sky.

"Allen." He smiled. "Hello."

Allen stared at him. "What are you doing there?"

"Some business came up." Sadji looked apologetic. "I'm afraid I can't make it until tomorrow afternoon."

Allen scowled. "Dad, what's going on?"

"Nothing. I just got held up."

"Nothing? What the hell do you mean, 'nothing'?"

Sadji frowned. "Allen, I've talked to you before about your language." He drummed his fingers on the desk. "I'm sorry I'm late. But matters needed attending to. I'll see you tomorrow." Then he cut the connection, the holo blinking out of existence as if he had dematerialized.

I stared at Allen. "That's *it*? After everything he put us through?"

"If you think that's bad, look at what else I found." He touched a button and light flooded into the garage from behind me. I turned around and saw lamps bathing the mansion with light. They showed the cliffs plunging down on the west side of the house in sharp relief. But instead of a sheer drop on the east, there was a snowy hill only a few feet below the level of the ledge where we had fallen: no holocliff, no holoclouds, just a nice, innocuous hill with pieces of the broken ledge lying half buried in the snow there.

I turned back to Allen. "I can't believe this."

"Well, I know one thing. I'm not going to stay here." He stood up. "He can spend Christmas with himself."

"This just doesn't seem like Sadji."

After a moment Allen's frown faded. "He's been late before. A lot, in fact. But he's always made sure we knew right away. And I've never known him to run a holoscape when he wasn't around to monitor it."

None of it made sense to me. "Do you know why this business trip had him so worried?"

He scowled. "Victor Marck went after Parker Industries again."

"Again?"

Allen nodded. "A few years ago he tried to take us over. Almost did it too. But Dad stopped him. He stopped him this time too." He grimaced. "Marck can't stand to lose. That's why he hates my father so much. Not only has Dad plastered him twice now, but both times he really whacked Marcksman Corporation in the process. Already this morning the Marcksman stock had dropped by a point. It's going to get a lot worse before it recovers."

I tried to catch my elusive sense of unease. "If we hadn't been caught in that holoscape, would you have thought anything was odd about our holocall to your father?"

"I doubt it. Why?"

"Maybe someone tampered with the computer."

For a moment Allen just looked at me. Then he said, "There's a way to find out." He turned back to the console and opened a panel, revealing a small prong. He pushed up his shirt sleeve and snapped the prong into a socket on the inside of his wrist.

I drew in a sharp breath. It was the first time I had seen someone make a cyber link with a computer. It meant Allen had a cybnet in his body, a network of fibers grown in the lab using tissue from his own neurons and then implanted in his body. Sadji had wanted to have it done, but he couldn't find any surgeon willing to perform so many high-risk operations on a man who had more power than some of the world's heads of state.

Allen had an odd look, as if he were listening to a distant conversation. Then I realized his "conversation" was with the computer.

"There's a virus," he suddenly said. "No, not a virus. A sleeper, a hidden program. It has an interactive AI code that emulates my father's personality." His forehead furrowed. "It also predicts how he'll move down to the smallest gesture, then works out the hologram each rendered figure of him would make if it were real. And it's *fast*. It can calculate over sixty interference patterns per second." He whistled. "It's making holomovies of him."

I stared at him. "You mean that holocall was fake?"

"You got it." Allen swore. "The sleeper is also set up to record arrivals and departures. After you and I go it will destroy itself, leaving a record of our presence disguised to look like the operating system made it." He paused. "But whoever set it up didn't know about Dad's holoscape. When the sleeper identified me, it set off a part of the holoscape that was supposed to identify us on New Year's Eve."

This sounded stranger and stranger. "So those holos in the house weren't supposed to be going when we came?"

Allen nodded. "We weren't meant to fall out that window either, at least not how it happened. There are safety nets, but the routines that control their release aren't running." He regarded me. "According to Dad's calendar, he meant to be here when we arrived. And it's obvious he never meant for us to be imprisoned in the holoscape. It's just a game he had set up for New Years Eve."

I frowned. "Then he couldn't have written the sleeper."

Allen pulled the prong out of his wrist. "I know only two other people who have both the ability and the resources to do it: Victor Marck and me. And I sure didn't."

"Why would Marck want evidence to prove we were here?"

Allen paled. "Can you imagine what it would do to Parker Industries if both my father and I were suddenly, drastically, out of the picture? It would be a disaster." He gritted his teeth. "And I can guess whose vultures would be ready to come in and strip the remains clean."

I spoke slowly, dreading his answers. "How could he get both you and Sadji so thoroughly out of the picture?"

His voice shook. "Implicating me in my father's murder would do just fine."

"No. Allen, no." Sadji *dead?* I couldn't believe it.

"We've been fighting Marck for years. I've seen how his mind works." Allen took hold of my shoulder. "How do you think it would look: you and I come here, spend the night, then leave. A few days later my father's body is found on the grounds, time of death placed when we were here or not long after we left."

I swallowed. "No one would believe we did it."

"Why not? Who has a better motive than me? I stand to inherit everything he owns. The greedy son and beautiful seductress murder the holomovie king for Christmas. It would splash across every news report in the country."

"Sadji's alive. *Alive.*" I put up my hands, wanting to push away his words. "No one would dare hurt him while we were here. The computer would record their presence just like ours."

Allen had a terrible look, as if he had just learned he lost someone so important to him that he couldn't yet absorb it. "Not if they left him to die before we came. They could have used a remote to turn on the system after they were gone."

"But Sadji's not *here.* We've been through the entire house."

Sweat ran down Allen's temples. "The damn computer keeps telling me he's in his office."

"Marley!"

"What?"

"It's a sensor Sadji set up for the holoscape. It knew exactly where you and I were."

Allen grabbed my arm. "Show me."

We ran back to the holoscreen room in the dance studio. My holo of the medallion was still in the lock, keeping the room open.

"Marley." I struggled to keep my voice calm. "Can you locate Sadji Parker?"

"Yes," Marley said.

I almost gasped in relief. "Where is he?"

"I can't tell you."

"This isn't a game. You have to tell us!"

"I can't do that."

Allen slammed his fist against the wall. "Damn it, tell us!"

"You must supply me with the proper sequence of words," Marley said.

"Words?" I looked around frantically. "What words?"

"The ones printed on the key." Marley sounded smug, like a game player who had just pulled a particularly clever move. Then it closed a panel over the holo medallion, hiding it from our sight.

I whirled to Allen. "The medallion! What's written on it?"

He had already pulled it out of his pocket. "'Proverbs 10: 1,'" he read. "'A wise son makes a father glad.'"

"That is the correct sequence," Marley said. "Sadji Parker is located in storage bin four under the floor in the northeast corner of the garage."

Allen grabbed my arm, yanking me along as we ran back to the garage. He hurled away the rug in the corner and heaved on the handle of a trapdoor in the ground there. When it didn't open, he ran across the room and grabbed an axe off a hook on the wall. Then he sped back and smashed the axe into the trapdoor, raising it high and slamming it down again and again, its blade glittering in the light.

The door splintered, disintegrating under Allen's attack. He dropped the axe and scrambled down a ladder into the dark below. As I hurried after him, I heard him jump to the floor. An instant later, light flared around us. I jumped down and whirled to see Allen standing under a bare light bulb, his arm still outstretched towards its chain as he looked around the bin, a small, dusty room with a few crates—

"There!" I broke into a run, heading for the crumpled form behind a crate.

He lay naked and motionless, his eyes closed, his mouth gagged, his wrists and ankles bound to a pipe that ran along the seam where the floor met the wall. Ugly bruises showed all over his body. Dried blood covered his wrists and ankles, as if he had struggled violently against the leather thongs that bound him.

I dropped on my knees next to his head. "Sadji?" In the same instant, Allen said, "Dad?"

No response.

I undid his gag and pulled wads of cloth out of his mouth, trying desperately to remember the CPR class I had taken. "Please be alive," I whispered, tears running down my face.

Slowly, so slowly, his lashes lifted.

I heard a choked sob from Allen. Sadji looked up at us, bleary eyed. As Allen untied him, I drew Sadji's head into my lap and stroked the matted hair off his forehead. He tried to speak, but nothing came out.

"It's all right," I murmured. "We'll take care of you now."

It seemed like forever before they all left, the police and the doctors and the nurses and the multitude of Parker minions buzzing around the mansion. But finally Allen and I were alone with Sadji. No, not alone; the bodyguards hulking discreetly in the background would never again be gone, neither for Sadji nor for Allen.

Sadji sat back in the cushions next to me on the couch, dressed in jeans and a pullover. He had refused to go to the hospital, but at least he was resting now, his furiously delirious attempts to go after Victor Marck calmed by food, water, and medicine. His face was pale, his wrists and ankles bandaged, his voice hoarse. But he was alive, wonderfully alive.

He watched Allen and me. "You two are a welcome sight."

I took his hand. "Do you think they'll be able to convict Marck?"

Sadji's face hardened. "I don't know. That hired thug he had waiting up here for me will be out of the country by now." He spoke quietly. "But no matter what happens, Marck will pay a price far worse, to him, than any conviction."

Allen regarded him. "The only thing that could be worse to Marck than the electric chair would be losing Marcksman Corporation."

Although Sadji smiled, it was a harsh expression far different than the gentleness he usually showed me. "He'll lose a lot more than Marcksman. The publicity from his arrest will finish him even if he's not convicted."

I didn't ask who would be the driving force behind the public hell Victor Marck was about to experience, or who would be there to scavenge the remains of his empire. All I could see was Sadji lying beaten and bound, dying of exposure and thirst.

Sadji looked at me, his expression softening. "When I opened my eyes and saw you, it was . . . appreciated."

Allen snorted. "An angel rescues the man from a horrible death and the best he can come up with is that he 'appreciated' it." He leaned towards his father. "I'm going to the kitchen to get some of that pizza your Parker people brought us. I'll be gone for a while."

Sadji scowled at him. But after Allen left, he laughed. "My son has the subtlety of a sledgehammer." He paused, clearing his throat with an awkwardness incongruous to the self-assured man I knew. "I was going to wait until Christmas. But perhaps now is appropriate."

I regarded him curiously. "For what?"

"I know the prospect of having Allen for a stepson may look daunting. But he really can be pleasant when he wants."

I smiled. "That sounds like a marriage proposal."

He spoke quietly. "It is."

I tried to imagine marrying Sadji. I loved him, and he understood about my dancing. But was I ready for the life he led? "I have to think about it."

For a moment he looked excruciatingly self-conscious. Then he covered it with a glower. "Why," he growled, "do women always feel compelled to say that?"

I slid closer and put my arms around his neck, more grateful than I knew how to say that he was alive, growls and all. "Merry Christmas, Sadji."

"It's not Christmas."

"It's close. Two more days."

"Are you going to marry me?"

I kissed him. "Yes."

His face relaxed into a smile. We were still kissing each other when Allen came back with the pizza.

Who killed cock robin? Just wait 'til next Christmas.

CHRISTMAS GAMES

David Langford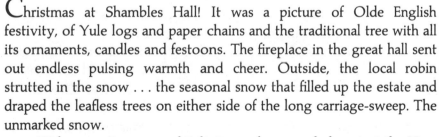

Christmas at Shambles Hall! It was a picture of Olde English festivity, of Yule logs and paper chains and the traditional tree with all its ornaments, candles and festoons. The fireplace in the great hall sent out endless pulsing warmth and cheer. Outside, the local robin strutted in the snow . . . the seasonal snow that filled up the estate and draped the leafless trees on either side of the long carriage-sweep. The unmarked snow.

"Of course," murmured Felicity as she snuggled against the Hon. Nigel in the window-seat, "we are quite, quite cut off from the outside world. If anything were to *happen* . . ."

Over the mantelpiece in the lofty dining-room hung the one statutory reminder built into every sequence: here, a probe's impression, done into oils, of the dim landscape to be expected on a certain world circling Barnard's Star. It was topped with a sprig of mistletoe.

Lord Blackhat the City financier had ruined countless men and tried hard to ruin as many women, yet he had a lingering sentimental streak and always invited his victims to Christmas at Shambles Hall. It was his whimsical way of dicing with Fate. He never troubled to remove or secure any part of the weapon collection from his youthful, sporting days which so extensively adorned the oak-panelled walls. Broadswords, crossbows, rapiers, shotguns, bludgeons, morningstars, strangling wires and vials of prussic acid were always to hand at the Hall. Today he had added spice to the festive season by blackmailing the crusty old Colonel and forbidding his own son's intended marriage to Felicity.

This year, the Duchess of Spong's fad was fortune-telling with a wicked pack of cards. As an old family friend who had swindled her out of her inheritance, Lord Blackhat liked to humour her. "This covers you, this crosses you," she intoned as she dealt out the pattern. "This is your heart and this is your head and this your destiny as of approximately supper-time."

"Funny," said his lordship without real surprise, "how all of them seem to be the ace of spades."

The Colonel and the Professor were taking a turn along the Yew Walk, swapping anecdotes of relativistic physics and the tiger hunt at Poona. "My God," said the Professor suddenly. "These seem to be . . . the footprints of a gigantic hound!"

"Lodge-keeper's dog, I believe. Bloody great animal."

"For a moment I thought that, even though it is Christmas Day, some sinister element might yet enter our revels, ha ha."

The Colonel laughed shortly. "Someone here'd make short work of any mystery, Prof. Funny thing, really, that we should have with us as a fellow house-guest the eminent amateur detective Chester Dix, who's sent so many foul murderers to the dock!"

"Oh yes, in my absent-minded way I had almost forgotten. But, Colonel, surely Dix couldn't be here on . . . business?"

"Nonsense! Balderdash! Pull yourself together, man!"

The Professor started. "Er . . . what was that?"

"Just an ominous magpie, Prof. Flying across our path. Symbol of sorrow and bad luck, they say, like those thirteen black cats over there."

"The scientific mind is above such nonsense," the Professor said conscientiously, walking under a ladder. From within the Hall came a crash as the tween-maid broke another mirror.

"Such a thing as overdoing the atmosphere," muttered the Colonel. "Oh well, it's only Christmas once a subjective year."

Chester Dix examined himself in the dressing-table mirror. Waxed moustache, deerstalker, monocle, magnifying glass—all seemed adequate. "One employs the little grey cells," he said experimentally. "By Jove, what? When you have eliminated the impossible, then what remains, *no matter how improbable* . . ." Losing the thread, he began again.

"Mortimer," said the dashingly handsome but amnesiac stranger who had so mysteriously turned up at Shambles Hall before thick snow isolated it for all practical purposes from the nearby village of Mayhem Parva. "Sebastian. Cholmondeley, pronounced Chili. It was something like one of those."

"Aldiborontiphoscophornio," Felicity suggested at random. "Chrononhotonthologos, pronounced Chris. You ought to recognize your own *name* when you hear it."

"I'm sure I shall. Fred. *Fred!* No . . . no, not Fred."

The Hon. Nigel Scattergood, son and heir to the tainted Blackhat fortune, stared moodily into the great fireplace. "Four bloody Christmases since launch day. I wish someone else got a chance to play detective just for once."

Felicity said, "Well, he *is* chief programmer, darling."

"Victor. Vitamin. Vitellus. Virtual Reality," muttered the stranger. "No, I'm fairly sure that isn't it either."

"Can we all try to stay a trifle more in character?" said Felicity. She tweaked at the hem of her short skirt. "Nigel, I shall be seriously annoyed with you if you don't *do something* about Lord Blackhat's pig-headedness. I want to marry a *man of action.* I. . . . Was that someone listening at the door?"

"That amnesiac chap," mused the Professor to the Duchess, "reminds me oddly of our host's younger brother; you know, the one long thought dead under suspicious circumstances in that Antarctic expedition from which only one survivor, Blackhat himself, returned. Odd how one gets these fancies."

"Another odd thing that few people know," said the Duchess, "is that identical twins run in that family."

The Christmas dinner was excellent as ever: the turkey vast and succulent enough to feed a family for a fortnight, the plum pudding flaming in brandy, the crackers exploding with satisfying bangs which, this year, did not once serve to cover a pistol-shot. But there seemed to be a strange atmosphere at the merry table. After pulling crackers with all twelve guests, Lord Blackhat idly unfolded the screw of paper bearing the last amusing cracker-motto. It proved to have been constructed from letters cut from a newspaper and pasted down, reading: "yOU *will* DiE toNIGHT."

The other eleven were substantially the same.

"One recognizes, does one not, the characteristic Baskerville typeface of the *Wessex Methodist Gazette*?" murmured Dix at his elbow. "*Alors*, my friend, we progress."

"Bah, humbug," said his lordship, and beckoned to the butler. "Starveling, I shall retire to the library and pass the evening altering my will. You might look in towards midnight with a whisky-and-soda, and see that I am . . . in good health."

"As your lordship pleases," said Starveling.

Firelight flickered in the dining-room where Chester Dix, brilliant amateur detective, brooded with steepled fingers and half-closed eyes over the remnants of the feast. No doubt each member of the party in turn would be paying a deviously motivated visit to the library. In due course there would follow a resounding crash of silver tray and shattered glass as the impeccable Starveling strove to be surprised at what he found slumped over the antique mahogany desk in Lord Blackhat's library. And then the investigation would. . . .

There was a frightful discontinuity.

"Lightning?" said the Professor.

"In a dead clear sky?" said the Colonel.

Upstairs, Felicity and the Hon. Nigel had been busy failing to establish a convincing alibi. "Did the earth just move for you?" she asked.

"Dash it all, I'd hardly touched you."

In the smoking room, the amnesiac stranger explained to Starveling, "I had it, I had it right on the tip of my tongue, and then that earthquake distracted me."

"Most regrettable, sir."

Alone in the Heliotrope Room, the Duchess turned over the thirteen fateful cards and found that all of them were Mr. Bun the Baker. She frowned.

Lord Blackhat, caught unawares in mid-disinherit, felt himself all over. He seemed intact. "Thought they'd got me with an electrified codicil that time. Be a damned clever notion. . . ."

"I have gathered you here," spluttered what seemed to be the brilliant amateur sleuth Chester Dix, "because one of you is guilty. Before twenty-four hours have passed I shall name the guilty person." He had a shaky, semi-transparent look.

Starveling bowed imperceptibly. "Sir," he said, "the fiendish criminal who so cunningly struck down Lord Blackhat in his prime has . . . er . . . has not done it yet. There would appear to be no crime."

"*Nom d'un cochon! Merde!* It is *I* who have been murdered, and I will know the reason why!"

"I say, the game's afoot, what?" marvelled the Colonel. "This is a new one."

The VR system, making the best of it, was seen to be maintaining two versions of Dix: the angrily gesticulating one, and an evident corpse slumped among the dessert plates and port glasses on the great oaken dinner-table.

Climbing with some difficulty out of her character as a bright young debutante, Felicity said: "This is the spare you talking, right? The machine analogue you programmed in. So the real you's gone to sleep in the VR tank or something. So what?"

The sleuth twirled his moustache with a flourish. "Mademoiselle will kindly employ her little grey cells. Chester Dix does not 'go to sleep' during an investigation. Archons of Athens! There has been foul play."

"All right, all right, game's over," snapped the Hon. Nigel. "Terminate. Terminate. If something's happened to Chester we need to go realside and take a look. Sorry to spoil the fun, everyone. Terminate, terminate.—Why the hell isn't it terminating?"

"A thousand pardons. I have taken the small liberty of activating a, how you say, a gamma-gamma override. *No one* shall be permitted to leave Shambles Hall until this mystery she is solved."

He stalked haughtily from the room.

"Jesus Christ," said Felicity.

"Anyone for tennis?"

"That's not funny, darling," said the Hon. Nigel, shivering in a chill like interstellar space. They were using the racquets as improvised snowshoes and had made it almost half a mile down the empty white lane. Although (as the Professor had pointed out) the benefits of reaching the police station in the village were extremely unclear, it seemed something that had to be tried.

"*While the snow lay round about, Deep and crisp and eeeven,*" Felicity chanted. "Cut off, indeed. It's not six inches deep anywhere."

Then they rounded a corner of the sunken lane and met an infinite wall that somehow hadn't been visible before, rising forever, the colour of the dark behind one's eyelids.

"That's what I call cut off," said Nigel gloomily.

"That's what I call shoddy programming," said his companion.

The suspects gathered in the library while the detective was occupied taking plaster casts of the strange new footprints he had found leading down and back up the snow of the carriageway.

"I don't understand," said the Duchess.

"Then I shall explain the situation to you as though you knew nothing of it," the Professor began.

The Hon. Nigel broke in hastily. "It's obvious. Chester dropped out of the gamesmaster link—that was when everything sort of quivered—and this bloody stand-in program of his took over. We'll need to give it some kind of solution to get out of this. Someone will just have to confess."

They cut cards for it, and the mysterious stranger lost.

"But I still don't even know my name," he whimpered.

"Constraint of the scenario," said the Professor helpfully.

The Hon. Nigel fiddled irritably with the carvings on the library's old oak panelling, and one of the wooden roses sank into the wall at his touch. At once a tall case of Agatha Christie titles swung aside to disclose a secret passage.

"Oh *f*—" Nigel began before the scenario constraints stopped him. "I mean, oh dash it all."

"I am in fact Lord Blackhat's identical twin brother, with our close resemblance disguised by plastic surgery," the supposed stranger said with growing confidence. "In my extensive travels in South America I acquired a quantity of an arrow poison compounded from tree frogs and almost unknown to science. This I planned to administer in the special Stilton cheese reserved for Lord Blackhat, who unfortunately took the precaution of exchanging his plate by sleight of hand with that of the person next to him, the unfortunate sleuth Chester Dix. Meanwhile I had established an alibi with a fake telephone message from Warsaw, actually my confederate speaking on the extension phone in the butler's pantry. Now I see you are hot on my trail and my only option is to confess. It's a fair cop."

"An amusing fantasy," smiled the detective. "But you have failed to explain the singular incident of the dog in the night-time."

"What was the curious incident of the dog in the night-time?"

"It was spelt backwards." The great sleuth looked momentarily confused. "Ah. Never mind that. There is one fatal error in your story, my friend. I have examined the body minutely. You know my methods. It is clear that the unfortunate victim has suffered a cerebrovascular accident, a stroke. Not, I fancy, a little-known arrow poison . . ."

"He's got access to the ship systems," Felicity whispered. "*That's* what happened to poor old Chester. I always thought he must have fiddled the physicals to get selected for this trip."

"Natural causes!" said the Hon. Nigel, pouncing. "There has been no murder. The case is closed."

"That, of course, is what the killer would *like* us to think. We are dealing with a very clever criminal, my friends. I see half of it now— but only half."

"Oh . . . botheration," Felicity said.

A loose group had formed around the glittering Christmas tree in the great entrance hall. "If we all committed suicide . . ." the Duchess suggested vaguely.

"Would just go non-interactive," Lord Blackhat grunted. "Used to like that bit the best, drifting round like a ghost and watching you all hash up the investigation."

"Then the case might never be solved," said the Hon. Nigel. "Would the scenario terminate if it recognized an insoluble problem?"

Felicity pouted. "God knows. Well, only God and Chester."

"Dammit," said the Colonel, "one of us will just have to be caught red-handed. No time for more fooling around. Got a starship to run."

"Ah, a second murder!" Nigel snapped his fingers. "Time to draw lots again."

"Ought to be me who's bumped off," said the mysterious stranger. "The person suspected of the first murder should always be the second victim. It's part of the classic unities."

"No. Build-up was for Blackhat," rumbled the Colonel crustily.

The Duchess sighed and broke the seal on a fresh pack of cards.

"Oh!" cried Felicity in synthetic alarm as the library door creaked open. "Oh! I was just passing by and happened to pick up the knife, forgetting everything I know about not touching anything at the scene of the crime. . . . Who would have thought the old man had so much blood in him?"

(The silver fish-slice had been an awkward choice of weapon, but Nigel thought it rather picturesque. "It's more of a blasted blunt instrument," Lord Blackhat had groaned irritably as he expired.)

The great detective took in the scene at a hawk-eyed glance.

"No," said Felicity. "It's no use. This huge bloodstain on my dress . . . the six witnesses in the corridor outside who will swear that no one but myself has entered this room since his lordship was last seen alive . . . I can't conceal my blatant guilt from you."

Alternately puffing at a huge pipe whose stem curved like a saxophone and sipping at a rummer of priceless old liqueur brandy, the sleuth made his way along the floor on hands and knees. Then he rose and touched a place in the panelling. The secret door opened on well-oiled hinges.

"Burn and blister me! Not quite a locked room after all, I fancy. Now I have just one question for you, my dear girl. *Whom are you shielding?*"

Felicity pronounced a word under her breath.

"Is there not," said the Professor with a certain academic distaste, "a criminal device known in the literature as a 'frame'? Now what I propose . . ."

Starveling the butler made a pathetic corpse in his pantry. He was only a program construct and not a live player, but the Hon. Nigel had felt a pang of real remorse as he did the deed and arranged the evidence.

"*I done it. I can live with myself no longer. Farewell cruel world. Tell the maid to decant the '49 port for Boxing Day,*" the investigator read aloud to the suspects. "Very determined of the fellow to write all that in his own blood on the table, after shooting himself through the heart. Using a disguised hand, too."

"Ah," said Nigel guiltily.

"Yes, what the murderer forgot was, firstly, that yellow stitchbane is not yellow at all but a pale mauve . . . and secondly, that Starveling *was left-handed.*"

Nigel gave a muffled exclamation, laden with even more guilt.

"Fortunately my snuff-box is invariably charged with fingerprint powder . . ." To an accompaniment of impatient shufflings, forensic science proceeded on its remorseless way.

"No! There must be some mistake!" cried Nigel unconvincingly.

"God, Captain, you're a lousy actor," Felicity whispered.

"Satisfactory. Most satisfactory. And what do we deduce from this exact match between the prints on the automatic and those of the Hon. Nigel Scattergood? Why, of course, that he must have handled the gun innocently at some earlier time, else he would have taken care to wipe it clean!"

The Colonel made some feeble suggestion about double-bluff, but the sleuth was happily launched on a flight of deductions about the unknown murderer's careful manipulation of the gun in a wire frame that left the prints undisturbed . . .

"We're being too rational," said Felicity. "This imitation Chester is soaked and saturated in detective stories just like the real one. We can't out-subtle him."

"Thanks so much, darling," said the Hon. Nigel with venom. "thanks for explaining that things are utterly hopeless."

"Ah, but if we could use the ship-system AI it could fudge up a super-clever pattern that any Great Detective would fall for."

"If, if," grunted the Colonel. "If pigs could fly we could all make a getaway on porkerback, if we had some pigs."

"Wait," said Felicity. "As *he* would say—when you've eliminated all logical solutions you have to try something that's stark raving bonkers. Duchess dear, where's the ouija board from our séance on Christmas Eve that gave us all those sinister and atmospheric warnings?"

"This is ridiculous," complained the Hon. Nigel as the planchette began to slide across the lettered board. Under all their fingertips it moved uncertainly at first, then with more seeming decision. "Is it spelling anything out?"

"L-O-G-I-N," said Felicity. "That looks promising. Now we're going to need a *lot* of pencil and paper."

They were busy through the small hours placing a wild variety of clues everywhere the Astral Intelligence had advised.

Bleary-eyed and feeling hungover, the Hon. Nigel lifted the silver cover of the largest dish on the sideboard. It contained, perhaps inevitably, red herrings. He settled for bacon and egg. The others were already gathered about the breakfast table, and after an early-morning hunt for evidence the world-famous sleuth was clearly ready to hold forth.

"This has been one of the most baffling and complex cases that I have ever encountered. Even I, Chester Dix, with my sixteen heraldic quarterings and unparalleled little grey cells . . . even I was stretched to my deductive limits by the satanic cunning of this crime. But now I have the answer!"

Felicity led a discreet patter of applause.

"What first drew my attention was that the seemingly false alibi with the phonograph record of the typewriter was a clever decoy. Second came the realization that when the tween-maid glimpsed the clock through the window of the supposedly locked room, *she saw the clock-face in a mirror* . . . producing an error of timing that has literally turned this case upside down. Next, the drugged cigar-cutter . . ."

The breakfast party found the thread a little hard to follow: there was mention of the legendary Polar Poignard or ice dagger that melted tracelessly away, of a bullet misleadingly fired from a blowpipe and a hypodermic filled with air, while disguises and impersonations were rampant. Keys were ingeniously turned from the wrong sides of doors, and bolts magnetically massaged. In the end it seemed on the whole that Lord Blackhat himself was the villain, having faked his own murder and posthumously blackmailed Starveling into doing much the same.

"Didn't quite follow the bit about the murderous dwarf hidden under the cover of the turkey dish," said the Colonel.

Felicity explained that that notion had been seen through by the detective as a diabolical false trail. She thought.

"And so, ladies and gentlemen, you are all free to depart. Merry Christmas!"

"Merry Christmas! I've never looked forward so much to boring old shipboard chores. Until next year—" said Felicity, and winked out. The others followed suit.

Alone again in the great dining-room, deep in the ship-system's bubble memory, the sleuth smiled a small, secret smile. He moved to the telephone and lifted the receiver. "Get me Whitehall 1212. Inspector Lestrade? . . . I have solved the mystery at Shambles Hall. Yes. . . . In the end I deduced that, unprecedentedly, *every member of the house party* conspired to commit the original crime. The method, I fancy, was suffocation—it was their good fortune that the victim suffered a stroke when part-asphyxiated. All of them were in it together. The ingenuity of their false clues proves it. *Sacre bleu*, they think me a fool! Being outnumbered, I lulled their fears most beautifully by announcing the solution they wished. They will return here—do we not know that the criminal always returns to the scene of the crime?—and we shall set a trap. . . . Yes. Yes, that murderous gang will not find it so easy to escape Shambles Hall *next* Christmas!"

TOY CHEST RIVER

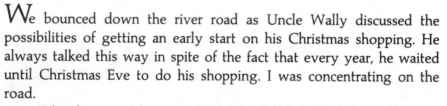

Paul C. Tumey

We bounced down the river road as Uncle Wally discussed the possibilities of getting an early start on his Christmas shopping. He always talked this way in spite of the fact that every year, he waited until Christmas Eve to do his shopping. I was concentrating on the road.

"Lloyd, are you listening?" With his beefy left hand, Uncle Wally grabbed the steering wheel. "Loosen your grip! Your knuckles are turning white!"

I took my eyes off the road for a millisecond and flashed a grin at his eyes, enlarged by the thick lenses he had taken to wearing. "Maybe you should drive the rest of the way," I said.

"Don't worry about the river. Pretend it's not there. There's no traffic and there's no hurry." His voice was as smooth and worn as a wooden carousel horse whose ornamented bridle and saddle had been touched by thousands of tiny hands. I relaxed.

Off in the distance, the great Toy Chest River Bridge arced into the clouds. The rusty orange girders crossed and recrossed each other so many times the silhouette was nearly solid. Such a sturdy-looking bridge from far away, I thought. A caravan of cars, some with their headlights switched on, crawled across the hump, while the Toy Chest roared underneath. They reminded me of my beloved toy cars and I wondered for the hundreth time where the missing one in the set had disappeared to.

My favorite car in the set my father had made for me was a miniature replica of our family car, a turquoise-blue Olds Rocket 88. It was so well-crafted that a single push would make it roll for yards. Perfectly detailed little people sat in front of a familiar dashboard. In the back sat a smaller figure, me in my two-year-old outfit of shorts and striped T-shirt. I took toothpicks and unsuccessfully tried to pry the people out, for I could never get over the feeling that they were trapped inside. Later, I felt as though I were trapped *outside*, never to be in my own car. It had vanished from my life at an early age. Now, at fifteen, I had the real thing.

About ten yards ahead, I saw a turtle in the road, mechanically inching his silver shell across. I slammed the brake pedal into the floorboards, the station wagon fishtailed, and a horrifying moment took a year to pass. I shut my eyes.

We stopped off the road, half a foot from the river's edge. The water boiled up at me. My heart was pounding. I glimpsed a turquoise-blue Rocket 88 tailfin moving deep under the water.

"Why'd you do that?" Uncle Wally shouted at me, his face drained of blood. "You could've got us killed."

"I didn't want to run over that turtle in the road." The turtle sat a few feet behind us, his head and feet retracted into his shell. Uncle Wally peered at him angrily.

"Lesson number one," Uncle Wally said, gasping for breath. "Don't hit the brakes so hard. They lock up and you lose control. Easy does it. Okay?" And he got out and gently moved the turtle off the road, never turning his back to the Toy Chest River.

I swear I saw a silver winding key on the turtle's back.

I'm sitting in the back seat of the Olds Rocket 88 at night. Mom and Dad are up front, talking and laughing. The lights of Xmas, Louisiana, play across their silhouettes and the car's dark interior in slants and circles.

When I was three, my parents drove onto the rusty old Toy

Chest River Bridge into Xmas one rainy night on their way back from a Christmas shopping trip. They lost control of their car, crashed through the iron railing and drowned in the river a hundred feet down.

I have the yellowed newspaper clippings in which people who had been in the cars behind them described the accident. The collision snapped the trunk open, leading one woman to describe "a beautiful waterfall of toys" chasing the car into the water.

Neither the car nor their bodies were ever found. I used to lie awake on hot summer nights in Uncle Wally and Aunt Esther's Airstream and imagine my parents driving through the murky waters of the Toy Chest in their Rocket 88, headlights illuminating the muddy river bed.

Other times I would dream I was down there, and they would open the trunk, filled with the most wonderful toys I had ever seen.

The fishing business, I believe, came from Uncle Wally's idea of what fathers and sons ought to do together. Of course, he wasn't my father and what he *really* wanted to do was search for junk.

The lot behind our trailer was packed with stuff from six states. He never stopped thinking about it. Our fishing trips always climaxed in a search for a flea market, garage sale, junk shop, or even a tempting pile of trash by the road.

"There's one, over there," he said, pointing to a moss-draped oak tree on which a hand-painted sign read GARAGE SALE. "Hey, we can get some Christmas shopping done."

I bravely parallel parked, getting it on the third try. "Maybe we can scare up a new set of salt and pepper shakers for Aunt Esther's collection." I said.

"That's a treasure trove if I ever saw one, Lloyd," Uncle Wally said, lighting his favorite pipe, carved in the shape of an alligator. The tobacco was tamped in the gator's gaping mouth and his tail served as the mouthpiece.

Uncle Wally had found it in a sewer grate thirty years ago. He had pried open the nearest manhole cover three blocks away and rescued the pipe after taking a wrong turn and wandering lost through miles of labyrinthine sewer tunnels. Thirty years later, the pipe still imparted a certain grimy smell to the tobacco.

On the concrete apron in front of the garage, cardboard boxes of various items for sale sat on metal shelves and folding tables. A few people poked around.

It was twilight now and, as we watched, the hundreds of multicolored Christmas lights strung across the roof and down the sides of the house winked on. A somewhat yellowed three-foot-high Santa shouldering his bag of presents stood guard over the light-bedecked hedges, competing with the plastic deer and the smaller black jockey that I imagined were year-round yard fixtures. His nose winked on and off.

We crossed the street, passing two pear-shaped women clad in polyester stretch pants and sleeveless cotton blouses with a little boy in tow, and went to work. Mostly boxes of worn tools, pickle jars filled with thousands of screws, nails, and nuts, and several cartons of miscellaneous electrical components.

I scrabbled in the single box of toys, but was disappointed to find no cars. I excavated a box shaped like an oversize die and held it up for inspection. A slinky burst out and hovered in front of my eyes for a second before wrapping itself around my wrist. The other end yanked me toward the hedges. I struggled, but it was amazingly strong, cutting into my skin. Uncle Wally intercepted me, brandishing a long metal pole.

"Lloyd! Look at this!" The slinky gave up the tug-of-war and, with a metallic hissing sound, collapsed into a tight coil. "A pogo stick! I haven't seen one of these in twenty years!" I had rarely seen my uncle so excited.

"Yours for a dollar. Most people wouldn't even know what to do with them if they found one." A gnomic little man stood at the entrance of the massive garage. He wore a tasseled smoking jacket and ornate slippers. Enormous round spectacles rested on his even larger brow. From the dim light cast by a single caged fixture, I could make out a long, densely cluttered workbench running the length of one wall.

"Well, that's not me!" Uncle Wally hopped onto the stick and began to bounce around madly, his fishing vest popping off flies and lures into the air.

"I've been looking for one of these," Uncle Wally said, huffing. "You don't know. A dollar seems . . . ridiculous. It's worth ten times that."

I was in shock. I had observed Uncle Wally bargain people down from their asking price before, but this was the first time he insisted on paying *more*. He proffered a ten-dollar bill to the man, who looked at it as if it were a dead fish.

"I insist." Uncle Wally waved the ten.

"Okay. But he has to take the slinky, too."

"No, thanks." I hurriedly dropped it back into the box of toys. "But, do you have any little lead die-cast cars?"

"I have something better! Look at this beauty." He rummaged around a box and extracted a horribly wrinkled potato.

"Now, *that's* nice," Uncle Wally agreed.

I was mystified. "It's a dried potato," I said.

"Ah, but look closer," the gnome shuffled over to me and shoved the thing in my hands. It had a face, a goofy face.

"That's the original Mr. Potato Head," the gnome said, proudly.

A pair of flat blue eyes looked out from between giant ears and over a big green nose and cherry-red lips. The whole festooned spud was crowned with a purple plastic homburg hat. I pulled the nose out, surprised to see it was connected to a sharp little spear.

Suddenly the eyes developed lids and blinked. The lips moved and inside the mouth I could see a tiny tongue. The Mr. Potato Head looked me in the eyes. "We miss you, Lloyd," it croaked.

I fainted.

"He's coming around at last." The gnome's voice was high-pitched and squeaky, like air escaping from a pinched balloon.

I was stretched out on a couch. "When you passed out, Finglenook here brought you inside," Uncle Wally gently explained. "You were babbling that you missed us."

"Here, drink some of this." The little man handed me a wineglass filled with a dark, musty liquid. "It'll help."

I sat up and looked around. Finglenook's house was filled with broken toys. Busted mainsprings and beheaded dolls sat on shelves above piles of toothless cogs and twisted gears. Eyeless teddy bears embraced stringless yo-yos amid shelves cluttered with greasy crankshafts and snarls of electrical wiring. There was a mustiness to everything, as though it had just been pulled from water.

A Christmas tree sat in the corner, lushly decorated with glittering copper coils, eggbeaters, chrome brand names, and other bits of machinery. A sterling silver quarter-moon, perhaps once the hood ornament of a luxury car, crowned the whole affair. Aside from the decorations, something else was odd about the tree. I peered at it in the gloom of the living room. The greenery was not right. It was stringy and shiny. Like water weeds.

I ran my hand past the shattered screen of an etch-a-sketch tablet on the coffee table in front of me. The knobs twirled and words shakily drew themselves on the screen: TAKE ME TO THE RIV—

"Drink up!" Finglenook urged, raising his own glass. "A toast. To submerged souvenirs, childhood treasures, and graceful living." We tentatively raised the glasses to our mouths. The liquid was very bitter, tasting of bile and smelling of fearful sweat.

We lowered our glasses simultaneously. Finglenook looked disgusted. "I had such hopes for the book press," Finglenook said in disappointment. "But it has yet to manufacture anything but nausea."

"Book press?" Uncle Wally asked, lighting his alligator pipe.

"A recent invention." Finglenook looked confused. "Well, no sense in wasting a good book," he said, and collected the glasses.

He walked over to a long library table cluttered with machinery. Carefully, the little man poured the contents of the three wineglasses into an upraised spout. Then he spent the next five minutes monkeying with the machine and muttering to himself. Uncle Wally puffed thoughtfully.

"Wallace, I have need of your services," Finglenook said. "If you'll take your pogo stick and begin jumping. And perhaps your nephew has recovered enough to use this?" He held up a lime-green hula hoop.

We looked at him uncomprehendingly. "I need childlike activity to make this process work," he explained. "Playfulness, you see? Whimsy."

Uncle Wally shot me a glance that meant, *We'd better humor him.* He straddled his pogo stick. "In here?" he asked, indicating the living room.

"Yes, yes. That's fine." The gnome waved distractedly while climbing on a rocking horse. "Bounce for all you're worth. With three of us, it shouldn't take more than a couple of minutes."

Uncle Wally hopped. I stepped inside the hoop and began to gyrate my hips. Finglenook rocked and grinned. He pointed. The book press was steaming. Calliope music raged through the room. The machine ejected a black book.

Finglenook dismounted, picked the book up and tossed it into my lap.

It was hot, like a baked potato. *"The Complete Works of Edgar Allan Poe."* I read the cover.

"No wonder it was so bitter," Uncle Wally said.

"I thought it might taste something like blackberry wine." Finglenook looked disappointed.

"You need Bradbury for that." Uncle Wally sucked on his pipe.

I opened the book. "Hey," I said, "There's chunks missing. It begins on page twenty-three. And there's something different." In the Doré illustration for "The Cask of Amontillado," Fortunato dug his way through the bricked-up wine cellar with a toy steam shovel.

"That's the part we drank," Finglenook looked sheepish. "It smelled awful, but I had to see how it'd taste. I'll drink it nevermore."

"Have you tried a quaint or curious volume of forgotten lore?" Uncle Wally asked around his pipe.

"Though I tried it, nearly napping, I found it would not pour," answered Finglenook.

"Wait!" cried I in mock agitation, "Is there someone at the chamber door?"

Finglenook laughed. Uncle Wally laughed harder and his pipe fell from his mouth, spilling a hot coal of tobacco on the musty carpet.

"Hey!" Finglenook shouted. "The rug's on fire!"

Uncle Wally stamped ineffectively on the smoldering Persian carpet. Smoke began to billow up. He knocked a carton from an end table. A platoon of three-inch-high U.S. Army soldiers scattered out and began to toss thimbles of water efficiently onto the fire, generating a series of tiny hisses.

But the fire was too fast. It rapidly spread across the rug. When it touched Finglenook's odd, gnarled and twisted shoes, he recoiled, knocking the workbench to the floor in a crash of Erlenmeyer flasks and metal tubing.

"Look!" I pointed to a stream of water coming down the hallway floor. In seconds the water level in the living room rose to our ankles and snuffed out the rug fire. Finglenook looked panicked.

"It's coming from the kitchen!" Uncle Wally stood up to run to the back. The overstuffed loveseat in which he had been sitting was sweating little streams of water. In front of my eyes, it liquefied completely, holding the form of the loveseat for a moment, and then cascading to the floor and blending imperceptibly into the rising currents at our feet.

Other pieces of furniture—the couch, the workbench, end tables and shelves—all dissolved into a pool of brownish water. Doorways and interior walls came down like stage curtains falling. The water weed Christmas tree melted in seconds, leaving the copper coils, the aluminum brand names, and the quarter moon swirling toward the murky bottom of the water.

Uncle Wally shouted, "The river's flowing through this house!"

Finglenook gurgled. "I can't find my feet!" he shouted desperately. The water was now above his eyes.

"You're drowning!" shouted Uncle Wally, forging toward him.

"No, I'm fine," said Finglenook, pushing his arms out as if to hold Uncle Wally at bay.

"You're irrational. I'll save you in spite of yourself." Uncle Wally hooked an arm around Finglenook's chest. "This isn't personal," he said, carefully landing a massive fist against the little man's chin. "It's for your own good."

Finglenook's eyes rolled up into his head and his body became limp. Uncle Wally towed him out the front door. "Come on, Lloyd!"

I stood on tiptoes to keep my head above water. A rubber duck bobbed by. A string hung from its side. I pulled it. My mother's voice, distorted and tinny, said. "We love you, Lloyd." Something wrapped around my left ankle and yanked my feet out from under me. I splashed into the water and the world became eerily quiet. I fought back to the surface and my head bumped into the overhead light fixture. There was only a band of air perhaps a foot wide between the water and the ceiling. The toy soldiers crawled up my pants, wrapping tentacles of the Christmas tree around my legs. I went under. I *wanted* to go under. Underneath, it was calm and quiet, oddly comforting.

The little men let go and fled as a meaty arm came slicing through the water and pulled me to the surface. I gasped for breath as Uncle Wally pulled me out the front door.

"I want three cheeseburgers! Two with pickles and ketchup and one with—" Uncle Wally leaned back and looked questioningly at Finglenook, who was asleep in the back seat, clutching Uncle Wally's pogo stick.

"Make that *three* with pickles and ketchup. And three large swamp shakes." He gingerly drew back from the five-foot-high plastic alligator's grinning mouth. The intercoms at the Gator Dip were so old, you had to lean in and shout your order down the gator's painted throat.

"That'll be seven eighty-three. Grrr! Thank you for your order. Please drive up to the window!" Oddly, the speakers blasted *out* fine.

We parked under a moss-draped oak behind the Gator Dip, woke up Finglenook, and ate. For a time, the only sounds that broke the solemn silence were the fartlike noises our straws made as we worked on the swamp shakes.

"So what do we do now?" I finally asked.

"This is really good!" Finglenook held up his quarter moon of cheeseburger.

"I'm not sure what happened back there," Uncle Wally said, patting his pockets for his pipe.

"You pack a mean punch," Finglenook said, fingering his jaw.

"And I had to go back for Lloyd. I thought ..." He looked abashed. I realized he felt guilty for not pulling me out first. When he had got me out the front door of the house, it was as though a flood had come up over just that one plot of land. The water was already running off, seeking the lowest level. Uncle Wally had looked at me like he didn't know whether to hug me or hit me.

"Something was grabbing at me back there," I said. "Pulling me under. That's why I didn't come out." I didn't mention the rubber duck or the soldiers.

"And to think I lost my pipe in all that!" Uncle Wally looked at us in consternation.

Finglenook smacked his lips and said that he was going into the Dip to wash up. He left.

Uncle Wally turned in his seat, the steering wheel pressing into his stomach. "Lloyd, it's time I talked straight to you. Man to man. You're old enough now."

"Some strange things are happening to me," I said.

"You're fighting with the river," he said.

"How do you know?"

"Every boy fights the river. There is a time, you see." He looked uncomfortable explaining this to me. "A time in a boy's life when he's thinking about being a man but before he is one, when he can do amazing things. And if he does do them, then he's one kind of man, and if he doesn't, he's hardly a man at all." He sighed deeply and stared out the windshield. In the overgrown weeds at the base of the mossy oak, I could see rusty beer cans.

"What's that got to do with the Toy Chest River and Finglenook's house dissolving into river water?" I asked.

"There's great forces at work against a boy becoming a certain kind of man. Natural forces not necessarily malevolent or devilish.

"Many years ago, as long as anyone in Xmas can remember, the Toy Chest River overflowed. That happens, you see. Rivers overflow, people die, at times even the earth itself opens up and swallows anybody in its way. In our lives, the river took away our toys.

"You can tell a man who's kept the boy alive in him if he keeps his toy. *The* toy. The one toy that defined his childhood. If a man grows up and hangs on to that, then . . ."

"But doesn't everyone?" I asked.

"No. Not anymore. Toys wind up in the river, I think. My grandfather told me a story once. About a little man who came out of the river and rode a gray mule through the streets of Xmas, calling out for the children to follow him. No children came. They were scared of the man. No one knows to this day if he meant them good or ill. In his anger, he caused the toys to follow him back into the river. Most folks know this story when they are children, but forget it when they grow older." He absently patted a pocket, his sodden bag of pipe tobacco clutched in the other.

"If a boy forgets a toy for more than two birthdays," he continued, "which is a very long time to a boy, the toy feels unloved so it walks sadly by itself to the river. And when the boy becomes a man and remembers, he is grief-stricken with the loss. But the toy is dead and can never come back. Now where did I put my pipe?"

"Looking for this?" Finglenook's head was level with Wally's window. He held the alligator pipe.

"Thanks!" Uncle Wally was happy. "Where did you find it?"

"In my pocket. The oddest thing. The water must have put it there." Finglenook winked at me.

We took him back to the Airstream and set up a cot for him in Uncle Wally's workshop in the back lot. He seemed to feel comfortable there, curled up with the well-oiled tools, gleaming in the moon-spliced darkness.

"He's a strange one," Aunt Esther mused, after we had put Finglenook to bed. She munched on a bag of curly-cue fries we had brought her from the Gator Dip, salting and peppering them liberally from her dog and fire hydrant shakers.

A week later Finglenook was still with us and normality had settled upon our lives. He and Uncle Wally spent happy hours in the workshop while Aunt Esther watched her football games.

I lay in bed caught somewhere between a deep sleep and a daydream. It was Christmas Eve, a time when I traditionally slept fitfully, my feverish excitement generated by the pile of wrapped presents and bulging stockings in the next room.

It was hot and humid, a typical Louisiana Christmas. The odd breeze drifted in through my louvered window, bathing my sweaty body with a delicious immersion of coolness. I heard a sound like rain on a tin roof and felt oddly comforted. The rhythmic sound was too even for rain. I surfaced to consciousness.

Straining my neck, I lifted my head off the pillow and held my breath. It was close by. In the room. *Slinnnk! Slinnnk!* At the base of the bed.

I poked the eye of my Elvis lamp and felt around its high ceramic collar until my thumb and forefinger encircled the switch. The sound stopped.

I looked down, my hand still on the lamp switch. My eyes had adjusted to the darkness and I could see the slinky on the floor. *Chinnk! Chinnk!* It walked under my bed, like an overbalanced inchworm.

I slipped down and looked under the bed, my torso still halfway under the covers, to give me comfort. A green hula hoop glowed in the darkness under the bed, hovering quietly an inch above the short piled carpet. Behind it, the metal spirals of the slinky whispered in the darkness with kinetic impatience. I leaned in closer, curious. As swift as a striking rattlesnake, the hula hoop lassoed my head and dragged me crashing to the floor.

I sat up and fought the hoop with all my strength. It pulled me toward the window. The slinky danced around us excitedly. I put my hands on the varnished paneling beside the tiny window and locked my elbows. The hoop pressed harder, digging into the back of my neck, stretching out to a thin oval. The end opposite my neck poked through the window and bulged against the screen. The only way I would go through that slotted window would be in sections, like Play-doh squeezed through a radiator grill.

The lights burst on and the hula hoop turned to a necklace of greenish water which soaked harmlessly into my pajama top. Uncle Wally stood in the doorway, wearing his flannel pajamas. The slinky quietly skittered underneath the bed.

"What in Sam Hill is all this commotion?" he asked.

"Well," I waved my right arm in wide circle. "There was this hula hoop. And"—I pointed at the dark rectangle of shadow underneath the bed—"A slinky came into my room. They tried to drag me out through the window. I think it's still under there." I was shaking.

"Still fighting the river, I see." Uncle Wally sighed and came into the room, shutting the door quietly behind him, so as not to wake Aunt Esther.

He had his pogo stick with him. "I don't know why I grabbed this." He gestured sheepishly at the rusty red pole. "It seemed the right thing to do at the time."

"I'm glad you brought it," I said, remembering how the slinky at Finglenook's garage sale had gone limp when Uncle Wally had appeared with the pogo stick.

He sat on my bed and patted the balled-up sheets beside him. "Sit down, Lloyd. Let's figure this thing out once and for all. I'm worried. The next time I might not be around with the pogo stick to defend you."

I sat beside him, pulling my feet up into a cross-legged position. I didn't want to leave *my* bare ankles within nipping reach of that slinky.

He just sat there for a long time, staring at the pogo stick. His thick walrus mustache bunched up and he gave me a chagrined smile. "I thought if we had Finglenook under our roof, I would be able to anticipate his moves. I don't know, I even had a silly notion I'd be able to befriend him."

"It's not working, is it?" I asked.

"No, I'm afraid not."

"Why does the river want me?"

"I don't know. But I'll tell you this. The river calls for all of us. Every boy hears the call. You ever stand at the top of a tall building and look down?"

"Sure. The state capitol in Xmas. I went with Mrs. Higgen's fifth grade class, remember?"

"I remember. You came back and began jumping off old man Wortz's garage roof." Uncle Wally chuckled.

"You knew about that?"

"Of course. Before your father . . . left, he entrusted your care to me. I've never taken that lightly. I've always kept an eye on you, but I've tried to let you live your own life."

"I remember standing there at the top of the state capitol and seeing the whole city spread out before me," I said. "The buildings and streets were reduced to building-block size. I could see the Toy Chest River beyond the buildings. And then suddenly, I wanted to jump. Jump right off and sail down twenty-two stories."

"That was the river calling. It happens all the time."

"I was scared."

"Of course. It's so scary that a lot of boys grow into frightened, deaf men, spending their lives not hearing. They can't hear the river calling anymore, but neither can they hear anything else. Just the sound of their own hearts beating in fear."

"Did Mom and Dad hear the river calling?" I was uncomfortable, as if Uncle Wally was lecturing me on the birds and bees.

"Look here." He held the pogo stick up and pointed to some scratches on one end. "Can you read that?"

The neatly scratched initials *N.T.* glowed in the moonlight. I gasped. "Nick Tinker!"

"I wasn't exaggerating when I said it'd been twenty years since I'd seen one of these." His eyes looked out through the trailer window across the darkened treetops outside. Nick Tinker was my father.

"He always blamed me for losing it," said Uncle Wally ruefully.

"But you didn't lose it, did you? It went to the river, like all the toys do."

"Your father never wanted to admit that. He was a toymaker who'd lost his own toy." Uncle Wally shook his head.

"What happened the night Mom and Dad died? Will you tell me?"

"I don't know the whole story. I wish I did. All I know is that Nick and Annie came to me and asked if I would look after you. They wouldn't say where they were going or how long they would be gone. Nick looked pretty excited, I remember that clearly."

"Excited about what?"

"He said he thought he'd found a way to get his Pogo stick back. And my stuffed alligator toy. And Sarah's doll. And Esther's ball and jacks. Everybody's toys. He hated the idea of toys going out of people's lives. He would've risked anything short of losing you to recover them."

"And I guess he did," I said.

"Next thing I know"—Uncle Wally looked away from me—"a grim-faced Sheriff Hebert is rapping on the trailer door at three in the morning telling me your parents crashed over the Toy Chest Bridge. Damn." He smacked a fist into a meaty palm. "I should never have let them go."

"Uncle Wally, I think if the river wants me, I should go to it."

"No, Lloyd. You'll end up just like Nick and Annie. I can't let you go."

There was a clunk under the bed and then a grunt. Finglenook came slowly crawling out, turtlelike. Uncle Wally jumped up on the bed and brandished his pogo stick. "Get back, Lloyd. He's dangerous."

Finglenook sat on the carpet and looked up at us. "The boy's right, you know," he said.

"The hell he is," Uncle Wally glowered.

I extended my legs and stood up, acutely aware of my undefended bare heels exposed to the slinky I knew was hiding underneath the bed.

"Come with me to the river." Finglenook held out a crooked hand. I took it and pulled him to his feet.

"Lloyd, no!" Uncle Wally cried, reaching out toward me.

"It's the only way, don't you see?" I held out my palms to Uncle Wally, who looked crestfallen.

"I'll lose you too," he said dejectedly.

"Maybe so, but isn't it better than me living my life in fear? Never able to overcome my past? Don't you see I'll become just like one of those deaf men you were talking about? It's already happening. I can barely manage enough courage to even drive out into the world. And all my childhood treasures are transforming into bogeymen that hide in the shadows. I have to face the river, Uncle Wally."

He sat on the bed, his huge stomach bulking up as he did so. "I know you're right, Lloyd. You sounded just like your parents then. Compared to this, it was easy watching you jump off a garage roof and staying quiet. It was easy letting you take the wheel and praying nothing happened. This is the hardest thing I've ever done." He gently set the pogo stick down and left the room. I pulled on jeans and a T-shirt while Finglenook stood alert.

A few seconds later, Uncle Wally reappeared. He held out his hand. "Here's the keys to the station wagon. Take them and be the best man you can be." He pressed the cold metal keys into my hand.

"I'll be back," I said to him.

I turned to Finglenook. "Take me to the river."

The whole town was bedecked with multicolored lights, every street lamp adorned with a wreath. It was two A.M. Christmas morning and there were no other cars on the streets. The town felt as dead and lifeless as a toy with its mainspring busted.

We came to the Toy Chest River Bridge. "My father drove off on purpose, didn't he?"

"Yes," Finglenook croaked dryly. He grew more wrinkled by the minute.

We approached the ramp. In the moonlight, the corroded orange girders looked like Life Savers candy. I put both hands on the wheel and breathed deeply. I had never driven over this bridge. Even riding over it terrified me.

It was a narrow, two-lane bridge with a short railing that gave only a nod to the idea of safety. From the driver's seat, I was panicked to discover, the railing was so low it vanished from view. We climbed. My back pressed into the vinyl cushion of the driver's seat.

"I remember my mother hated going over this bridge," I said, talking just to keep my mind off my fear. "Aunt Esther once told me a story. She and Mom were riding over this bridge and talking away when Mom suddenly demanded that she take the wheel. Aunt Esther had to steer them across the bridge with her left hand while Mom just sat in the driver's seat, pressing the accelerator with her foot and chatting on as though nothing was happening. She never mentioned the incident to Aunt Esther. It was as though it had never happened."

The lights of Xmas were dots in my rearview mirror. The Toy Chest rushed underneath us. I risked a glance at Finglenook, who'd been silent since we boarded the bridge, and screamed.

A mass of slimy green water weeds in the shape of a short man sat in the passenger seat. The head turned. A hand dripping vegetable matter and smelling of decay pointed at the road. I looked up and hit the brake. We crashed through the railing and I turned the wheel wildly. The front wheels sank over the edge and there was a sickening feeling in my stomach as the full weight of the station wagon tipped us off the bridge and sent us plunging toward the black waters of the river below.

The car hit the water and I smashed my head against the windshield. We floated on the surface for a minute and then I felt water crawling into my shoes. The waterweed man in the passenger seat grabbed the door handle.

"No!" I shouted. He opened the door.

Water flooded in and the wagon sank. The waterweed man lost his human shape and floated toward me, a mass of groping slimy tentacles.

The world became silent with a dense, thick level of white noise. It was dark, muddy. The water-filled station wagon settled on the bottom. I pushed on my door, but it wouldn't open. I rolled down the window and slipped out, the exertion using up my oxygen at an alarming rate.

The waterweeds slithered after me and encircled my ankles. They pulled me to the river bed. I stumbled, blind, lost. The mud was littered with slimy objects. I tried to push off, but the weeds pulled me down, like a hungry octopus. I grabbed at an object in the mud trying to get to my feet, but it pulled free. I ran my fingers along the tubelike object. I felt slippery smooth glassy disks at both ends. On impulse, I put it to my eye. It was a kaleidoscope. It worked.

Though little light penetrated into the river from above, I could see clearly through the kaleidoscope. By turning the end, the fragments of the view came together enough so that I could make out details. The riverbed looked like the desolate surface of another planet. A few yards away, an entire house sat in the mud, decayed with gaping black holes for windows and doorways.

I was running out of breath. Two, maybe three minutes had passed since I had emerged from the wagon into the water. The free-floating weeds patiently inched me through the mud, toward the old house. In desperation, I scanned the river bed with the kaleidoscope, looking for anything that could help me, and saw what I needed. A Major Matt Mason space helmet, sitting on the muddy bottom just two feet away. The weeds were loose enough, but I had no energy left with which to fight them anymore. It was over. I opened my mouth to fill my lungs with river water and then I saw the Olds.

The headlights were close by, traveling steady, cutting through the swirling muddy currents, two cones of light that quickly came to rest beside me. Through the thick water I could hear the strong thrum of the Rocket 88 engine.

Using the kaleidoscope, I drew a bead on the space helmet and then took it away from my eye, blinded again in the murky water. The presence of my parents' Olds gave me strength. I reached over with the kaleidoscope, hooked the jawpiece of the helmet, and dragged it to me. I shoved it on my head, lowered the tinted visor, and, as I had hoped, I could breathe and see again.

I sat there gasping and looking at the car just as I had dreamed it so often on many a hot summer night, with headlights throwing cones in the dark, muddy water. Mom sat inside with her red hair swirling in the waters and her hands pressed against the window. And Dad sat on the driver's side, smiling at me, his arm leaning on the steering wheel.

After a moment, I had enough strength to fight my arms free of the waterweed straitjacket. I reached down and ripped the tendrils off my legs. I was free for the moment.

I swam over to the Olds. The weeds followed. I tried to open Mom's door but it wouldn't work. I had an idea that I could save them, break them free, and we could all escape. I gestured at the lock but she shook her head sadly. I put my fingers against the glass and she wistfully mirrored the movement on her side. She unrolled the window a little. The weeds encircling my neck, I reached inside and touched her fingers. Dad looked over her shoulder and smiled, pointing up at the surface. *No!* I shouted, my voice flat in the space helmet. *I want to stay here with you and Mom!*

She pushed something through the window into my hands and Dad revved the engine hard. They both waved and smiled at me. Instantly, the weeds slid off me, water flooded into my Major Matt Mason space helmet, and I shot toward the surface of the river.

I fought hard to swim back, but the object in my outstretched hand drove me toward the surface. I looked around for the Olds and made out the old house on the river bottom, now all lit up with candy-colored Christmas lights. The same lawn ornaments I had seen at the garage sale, including the faded yellow Santa with the winking nose, stood in front of the house, embedded in the mud. Finglenook was framed in the brightly lit doorway, a full wineglass in his hand. He grinned and toasted me, then turned back into his house.

I broke the surface, gasping. I tore off the space helmet and floated on the surface of the Toy Chest River, stunned. Something surfaced beside me, shooting out of the water and falling back in. A smiling rocking-chair horse, its gold-painted bridle shining in the moonlight. I hugged its neck, keeping my head above water. Behind me I heard another splash. Then another. In seconds the river became filled with toys, their gay colors changing its appearance. Countless dolls, dollhouses with tiny chairs and tiny tables, clowns, balls, stuffed tigers, wagons, teddy bears, tricycles and skateboards, and hundreds upon hundreds of toys, freed from the mud on the river bottom, had risen to the surface.

"Hey, Lloyd!" Uncle Wally waved at me from the river bank, his Pogo stick in hand. Our neighbor's Pinto was parked behind him.

I waved back broadly. A string of three Velveeta-yellow rubber ducks bobbed by. The menacing Toy Chest River had become nothing more than a giant bathtub filled with toys. Then I remembered the hard little object Mom had pressed into my hand. I slowly unclenched my fist.

It was my lost car.

That Christmas people went down to the banks of the river and reclaimed their lost toys. Children spent the day playing in the streets of Xmas with the very toys their parents and their grandparents had loved.

Aunt Esther fixed us a turkey dinner and then we left her to her football games, going for a walk around the trailer park. It was twilight and the crickets were beginning to trill. We stopped on the road that ran in front of the trailer park. Uncle Wally lit a match, momentarily flaring his face in warm orange light, and puffed on his alligator pipe. "Well, Lloyd, you faced the river and won."

"Sort of." I shrugged, feeling melancholy.

"Your parents?" A huge hand descended gently on my shoulder.

I took the toy Olds from my pocket and pushed it across the crevices in my outstretched palm. "I should have saved them."

"Let me see it." He held his hand out.

I handed it to him. He knelt down and set the little leaded car on the road.

"The way you explained it to me, you'd have had to let go of the car to go back down. There's no guarantee that you'd been able to help them, anyway. No, I think, wherever they are, Nick and Annie are happy. That car is their gift to you." He stood up.

I knelt down and studied it. It was perfect. I could push it and set it going, and it would travel down the road and never stop. It would turn corners and flow down streets that joined larger streets that poured into highways that went all over the land. A flick of the finger and it could roll forever.

"I know," I said, and put the car in my pocket.

A Christmas disaster becomes a triumph.

A PRESENT FOR SANTA

Hilbert Schenck

1

Anne Hastings came out of the elevator on the sixth floor of Boston
Municipal Hospital like a shot from a cannon, turned right and set off
at a near run down the long corridor heading to the critical wards.
Anne was a small, still-attractive woman of eighty years, her face set
in determination, her high heels clicking rapidly on the waxed floors.
Behind her, jogging along, trailed Freddie, the much-taller grandson of
her sister, his college-boy face filled with apprehension.

They reached the nurses' station where several wheelchairs
waited. "Take that one, Freddie," said Anne in a tight but clear voice,
then went along the corridor to the third door on the left. Freddie
followed pushing a chair while the head nurse looked out over a
counter, then picked up a phone and said a few words.

Once in Henry Hastings's room, Anne busied herself getting

Henry from the bed to the chair, helped by Freddie, and muttering to herself. Henry moved with difficulty for he had only one leg, the other one gone three weeks ago to diabetes-caused circulation problems. Henry still had a bushy thatch of white hair, since they had waited on the chemotherapy for his prostate cancer until they could do his multiple-bypass heart operation. His old and wrinkled face was filled with a mixture of apprehension and hope.

"It can't be this easy, Annie," he said softly.

Anne threw his clothes onto his lap. "We live in a free country!" Her voice was sharp and determined. "Let's go, Freddie, he can dress in the car."

They surged out of the room, Anne leading, Freddie pushing, and headed down the corridor towards the distant elevators. The head nurse, a plain, middle-aged woman with thin, calculating eyes, intersected their path as they passed her station, and spoke loudly. "Mrs. Hastings, what are you doing? You can't take Dr. Hastings out like this!"

Anne did not look back. "Send us a bill! You know damn well that we're good for it!"

The nurse trailed along behind, protesting and waving her hands. Ahead of them an elevator door opened and three men came out. Two of them were young, one white and one black. They were dressed in green tunics and wore white badges, symbols of the medical staff, but it was obvious they were not interns or techs. The black employee had a long cheek scar and his lumpy knuckles showed him to be a street-fighting adept. The other, larger guard, had a crew-cut and his bull neck defined him as a weight-lifter. Both of them, Anne noted, wore identical expressions of menace.

Between them stood Doctor Frank Parkinson, senior staff and Chief of Surgery, his neat beard jutting out and his eyes even colder than those of the security toughs flanking him. "We cannot permit you to take Henry home, Mrs. Hastings. Our responsibility for his health and the law of this state make that impossible."

"Listen, Parkinson," said Henry Hastings in a strong and bitter voice, "I managed a look at my file two days ago. You're planning a multiple bypass for me. I'm dying and you're going to put me under the knife for major surgery!"

"Henry, this is a hospital. You are here to be cured, to have all your medical problems analyzed and competently treated. Your best interests are our only . . ."

"Don't you call me Henry, you greedy phony! I am Professor Hastings to you. You are a quack and the only competence you possess is bilking money out of my medical insurance!"

Dr. Parkinson's face turned bright red. "Take Professor Hastings to his room, nurse," he said quickly. "You gentlemen," he spoke to the two security guards, "please escort this young man to his car," and he indicated the white-faced Freddie. "I think you and I, Mrs. Hastings, should go for a talk with Ralph Steen, our Chief of Hospital Security. He's a busy man, but he has agreed to see us now."

The thin-eyed nurse turned Henry's chair around and moved him quickly back down the hall, to a chorus of shouted complaints from her patient. Freddie, each arm in the grip of one of the guards, was whisked into an elevator. Anne walked in shocked silence into a second elevator with Dr. Parkinson and rode quickly up to the tenth floor of the hospital.

The offices of Security Chief Ralph Steen were large, and one of his three secretaries nodded, then gestured toward the inner sanctum.

Ralph Steen rose to meet them, an oily smile on his wide face. He was almost grossly fat, his belly jutting out of the vest of his three-piece suit, his coat open and obviously impossible to button.

"Sit down, Mrs. Hastings," he said in a smooth voice.

She shook her head. "Whatever you have to say, I'll stand to hear it."

Steen's expression tightened. He reached into a desk drawer, pulled out a printed sheet of paper, and held it out to her. "Here is the agreement both you and your husband signed when he was admitted. Have you read this?"

Anne shook her head. "My husband was ... is ... dying. I've had other things to concern me."

"Under the Massachusetts Hospital Reform Act, passed three years ago and operative in every health care facility in the Commonwealth, critical patients are completely our responsibility. This includes medication, treatment decisions, everything leading to a successful resolution of their difficulties."

"This is America," said Anne stoutly. "You can't hold my husband here against his will!"

"Your husband's will, as you put it, is subordinate to our mandate to make him well. That is the law. The time when relatives could subvert the best interests of patients is over, at least in this state."

Anne reached to take the form from Steen, crammed it into her purse, and turned to leave. "My attorney will be in touch with you, Mr. Steen," she said in icy tones.

"Ah . . . one more thing, Mrs. Hastings," and Steen's small eyes glittered as Anne half-turned back. "If there are any more repetitions of what happened this afternoon, any more disturbances, we will be forced to remove you from the list of Dr. Hastings's allowed visitors. He does have a life-threatening heart condition."

That hit Anne like a blow to the face. Her eyes filled with tears and her voice cracked. "You . . . you could keep me from Henry? When he's dying? You would do that?"

"Our responsibility is to your husband . . . no one else."

"You *are* bastards . . . both of you!" Anne turned and dashed from the office.

By the time she reached the sixth floor, she had regained control of herself and she stalked back to the critical ward. The head nurse was waiting. "Mrs. Hastings?"

Anne turned. "Yes?"

"We were forced to sedate your husband. His blood pressure was at a dangerous level. You really should think of that before you do this sort of thing. He won't be awake until much later, so I would suggest you do not come back until tomorrow's visiting hours."

Anne stared with pure hatred at the woman. "Too bad you were born so late. You would have made a wonderful nurse at Dachau or Bergen-Belsen."

The nurse's face stiffened in shock and Anne suddenly regretted such a savage response. "I'm sorry. I didn't mean that. We're both powerless here and I'm sure you have children to support. Why should you risk your job for an old man and an old woman you don't know?" She turned and went to the elevators.

Freddie was waiting in his car and drove up the visitors' ramp when she appeared at the main door. Once in the car, Anne broke down again weeping, and Freddie reached to touch her hand. "I didn't do so good, Auntie. I'm sorry. Let me take you to Mom."

Anne sat up straight and wiped her eyes. "You did your best, Freddie. Take me home. This isn't your mother's problem or anyone else's. It's mine."

Once she was in her big, old house, Anne felt better and mixed herself a stiff drink. After some thought, she called her old family doctor, Fitzgerald Hamilton, and when his answering service finally found him, described her afternoon.

Dr. Hamilton seemed strangely withdrawn. Finally he said, "Annie, you're still friends with Betty Freeman, right?" Anne said she was and the doctor continued. "Okay, call her right now and tell her what you just told me. She can help."

Anne did that, explained her problems and asked for advice.

Like Dr. Hamilton, her old friend suddenly spoke in almost a distant manner. "Write down this phone number and address. Call them at once and say I told you . . ."

The number answered immediately, a guarded woman's voice. "My friend, Mrs. Freeman, suggested I call you," and Anne went on to describe her problems with the hospital and her husband.

"You've got our address," said the voice. "Can you get here by ten tomorrow? The sooner we can get together, the better."

"Yes, I can do that," said Anne. "Are you lawyers, legal people?"

There was a pause and the voice now sounded amused. "Sort of that, Mrs. Hastings, but you shouldn't mention us to anyone, not your husband, nobody. Do you understand?"

"Well, I guess I do," said a puzzled Anne as the woman hung up.

Anne somehow felt better, although she couldn't have explained why. She made her supper, had a couple more relaxing drinks and fell asleep long before she thought would be possible. After midnight Henry woke from his drugged sleep and called in a rage to urge her to go to a lawyer as soon as possible. Anne sleepily agreed, told him that her old friend, Betty Freeman, had suggested a legal firm and fell back to sleep.

She dreamed that night that she and Henry went magically out through the window of the day room at Boston Municipal Hospital and flew to a place where they were young again and nothing hurt.

2

The taxi came to a stop in the middle of the block and Anne Hastings peered out the window with a sense of sudden unease.

"This is the address you gave me, lady," said the driver defensively, himself staring out at a blank-walled, two-storey building with a small door in its exact middle. The street was one of the few in downtown Boston that had not been renewed in recent history and the small and disheveled buildings along it spoke of decay and quiet failure.

Anne paid and tipped the cabby, then stepped resolutely out onto the sidewalk.

"You want me to wait, lady?"

"No thank you, driver, I may be here for some time." She moved up to read the brass plaque under the doorbell. "Tradewinds Exports Incorporated," she said half to herself, then pushed the bell.

The door opened at once and Anne blinked up at a tall, black woman in a simple black dress. She was thin and statuesque with an impassive ebony face like, Anne thought to herself, that Nefertiti bust you see so many pictures of.

"Mrs. Hastings?"

"Yes."

The woman reached and took her hand. "We've been expecting you. I'm Sharon Goodspeed. I spoke to you on the phone. Please come in."

Anne followed the tall woman down the hall which Anne saw with shrinking hope was old and dirty. The woman opened a door to the back section of the house, a windowed, almost-empty room. The only things in the room beside the desk were three chairs and an elaborate computer workstation next to it. Here stood a young man of average height and rather average looks, his hand extended.

"Hi, Anne Hastings," he said in warm and familiar tones. "I'm Ben Newmark, Ben if you would. Grab that comfy chair next to the desk."

Sharon Goodspeed sat down on the other side of the desk as Ben gestured rapidly.

Anne sank somewhat stiffly onto the front edge of the chair and looked back and forth at the two strangers. Sharon was cool and elegant. She moved and sat with an easy confidence that was somehow calming. Ben Newmark was quite different: frenetic and restless. The foot of his crossed leg was wiggling rapidly while he busily gestured at her with both hands to sit back and relax. He smiled and blinked rapidly. "Mrs. Freeman gave you our number?"

Anne nodded. "Actually my doctor, Fitzgerald Hamilton, suggested I call Betty Freeman, after I told him what happened at the hospital."

Ben jerked his head toward Sharon and his eyes narrowed. "So old Fitz isn't acting as a contact. He passed her off to someone he knew would get her here. He's worried . . . looking for deniability."

Sharon lifted her eyebrows. "If you had four kids in Ivy League schools and the local medical society was trying to get your license, you'd look for deniability too."

Ben's scowl turned to a smile again and he turned back to Anne, but her face was now pinched in concern. "Is Fitz Hamilton in some sort of trouble? Why I can't believe that for a second! He's a past president of the General Practice Society!"

The young man waved his hands at her again. "Mrs. Hastings, ah . . . Anne . . . okay if I call you that?" She nodded and he continued. "I think the best way to start this is for us to explain how we helped Betty Freeman. Did she ever talk to you about her husband's final year?"

Anne shrugged. "She told me that Gil had a terrible cancer. He was in the hospital for a while. I visited him there. But then he came home and they went with a nurse to Bermuda for three weeks, sort of a final honeymoon she told me, and he died soon after."

Newmark nodded rapidly and made encouraging noises. "That's right. That's right. Our part came in getting him out of the hospital for that last honeymoon. Gilbert Freeman was, as I'm sure you know, the retired head of one of Boston's top bond-trading operations. As such, he had a Medicare supplement policy that would have paid to send him to the moon, if the hospital could find a doctor or medical committee to claim that treatment would extend his life."

The young man turned and punched some letters on his computer keyboard, then stared at a green unrolling of words. ". . . Oh, yeh, now I remember. Gil had a really bad thing, liver cancer. They were planning a transplant attempt at Boston Muni, the same place your husband is at. Now even ten years ago, liver transplants were running a half-million-plus. It's two-mil-plus now. They often need several tries. There's the possibility of a primate donor, and you can't imagine how expensive a healthy baboon with a healthy liver is today!" Ben gave her a boyish grin.

"Gil came under the same state law that fatty Steen read to you yesterday, and since he was of sound mind and fully conscious, even if he was eighty-two, his living will was not operative. Did fatso explain all that to you, Anne?"

She nodded and her small face contorted in anger. "It's all in that stupid paper he gave me."

"Well, your friend, Betty, located us . . . through Doc Fitz in fact . . . and we worked on a way of getting Gil out of Boston Muni. Fortunately, he could walk . . . not like your husband's situation."

"How did you know my husband can't walk? I didn't mention that to Ms. Goodspeed on the phone!"

Ben gestured at his computer. "We have access to most medical records, either through the good offices of friendly hackers or through the help of suborned hospital employees. Most hospitals in this state employ Latinos, blacks and Filipinos as hourly staff, and the hourly pay is pretty awful. So we augment that minimum wage and they will repay us by helping get people out. We also have access to friendly older people, our 'actors' we call them, usually people who had a relative rescued and brought home to die. Since Gil had no hair left . . . they fed him maximum chemo to slow the cancer . . . we found a look-alike about his age and bald as a billiard ball. We wigged him, recruited an elderly lady . . . about your age, Anne . . . and sent them up to Gil as visiting old friends. Once in the room, the lady stood watch at the door while Gil and his double switched outfits and Gil put on the wig. After a decent interval of chatter . . . the rooms are all bugged . . . our changed couple left the hospital, while Gil's double lay facing the wall, his bald pate shining. As soon as enough time had passed for the escapee to get clear, the substitute went into the bathroom and changed into a hospital employee outfit and another wig our visitors had sneaked in under some flowers in a box. We had instructed him how to leave the ward and the hospital and he was soon off in another car. That was an easy one. A real textbook rescue!"

Anne was now staring in astonishment at Ben Newmark. "And this was all illegal? Did they come and try to get Gil at home? Can they do that?"

Sharon Goodspeed sent Anne a cool, yet reassuring, smile. "Our lawyers believe that the Hospital Reform Act gives the care facility the right to come after a patient. They've never dared try that yet, but we don't take any chances. When we get somebody out, we don't take them home. We have safe houses where they can wait until we legally switch their medical supervision."

Ben noted Anne's complete astonishment at this story and he spoke directly to her. "Anne, listen . . . Gil and Betty went to Bermuda once, on their honeymoon, at the end of the thirties. Two months before he died, they went again. There's no way he could have done that after the transplant procedure . . . even if he lived!"

Anne nodded. "I don't have any problem with the illegal part, Mr. Newmark . . . ah, Ben. I just don't understand how any of this is possible and why people like Gil, and my Henry, have to be *rescued* from a *hospital!* I mean, what ever happened to the U.S. Constitution . . . habeas corpus . . . ?"

Ben Newmark leaned back in his chair and spoke in a thoughtful voice. "Yeh, how did it start? Do you remember . . . ten, fifteen years ago . . . when there was that rash of publicity about people in comas, on life-support systems? Relatives would go into court to pull the plug and some local politico, playing to some religious lobby, would put the state on the side of keeping the dead thing alive. Well, almost every time, the hospitals sent their lawyer in on the side of the state to fight the tube-removal request."

Ben lifted his eyebrows. "Hey, why not? Coma patients don't bitch about the food. They don't need counseling, and they often generate thousands a day. But the hospitals overplayed that policy and the result was a boom in living wills, legal systems set up to stop the health-care operation from prolonging life after death. At about the same time, people in their thirties and forties were getting into jogging, home exercise, diet, stopping smoking. So the oldsters were opting out of extreme measures and the younger customers were delaying the onset of that expensive heart attack. Remember this: it's the people without the open-ended insurance, the Medicare supplements, and the attachable savings who are also the smokers, the fatties, the druggies, the drunks, and the majority of a hospital's customers . . ."

"And . . ." said Anne, nodding at him, "Every year they develop wonderful new medical gadgets and tricks that cost patients the national debt."

"Right," said Ben. "Just as the health empire was towering, growing all-powerful, the clientele that could pay was shrinking and dwindling away. Then about four years ago, 1995 or so, a series of unhappy episodes burst upon our national consciousness—helped, I'm sure, by the health-care lobby. Grasping, scheming, manipulating and usually younger, relatives of ancient, bewildered, feeble patients were talking Granny into coming home to die, whereas in fact, Granny had many good . . . anyway expensive . . . years if only the experts could be allowed to fix her up. There was one devastating case, out in West Newton, where a very senior lady was taken from a hospital that had strongly urged further treatment and fell over dead on her front step with all the neighbors gathered to welcome her home." Ben shook his head in dismay at the memory. "To put in a nationwide hospital reform act is not yet possible. The senior-citizen lobby has too much muscle at the national level. But Massachusetts is different. It's always been in the forefront of Big-Brother-style government. Also, science and research has often been a last resort here, the final thing to save us from the latest recession. And the hospitals are certainly part of that. So when the medical societies and the hospital administrators went to the legislature and said it was wrong and immoral that people being saved by high-tech . . . and high priced . . . miracles should be taken away by young and forceful greedies, thus came the Hospital Reform Act, which the abominable fat man tossed at you yesterday, and which you and your husband signed onto prior to his leg amputation."

Anne Hastings hung her head. "I remember some of that when it happened, but Henry's diabetes was bad then and we sort of stopped paying attention to outside things. Should I have not signed that, Ben?"

"Only if you wanted to get back in the ambulance and start driving around, hunting some sort of health facility that didn't insist on you signing it, and you would have had to go to New Hampshire or Connecticut for that. No, patients don't have too much choice when bad things are happening quickly."

"And nobody has objected to this? Nobody is fighting it?"

Ben grinned more widely. "You bet they are. The old folks' lobbies. The civil liberties people. The insurance industry. There's a dozen cases now headed for the State Supreme Court, but that bunch will probably find for the legislature and send the plaintiffs up to the U.S. courts. Meanwhile, the people for whom the suits are named are dead after God-knows how many expensive, invasive, and painful procedures. What you've got to realize is that the docs and the health-care lobby are number one in PACs and contributions, statewide and nationwide. If they can get this law past the U.S. Supreme Court, who knows what comes next."

He stared at her somberly. "Your husband's bypass will generate at least one-third of a million dollars for Boston Muni. If he should get past that, his prostate treatments and eventual surgery could generate almost as much again. Gil Freeman, Henry, a few hundred other people in the entire state have unwittingly fallen into a situation that has turned them into medical cash cows. They have expensively treatable diseases and Medicare supplement policies that won't quit. It's not fair. Your husband is being victimized. But that is the actual situation."

Anne nodded once. "What can you do for Henry?"

"Tell us about what has happened, about your situation."

Anne took a deep breath. "Well, yesterday I went with my sister's grandson to get Henry . . ."

Ben held up his hand. "Before that. Give us some background on you and Henry."

Anne paused to shift her thoughts. "I was at Smith College in the late thirties. Betty Freeman was my roommate for two years. My family was well-to-do. I went to private school and all that sort of thing. Henry was a Yale boy, very much a Yale boy, I'm afraid, but I could see he had a warm heart. We married when I graduated, in 1939, and went to live in New Haven while Henry started graduate school. Of course the war was coming and Henry went into the Naval Reserve and got his commission in 1942. I was a Navy wife then and Henry was on a ship, a destroyer, in the Pacific. Near the end of 1943, Henry's ship attacked a big Japanese convoy. There were supposed to be other ships in support but they never got there and Henry's destroyer was blown apart, set on fire and sinking. After many of the men got onto life rafts, everybody realized there were other men trapped below decks. Henry, he was executive officer, and two other men went back aboard and dragged some of the men up from the fires. Eventually, two PT boats came and took all of them aboard and off to safety. Henry's hands and arms were badly burned from opening those hot steel doors below decks so they flew him back to a hospital in Maryland and a year of skin grafts and treatment.

"In 1944 there was a medal ceremony at the White House. Many Navy men were there to get important medals pinned on them by Mrs. Roosevelt. Henry was in the line with his hands and arms still bandaged and when Mrs. Roosevelt got to him she said, 'I can't shake your hand, Lieutenant Hastings, but I can certainly do this,' and she gave him a big hug and kissed his cheek. Some newspaper people were there and it was a famous picture afterwards, a full page in the old *Life* magazine and on front pages everywhere."

Anne's eyes were bright and her voice seemed younger and Ben Newmark saw what a pretty, loving young woman she had been and he envied them both for living through a time that, if it wasn't really better, certainly seemed better.

Anne blinked back a tear or two. "Being a hero doesn't last long and Henry went back to school and spent the rest of his life teaching philosophy. He wrote books and finally went to Harvard as chairman of a department . . ." She bit her lip. "One of the reasons he took that job was because the health program was so generous." Now the happy memories were gone and her old face was gaunt and wrinkled, her voice bitter.

"Do you have children, Anne?" asked Ben gently.

"One. We had trouble and that was the best we could do. Mark is living in France now. He's head of an important publishing house. He keeps telling us to come over there where medical treatment is free and they let you decide what the doctors can and can't do, but it's gotten a little bit late for that, I guess."

"Let's get to yesterday," said Ben. "You don't have to give us any details on your husband's diabetes and heart condition. We've got that all in the computer."

Anne's voice became hard and tight as she described the events of the previous day. When she got to the moment of confrontation in the corridor, Ben held up his hand. "Your husband called Frank Parkinson a phony and a quack?" He shook his head. "Dangerous stuff, Anne! Parkinson is one of the rats who helped write the reform act. He's mean and powerful. Also, he makes more than the C.E.O of Ford at this point."

Anne looked down at her small hands, twisting in her lap. "We were stupid, I know that. It was panic, I guess. Panic and rage at being so powerless." She finished her account by describing the interview with Steen and the sedation of her husband.

"So you haven't been back since and you haven't mentioned us to Henry on the phone?"

Anne shook her head. "No, Henry called me last night, after he woke up, to tell me to get a lawyer to stop the bypass operation. I didn't know about you then."

"Good. All the rooms are bugged at Boston Muni and the patient's phones are tapped. Voice-activated tape machines go on when needed. Security there probably doesn't monitor them all every day, but after your little scene, you can bet they're watching Henry every minute. Now, do you have a lawyer that you can call?"

"I guess we do, although we don't call them much. Krider and Petersen. It's a big firm."

"Great," said Ben. "What I'd like you to do is call them right now and make an appointment for this afternoon, as soon as possible. It doesn't matter whom you see; some kid or junior partner is fine. Just say it's very urgent, crucial."

Anne found the number in the phone book and made the call. After a brief discussion she hung up and smiled at Ben. "One o'clock today with a Mr. Belsen, who sounded quite young."

Ben jiggled both hands excitedly. "Super! Now I'm going to make some notes for you, but pay attention while I do. It's crucial that the overweight Eichmann at Boston Muni be convinced that you believe that you can stop them legally and that you'll go to the end of the earth to do it. Give your lawyer a copy of the paper they gave you about the reform act. Tell the attorney to call, right then while you're with him, to get a Medical-Legal Profile of your husband. When he calls, some flunky at Boston Muni will stall him, claiming they must have the request in writing. Tell the lawyer to get their fax number and, after he hangs up, to have his secretary type and fax the request right then and there. You've got to play a part in this, Anne, the part of an angry, determined woman who is fighting against time to stop something terrible. Don't let this fledgling legal eagle put you off. Press him! Raise your voice! Okay?"

Anne nodded. "I can certainly do that. I'm living the part."

"When will you see your husband again?"

"This afternoon, I guess, after I leave the lawyer."

"Okay. If you want to prepare Henry for us, you have to do it with a note. Don't speak of us. You should talk to give the impression that you believe the operation can be stopped by court order. They will be listening to that tape and they will have to be convinced that they need only fight you at law. If you should write Henry a note, your first sentence should be, 'This room is bugged. Be careful!'"

Anne nodded and took the folded paper. "We've got to be quick with this," said Ben. "The hospital Critical Care Committee that rubber-stamps major operations for the very sick didn't meet last week because of the coming holiday, but they will meet again after Christmas, in three days, okay Henry for the bypass, and it can happen any time after that. Even if your hot-shot law firm moves much faster than they usually do, they'd never get a judge to restrain before the hospital had made it all moot. And we haven't had much luck with Boston judges on this anyway. They're mostly political hacks. Sharon, can Anne do anything else for us at this point?"

Sharon's eyes were hooded. "Wheelchair?"

"Right," said Ben. "Have you been getting Henry into a wheelchair, Anne?"

She nodded. "Sometimes I wheel him into the day room so he can look at the harbor. I can get him into it by myself."

"Is there someplace in his room where a collapsed wheelchair might be hidden?"

Anne thought a moment. "There's that folding screen they can put around the bed. I suppose a chair could be hidden behind that."

"Okay. That's it for now. Can I get you a cab?"

Anne shook her head as she got to her feet. "No thank you. The lawyers' office is only a few blocks away and I can get a sandwich on the walk over."

Sharon helped Anne Hastings on with her coat and the old woman shook both their hands again, then paused and cocked her head at them. "How and why are you doing this, Ben?" For the first time her tone was wary.

"The answer to 'how' is that the people we rescue have relatives and friends with resources. When we need help, of any sort, we go to them, just as we will probably go to you and Henry, after he gets home."

Ben paused, and his normally cheerful expression became grimmer, his eyes thinner. "As to 'why,' our story is cruelly simple. My Dad had a world-class stroke that took his mind, his speech and his respiratory reflexes. They kept him going at Boston Muni on a respirator and assorted tubes. Mother and Dad had both executed living wills, but the Reform Act had just been passed and the hospital was taking the position that it superseded any living-will provisions. We went to court to have Dad taken off life-support but the judge refused to act until the legislature had clarified its intention vis-à-vis prior living-will legislation. Eventually, the hospitals lost on that one.

"After the judge refused to intervene, I took my mother home and went off to see my lawyer. She immediately got a cab and went to the hospital, taking one of those steel bars you can jam under a door knob to prevent anyone from kicking open a door. She went into Dad's room, jammed the door, and pulled all his plugs and tubes."

Ben paused and took a deep breath. "Sharon was head ward nurse on that shift, and she saw my mother go by her station. When the alarm went off on Dad's respiration monitor, she knew what was happening, turned off the alarm and did nothing. The other duty nurse had gone for some coffee. When she came back she noticed the flashing lights and tried to get into Dad's room. Eventually, Mr. Obesity's S.S. troopers came and battered in the door, helped by two cops. They were confronted by my mother using a metal bed pan as a weapon to try and keep them away from Dad to let him die . . . which had actually already happened. When they grabbed her she fell down with a massive coronary . . . she'd had a history of heart problems . . . and she died on the spot!"

Ben paused, then managed a half-grin. "Sharon claimed she had shut off Dad's monitor by mistake, but they knew better and instantly fired her. They also blackballed her on nationwide hospital personnel reference files, so she'll never work in a ward again. She was the first person to be named a 'health terrorist' by the medical P.R. lobby."

Sharon gave an easy laugh. "I'm as proud of that as your Henry is of his medal," she said.

Mrs. Hastings gave a sigh of compassion. "How awful! And how *hateful!*"

"Indeed it was," said Ben, now waving his arms in his usual cheerful way. "Afterwards, Sharon and I got together. I had been a C.P.A. with a medical specialty firm, so I knew quite a bit about the dark underbelly of hospital management, while Sharon is the nuts-and-bolts expert on in-house hospital operation. We approached some people my Mom had met during our struggle with the courts and worked out some rescues. Soon, we were off and running."

Mrs. Hastings set her jaw and turned to leave. "What a wicked world it is," she said softly.

3

After Anne Hastings left, Sharon and Ben sat in silence, staring at the blank walls. "Well," said Ben finally, "we've bitten one off this time, I guess."

Sharon sent him a thin smile. "I thought we agreed, over a year ago, never to attempt a rescue with somebody who can't *walk* out?"

"He got a medal and a kiss from Mrs. Roosevelt, for God's sake! We *owe* him, Sharon!"

"Yeh, I know. So, how do we do it?"

Ben waved a hand at her. "Okay, substitution won't work, even if we get him a fake leg to sit in the wheelchair with."

"I'll say it won't!" laughed Sharon. "After what the two of them did yesterday, can you imagine what would happen if we wheeled in a supposed old buddy in a chair?"

"They'd be on us like a duck on a June bug. One of those thugs dressed as an electrician or phone tech would be fussing in Henry's room the whole time our substitute was there." He thought a moment. "What about replacing the third-shift nurse . . . like in that Springfield rescue?"

Sharon moved around to sit next to Ben and punch the computer. "Impossible. This is an intensive-care ward. They never have just one nurse, even on third shift. And look at this sixth-floor map. Henry's room is on a corridor that dead-ends at the day room. To get him to the service elevator you have to go past the nurses' station."

"But wait a minute, Sharon. Those nurses are there watching the heart monitors, right? Henry's plugged in. Everybody on his ward is."

"Sure, but we can use one of Manny Feinstein's electronic heart simulators to get by that when we go in after Henry. We've used those a couple of times already."

"I know that," said an excited Ben, "But maybe Manny can fix up one that switches from normal heart action to fibrillation. We stick it in a nearby room with a comatose patient. The nurses run to that room and while they're busy, we wheel Henry past the station and to this freight elevator." He pointed at the diagram on the computer screen, then stared at her with a grin of triumph.

Sharon nodded. "Okay, and somebody has to go in there and do all this stuff: get Henry ready in a planted chair, bug some other patient's heart monitor with Manny's new toy, wheel Henry to the elevator, and get him down someplace where we can put him in the ambulance."

Ben pursed his lips and his brow wrinkled. "Hiding the chair in the room, that we can deal with. We'll get Juan Cordova to do that. He's on all the floors during the day and nobody will notice him. And he's a tough, gutsy kid. But he can't do that other stuff. They'd throw the book at him if he were caught. I don't think Juan even has a work permit."

They both sat silent for a while and Sharon's idle gaze shifted from the computer screen to the few things on Ben's desk, finally settling on his calendar.

"Santa Claus," she breathed.

"Huh?"

"Santa Claus, Ben! Tomorrow is the day before Christmas. The one day a stranger in a red suit can wander at will, in and out of rooms, past nurses' stations. Boston Muni hires a Santa for each floor . . . to dish out their sleazy little gifts to the patients: the hand-held computer games, the battery-run CD players with earphones. Santa could get Henry into the unfolded chair, place the simulator, then wheel him out of the ward. Any passing employee would think nothing of Santa taking some old gaffer for a ride."

Ben nodded with enthusiasm. "You've got it! You have definitely got it! Now, how do we infiltrate the ranks of Santas? When you worked there did they use staff?"

Sharon shook her head. "I don't think so. They used an agency."

"I'll call Jim Bosworth at MassTemps. He owes us. We got his mother out six months ago and she's still going strong." Ben rang the number, then spoke rapidly to an underling at the employment agency. After some shouting, Ben's face relaxed.

"Hi, Jim. Ben Newmark here. Thanks for sparing me a sec. You sound busy as hell. What I need to know is, who supplies the Santas to Boston Muni tomorrow? . . . Uh, *you* do! Wonderful! Okay, here's what we need . . ." Ben explained the plan quickly. After he finished, he listened and made some notes. "Yeh, I'm going to go in. You'll need a pic for the phony ID, right? Oh, so we arrive at Boston Muni with beards, all dressed. So any ID will do then. Can you be sure I'll be assigned to the sixth floor? . . . Great. I'll be there tomorrow afternoon at three, ho-hoing my head off. See you then."

Ben spun around beaming at Sharon. "This is going to work, sweetie. Jim says the hospital has him assign the Santas, so he can put the best ones into the kids' wards and stick the old poops up in places like floor six where half the patients are ga-ga or completely out. I'm all set."

"Providing Manny can make the gadget by three tomorrow."

"Right," said Ben. "I'll get him. Pray he's not flying to Russia."

Reaching the Chief of Research at Meditronics took almost forty minutes of calling to his car phone, but eventually they reached him in Worcester. Ben quickly explained his ideas and needs. "You've got to put in an adjustable time-delay between the set time and the onset of the fibrillation signal. Up to a minute, maybe . . . great, great!"

Ben seized Sharon's hand and leaned to give her a kiss. "He'll work on it tonight and get it to us tomorrow morning. They have a kid on a motorcycle who gets things around the city fast. And he's sending a straight healthy-heart simulator plug for Henry's room. Now, what else?"

"Where does that elevator go?"

Ben busied himself with the computer keyboard, bringing up each lower floor in turn. "Okay, the shaft terminates in the sub-basement, where they get truck deliveries. See, there's a loading bay you can back the ambulance up to. Nobody will think much about that. You could be there to retrieve a chair or a stretcher that went with an emergency case into the operating room."

Ben enlarged the map to show the surrounding streets, then copied the image on his printer. "There's the approach map. I'd come in here off the Artery, then go there."

Sharon thoughtfully studied the map. "I think I should get on the old uniform and go in tonight, Ben. I'll take my car and put it in the employee lot. We've got stickers. I'll change my hair and do some other disguise stuff. When do you figure to bring him out?"

"Let's see. Visiting starts at seven in the evening, and Jim said the Santas are supposed to be up in the wards by six. It'll be good and dark by six-thirty, so sometime between then and seven I'll get Henry into the elevator."

"Then I'll go in tonight at that time and see how busy that sub-basement is."

"Okay. All we need now is Juan. He should be home. He's a second-shift attendant. I'll let him figure out where to get the chair and how to get it into Henry's room. I should think five or so tomorrow afternoon would be good. Henry gets his food then, but the attendants do all that and they wouldn't think anything was funny if they noticed a chair folded in Henry's room. When do they medicate him?"

Sharon leaned and poked at the computer keys, then peered at the lines of print scrolling downward. "Two in the afternoon, then nine at night, so if Henry is discreet, there shouldn't be any unexpected nurse visits at the crucial time." She paused, then turned to look into Ben's face, her own long forehead now furrowed. "Ben, when that fibrillation alarm goes off and the nurses push the panic button to call the resuscitation team to the ward, that alarm will ring at security too. And the call being from the sixth floor will set them moving as well as the team. You know that's true!"

"Right, but we will already be moving. They have no idea what we're doing or if we're there at all. With any luck, we're out of there before they realize the injuns are in among the wagons."

Sharon sniffed. "Keep talking. If that lard-ass security boss is any good, he'll have his goons block the parking-lot exits when the balloon goes up. No amount of flashing lights and siren wails will get us past cars broadsided on those ramps!"

Ben shook his head. "I'm telling you, we're going to be out of there before he can do that kind of stuff."

Sharon Goodspeed sighed, leaned forward, and gave Ben a long kiss. "You'd like to have been a hero, like Henry, wouldn't you, baby?

Saving those guys who were burning up? Standing at attention on the White House lawn?"

Ben grinned and shrugged. "I'm not much where pain is concerned. Maybe that's why I like helping old folks avoid it. But the hero, the medal part, I wouldn't mind that a bit."

Sharon smiled back. "When that spunky old lady says, 'Thanks, you were great, Ben,' I don't think you'll need a medal."

4

"We're getting your husband out around seven tonight," said Ben Newmark to Anne the next morning. "How did the lawyer thing go?"

"Just as you predicted. But the young man was very sympathetic and enthusiastic, so I didn't have to shout much. He called me this morning and said they had Henry's records and that he would be taking them to an alternative doctor today and if there was agreement that the bypass should be delayed, he would be in court after a restraint next Monday morning."

"Don't put hopes on that, Anne. If they schedule Henry for six A.M. Monday, the operation will be history before the court opens." Ben's voice was sharp.

"Ben, I'm only telling you what the lawyer told me. If Henry can come out tonight, I want that more than anything else."

Ben leaned to pat her hand. "Sorry, Anne, doing these rescues has made me wary of the legal bullshit. You can't trust it." He smiled to reassure her. "Anyway, Sharon is out checking on our rescue vehicle, and I've written Henry a note which you should give him this afternoon. While he reads it, you can talk about what the lawyer told you, emphasizing that the young man genuinely believes he can stop the bypass operation and eventually get Henry out of Boston Muni. Now, I'll read it to you to be sure you understand what will happen."

As Ben read the note aloud, explaining about the heart-beat simulators and the role of Santa, Anne's eyes grew even wider than they had the day before. "My goodness," she said finally, "It's sort of like one of those spy movies on TV, or those old James Bond reruns, isn't it?"

Ben waved his hands rapidly and horizontally as though he were rubbing out spots. "Nothing like those things. Nothing! We hope it will be so quietly done that the nurses won't miss Henry until his nine o'clock medication."

Anne peered at him. "What is the chance of this working, Ben?" Her face was old, her expression dark.

"I'll make it work. Now, when you go home this afternoon, someone will be there to pick you up. Do you have any pets or things that need doing at your house? You may be gone a week." She shook her head.

Ben got to his feet and, as she rose, took her hands in both of his. "We've done this stuff plenty of times. It's a piece of cake!" But he saw that her thoughts were elsewhere and her concern all-encompassing.

At five-thirty that night, a line of nine identical Santas waited patiently in an employee lounge at Boston Muni to be given their pack of presents and sent off to their assigned floors. When Ben reached the bored, middle-aged lady in charge, he was handed a plastic pack and a sixth-floor map with a patient list. "About a third of the people on this floor will not be in very good shape to accept their present or even know what it is," she said. "Just do your best. They need cheering up."

Ben nodded and gave her a cheery wave, then stumped off to an elevator. The sixth floor was quiet, only two student nurses coming toward him heading for their supper. "Ho-ho-ho, my dears!" he boomed at them and they waved and smiled back as they walked into the elevator.

At the nurses' station, Ben carefully consulted the floor map while looking about, as if he were attempting to orient himself. It was 6:10 and he had about a half hour to kill, so he decided to start down the row of rooms across from the row containing Henry. Several of the patients were awake and talkative, so that by 6:35 he was still two rooms away from Henry's. The first room had an oblivious patient, and Ben noted where the heart monitor cord plugged into the wall. In the next room a bird-like, ancient lady was picking at her supper and he ducked past before she noticed him. He darted into Henry's room and began his "Ho-ho-ho," as he snatched out the collapsed wheelchair left by Juan behind the screen, unfolded it, and pushed it over to the bed.

"And what can Santa bring you this Christmas, ahhh . . . Professor Hastings?" he rumbled, as if he were looking closely at a list to get the name right.

"What about a right leg, Santa?" said Henry Hastings, his old face alight with interest and hope as he intently watched Ben unplug his heart monitor and simultaneously plunge the simulator, built into an identical plug, back into the wall.

"Well, well, Professor. That's sort of a tough request. Have to talk to the elves about that, I think. What would you like your leg made of, I wonder? What about ebony or mahogany . . .?" He was hurriedly shifting Henry from the bed to the wheelchair.

"What about whalebone, Santa. That would be different," said Henry as Santa threw an open sweater around his shoulders.

"Aye, want to be Captain Ahab, do ye?" said Ben in his best Yankee sailor accent. "We'll see if the elves can find the bone from a white whale, matey." He tossed a folded blanket over Henry's knees.

"The Moby Dick that took my leg is all around us, Santa," and Henry's voice was suddenly sharp and bitter. "We're living in the belly of the beast at this very moment . . ."

But Ben now wheeled him nearer the door and gave him a warning shake of the head. "I'll stop back later, Professor," he said in his heartiest tones. "A Merry Christmas to you, sir."

Ben darted back down the corridor but this time he could not get by the lady who had been eating her supper. "Yoo-hoo, Santa," came a high, cracked voice.

He rushed into her room beaming and ho-hoing. "A little something for you, my dear Mrs. Rutledge," he said as he handed over a package. But Mrs. Rutledge was not going to miss a chance at conversation, and Santa found himself hearing about her medical prognosis, her special diet, her doctor's qualities, and her grandchildren. Santa, sneaking a look at his watch, saw it was already almost seven, but the grandchildren saved him.

"Are they coming in to see you tonight?" he asked, pulling impatiently at his beard.

"Oh yes," said Mrs. Rutledge. "My son is giving them my presents early and they're going to bring them in."

"Why don't I come back later?" said Santa, backing toward the door. "I can say hello to them and find out what else they might like. You can introduce me as your own private Santa."

"What a wonderful idea!" beamed Mrs. Rutledge.

"I'd best see to some of the others then, so I'll have more time for your youngsters. . . ." and he backed through the door and turned to dash down the hall to the next room.

In a single gesture, he pulled the comatose old man's heart monitor plug out of the wall, shoved the simulator in, then popped the other plug back on top. Manny had cunningly made this simulator so small that it hardly showed when fitted between the receptacle and the standard hospital plug. Ben had set the time delay for thirty seconds.

He peeped out the door in both directions, saw nobody, and darted two doors up to Henry, putting a finger to his lips as though he were about to rise up a non-existent chimney. He stared tensely at his watch as time crawled by. An eon later the low, insistent warning beep of the monitor alarm at the nurses' station began to sound. This is when your stomach really goes empty, thought Ben, as his heart paced the steady beep-beep-beep.

Two nurses dashed out of the station and around the corner while Santa's heart fell into his phony black plastic boots. There had been three women at the station when he came into the ward.

But then the third one came racing by, an electronic resuscitation suitcase in her hand. As she turned into the room two doors down, he wheeled Henry into the corridor and set off in the other direction. They rounded the station and moved quickly down a long corridor that went off at right angles to the one from the main elevators. Behind them, an emergency team dashed by and Ben wanted to run too but he forced himself to keep to a brisk walk.

They finally reached the service elevator and Ben pressed the call button. Sharon had said the elevator moved like a snail and the two men watched, in total silence, as the indicator left its upper pin and swung slowly, agonizingly slowly, downward. At last the arrow reached six and the big door groaned ponderously back.

And there before them, smiling and confident, stood Ralph Steen in his three-piece grey suit and the bull-necked guard who had confronted the Hastings two days before.

"Well, well," said Steen to them. "Santa Claus, no less. You people are getting so clever and tricky . . ."

But he did not continue this sarcasm because Henry Hastings had taken out from under the blanket covering his legs a large, old, but rather deadly-looking forty-five service automatic. "Shut up and move back in the car, you two!" Henry's voice was a hiss of menace. "Up against the back wall . . . as they say in the cop shows."

The two men stood in shocked silence, not moving. Steen moved his hands as though to push away the gun. "Dr. Hastings . . . please . . . this is not . . ."

But Henry now put his elbows on the chair arms and slid down in the seat so he could sight along the barrel of the pistol. "I'm dying. Killing you two would be a gift to humanity. Nothing, absolutely nothing, that I might suffer as a result would match what you and this place have planned for me. Hands on your heads and *move!*"

They backed up then and Henry, watching them closely, said in some impatience, "Santa?"

Ben Newmark was jolted from his shock-induced paralysis. "Yeh, sorry, Henry," and he pushed the chair into the deep elevator and hit the door-close and sub-basement buttons. Sharon had discovered that, if you continued to hold the door-close button in, the elevator would not stop at any other floor, and they moved slowly downward.

Ralph Steen continued to shake his head. "Dr. Hastings, I know you are not well, but we are here to help you, to make you well, to give you life. . . ." As he said this he dropped his hands to his side and began to move forward.

The old Colt went off with a shocking, enormous slam and a shower of sparks flew from the back wall of the elevator next to Steen's head. "Against the wall, I said, Steen," came Henry's old, hard voice. "I missed you then because I intended to. That was your last chance unless you pay attention. . . ." At that moment the elevator stopped and the door opened while everybody's ears rang.

"Which way, Santa?" said Henry without shifting his eyes.

"To your right," answered Ben in a breathless whisper.

"Roll me back then," responded Henry, "So they can't get close. Okay, you two, come on out and go to your left," and the little parade began a long walk down a dim and empty corridor. Around a corner they came to a loading bay, big open doors, and Sharon in a wig and a natty E.M.T. uniform staring at them in suspended amazement. A dark rescue-squad ambulance waited, backed against the elevated apron, its rear doors open.

"Stop!" said Henry in a sudden bark. "Wheel me backwards into that thing, Santa." After he was up at the cab end he waved the gun muzzle. "You two. Get in here. Quick!"

The two men moved slowly into the ambulance and Henry now pointed the gun muzzle in a downward direction. "Shut the doors and sit on the floor. Come on!" As the doors were pulled shut Henry let out his breath in a gasp of urgent command. "Move it, Santa! Get out of here!"

The ambulance accelerated quickly up the ramp, through a parking lot and up another ramp. As they headed toward the Artery, Henry turned his head slightly, still intently watching the two men sitting on the floor. "I don't know where you're going," he said to Ben, "But maybe there's some place along the way we can set this pair adrift, sort of away from phones and houses?"

Ben leaned forward to talk to Sharon through the window to the driver's cab, then turned and whispered in Henry's ear. "Thirty to forty minutes," and Henry nodded.

"Well, we have some time to discover how you people knew so quickly that I was leaving. Did you just happen to be making an elevator inspection at that moment, or what?"

They stared at him sullenly and said nothing. Henry gripped the gun with menacing intent and narrowed his eyes to sight more carefully along the barrel. "If I shoot you, Steen, in one of your beefy thighs, you won't die but you will sure as hell hurt. I ask you again, how did you know we were coming to use that elevator?"

Steen's tone was a self-righteous whine. "When you talked to your wife on the phone two nights ago, she mentioned the name of Betty Freeman. Mrs. Freeman is in our computer as an agent of the group that is doing this kidnapping of sick patients so their relatives can save money. So we knew you would be coming," he indicated Santa. "And we soon realized that if anything unusual happened on the sixth floor, you would probably have to use the freight elevator to get out. When the call for an emergency team reached us, we got in the elevator and waited for you to bring us down, as you did."

"Room taps, phone taps, computer lists of enemies, young thugs to terrorize old people . . ." Henry curled his lip. "But this isn't the Communist party or the Nixon White House. You're supposed to be an organization devoted to service, to healing . . ."

The two men on the floor said nothing and they rode in silence toward Cape Cod. Beyond Plymouth, Sharon turned off the main road and headed into the dark surroundings of the state forest. In the middle of a long dirt road she came to a stop. "We're out in the wilds," she said quietly through the rear window.

Henry sighted carefully along his gun again. "Reach up, each of you, and open those doors. . . . That's it. Now . . . climb out backwards. Right. Now, start running down that road, straight away from us."

Ralph Steen lifted grasping hands toward Henry. "Dr. Hastings, please, you're making a terrible mis—"

The gun went off with a flat, jolting explosion and the two men dashed away. "Go, Sharon!" shouted Ben as he lunged to shut the rear doors and almost fell out as the ambulance spun its wheels and shot off in the opposite direction to the running men.

Everything was quiet for a few minutes as Sharon regained the main road again and headed for the Canal. Ben finally peeled off his glued-on beard and shook his head. "Wow!" was all he could say.

Henry stared down at the gun, now lying in the blanket over his lap. "I wouldn't have shot them, you know. No matter what happened, I couldn't do that. The gun was for me alone . . . if things deteriorated. Maybe I could have killed myself . . . maybe not."

Ben nodded. "Anne brought the gun in?"

"This afternoon," said Henry. "She promised months ago she would do that if I insisted, which I did when she first wrote me yesterday that you folks were going to try to get me out."

Ben shrugged. "Hey, it worked. We would have never gotten out without it . . ." his voice trailed weakly away.

Henry smiled at him. "I'm sure you've rescued people with past lives more active than mine, Ben. A professional philosopher may not be a soldier of fortune or a secret agent, but ideas of personal control, of self-worth, are central to my life. We don't make good patients, I'm afraid, always wondering about ethics and a healer's motives. When I realized that the agenda of Boston Municipal, as far as I was concerned, was to use me rather than to heal me, it was intolerable!" He paused, then peered intently at Ben. "Yes, I would have killed myself. I'm sure of that."

Ben Newmark, trying to imagine a patient's suicide with a firearm in the middle of an escape attempt, said nothing and spent the rest of the ride taking deep, grateful breaths.

The ambulance crossed the northern Canal bridge and headed along back roads bordering Cape Cod Bay. They finally bumped down a dirt road, the ocean ahead, and came to a stop in front of a big, modern, one-story summer home perched on a bluff and looking out at a full half-circle of ocean and stars.

As Ben and Sharon huffed the wheelchair down a retractable ramp, Anne dashed out and bent to seize her husband in a passionate hug. "Henry, dear Henry! Was it awful?"

Henry looked up at her with a lopsided grin. "It was exciting, Annie." She saw the gun in his lap and nodded with a shiver.

They wheeled him up a ramp into the wide living room with its glass doors leading to an open deck.

"Fitz brought me here," said Anne, now smiling and completely happy. "He's going to be your new doctor-of-record."

Dr. Fitzgerald Hamilton was a tall, distinguished sixty-year-old who came up on the other side of the wheelchair. He leaned and patted Henry's shoulder. "Long time, no see, old friend. How do you actually feel, Henry?"

"Like a kid," said Henry grinning up at him. "Well . . . like a kid with one leg. Listen, wheel me out on that deck, you two. I never thought I'd see the stars like this again. Look at that spangle! What a marvel!"

The three stood looking up from the deck when Ben and Sharon came out to them. Ben had shed his Santa stomach and he put his hand on Henry's shoulder. "Fitz called us and said he wanted to do this, Henry. He's taking a chance with the medical society. They're after the docs who take over with the rescued patients."

Fitzgerald chuckled. "Let's not concern ourselves with the behavior of insect life, Ben."

Henry sighed and looked up from one to the other. "Using that gun has compromised you people, hasn't it? Especially in this state."

Ben shrugged. "I doubt it. Fatso Steen and his crowd aren't likely to go to the law about this episode. Think of the newspapers, 'Distinguished Professor Forced to Shoot His Way out of Boston Muni.' That's a headline they don't need!"

"Well," said Anne in sudden excitement. "Then why don't *you* tell the papers, Ben? There must be some people you've saved who have relatives in TV or the newspaper business."

Ben shook his head. "You two don't have much time together. I wouldn't think of putting you through something like that."

Henry reached to take Ben's hand. "Would that help, Ben? If we went public. Would it do any good?"

The idea hit Ben like a stroke of lightning. "Yeh . . . yeh, I think it would! We'd have to get you out of the state first. They would probably let you plead to a lesser charge on the firearms offense, Henry, like they do with the kids in Roxbury that shoot each other. You wouldn't do the mandatory one-year sentence, but they would sure charge you and get you into court."

"We could take them to the Connecticut place, on the Sound," said Sharon excitedly. "Set up secret meetings with the TV talk-showpeople. This state would never dare try to extradite, but all that hocus-pocus with go-betweens and limos with dark windows gets everybody stirred up."

"Right!" Ben's eyes were bright and he dashed around in front of them all. "I'll call a *Globe* editor, give him an anonymous interview. We've got to find that picture of you and Mrs. Roosevelt. It must be in dozens of morgue files. . . ."

"Waiting for my obituary," said Henry in a dry, amused voice.

"But imagine it five columns wide . . . on more front pages than the first time around," breathed Ben. "Can we say the gun was for suicide in case of failure, because you felt abandoned due to the state's appalling failure of medical ethics?"

"Absolutely," said Henry. "I'll say that myself if you can get Annie and me on TV."

"And as Henry's personal physician," said Fitz Hamilton in a mock-stern voice, "I will certify that not only is Henry of sound mind, but that he remains the same sensible, courageous man who was kissed by Mrs. Roosevelt those many years ago."

Ben was running his hands through his white, Santa hair and the hands now shook in pure excitement. A dozen schemes and images ran through his mind, multiple visions of total victory. "They'd *never* stand against that, *never!* The legislature, the courts, the medical societies, the health lobbies. They'll be groveling, crawling to get out from under a pile of do-do higher than Mount Everest!"

"Dear Ben, of course we'll do that," said Anne, coming up to kiss his cheek. "We owe you that and much more. Great victories are never denied a bold commander!"

And as they stood, grinning at each other, visualizing a success beyond former hope, beyond earlier imagining, Sharon came to put an arm around Ben on his other side. "When the distinguished membership of our esteemed State Legislature repeals the Hospital Reform Act, as they surely will, our little organization is finished too. What will we do then?"

Ben leaned to give her a tender kiss. "I don't know about you," he said with a wink, now looking down at his collapsed and disheveled Santa outfit, "But I thought I made a convincing Santa. I just might make a career of it . . . ," and as they all laughed, he shrugged and winked again. "The pay isn't much, but you sure can't beat the vacations."

A Christmas fairy tale.

EASY AS PIE

Rudy Rucker

In a far corner of a distant galaxy spins planet X, a place quite similar to our wonderful Earth. Like Earth, X is in a planetary system with a chaoticity of six parts per million and, like Earth, X orbits its sun in the third resonance band of its planetary system's attractor.

Planet X wears a lifeweb much like our holy Gaia, mother of life. Planet X once had a living neighbor, a planet Y, but eons and eons ago, the lost inhabitants of Y mastered direct matter control—and ended up by turning themselves and their planet into a great band of dust.

Each year there is a day when planet X is the farthest from its sun and the closest to the orbit of the shattered planet Y. The people of planet X call this day Xday, and they cheer themselves through it with eating, drinking and the giving of gifts.

This is the story of what happened one Xday season to a selfish peasant named Karl and to his kind, long-suffering wife Giselle.

Karl and Giselle's hut was on the outskirts of a large ugly city. As a young man, Karl had been lively and wise, but time had crusted his heart over with self-indulgence and idle lechery. With his and Giselle's children grown and gone, Karl's only remaining smiles were for dancing-girls, for smoke, and for drink.

Like many women, Giselle thought first and foremost of her family and her home. If Karl was increasingly unpleasant to live with, there were still things to be set right in their hut and, above all, there was the Xday visit of the children to prepare for.

Six weeks before Xday, Giselle began talking to Karl about the coming holiday. Karl tried to put her off with sullen grimaces and discouraging words, but Giselle kept up her happy plans and chatter. What Giselle thought, she frankly said, and now she was thinking about the holiday.

"You say we can't afford a goose, but at least we have to put up some garlands, Karl. And the hut needs to be cleaned from top to bottom."

"Oh, what for? The hut looks fine. And you didn't like the garlands I put up for you last year."

"I think that this year we'll use ivy for the garlands," continued Giselle. "Ivy will stay nice and green."

"Where are we supposed to find ivy?"

"Don't you remember? There's a big patch of ivy near the top of Summer Hill! When the children were younger, you and I used to walk there with them all the time. It's not far. Come, Karl, let's go to Summer Hill and gather ivy."

"You're always asking for something, Giselle. I'm about to go to the inn. I'll get ivy another day. Or *you* get it."

"The inn is what you love, Karl, and I don't begrudge you; you worked hard for many years. Now you're an idle red-faced lecher who stares at hussies, fine. Nobody's perfect. But come with me to Summer Hill for an hour now." Giselle smiled fetchingly at Karl and ran her gentle hand across his stubbled cheek.

"I'm not a red-faced lecher," blustered Karl.

"Then don't act like one. The inn's empty at this time of day anyway. If you go there now, you'll be a *desperate* red-faced lecher." Giselle laughed so merrily that Karl's anger was undone.

Karl and Giselle left their hut and wound their way through their neighbor's huts and up the slopes of Summer Hill. Soon there were no more dwellings. Hilltops were viewed as sacred on planet X, and all hilltops were left empty for the wind, the people, and the Gaia of X.

As they gathered ivy high on the hill, the peasant couple could see out over the great imperial city of Mur which lay to their north. In the center of Mur rose the far tiny spires of the emperor's palace. The air near the palace was enlivened by the comings and goings of the gleaming metal flying saucers that the emperor Klaatu and his court used.

Karl and Giselle had often been into the city for market day, but neither of them had ever stood directly before the imperial palace. Peasants were not much welcomed in Mur outside the market district, and a peasant who tried to walk all the way to the palace was likely to be beaten and robbed—if not by a thief then by an officer of the imperial watch.

Though his palace was off-limits to the peasants, the emperor's airships often came to claim goods from the market. Over the years many of the great silvery saucers had grown to a size of over fifty feet across—yes, *grown*. The metal saucers were living things that grew and learned and eventually died. The saucers' silver surfaces were intricately chased with filigreed coppery lines that branched and intertwined as a saucer grew. No two saucers were quite the same. With exercise, polishing, and plenty of sunshine, a flying saucer could grow for many a year, perhaps as much as two centuries. When a saucer got quite old, its skin would thin out to nothingness and the whole thing would suddenly crumble into a drifting dust like mushroom spores.

Where did the saucers come from? They spawned on the ribs of planet X herself. Every few years in some deep cave of planet X—and never twice the same cave—a few baby saucers would be found stuck to the walls like limpets. All saucers that were found became the property of the Klaatu dynasty. And the finder—invariably a hardy young peasant—would be granted imperial favor, a purse of gold, and the rank of baroness or baronet.

The sages of planet X classified the saucers as Spore Magic. Spore Magic included all the inexplicable events that had puzzled the citizens of X throughout history. The fact was that very odd things happened regularly on planet X—especially around Xday.

When the bright shape came flying down at Karl and Giselle on Summer Hill, they may have thought for an instant that it was a saucer—but it was a goose with snowy white plumage and a wedge-shaped orange beak. The goose stood there on her orange webbed feet, curving her neck this way and that, looking at Karl and Giselle.

Finally she began slowly to waddle about, pecking up snails from beneath the ivy.

"Catch the goose, Karl," exclaimed Giselle. "We can eat her on Xday!"

Karl was reluctant. The goose looked alert and powerful. Karl didn't much fancy being pecked, clawed, and wing-beaten by the beast. "Why can't our Xday meal be turnips like it is every other day?" said Karl. "Leave the goose alone, Giselle. They'll have goose at the inn on Xday in any case. If I happen to go there, I can bring a wing home for you."

"Selfish old fool," said Giselle. "*I'll* catch the goose."

Giselle marched towards the plump white bird. Far from looking alarmed, the goose looked interested. She stuck her neck up to full height and regarded Giselle. The goose had shiny blue eyes. Giselle made feeding motions with her fingers, though she had no food to give. "Nice goosey loosey goosey girl," sang Giselle. "Goose, goose, goose!"

The goose honked, and when Giselle turned and walked away from her, the goose followed. When Karl, Giselle, and goose were down among the huts, the goose willingly jumped into Giselle's arms and let herself be carried back to the peasant couple's hut.

Giselle cut a turnip into small bits and fed the bits to the goose, who gobbled them down avidly, stretching out her neck to swallow each morsel. Before letting the goose go outside, Giselle tied a heavy stone to one of the goose's legs. Slowly dragging the stone, the goose waddled about the yard, contentedly rooting for slugs, bugs, and snails.

"What a beautiful bird, Karl!" exclaimed Giselle. "We'll fatten her till the day before Xday, and then you can butcher and bleed her for me. I'll pluck, singe, draw, and cook her! We'll have goose for Xday! The children will be thrilled!"

"I hope Tolstan, the cook at the inn, can help me with the butchering," grumbled Karl. "I don't know anything about killing a goose. Yes, I'd better go talk to Tolstan."

"That's fine, Karl, but before you go off to the inn, I still want you to help me put up the ivy."

"Will you never be done, woman?" cried old Karl, but help with the ivy he did, and only then, finally, could he go to the inn to smoke and drink and stare at women until it was time to totter home and fall into his and Giselle's bed.

In the coming days, the goose became more and more Giselle's pet. The goose quickly found a way to free her foot from the rope and stone, and could easily have flown away—but she chose not to. At every hour of the day she was inside or outside the peasant couple's hut. When Giselle was active in the hut, the goose would honk plaintively until Giselle would pull aside the hut's wicker door and let the goose in. Once in the hut, the goose delighted in following Giselle, who often fed the goose scraps. The goose liked meat as well as vegetables, indeed she would even eat small pebbles and pieces of wood. Not that the goose was going hungry—the more time she spent in the hut, the more snails and bugs there seemed to be on the hut's floor. Giselle noticed that, for a special wonder, the goose seemed to know not to foul the floor, no matter how much she ate.

A few days later, Karl was due to pay off his quarterly debt at the inn. He and Giselle dug their small bag of savings out from under a stone at the back of the hearth. There was no way to reach the hoard without getting ashes all over oneself, which was the peasant couple's way of being sure that neither of them dipped into the savings alone.

The small leather bag held some silver and copper coins saved from Karl's occasional earnings, along with sixteen gold coins that remained from the inheritance which Giselle's parents had left her several years before. Ever since Giselle got her inheritance, Karl had worked as little as possible. He thought of Giselle's money as his own.

As was their custom, Karl and Giselle spread the coins out on the table and counted them together, a ritual they went through each time the coins appeared from beneath the stones of the hearth. The goose stood next to the table, watching with glittering eyes.

"Let me take a gold coin to the inn," wheedled Karl when they were done counting. "Then I'll have credit clear into the spring."

"Very well," said Giselle. "And I'll take a gold coin to spend on gifts for the children."

"One silver coin would be more than enough for them, woman!" snapped Karl. "The children are grown; they should take care of themselves!"

"It's my gold, Karl. You should be grateful that I'm so foolishly generous to you."

"Then I get some coppers as well," shouted Karl. "I earned the copper and silver in the turnip harvest this fall!" Giselle nodded curtly, and slid two gold coins and three coppers to one side of the table.

Leaning forward, the two peasants began telling the remaining coins back into the bag.

But now all at once the goose darted forward and gulped down the two gold coins, pumping her neck to get the hard metal disks all the way down from craw to crop to gizzard.

"No, Goosey!" cried Giselle.

"Grab her," said Karl, drawing his knife. "I'll cut her open!" The goose made a frightened noise like a rusty metal hinge, and waddled rapidly out of Karl's reach.

"Stop, Karl!" cried Giselle. "She can't digest gold. The coins are safe in her stomach. It's still four days until Xday. If we butcher Goosey now, her meat will spoil."

"What if she shits the coins into the street?"

"I'll make a nest for her inside our hut," said Giselle. "Anyway, haven't you noticed? Goosey never shits. She just grows."

"Well, nobody's taking any *more* of our gold," snapped Karl. He pocketed his three coppers, swept the remaining coins into the little sack, tied the sack tight, and crawled into the hearth to bury the sack again. "The inn's coin and the children's presents will have to wait until your precious goose is ready," he told Giselle. And then Karl went down to the inn to spend his coppers.

The next morning, Giselle found four gold coins in the nest beneath the goose. She bit them and rang them; they seemed true as any coin. Karl, waking late, sat up blinking to stare at Giselle. "What's happened?"

"The goose, Karl! She turned our two coins into four!"

"What!" The old peasant sprang out of bed to see. Four bright coins lay in Giselle's dainty hand.

"Give me my two," demanded Karl.

"You get *one*, Karl," said Giselle and gave it to him. "I'll keep one for the children, and I'll feed these other two to Goosey to see if it works again! Then we'll have *four* extra gold coins! Here, Goosey!"

Karl watched excitedly as the goose ate two gold coins from Giselle's hand. He stayed in the hut at Giselle's side all day, and finally, near dusk, the goose gave a warbling honk and rose to her feet. Gold glittered from the goose's nest—and this time it was not just four coins, it was a heap that Karl feverishly counted as seventeen coins! Their fortune had more than doubled in one day!

Karl snatched up two gold coins for his own and hurried off to the inn, leaving Giselle to hide the new treasure. Once at the inn, Karl behaved very foolishly: he got drunk and began bragging about his white goose that laid golden coins. One of the emperor's soldiers happened to hear him, and the next morning Karl awoke from his sodden slumber to hear Giselle arguing with someone while angry Goosey made her rusty hinge sound.

"It's just an ordinary goose," Giselle was saying. "We caught her on Summer Hill."

"The goose may be Spore Magic," came the stranger's voice. "I'm here to claim her for the emperor."

Any miracle that might be as valuable as the flying saucers was called Spore Magic. And, by ancient imperial decree, all Spore Magic was the property of the Klaatu dynasty.

Goosey came running to the corner of the hut where Karl lay. *If the goose is Spore Magic like the saucers*, thought Karl, *then the emperor will grant imperial favor to the one who brings her to him*. Karl grabbed Goosey in his arms and went out to face the stranger.

It was a young knight of the emperor's guard, smartly dressed in flowing silks and furs. One of the emperor's flying saucers rested in the dirt of the peasants' yard; the saucer was a young twenty-footer, still but lightly filigreed. All the peasants from the neighborhood had gathered, or were still gathering, to watch. None of the emperor's saucers had ever landed here before, and none of the peasants had ever been inside a saucer.

"I will come with you to bring the goose to the palace," said Karl, his voice trembling at the enormity of the proposal.

"No, Karl," cried Giselle. "The goose is mine. And I fed her two more coins this morning."

"Silence," said Karl. "We cannot argue with the emperor. I will bring the goose to him, and he will grant me imperial favor. He will give me a bag of gold and the rank of baronet. Have a care, woman!" Karl held the goose tight and stepped away from Giselle.

The young knight looked at Karl doubtfully, but then said, "Very well. Carry the goose into the ship, peasant. But don't touch anything. You're filthy and you stink."

The inside of the saucer was of smooth silvery metal delicately veined with copper. There was a bulge in the wall that made a bench that ran all around the circular cabin. As well as the open arch of the cabin door, there were round, open portholes ranged along the walls. So as not to sully the fine fabric of the cushions on the seats, old Karl sat on the floor with Goosey cradled securely in his arms.

The knight controlled the saucer's flight simply by talking to it.

"Fly back to the courtyard of Emperor Klaatu's palace," said the knight, and the saucer lifted into the air. Wind whistled through the open door and portholes. The view was dizzying. What with the uneasiness in his stomach from last night's debauch, it was too much for Karl, and as the ship turned to angle down to the emperor's palace, he vomited between his legs onto the floor. Goosey pecked at the vomit.

"You cursed old fool," cried the young knight, and favored Karl with a sharp kick in the ribs. Karl endured the abuse with no complaint. At least he had now flown in one of the emperor's airships.

The saucer landed in the palace's walled courtyard. The knight called for a scullion to clean up Karl's mess, then led Karl across the courtyard and into the palace. Still clutched in Karl's arms, the goose turned her head this way and that, watching everything with her clear, blue-irised eyes.

The Emperor Klaatu was a small bald man with a dark beard and a penetrating gaze. Sitting at the emperor's side was his fool, or minister, a fat clean-shaven man with a loose smile.

"Is this the goose that lays golden coins?" demanded the emperor.

"Yes, sire," said Karl. "And I freely bring her to you. Will you grant me imperial favor?"

"Favor?" asked the emperor.

"A purse of gold," said Karl. "And I should like to be made a baronet. I could rule my neighborhood in the name of the empire. Even my wife would have to obey me." He bowed low and set the goose down on the floor at the emperor's feet.

The goose gave a rusty honk, waggled her bottom, and squeezed out a foul-smelling puddle that resembled Karl's vomit.

"I'm to grant a baronetage for goose-droppings?" roared the emperor. The fool, or minister, cuffed Karl on the head, and the knight screamed for a scullion to clean up the mess.

"I think you have to feed the goose gold coins first," stammered Karl. "She needs gold to make gold. She shits out copies of whatever you feed her. Do you have a coin you can feed her, sire? Or a large gem?"

"Oh, so I'm to give you jewels as well as gold?" cried the emperor. "Knight, lock this charlatan and his goose in the dungeon. If the goose lays no gold by tomorrow, then put them both to death. I'll have the goose roasted with turnips."

"Oh, wait, please wait," cried Karl, as all his courage fled from him. "If you want gold from the goose then you should cut her open right away. She still hasn't shit out the two coins my wife fed her this morning." The goose gave Karl a startled look as the peasant caught hold of her.

"Go on," Karl begged the knight, stretching out the goose on the floor with her neck in his left hand and her feet in his right. "Cut the goose in half with your sword, sir knight. Cut right where she's the fattest. I know there's gold in her. Take the gold and flog me and set me free. Please spare me, my lords, as it is nearly Xday. I thought the goose was Spore Magic. I meant no harm."

The emperor nodded to the knight, and the knight brought his razor sharp sword down on Goosey's back, quite severing her breast and head from her feet and tail. What a shriek the poor goose gave!

Instead of gushing blood, the cut surfaces of the goose's body were damp but firm, with the consistency and color of a ripe avocado. In the center of each surface was a hemispherical depression: Goosey was hollow at the center, hollow as an avocado without a pit. From the two halves of the cut-open cavity there oozed onto the stone floor a shiny fluid that quickly hardened into a puddle of gold.

Karl had let go of the goose as the sword struck. Now the goose's rear section rocked back and began waddling around on its feet, while the front section settled its flat cut surface onto the floor and began honking and beating its wings. As the seconds passed, the rear section bulged up its top surface to grow a new breast, neck and head. At the same time, the front half of the goose rose slowly up onto a fresh-grown belly and legs. The flesh and feathers of the geese flowed and shifted as these transformations happened, so that the two new geese were each of half the weight of the original goose, with each new goose being about four-fifths the original size.

One of the geese hopped onto the emperor's lap, and the other one waddled over to Karl.

"You . . . you see!" blustered the peasant. "The goose *is* Spore Magic. And look!" He leaned forward and pried the golden, somewhat vomit-reeking, puddle off the floor and presented it to the emperor. "Here is your gold, sire. Now please let me go home. My family needs me for Xday. Oh please, sire, let me go to them. I love them so."

"Very well," said the emperor. "But I will keep both of the magic geese. And you shall receive no gold, nor any baronetage. You have tried my patience too sorely."

So Karl spent Xday with his family, laughing and feasting on a roast goose—which Giselle bought from a poultry dealer. So relieved was he to be alive that old Karl opened up his heart to his loved ones as never before—and the good feelings lasted on through the rest of the year.

And the emperor? The emperor grew ever richer as he ran the contents of the royal treasury over and over through the bodies of his ever-growing flock of repeatedly subdivided magic geese, who stayed with him for a whole year. But on the eve of the next Xday, the geese herded the emperor, and all his family, and all his court, into the emperor's flying saucers and flew them away forever—easy as pie. With no more emperors, planet X became a more sacred place.

Hail Gaia, full of synchronicity, the universe is with thee. Blessed art thou amongst dynamical systems, and blessed are thy strange attractors. Holy Gaia, mother of life, pray for us sinners, now and at the hour of our death, Amen.

THE TAMERLANE CRUTCH

James Powell

Marley was dead, to begin with. There was no doubt whatever about that. Old Marley was as dead as a doornail. And when a man's partner is killed he's supposed to do something about it. It doesn't make any difference what you thought of him. He was your partner and you're supposed to do something about it. Ebenezer Scrooge, in nightcap, dressing gown and slippers, took another swallow of lukewarm gruel before moving closer to the tiny fire in the grate. The fog creeping through the keyhole had brought the frosty night in with it. Staring down into the flames, the miser reviewed the events of the calamitous day. How had it all begun?

Early that cold, bleak morning while Scrooge sat busy in his countinghouse office, door ajar to keep an eye on his clerk, Bob Cratchit, who would rather warm his fingers at the candle than copy letters, the door to the foggy courtyard had flown open. The handsome middle-aged woman who stepped inside had excited and gladsome eyes although the golden hair that peeked from under her bonnet carried a heavy burden of silver. All this Scrooge caught in one glance before returning to his banker's book. Scrooge had nothing against a pretty face. But such a visitor at this season usually meant he was about to be dunned by another charity such as this year's madcap project to provide every poor, able-bodied child in London with an orange on Christmas morning and every crippled one with a crutch. Scrooge regretted having instructed Cratchit to turn such busybodies away. He should've handled the matter himself. "Are there no prisons?" he'd have asked. "And the Union workhouses, are they still in operation? The treadmill and the Poor Law are in full vigor then?" And what could anyone answer to that?

He was interrupted from this pleasant reverie by Bob Cratchit. "A lady to see you, sir," said his clerk, adding a hasty, "on a matter of business."

"Have I the pleasure of addressing Mr. Scrooge or Mr. Marley?" asked the woman in a musical voice.

"Marley has departed," said Scrooge, without rising from his stool.

"My name is Dirndl Wunderlich, Mr. Scrooge. I understand you are a miser, quite a tight-fisted hand at the grindstone."

Scrooge bowed modestly, at once pleased and made wary by the flattery.

"I have arrived in your country in search of a man, a Muscovite who has come into possession of an heirloom belonging to my family. I am prepared to pay you the sum of twenty guineas for its recovery."

Scrooge sighed. "Let us not waste our time, Madame," he said. "We misers are not in the business of recovering things belonging to others." As he spoke he searched among the papers on his desk until he found the address of Messrs. Spade and Archer, two gentlemen considerably in arrears in what they owed the countinghouse. Making a mental note never again to loan out money to a man who called him "Sweetheart," Scrooge said, "However, let me put you in touch with two private investigators who will handle this matter quite to your satisfaction."

"Such people do not work on Christmas Eve, Mr. Scrooge," insisted Dirndl Wunderlich. "Misers do. Indeed, I understand you are a master at the art of extracting your due by threatening people with the law. I wish to rent that skill."

"For the sum of twenty guineas," added Scrooge.

The woman gave an eager nod. "Come, I'll lead you to the man this very minute. A while ago I left my hotel in search of a restaurant selling those new what-do-you-call-'ems, the fried meat patty on a bun."

Scrooge scowled. "Bah, hamburg," he said for he did not care for London's latest eating craze.

Miss Wunderlich continued. "Anyway, by some stroke of luck who should I see hobbling along in the fog ahead of me in Piccadilly Circus but my fat Muscovite. I followed at a distance, hoping he'd lead me back to his hotel where I could set someone like yourself on him. But he just kept walking around and around Piccadilly Circus. Finally I decided to chance it and dash here. If we move quickly . . ."

As she spoke the outer door flew open and there, an apparition against the palpable brown air swirling in the courtyard, stood a moaning figure with a face like a door knocker, a figure weighed down by chains, ledgers, padlocked cash boxes and heavy purses wrought in steel. Scrooge had always regretted Marley's tendency to flaunt his miserliness. "My partner," he explained to Miss Wunderlich.

"The departed Marley's ghost!" she gasped.

"Hardly," said Scrooge. "Jacob departed for home a while back to get some hot salt in a black sock for his toothache." Indeed Marley sported such a poultice in a folded kerchief bound round his head and chin. "Come in, Jacob," invited Scrooge. As he outlined Miss Wunderlich's offer, he gestured at his ledgers and added, "I've got my hands full here. But a bad toothache'll put you in just the mood to shake a Muscovite loose from ill-gotten gains."

Marley rolled his eyes and, groaning like a spectre, he followed the woman back out into the fog.

Several hours later, an astonished Scrooge was following a police constable's broad back through the cold, bleak, biting weather on his way to identify a murder victim believed to be his partner. Marley murdered? Jacob Marley dead?

The lamp outside the police station was a ruddy smear upon the fog. Inside the Day Inspector stood like a maître d' beside his reservations book. That gentleman put down his pen and giving Scrooge a look that said, "We know your kind, Mr. Scrooge. You'll get the table you deserve from us," he escorted the miser to an outbuilding in the yard, where Marley's body lay, eyes weighted down with two large pennies. "Found in an alley behind the Bristol Hotel. Do you know it, sir?"

Scrooge nodded. "A fleabag."

The Day Inspector's solemn nod confirmed this. "You will note, sir," he continued, "that the victim was shot twice. Once in the ankle and once in the heart. A peculiar thing that." Here the Day Inspector withdrew to give Scrooge a few moments to mourn his late partner.

Scrooge looked down at the dead body. Well, Jacob, he thought, you've been murdered. Tell me, what would you do about it if I was lying there and you were standing here? Nothing. There's no profit in sentiment. So why do I feel I should do something? Scrooge shrugged and, pocketing the two coins from the dead man's eyes as Marley would have done, he returned to the police station proper. The Day Inspector was waiting at the front door. As Scrooge passed the man held out his palm without speaking. Scrooge dutifully deposited the two large pennies there. Yes, they did know him around here.

Outside the fog and darkness had thickened. People ran about with flaring links, proffering their services to go before horses in carriages, and conduct them on their way. Foggier yet, and colder! The gruff old bell in the ancient tower of the church near the countinghouse struck the hour with tremulous vibrations as if its frozen teeth were chattering in its frozen head. In the main street before the courtyard labourers repairing the gas pipes had lighted a great fire in a brazier, round which a ragged party of boys were gathered, warming their hands and winking their eyes before the blaze in rapture.

As Scrooge passed a small man who had been watching these boys with considerable interest separated himself from the holly sprigs and berries of a poulterer's window and fell in step with the miser. "Mr. Scrooge," said the man in a high pitched thin voice, "My name is Niles Truck. I am trying to recover a crutch that has been—shall we say?—mislaid. I thought, and hoped, you could assist me."

Scrooge looked Truck up and down. He was a small-boned dark man of medium height with Levantine features. He wore gloves of yellow leather, fawn half-gaiters and a tight wool coat. The miser shook his head. "A person mislays a bumbershoot or a parasol or a walking stick," he insisted. "Not a crutch."

"Nevertheless, I'm prepared to pay one hundred guineas for its recovery," said Truck, as they turned into the countinghouse courtyard. "No questions asked."

"Who says I've got your damn crutch?" snapped Scrooge.

Truck answered by ramming a blunderbus barrel into the miser's kidneys. "Please clasp your hands together behind your neck," ordered the Levantine, prodding the miser forward through the countinghouse's chill outer room to the chill inner-office. With whining complaints about the English climate, Truck tried to light the candle with a trembling match.

Scrooge chose that moment to spin around, knock the blunderbus aside and apply the Penny Pincher's Nerve Pinch, one of the finest moves in the misers' martial arts arsenal. Truck slumped where he stood, the weapon slipping from his fingers. Holding the man up with one hand Scrooge rummaged through his pockets with the other, dumping their contents on the ledger open on his sloping desk. Then he forced Truck up onto a high stool and left him to recover. Rummaging through the items on the desk he found a Greek passport that identified Truck as a currant merchant. (Scrooge wondered if the man ever dealt in a new strain called the Humboldt, having himself lost a bundle a year or two ago investing in Humboldt currant futures. "Bah, Humboldt," he scowled.) The contents of the pockets also included a paper cone of violet pastilles and an advertising broadside. Sucking on a pastille Scrooge perused the announcement for the Christmas pantomime entitled "Ali Bow-Wow and the Forty Fleas," to be performed by the resident company in the lobby of the Bristol Hotel. Here Truck groaned, stirred and might have fallen from his perch if Scrooge hadn't cuffed him awake. "All right, Mr. Truck," he snarled. "Spill everything or you'll get another taste of the pinch."

Truck licked his lower lip nervously. Then the thin high-pitched words came tumbling out. "I was taking my morning constitutional in Piccadilly Circus when I saw her, Dirndl Wunderlich, the woman who stole the Tamerlane Crutch from me."

"The what?" demanded Scrooge.

"A priceless jewel-studded crutch with a provenance lost in the mists of history," said Truck, adding in a voice turned shrill, "But it belongs to me. It's mine! I paid for it with three years of shame, humiliation and ...." Strong emotion choked off the Levantine's words. He breathed deeply several times and went on in a more subdued voice. "Keeping my distance I followed the thieving woman around and around Piccadilly Circus for a good hour hoping she'd lead me to the crutch. But our first stop was when she broke off and led me here. Then I followed her and this old guy wearing a lot of chains and cash boxes back to Piccadilly Circus. Then they headed off to a rundown part of town and a hotel called the Bristol. Well, I waited in the street but they never reappeared. They must've slipped out the back." As he spoke Truck poked two fingers under his shirt and scratched absently. "So I came back here, hoping to pick up her trail again. I. . . ." Truck's eyes followed Scrooge's gaze as it moved from his scratching fingers to the broadside about Ali Bow-Wow and the Forty Fleas.

"You lying Levantine ankle-shooter," snarled Scrooge, knocking the little man off of the stool with a backhand slap. "You followed Marley into the hotel and out the back door. First you shot him in the ankle so he couldn't escape. Then you reloaded and shot him in the head." Scrooge advanced on the prostrate man. "Listen," he said, "when a man's partner is killed he's supposed to do something about it. It doesn't make any . . ."

"But why would I shoot him in the ankle first?" whined Truck, pushing himself backwards along the floor with his heels. "Why wouldn't I just shoot him in the head and get it over with?"

Scrooge stopped. The man had a point.

Truck sat up and rubbed his cheek. "Boy, I don't know how that 'ankle-shooting Levantine' crack ever got started. We really aren't that way," he insisted. "But, you're right, Mr. Scrooge. After a bit I did go into the hotel lobby. There was a very shaggy dog dressed in a big green turban and a red vest lying in one corner of the lobby while a modest crowd stared at it through rented magnifying glasses. When I saw the place had a back door to it I hurried out into the alley. But they were long gone. Then I saw a foot sticking out of the doorway. It was your partner, dead as a doornail."

"And where does the fat Muscovite fit in?"

Truck's olive features took on a grey cast and his eyes filled with fear. He scrambled to his feet. "Gutmanov? Gutmanov here?"

Jabbing a bony finger into Truck's chest Scrooge urged, "Do yourself a big favour. Tell me what's going on."

Truck thought a bit. Then he shrugged his shoulders and told his story. If the man was to be believed he had spent his life tracking the whereabouts of a mysterious object called the Tamerlane Crutch, collecting and cataloguing any shred of information, each rumor and every story no matter how wild. Suddenly one day all signs pointed to the island of Malta where a reclusive multimillionaire named Constantine lived with his very extensive crutch collection—no two alike—kept from rival collectors in a well-guarded vault deep in the cellars of his impregnable home. But Truck thought he'd concocted a way to penetrate the Constantine vault. To this end he spent three years touring the Mediterranean as a receiver with a troupe of low vaudevillians. Night after night he took custard pies in his face, was beaten about the head with rubber chickens and endured having his suspenders snipped with big shears to expose his bright underdrawers. At last the troupe was booked into Malta's Valletta Opera House. Constantine had a box seat for opening night for, as Truck had calculated, any man with so large a collection of rubber crutches would be a big fan of low vaudeville and could be expected to come backstage after the performance to meet the cast. But to Truck's dismay he saw Dirndl Wunderlich in the audience. If she'd followed him to Malta then Gutmanov, the fat Muscovite, couldn't be far behind. Truck had no time to lose. After the performance he showed enough interest in rubber crutches to earn an invitation to see Constantine's collection that very night.

The vault resembled a curative religious shrine with crutches hanging everywhere. After putting Constantine and the heavily armed watchman in stitches by stumbling around with rubber crutches in his armpit, Truck was rewarded with a conducted tour of the collection. The object he coveted so much was not behind glass with the finer pieces. Disguised with black paint it stood among others in an open barrel labelled "Assorted Novelty Items." The crutch was tagged, "Fifteenth Century item from Samarkand vicinity. Black enamel over raised baguette and cabochon design."

As he bid the millionaire good night Truck mentioned he had a crutch, an old family heirloom, which he would like to donate to the collection. When Constantine expressed interest Truck rushed back to his hotel and working from memory, built a reasonable facsimile of the crutch in the barrel. "Fifteenth Century Samarkand, you say?" said the doubtful collector the next evening. "Well, I could be wrong but I think I've got one of those. But let's take a look." Back down in the vault the millionaire quickly located the crutch in the barrel. "Thank you very much, young man," said Constantine with a shake of his head. "But 'no two alike' is my motto." Then while the watchman tried to doze in his chair in the corner and Constantine demonstrated some of his finer musical crutches Truck deftly switched his imitation for the real Tamerlane Crutch.

Back out on the narrow winding street it seemed to Truck that every passerby's glance pierced the crutch's black enamel to the treasure beneath, every shadow harboured a gang of thieves and each footstep behind him spoke menace. He sought out the brighter streets and came back to his hotel by a roundabout way. But as he stepped inside his room he was struck a great blow on the head. When he recovered consciousness the crutch was gone. The smell of Dirndl Wunderlich's edelweiss perfume still hung in the air. So the Levantine set out after her and his search had brought him to London.

At the conclusion of the story Scrooge showed Mr. Niles Truck the door, saying, "You want your damn crutch? Be at my apartment tonight at the stroke of twelve." Then, alone, he rubbed his stubbly chin and resolved to discover the identity of Marley's killer. A man should certainly do what he can to help a murdered partner find rest—provided it didn't cost him anything. Would Truck come at the appointed hour? If he did, Scrooge suspected that Dirndl Wunderlich and the fat Muscovite wouldn't be far behind.

Scrooge took another sip of gruel, scowled and spat it into the fire. The damn stuff was stone cold. How long had he been sitting there? And why did misers have to drink gruel? Why not a whisky of the Scottish persuasion? Scrooge had to smile at himself. No. Gruel came with the miser territory. He'd known that from the start. Years ago whenever his schoolmates talked about what they'd be when they grew up he'd always said, "A miser." How they'd laughed! Yet one of them wanted to be a surgeon and cut people up and another a soldier and blow strangers' arms off and a third a judge who'd make men dance at the end of a rope.

Scrooge pulled still closer to the fire but found small comfort there until among the little tongues of flame another scene from the past came to life again. He saw himself, Scrooge the young man, sitting in a bower with a beautiful young woman. It was Belle! Dearest Belle. No, he'd never forget that moment. She had just broken off their engagement. She wouldn't marry an aspiring miser. "But, Belle," he'd insisted, "you should love a man for what he is, not how he makes his livelihood. Come marry me. Be a miser's wife and live in a miser's house with all the miser's little children running around inside. Oh, what fun we'll have!" But Belle didn't share Scrooge's conviction that miserliness and laughter could go hand in hand. Had she been right? Could Scrooge's whole life have been a mistake?

At first, after their break-up, he'd fallen in with a crowd of young spendthrifts and prodigals. Who else would accept a man who never bought a round of drinks or picked up a dinner check? And when Scrooge's companions grew low on money he obligingly loaned them funds at as reasonable rates as they'd have found anywhere. But that man spoke true who said there was no better way to lose friends than by lending them money. Yes, being a miser proved a lonelier life than he'd expected. So he'd gone into partnership with Marley, thinking two misers might get along famously. But Dutch treat was tedious. Bah, humdrum, thought Scrooge. Yet in his heart of hearts he still thought that misers could have fun, too.

Suddenly the chimes of a neighbouring church struck twelve and roused Scrooge from his reverie. He'd left the apartment door unlocked for Truck. But even before the chimes died away the miser heard a foot and an active crutch approaching from room to room. Suddenly the door flew open and an immensely fat man with glossy cheeks, a tall fur hat and one foot swathed in bandages limped into the room with the help of a black crutch. The man's face brightened when he saw Scrooge. "Allow me to introduce myself, sir. I am Caspar Gutmanov. We begin well, sir. A man who locks his doors reveals a suspicious nature. Suspicion breeds treachery." The Muscovite looked around the room warily. "I'd hoped to find Mr. Niles Truck here. He must've given me the slip along the way."

"I thought he'd get here first, too," admitted Scrooge, gesturing the fat man into a chair. "Without him to lead you, I'm surprised you knew where to come."

"Fortunately I saw a door knocker down below that was the image of your partner Jacob Marley."

Scrooge bowed to the man's power of observation. Then he suggested, "If Truck's given you the slip maybe he's figured out the Piccadilly Circus business too."

"Gad, dovechick, you amaze me," smiled the Muscovite with admiration. "Yes, perhaps you're right. A droll thing the Piccadilly Circus business. You see, this is the season when I most like to lug my belly out into the streets, gouty foot and all, if that curse is upon me. I really want the little people to see me as they rush about with their widow's mites and sweaty farthings trying to scrape something together for Christmas. I want them to know that every single night of the year I consume ten of their petty Christmas dinners. Yes, I like that. But today as I walked in Piccadilly Circus who should I see mincing along ahead of me but Niles Truck, the very man I outwitted to obtain this." Gutmanov banged his crutch on the floor. "To see what he was up to I trailed him around and around Piccadilly Circus and then to your countinghouse where I discovered Truck was following a disgruntled ex-employee of mine, a Miss Wunderlich. When she and your partner Jacob Marley hurried back to where we'd started with Truck on their tail I followed along behind. After we'd made two or three more swings around Piccadilly Circus, I following Truck and Truck following Miss Wunderlich, I realized to my amazement that Miss Wunderlich was following me. How could I elude her without losing Truck? I decided to lead the way to the Hotel Bristol, an establishment which had a rear entrance. By slipping out the back and hobbling around to the front I hoped to escape her while taking up position behind Truck. But Marley knew about the back door. Out in the alley he shouted to Miss Wunderlich, 'You go that way. I'll go this.' So I ducked into a doorway hoping he'd walk right by."

"But he didn't," said Scrooge. "So you shot him in the ankle with that pistol you've got hidden in your foot bandages. When he fell to the ground you reloaded and shot him in the head. But you won't get away with it. I'll see to that. Listen, when a man's partner's killed he's supposed to do something about it. It doesn't make any difference what . . ."

"Dovechick," said Gutmanov, "I could've killed your partner with one shot. Nothing easier. He was a miser after all." Scrooge's incredulous laughter made the fat man shrug. Then, as if to change the subject, he said, "Ah, my dear fellow I believe you've dropped a sixpence there on the floor."

Scrooge bent over quickly. Then, with his cheek against the floor, he found himself staring down the barrel of the bandaged foot. The Russian's heels were cocked. Scrooge knew that by tapping them together the man could trigger the hidden gun.

"Yes, I could've killed Marley," smiled Gutmanov. "But I just wounded him in the ankle. I wanted to get out of there and get back on Truck's trail."

Scrooge glared at the man. "A crime like that could mean transportation to New South Wales. Sydney."

"Capital," chortled the fat man. "Very well, call the police. I am an agent of the Tsar of Russia. All they can do is deport me and my crutch back to my homeland." He smiled at the thought, stroked the black enamel and said, "Let me tell you about this crutch. Four hundred years ago a mighty warrior called Tamerlane or Timur the Lame held sway over all the lands and peoples from the Volga to the Persian Gulf and from the Hellesponte to the Ganges. After each of his great military victories his subjects presented him with a ceremonial crutch decorated with precious inlay and priceless gems, but none more sumptuous than the one after his defeat of the Ottoman Sultan Bazajet whom Tamerlane afterwards carried about with him imprisoned in an iron cage for all to see." While he spoke Gutmanov took out a pocket knife and began to scrape at the black enamel as if to prove his words. "So valuable was this crutch that even Tamerlane, who was not shy about such things, wrapped it in tissue paper and put it away for special occasions. Perhaps this was why it alone survived the turmoil following Tamerlane's death.

"Oh, many like Niles Truck have pursued the crutch across the centuries just for the monetary worth of the thing. My Imperial master cares little for that. But he knows that every wild tribe from Samarkand southward would follow the man who possessed this symbol of ancient authority to hell and beyond. With the Tamerlane Crutch as our battle flag Russia will sweep down through India, conquer Burma and, avoiding the invincible defenses of the Great Wall, strike a mortal blow at China's soft underbelly."

Here the fat man brushed away the enamel scrapings to reveal a bright blue jewel. He purred approvingly and continued his story. "Well, if anyone was going to learn the whereabouts of the crutch I knew it would be Truck. So I hired people to keep a constant watch on him, not least among them Miss Wunderlich. The night he stole the crutch I was waiting for him outside Constantine's and followed him back to his hotel. But I found him unconscious on the floor of his room, the crutch at his side. I took it and fled across the rooftops, hurrying down to the harbour where I signed on as a deckhand aboard a ship bound for London under charter to the Valletta Crutch and Citrus Exporting Company."

Here Gutmanov offered the crutch for Scrooge's examination. But he stopped abruptly and frowned down at it. With a loud curse he fell to scraping wildly, his fat face trembling like an outraged pudding. Then he dropped the crutch, moaning, "They're not jewels! They're violet pastilles!"

The clatter of the crutch had scarcely died away when Truck appeared in the doorway blunderbus drawn. "You will please clasp your hands behind your necks, gentlemen," hissed the Levantine. Keeping his eyes fixed on them he came into the room and picked up the crutch. Fondling it lovingly he told Gutmanov, "When I heard you behind me in the fog, I ducked into an alley and let you get ahead of me. But before I could kill you and take my treasure you turned in here." Truck aimed his weapon at the fat Muscovite's chest. "Well, when it comes to dying, one place is as good as ..." Suddenly Truck felt the stickiness of the pastilles in his warm fingers. He looked down. "But this isn't the Tamerlane Crutch," he whined indignantly, "It's my fake!"

High heels approached through the apartment. "Quick, you two," urged Scrooge, "into that room over there." They obeyed, Truck handing over the crutch so the gouty Muscovite could hobble quickly across the floor. The door had scarcely closed when Dirndl Wunderlich, erect and alert, swept into the room. But when she saw Scrooge was alone she faltered and, it seemed to Scrooge, her hair took on more silver. Then she got a grip on herself. "I'm sorry about what happened to Marley," she said. "I didn't know Gutmanov was armed. You lost a partner. I lost my last chance to hit it big."

"The Tamerlane Crutch, you mean?" asked Scrooge. "Was that why you killed Marley?"

Dirndl Wunderlich turned those wonderful eyes on him for a moment. Then she said, "All right, I killed him." She licked her lips anxiously. "Look, there he was writhing on the ground, one hand around his ankle, the other holding onto that damn toothache of his. And me with the priceless crutch slipping from my grasp. I shouted for him to tell me which way Gutmanov'd gone. But his own pain was all he was thinking of. In a rage I gave him one of Mother Wunderlich's Lead Toothache Pills right in the noggin." She hung her head contritely. "I guess the laugh was on me because later I realized we'd all been following each other. I didn't have to kill Marley. By sticking close to Truck I'd have been sure to pick up Gutmanov's trail again. But now they've both given me the slip. It's all over."

"Why tell me?" asked Scrooge.

"Because I'm not as young as I used to be," said Dirndl Wunderlich. "Because I need to settle down in some cozy little business. You're short one partner. I've got a little money set by and some jewels. I could get the hang of misering. 'Scrooge and Wunderlich,' doesn't that have a lilt to it? Of course, that'd just be around the office. At home it'd be Ebenezer and Dirndl, Dirndl and Ebenezer. What do you say?"

Ebenezer and Dirndl? Damn, Scrooge liked the sound of it. Could life be granting him this one last chance to grab his dream of miser happiness? Perhaps. But first he had to explain that she'd killed his partner for a piece of wood studded with violet pastilles.

Dirndl's eyes grew wide as he spoke. Now they narrowed. "Listen," she said, "that night in Malta when the Tamerlane Crutch was stolen Gutmanov had ordered me to stand watch outside Truck's hotel. I remember seeing this skulky type wearing a long cape and a slouch hat down over his eyes slip into the hotel. I even remember remarking to myself, 'Dirndl, there goes a cape big enough to hide a crutch under.' At first I thought it was Truck. But he showed up a few minutes later, crutch and all. Gutmanov arrived a bit later just in time to pass the man in the cape coming out of the hotel. Now my little plan had been to wait for the fat Muscovite to come back out and then trade him one of Mother Wunderlich's Lead Barter Tokens for the Tamerlane Crutch. But Gutmanov skipped out over the rooftops. When I finally went up to Truck's room the little man was unconscious on the floor and the crutch was gone."

"I don't get it," admitted Scrooge.

"What's to get? Constantine spotted the switch, beat Truck back to the hotel, knocked him out and switched the crutches back. But Gutmanov didn't know that. When he found Truck unconscious he stole the fake. That means Constantine's still got the real one."

There was blunderbus play in the other room. When Dirndl and Scrooge burst through the door they found the fat Muscovite dead on the floor under the open window with the Levantine's body stretched across his. "Looks like they heard you," said Scrooge. "Gutmanov tried to get a head start for Malta. Truck stopped him dead but made the mistake of leaning over his victim to make sure. Gutmanov still had a heel tap left in his gouty foot."

"But don't you see what this means?" cried Dirndl. "This means we're the only ones left who know where the Tamerlane Crutch is."

"Except for Constantine," insisted Scrooge.

"I rather think Mr. Constantine thought he was just getting one of his crutches back from some thieving collector," said Dirndl. "No, only you and I know it's the Tamerlane Crutch. We'll work the years necessary to get another crack at it."

Suddenly Scrooge understood. "You mean custard pies and the whole bit?"

"A small price to pay," said Dirndl. "The Tamerlane Crutch'll makes us the miser Emperor and miser Empress of India and China. And, oh, what fun we'll have!"

Scrooge smiled sadly. No, it was too late for that now. "Listen, Dirndl," he said, "when a man's partner's killed he's supposed to do something about it. It doesn't . . ." Here there was a sound of many flat footsteps and policemen burst into the room. The clock said ten minutes to one. Scrooge muttered darkly. He'd told them to come at one on the dot. He handed Dirndl over to them, resigned that he'd never get to give his big speech.

Scrooge retired to his four-poster, snuffed out the candle flame and fell into a sound sleep. But his late partner's spirit was not quite laid to rest. Scrooge dreamed that Marley's ghost took him by the elbow and, both invisible, they flew out of night's darkness into the brightness of Christmas Day and flitted all about the city looking in at revellers' windows. They watched the Lord Mayor, aided by his fifty cooks and fifty butlers, keeping Christmas as a Lord Mayor's household should. And they visited Camden Town and Bob Cratchit's little house where they found Scrooge's clerk serving up some hot mixture compounded with gin and lemons which simmered in a jug on the hob. "A toast!" he cried. "I give you, Mr. Scrooge, the Founder of the Feast!"

"What a fool Bob Cratchit was," thought Scrooge. "Was there ever such a goose?"

Here Tiny Tim, the Cratchit's little crippled son, tottering happily about the room with the charity crutch he'd found in his Christmas stocking, cried out a joyful, "God help us everyone!"

Marley's ghost moaned agreement, squeezing Scrooge's forearm to draw attention to the crippled boy, his door knocker of a face giving his partner a meaningful look. Scrooge nodded. Yes, he understood.

Grinning delightedly, Jacob Marley's ghost rushed Scrooge away from the light of Christmas Day and back into the darkness from which they'd come.

Scrooge awoke from this crowded dream with the sunlight lying heavy on the floor of his bedroom, a smile on his face and the sure conviction that he had smuggled a very important discovery from the land of sleep. But what had it been? Ah, yes. All that flying about from window to window had inspired him. He'd design and market a contraption, a kind of magic window frame for the kingdom's poor to sct in the middle of their modest living rooms and use it to peek in at the dining rooms of their betters. Yes, he, Ebenezer Scrooge, could bring about a frugal world where one goose could as good as feed ten thousand people and the nightly joys of one small prosperous jocular family could supply the domestic pleasure of an entire nation. And every few minutes tradesmen would pay Scrooge for the privilege of appearing in the window to hawk their wares. Scrooge was warming his hands at that happy thought when the whole thing evaporated as the fantasies of sleep do in the morning light. "Magic window frames for the poor? What a far-fetched idea! What humbug!" thought Scrooge.

The miser sat on the edge of the bed and shook his head, still haunted by his dream. Then he remembered old Marley's ghost pointing out Tiny Tim to him. That was it! With a whoop of joy Scrooge ran to the window, opened it and put out his head. "You there," he called to a child he recognized who was passing by sucking an orange. "You're the talkative boy, aren't you?"

"I'll tell the world," said the boy.

"An intelligent boy," declared Scrooge. "And, do you know where my clerk, Bob Cratchit, lives?"

"I'll tell the world."

"Then run there at once. Tell him Mr. Scrooge says a crutch worth its weight in jewels was mistakenly mixed in among those distributed to the crippled poor this morning. Tell him to expect offers for Tiny Tim's crutch but not to sell it until Mr. Scrooge puts his bid in. Hurry now. There'll be sixpence in it for you if you get back here before I change my mind."

Scrooge closed the window and laughed out loud. Yes, within the hour all London would know the news and be bidding up those crutches. With one glorious lie Scrooge had accomplished more for the city's crippled poor than any charity subscription. And it hadn't cost him a penny.

"A Merry Christmas to us all!" cried the miser. Then with a gleeful laugh Ebenezer Scrooge, of Scrooge and Marley, leaped into the air and kicked his skinflint heels.

CHRONOS'S CHRISTMAS

Rhea Rose

Any minute, two more kids would be arriving at Daycare. *Two* replacements at once. That was unusual. Normally we arrived one at a time. Two would give us a small advantage over Deemi's Daycare unit, but I'd already decided not to keep them both. I'd give one to Deemi. That would make for fair play, and I figured that this year my unit could still beat Deemi's to Christmas.

Three of us sat in different corners of the large activity room, across from Ceep who filled an entire wall of the pentagonal room. Except for his flashing red eye and the blue glow from his vidscreen, we waited in the dark; it was better for the arrival of the replacements, less of a shock for them.

I could hear Snuks sucking her thumb, and I tried to see where she was hiding. She must have noticed, because she leaned out of the shadows and into the vidscreen's blue glow, looking eerie. Her round eyes made contact with mine.

Ceep's red eye, located at the other end of the room where Geebo waited, became a steady red.

"They're coming," I said to the others.

"Chronos?"

It was Ceep. "Here," I answered.

"Stand by for replacement 1313M and replacement 1315M, both chronological four."

"Double chrono four?" I asked. I thought that was strange. I went over to Ceep and touched him for a pause and repee. He repeated, and I'd heard the computer correctly. Chrono fours, *two* of them. Snuks, Geebo and myself had all arrived when we were five, and as far as I knew the kids at the other unit had all arrived when they were five, too. This Christmas I would be nine and Snuks would be six. This was her first Christmas at Daycare.

"We're ready here, Ceep," I said. Instantly, above our heads, a pink finger-thin laze shot across the room. It was a soothing, hypnotic color, and I had to look away for a moment. The beam began to pulse, expanding in all directions and filling the room with a warm sleepy glow. A low hum caused vibrations in the floor and walls. I looked over at Snuks. Her hiding place was exposed by the light, and she was really pulling on her thumb. She'd never seen the arrival of new kids.

At the center of the room appeared a blue dot as big as a fingernail. It hung in midair and then another appeared beside the first. They grew simultaneously. Snuks was engrossed by the process, or maybe she was just affected by the light. Whichever the case, she appeared to be watching very carefully. The miniature blue dots started to take shape. The tiny human forms looked like holos suspended just above the floor. They stayed that way for a moment, then quickly grew. The pink light intensified, became brighter, and a sudden white flash blinded us for an instant.

"How long?" I asked.

"Two hours before they are fully awake," Ceep replied.

I heard Geebo set down the gadget he'd been tinkering with while the new kids arrived. He'd been preparing the gadget for Christmas, but now that the replacements were here, he was more interested in them. He began looking the new arrivals over, checking their pockets, cutting the velcro from their clothes and stuffing the strips into his own pockets. Ceep's red light shone in Geebo's hair, making it almost the same color as mine. It was the only time Geebo and I ever resembled each other. We were the same age, but he was a head shorter than I. His dark eyes were almost black, while mine were pale, almost colorless. I was the only one at Daycare with freckles.

I could see that Geebo was completely absorbed with the sleeping kids, while Snuks sat back in the shadows like she always did when something was new to her. There was little to do except wait for the arrivals to wake up so that we could orient them to Daycare and Christmas, which would be the next day. Deemi and his unit would be anxious to beat us to it, if they could. But we were ready, too.

"You gotta see these kids, Chronos," Geebo said. He came over to me, brushing his dark hair out of his eyes and exposing a thin, raised white line that ran horizontally across his forehead—a scar from a gadget that had backfired on him when he was younger. Geebo hadn't been much of a talker when he first came to Daycare and after he was killed the first time, he spoke even less. The only time I'd ever seen him excited was over a new gadget he'd created and now, with these new kids. He tugged my sleeve insistently.

I followed him, and we crouched over the small bodies. He pulled a tube of glow grease out of his pocket, squirted some into his palms, and then rubbed them rapidly together.

Snuks crawled over from her corner. Her long golden hair, curling delicately at the ends, became blue as she passed through the light cast by the vidscreen at her end of the room. Sitting cross-legged, she looked at the sleeping arrivals, then at me. One of her fingers was curled over her nose as she sucked her thumb. Geebo had made her a warm-doll which she held by its head in the crook of her arm. I thought the doll was dumb, with its gaping mouth exposing its large front tooth, but Snuks would fight anyone who tried to take it from her. She took her thumb out of her mouth. "Ith that how I came here?"

"Yeah, 'cept you were a pink dot, not blue," I said.

"Why?"

"'Cause you're a girl."

"Why am I the only girl?" she insisted.

"I asked Ceep about girls once," I told her. She shifted her warm-doll from one arm to the other. "He said that girls used to be a lot more popular, but for a long time now girls haven't been requested as much."

"Why am I here, then?"

"I don't know," I lied.

"Doth Theep know?" She looked from me to Ceep.

I was relieved when Ceep didn't say anything. Sometimes he'd give answers and other times he wouldn't, but by that time he'd only told Deemi and me about girls like Snuks. He said that she was a longlifer. All girls were. It's the way the dults wanted them. When she was ready to leave Daycare the dults would eventually trade her to Offworlders. She wouldn't get to be immortal like me and Geebo and the others at Daycare, like the dults. Ceep told me not to tell Snuks just yet, but sometimes the dults took girls away at Christmas. When I asked Ceep who the Offworlders were and why they weren't immortal, he just stayed quiet.

"Look." Geebo elbowed me. He grinned and held a green glowing hand over the face of each replacement. I was surprised to see their faces were identical, and I had a feeling these two would be special. Christmas, and now the replacements, had me excited and a little nervous.

They awoke earlier than Ceep had calculated and sat quietly in the same place they had been deposited. Fair-haired and shy, they looked up at Ceep. He was talking to them, telling them about Daycare.

"Since the skirmishes with the Offworlders first began more than a century ago, it became economically unfeasible to restore Daycare to its original standards. When those in charge of maintenance were destroyed in a particularly violent encounter with the Offworlders, the dults, who long ago lost the ability to nurture their own young, also lost the maintenance knowledge needed to make sure I continued to perform the task for them. Now it is entirely up to me to make the necessary adjustments in both of you if you are to fulfill the role the dults have prescribed for you."

"What adjustments?" one of the replacements asked Ceep.

"Those cannot be determined until you have spent more time at Daycare," he replied.

I knew that Ceep was talking about the times they'd be killed. Any desired abilities they displayed before their first three deaths would be 'sharpened' by him.

Ceep continued: "A basic foundation of knowledge is given to all of you before you come to Daycare, but the dults can never be sure, any more, what your pre-Daycare knowledge along with your adjustments and experiences at Daycare will result in. It is during your time in Daycare that your intrinsic abilities will—or will not—manifest."

One of the little kids turned to me. "What do you call him?" he asked.
"Ceep."

"Why do you call him Ceep?"

"He makes a noise that sounds like 'ceep.' But forget him," I said. If these two were going to participate in Christmas, we would have to orient them to Daycare pretty quickly. Officially, Christmas started at 1900 hours, now only a few hours away.

"One of you has to join Deemi's Daycare unit. Now, who wants to go?" I looked from one to the other.

"Does Deemi have one of those?" One of them pointed at Ceep.

"Yeah. His unit's identical to this one, and Ceep is over there, too."

"I'll go," said the one who'd been doing all the talking so far.

"Good. Ceep, has Deemi responded to my message about the new arrivals?"

"Yes. He says that if you want to take Christmas this year, you should keep them both. You need all the help you can get."

I ignored the message. When I first came to Daycare, I arrived at Deemi's unit. He taught me everything he knew about getting Christmas. Together, Deemi and I used to be on the same team; we were invincible. Every year, Christmas was ours. But when he started making his own rules, I left his unit.

I looked over at Geebo. He seemed to have forgotten the new kids and was completely absorbed with his tinkering. I waved over the kid that had volunteered, and he followed me to the exit.

"Except for Deemi, Geebo and I are the oldest at Daycare," I explained to him. "Deemi's eleven, the oldest and biggest kid Daycare's ever had. He'd never been killed before I took over this unit, but I've killed him three times." I looked him straight in the eye. "And I plan to kill him and whoever gets in the way of me and Christmas." He just looked up at me with an innocent and shy expression. I told him how to get to Deemi's unit, and said that he should follow my directions exactly. If he wandered or dawdled there was a good chance he'd be killed by one of the many traps which both units had spent the rest of the year setting up. I watched him walk down the stairs to the sidewalk. He stopped and looked up at me.

"Bye." He turned and never looked back. I really hoped he made it to Deemi's, and I hoped Deemi liked him. At least this kid wasn't a girl. One of the rules Deemi had decided on, while I was still with him, was no girls. Once he was sent a girl, and he killed her himself.

What a waste. He never even tried to use any of her abilities for Christmas. Every time Ceep restored her, Deemi'd just kill her again until after the fourth time Ceep never brought her back. No one came back to Daycare after the fourth death. I thought it was really a shame; I felt sorry for the girl. No one *wants* to leave Daycare. I've never traded a girl to Deemi's unit, and I don't think Ceep's ever sent him another one.

When the new replacement was out of sight, I looked up at the light dome high overhead. It was the ceiling to the walls that enclosed the one and a half square kilometres of Daycare. Ceep had the overcast filters up.

I went back to the activity room, and my knee started aching. I'd been killed three times, twice by Deemi, and my knee hadn't been repaired properly. It usually started bothering me around this time, when I was worrying about Christmas. Ceep said there was nothing the matter with it, but I knew he had to be wrong.

When I walked into the activity room, I saw Geebo watching the remaining kid who was standing on a stool and halfway inside Ceep. The vidscreen light was out and the screen was off and *on the floor.* Geebo gave me a worried look, but the kid kept working. "Ceep, are you still there?" It made me nervous, seeing him in pieces on the floor.

"I'm here, Chronos," he answered. He sounded different. His voice was the same, but there was something different. By this time the blond kid was looking at me. He smiled.

"Geebo, what's he doing? *You* know Ceep's off limits. We all know that," I said. Snuks sat in the corner, her face painted white. She was about to apply more colors. At least someone was getting ready for Christmas.

"I gave that new kid a name," Snuks said. "Teb."

"Ceep asked Teb to do this," Geebo said.

"Do what?" I asked.

"Fikth him," Snuks answered. She went back to coloring her face. Teb still worked on Ceep.

"Is that true, Ceep?" I asked, half expecting him not to answer.

"Yes, Chronos."

"But why Teb? Why not Geebo? You know how he loves to do that kind of thing. And why now with only one hour until Christmas? We've got to be ready. Deemi will be ready."

"Geebo wasn't bred for this kind of job, Chronos. I couldn't let him work on me."

I recalled the one time Geebo had attempted to tinker with Ceep. Geebo hadn't been here too long, and Ceep had zapped him so badly that I thought he'd been killed for sure, but he hadn't.

"Geebo would have changed me. He would have made me something more—or less."

"I wouldn't," Geebo protested.

"Yes, you would have. Don't feel bad, Geebo. That is your specialty. It has become more and more obvious. Your creativity is greatly needed and desired."

Ceep was absolutely right. Geebo's genius had come in handy more than once and would be greatly desired in less than an hour.

"Besides," Ceep continued, "Geebo's hands are too large for this procedure. I could not be sure that Teb or the other replacement would survive this Christmas, and this adjustment could not wait much longer. Do not worry about being prepared for Christmas. You are prepared."

By the time Ceep had finished explaining, Teb had completed what he was doing, and Geebo replaced the vidscreen and turned it back on. We always kept the vidscreen on. That way it felt like Ceep was really there.

"Teb, have you looked at Ceep's Christmas catalogs and given him your list?" I asked. His blond head nodded. It was strange talking to him when I felt like I had just said goodbye to him a moment earlier. "Snuks will help outfit you. Geebo and I have to get ready, too. Remember, it's only fifteen minutes to Christmas." Snuks looked nervous. I was nervous. But Geebo didn't look worried at all. "We've got fifteen blocks to cover by tomorrow, but then so does Deemi," I said.

We gathered on the concrete stairs outside of our unit. We looked at each other, admiring the faces we had painted on ourselves. Geebo and I snickered at Teb. He'd allowed Snuks to apply his paint to him, and she'd given him a clown's face, just like the ones she'd seen in Ceep's catalogs. Teb's nose and mouth were red, and his eyebrows arched into the blond bangs on his forehead. He looked like he'd been surprised by Deemi himself. He didn't seem to mind us laughing at him. Snuks wore a tight, black, stretchy outfit. Her hair was tied back and fastened down with a thong that looped around her neck.

"Watch this," Geebo said. He slipped off something that he had slung over his shoulder, then moved down the stairs and away from us. It was a flat chrome disc tied to the end of a plastic string. He held it out to one side. With a few twists of his wrist he had the disc spinning, and then he released it. Slicing through the air, the silver disc cut two branches from a nearby bush before it was stopped by a clump of twigs. Not until it had become lodged did we realize that the razor-disc was still attached to the string Geebo held. He flicked the string and the disc dislodged and came spinning back to him, stopping just short of his hand. He grinned, looking delighted with himself.

Geebo had other gadgets hooked to his belt. I recognized his grease gun and a few other things. Snuks wore her pellet shooter around her neck like a necklace. She blew through it a couple of times then tucked it down the front of her top. A small pouch of pellets hung by her hip. When she was ready, she slipped her thumb into her mouth and sat on the top step.

I was ready too, but I wasn't sure about Teb. I had no idea what his capabilities were. He probably wouldn't make it all the way through Christmas, but I was going to make sure we got as much use out of him as possible, at least until Deemi or one of his gang got him.

"Message from Deemi." Ceep's voice came through the com by the door.

"I'll come inside to take it." I didn't want to take Deemi's message while the others were listening. It might disturb them.

I left Geebo bragging to Teb about some gadget he'd created and walked into the silent activity room. Ceep was quiet.

Ceep was quiet!

That was it. Teb had fixed Ceep so that he no longer made the hissing sound we'd named him after. I stood in the silence and wondered what Deemi could possibly have to say just before Christmas. I decided that it was probably some kind of trick and was ready to walk back outside when Ceep spoke.

"Shall I communicate Deemi's message?" he asked.

"No." I really didn't want to hear it.

"I would like to talk with you before you go."

"There's not much time, Ceep." I felt uncomfortable.

"I have always considered your development, and the others at Daycare, my most important task, but until now, the way your time has been spent here has never been completely under my control."

"You've done everything for us," I said, wondering what Ceep was getting at.

"No. The dults neglected Daycare and were afraid of the children that were coming out of here because the children were violent. Conditions here demand that you be tough. I do what I can to ensure that you will survive once you leave here. The dults don't know how to stop Daycare, and at one time hoped it would break down completely—until they saw how they could take advantage of the children. They need you to defend them from the Offworlders. The dults introduced Christmas to Daycare to ensure the violence would continue—a motivating agent. They've been preparing you, the others and many before you to fight for them, to die for them—"

"But you won't let us die."

"You will be beyond my range once you leave Daycare," he said.

I felt cold.

"The dults who do not fight the Offworlders are not mine. They didn't come from Daycare. But you and others *are* mine. Especially you, Chronos."

"Me?"

"Yes. You love the other Daycare children, even those in the other unit. You even loved Deemi once, but you especially care for Snuks—"

"I'll be sorry to see her go," I mumbled.

"She will be traded to the Offworlders. You may kill her one day, or she you."

"Why does Snuks have to go there?"

"The Offworlders threaten to destroy the dults. They want the dults' secret of immortality. Unfortunately the remaining dults don't have that information. It was lost long before the first Offworlder skirmishes. The immortality gene was bred into you and the others—except for Snuks. Her offspring will be longlifers, and all females like her are traded to the Offworlders in order to keep the Offworlders from carrying out their threat. This trade appeases them for a while."

"Can *you* give the Offworlders the information they want?"

"No. I've lost large batches of information as a result of the degeneration that has taken place in Daycare and the outside world. Your immortality was already present in your gene pool."

"You don't think I'm going to survive this Christmas, do you, Ceep?"

"I did consider that possibility. I have reissued your genetic pool, Chronos, and have designed the two new replacements after you. Yet they are also significantly different from you."

There was a long silence.

"Are you finished?" I asked.

"Yes."

"I have to get back to the others."

"Goodbye, Chronos."

I stepped outside not wanting to think about why Ceep told me this. I just wanted to win Christmas.

"Let's get Christmas," I said, and we began.

We jogged down the street on which our Daycare unit was stationed. Snuks and Teb followed me with Geebo bringing up the rear. We moved in single file towards the center of Daycare.

Skirting potholes and debris from other Christmases, we traveled north. Daycare had been a small grassy park surrounded by many city blocks. The park was battered and worn from years of battle, but there were still patches of yellow grass to be found at the outskirts. The old tenement buildings that still stood were now empty shells. Some old street lamps still worked, and Ceep usually turned them on for Christmas.

We didn't move straight down the middle of the park but drifted west where the park foliage was heavier. Here, some of the trees were still real and alive, but most were imitations. None of us were even sure which were the real ones, though Ceep assured us that there were still originals. We had planted many of our own traps here and were able to move through the area in relative security.

The buildings on the outskirts were a kind of no-man's-land where both groups, Deemi's and mine, tried not to become trapped. The roads there did not lead to Christmas, but the buildings could provide cover from an attack.

It was getting cooler out. My breath came out in cloudy bursts, but it seemed too early for Ceep to be lowering the temperature. We came to the treed area, and I jogged to the base of a tree with low branches. Linking my fingers together, I formed a cup with my hands. Snuks ran as hard as her legs could go, stepped briefly into my hands, and leaped upward. With the momentum gained from the leap, she swung her body around the branch, straddled it, and was able to reach the rest of the branches to clamber high into the tree.

In a moment she was rapidly climbing down the tree. As she came to the last branch she leaped, confident that I would catch her.

"They're coming, three of them. They're just over the hill. Run!"

Our only chance was to head west towards the empty buildings and hide there. Snuks was ahead of me, her small legs pumping so fast that I couldn't keep up with her. I couldn't figure out why Deemi had deviated so drastically from the course that would take him to Christmas. Snuks headed for an old house. She took the steps two at a time and disappeared through a doorway. I followed her and, in the distance, could hear Deemi calling my name. I ran faster. Glancing over my shoulder, I saw his gang take cover behind a bush.

In the dim light, inside the house, I saw Snuks in a corner. From the window I saw the dome lights fade. For a moment Daycare was dark. The street lamps that still worked came on. Ceep even brought out a few stars and a moon. Snuks came over to the window and stood beside me. The moonlight sparkled in her eyes.

"Are you afraid to leave Daycare?" she whispered. I looked down at her. She seemed very small. I nodded.

"Why?"

"Because I don't know what's out there," I said.

"Deemi'th out there."

I scanned the street looking for some sign of Deemi. It seemed quiet, and I wondered why he'd called my name.

"Why do we need Chrithmath?"

"Because."

"Becauth why?"

"Because it's important. What else is there? I mean don't you like the idea of getting all those presents every year?"

"Yeah."

"That's why," I said.

"But why don't we share Chrithmath? Then we wouldn't have to kill each other, and then we could alwayth be at Daycare."

She had a point, but it wasn't the time to explain that Deemi would never agree to a truce; besides, before now, Ceep always encouraged us to compete for Christmas.

"Are you afraid of Deemi?" she asked.

"No. Just the dults."

"I'm afraid of Chrithmath. If Deemi killth you, you won't be back. I don't want you to go away, or Geebo."

I didn't know what to tell her, so I took her hand and held it.

Without warning, Deemi burst through the door. Snuks had time to pierce his cheek with one pellet. Then she jumped up onto the window ledge, somersaulted through it and landed safely outside. She ran towards the street. "Run!" I yelled after her. A member of Deemi's gang stepped out from behind a lamp post and caught her.

"Why didn't you answer my message?" Deemi said. He was holding his left cheek, blood oozing through his fingers.

"You mean back at Daycare?" I watched him carefully. I was at a disadvantage. I couldn't get to the door or window without fighting Deemi.

"That kid you sent to me never showed," he said.

I glanced out the window. Snuks struggled with a captor, much bigger than herself. "Damn."

"You should have got rid of her a long time ago." Deemi walked over to the window. His back was to me. I should've tried to kill him then, but I saw something whiz out from one of the shelled houses across the street. It struck Snuks's captor in the neck. He let her go and grabbed his own neck with both hands.

"Those replacements are missing. What's going on with them?" he asked.

"What?"

"The replacement you sent over to my unit—it never showed. Those new kids—they've done something to Ceep."

"How do you mean?" I tried to stall.

"Ceep's making the weather cold sooner than last Christmas. The night's come too soon, and I think it's those new kids."

Deemi was afraid. He leaned on one arm against the window frame, blocking my exit. When I looked for Snuks, she was gone. Her captor was on his knees with a red glistening stream spurting from between his fingers.

"Where's your new kid?" He glanced suspiciously around the room.

"He's not here."

Deemi was volatile and unpredictable. He gave me a violent shove against the wall and then grabbed me. "We've got to find them." He was desperate.

"You find them," I said and jammed two knuckles into his throat. He let go, and I jumped out the window and ran for the cover of the trees. I ran past the body of Snuks's captor and saw someone hiding in the bush ahead of me. It was Geebo. He motioned for me to follow him, and he led me to one of the traps we had set for Deemi's unit. He pointed to the strip of laze-eyes he had placed along one side of the trunk of a tree.

The trap had been tampered with. It should have let anyone from my Daycare unit pass through it without harm, but no one from

Deemi's. It had been dismantled, and Geebo couldn't figure out how it had been done.

"Did you see Snuks or Teb?" I asked him.

"Snuks got away." Geebo patted his bloodstained razor-disc. "But I haven't seen Teb since we left the unit."

I was relieved to hear that Snuks had gotten away. We left the trap and decided to try to make our way to Christmas.

We moved cautiously, encountering no difficulties. This unnerved us even more than if we had been attacked or injured by Deemi's gang or their traps. We walked through his territory as if he had never been expecting us. We found that Deemi's traps were dismantled, too.

We weren't far from Christmas when we heard a noise. I climbed a tree and was barely up and hidden when two shadowy forms came from opposite directions to converge on Geebo. He decided to stay and fight it out. Besides he couldn't follow me because he had too much junk strapped to himself. He had his grease gun out and sprayed the stuff all over, but they got him. He never made a sound. His body was heaped awkwardly on the ground, a dark silhouette against the soft green glow of the grease.

They tried to climb the tree after me but were covered with the slippery glow grease and even when they tried to hide, the thick foliage couldn't completely conceal their glow. They waited for me, so I couldn't climb down. I remembered a group of trees in this part of Daycare that were clumped together. Crawling through the tree, I hoped the neighboring one would be close enough for me to jump across to it.

Not knowing if the tree I was in was real or not, I moved out onto the branch as far as I dared. There was a good chance that the small branch of a real tree would not hold my weight. Flat on my belly, pulling my feet under me until I crouched, I got ready to jump to the next tree. Suddenly my knee started to ache.

When the pain subsided a little, I leaped. My knee cramped just as I took off, and I knew in midair that I did not have enough force to make the branch.

I crashed through the branches, grasping at twigs that tore the skin from my hands. Everything blurred as I plummeted and hit.

I'd been out for a while, but I wasn't sure how long. It was very dark out, and a light snow was falling, covering the ground. I was cold, but more worried that I had lost Christmas. I took a few things from Geebo's body, things that I thought I might need in case Christmas wasn't over. Carefully, I wiped off my footpads and followed a small trail through the brush. It was against all the rules for members of opposing Daycares to break away and form their own team, and I was beginning to suspect the new kids.

I came to the north gate where Christmas normally took place and didn't find anyone. I climbed another tree and waited there. Perched high in a branch, I could see someone hiding in a bush below. Christmas wasn't over yet! A portion of the north wall began to change color. Normally grey, it became a bright orange. Only a small section of the wall changed color and began to sink into the ground. When it had disappeared, a gush of air and mist blew into Daycare, then quickly dissipated. The black space left in the wall reminded me of the gap left in Geebo's grin when he'd lost his front tooth.

They entered Daycare cautiously and looked the way they had last year, tall, taller even than Deemi. They wore bulky white clothing, their heads helmeted. Their weapons were holstered, but their hands rested on them. More dults followed them. They brought Christmas into Daycare. Some had their arms full of presents while others carried glitter and lights. Another brought a tree.

They placed the parcels and packages on the ground and decorated a small area around the gifts. The tree was raised and powered up. It was a magnificent tree which rotated at the base with the center section slowly rotating in the opposite direction. The branches shone, blinking on and off in many colors. More and more gifts were brought in, until the area in front of the wall gate was nearly covered. The presents that didn't give off their own light reflected those of the Christmas tree.

Some of the tree ornaments played soft music which drifted upward to me. The tree smelled fresh, too. Everything was beautiful, better than the light shows Ceep would put on to entertain us. It was a warm, enticing scene and before I realized what I had done, I was down from the tree and wading knee-deep among the presents. I wanted to hold one, feel the smoothness of its wrapping and the crispness of a bow. I picked up a small package that glowed softly. It was wrapped in gold and trimmed with a pink ribbon and bow. I could smell the newness of it and felt whatever was inside slip and slide around. As I turned it over, the small identification tag lit up. It was for Snuks.

"Put that present down. It's not yours yet."

It was Deemi. I dropped the gift and ran towards a bush, trampling gifts as I went. I could hear Deemi right behind me as I dove for the bush. To my surprise Snuks had been hiding there all along, and she sprang at Deemi. I watched them tumble among the gifts and reached in my pocket for one of the velcro bombs I'd taken from Geebo. She was no match for Deemi, but she'd taken him by surprise. At last Snuks fell away from him, but when I stood to throw, I had a severe pain in my ribs. I couldn't throw the small explosive without risking the chance that it would miss Deemi and cling to Snuks. Suddenly, two of the dults were keeping Snuks and Deemi apart with the threat of their weapons.

They threatened to blast all the gifts if Deemi and Snuks didn't stop fighting immediately. They stopped, and Snuks walked back towards me. Someone touched me from behind.

It was the two new kids.

"I found them taking apart all the trapth in Daycare," Snuks said. "They don't want to fight for Chrithmath all the time."

"Geebo's dead." I looked at them. Snuks started to cry quietly. "Teb." I waited until one of the kids looked at me so that I could identify Teb, whose clown face had been wiped off. "What did you do to Ceep back at the unit?"

"Just adjusted the problem that caused him to make that funny noise. It would have eventually caused severe problems," he said.

"They fikthed Theep. Now he doth everything on time, like thnow for Chrithmath," Snuks said.

"That's all? You just fixed him?"

The kids looked at each other, and I had this sick feeling there was more.

"We did some security bypasses," Teb said, "Anyone killed this time won't be back until next Christmas."

"It was all done at Ceep's request, which was made before we arrived at Daycare," the other one added.

There was a commotion beyond the tree. We turned to see Deemi jump onto the dult guard who had separated him and Snuks. A second dult guard was on his way over. While Deemi struggled with the first guard, I saw my opportunity to win Christmas. Except for the kid who never actually joined his side, Deemi seemed to be the only survivor from his Daycare unit. Once I got rid of him, Christmas would be ours. And Deemi would be gone for good.

The second guard slowly wove his way through the gifts, weapon ready. Then it happened—my chance came. The first guard, weaponless, broke away from Deemi. I ran from the tree for Deemi, tackled him and struggled for the weapon he'd taken. The next thing I knew Snuks was yelling at me.

"Stop it, Chronos. Stop. Ceep can't bring you back if you die. Teb says Ceep can't hold any of us any more."

I let go of Deemi and shoved her away. "Go back!" I screamed.

The second guard grabbed Snuks's arm. "No!" I started after him, but he brought his weapon to her face. I stopped and watched him drag her, screaming, backwards through the gifts.

Behind me I could hear Deemi laughing, and I turned to face him. He had the weapon he'd taken from the first guard aimed at me.

"You lose," he said. And in that instant a hole burned through Deemi's neck as another guard shot him from behind. I thought I would be next but the guard walked away, following the one that carried Snuks. I watched the two dults take her out. Then they all left Daycare and Christmas.

"They won't be coming back," a voice beside me said. It was Teb. "Ceep's gonna let you decide what should happen at Daycare."

I saw the small parcel I'd seen earlier, the one tagged for Snuks. It was crushed; the lighting mechanism on the tag had gone out. I kicked it away. Ceep didn't want any more Christmases—not like this one. That was why he'd brought Teb and the other kid. I supposed it was the only way he could stop it. "Ceep!" I yelled up at the trees. "It's got to be different in here. I don't want any more Christmases like this one. I'm changing things. Do you understand me?"

There was silence.

Of myth and legend are:

WE THREE KINGS

Alan Dean Foster

It was overcast and blustery and the snow was coming down as hard as a year's accumulation of overdue bills. Within the laboratory Stein made the final adjustments, checked the readouts, and inspected the critical circuit breakers a last time. There was no going back now. The success or failure of his life's work hinged on what happened in the next few moments.

He knew there were those who if given the chance would steal his success, but if everything worked he would take care of them first. Them with their primitive, futile notions and dead-end ideas! All subterfuge and smoke, behind which they doubtless intended to claim his triumph as their own. Let them scheme and plot while they could. Soon they would be out of the way and he would be able to bask in his due glory without fear of theft or accusation.

He began throwing the switches, turning the dials. Fitful bursts of necrotic light threw the strange shapes that occupied the vast room in the old warehouse into stark relief. Outside, the snow filled up the streets, sifting into dirty gutters, softening the outlines of the city. Not many citizens out walking in his section of town, he reflected. It was as well. Though the laboratory was shuttered and soundproofed, there was no telling what unforeseen sights and sounds might result when he finally pushed his efforts to a conclusion.

The dials swung while the readings on the gauges mounted steadily higher. Nearing the threshold now. The two huge Van de Graaf generators throbbed with power. Errant orbs of ball lightning burst free, to spend themselves in showers of coruscating sparks against the insulated ceiling. It was almost time.

He threw the final, critical switch.

Gradually the crackling faded and the light in the laboratory returned to normal. With the smell of ozone sharp in his nostrils, Stein approached the table. For an instant, nothing more than disappointment brokered by uncertainty. And then . . . a twitch. Slight, but unmistakable. Stein stepped back, eyes wide and alert. A second twitch, this time in the arms. Then the legs, and finally the torso itself.

With a profound grinding sound, the creature sat up, snapping the two-inch wide medical restraining straps as if they were so much cotton thread.

"It's alive!" Stein heard himself shouting. "It's alive, it's alive, it's alive!"

He advanced cautiously until he was standing next to the now seated Monster. The bolts in its neck had been singed black from the force of the charge which had raced through it, but there were no signs of serious damage. Tentatively he reached out and put a hand on the creature's arm. The massive, blocky skull swiveled slowly to regard him.

"Nnrrrrrrrrrgh!"

Stein was delighted. "You and I, we are destined to conquer the world. At last the work of my great-grandfather is brought to completion." His voice dropped to a conspiratorial whisper. "But there are those who would thwart us, who would stand in our way. I know who they are, and they must be . . . dealt with. Listen closely, and obey . . ."

Outside, the snow continued to fall.

In the dark cellar Rheinberg carefully enunciated the ancient words. Only a little light seeped through the street-level window, between the heavy bars. Seated in the center of the room, in the middle of the pentagram, was the sculpture. Rheinberg was as talented as he was resourceful, and the details were remarkable for their depth and precision.

An eerie green glow began to suffuse the carefully crafted clay figure as the words echoed through the studio. Rheinberg read carefully, in a steady, unvarying monotone, from the copy of the ancient manuscript. With each word, each sentence, the glow intensified, until softly pulsing green shadows filled every corner of the basement studio.

Almost, but not quite, he halted in the middle of the final sentence, when the eyes of the figure began to open. Stopping would have been dangerous, he knew, and so he read on. Only when he'd finished did he dare allow himself to step forward for a closer look.

The eyes of the Golem were fully open now, unblinking, staring straight ahead. Then they shifted to their left, taking notice of the slight, anxious man who was approaching.

"It works. It worked! The old legends were true." Unbeknownst to Rheinberg the sheet containing the words had crumpled beneath his clenching fingers. "The world is ours, my animate friend. Ours, as soon as certain others are stopped. You'll take care of that little matter for me, won't you? You'll do anything I ask. You must. That's what the legend says."

"*Ooooyyyyyyyy!*" Moaning darkly, the massive figure rose. Its gray head nearly scraped the ceiling.

Within the charmed circle something was rising. A pillar of smoke, black shot through with yellow, coiling and twisting like some giant serpent awakened from an ancient sleep. Al-Nomani recited the litany and watched, determined to maintain the steady singsong of the nefarious poem no matter what happened.

The fumes began to thicken, to coalesce. Limbs appeared, emerging from the roiling hell of the tornadic spiral. The whirlwind itself began to change shape and color, growing more man-like with each verse, until the horrid humanoid figure stood where the smoke had once swirled. It had two rings in its oversized left ear, a huge nose, and well-developed fangs growing upward from its lower jaw. For all that, the fiery yellow eyes that glared out at the historian from beneath the massive, low-slung brow reeked of otherworldly intelligence.

"By the beard of the Prophet!" al-Nomani breathed tensely, "it worked!" He put down the battered, weathered tome from which he had been reading. The giant regarded him silently, awaiting. As it was supposed to do.

Al-Nomani took a step forward. "You will do my bidding. There is much that needs be done. First and foremost there is the matter of those who would challenge me. They must be shown the error of their ways. I commit you to deal with them."

"*Eeeehhhhzzzzz!*" Within the circle the Afreet bowed solemnly. Its arms were as big around as tree trunks.

Stillman was cruising the rundown commercial area just outside the industrial park when he noticed the movement up the side street. At this hour everything was closed up tight, and the weather reduced traffic even further. He picked up the mike, then set it back in its bracket. Might be nothing more than some poor old rummy looking for a warm place to sleep.

Still, the bums and the homeless tended to congregate downtown. It was rare to encounter one this far out. Which meant that the figure might be looking to help itself to something more convertible than an empty park bench. Stillman flicked on the maglite and slid out of the car, drawing his service revolver as he did so. The red and yellows atop the cruiser revolved steadily, lighting up the otherwise dark street.

Cautiously, he advanced on the narrow roadway. He had no intention of entering, of course. If the figure ran, that would be indication enough something was wrong and that's when he'd call for backup.

"Hey! Hey, you in there! Kinda late for a stroll, especially in this weather, ain't it?" The only reply was a strange shuffling. The officer blinked away falling snow as something shifted in the shadows. He probed with his flashlight.

"Come on out, man. I know you're back there. I don't want any trouble from you and you sure don't want any from me. Don't make me come in there after you." He took a challenging step forward.

Something vast and monstrous loomed up with shocking suddenness, so big his light could not illuminate it all. Officer Corey Stillman gaped at the apparition. His finger contracted reflexively on the trigger of his service revolver, and a sharp *crack* echoed down the alley. The creature flinched, then reached for him with astounding speed.

"Nnrrrrrrrrrr!"

Stillman said not another word.

His head was throbbing like his brother's Evinrude when he finally came around. Groaning, he reached up and back as he straightened in the snow. Memories came flooding back and he looked around wildly, but the Monster was gone, having shambled off down the street.

Eleven years on the force and that was without question the ugliest dude he'd ever encountered. Fast for his size, too. Too damn fast. He was sure his shot had hit home, but it hadn't even slowed the big guy down. Wincing, he climbed to his feet and surveyed his surroundings. His cruiser sat where he'd left it in the street, lights still revolving patiently.

His gun lay in the snow nearby. Slowly he picked up the .38, marveling at the power which had crushed it to a metal pulp. What had he encountered, and how could he report it? Nobody'd believe him.

A figure stepped into view from behind the building. He tensed, but big as the pedestrian was, he was utterly different in outline from Stillman's departed assailant. He staggered forward . . . and came up short.

The enormous stranger was the color of damp clay, save for vacant black eyes that stared straight through him.

"Good God!"

Startled, the creature whirled and struck.

"Ooyyyyyyyyyy!"

This time when Stillman regained consciousness he didn't move, just lay in the snow and considered his situation. His second attacker had been nothing like the first, yet no less terrifying in appearance. He no longer cared if everyone back at the station thought him crazy; he needed help.

Too much overtime, he told himself. That had to be it. Too many hours rounding up too many prosties and junkies and sneak thieves. Mary was right. He needed to use some of that vacation time he'd been accumulating.

Body aching, head still throbbing, he struggled to his feet. The cruiser beckoned, its heater pounding away persistently despite the gaping door on the driver's side. Recovering his hat and clutching the flashlight, he staggered around the front, pausing at the door to lean on it for support. The heat from the interior refreshed him, made him feel better. He bent to slide behind the wheel.

The seat was already occupied by something with burning yellow eyes and a massive, distorted face straight out of his worst childhood nightmare. It was playing with the scanner, mouthing it like a big rectangular cookie.

He'd surprised it, and of course it reacted accordingly.

"Oh no!" Stillman moaned as he staggered backwards and an unnaturally long arm reached for him, "not *again!*"

"*Eehhhzzzzzzz!*"

The wonderful profusion of brightly colored street and store lights slowed the Monster's progress, mysteriously diluted its intent. They were festive and cheerful. Even as it kept to the shadows it could see the faces of smiling adults and laughing children. There were the decorations, too: in the stores, above the streets, on the houses. Laughter reached him through the falling snow; childish giggles, booming affirmations of good humor, deep chuckles of pleasure. It inevitably had a cumulative effect.

Memories stirred: memories buried deep within the brain he'd been given. The lights, the snow, the laughter and ebullient chatter of toys and candy: it all meant something. He just wasn't sure what. Confused, he turned and lurched off down the dark alley between two tall buildings, trying to reconcile his orders with these disturbing new thoughts.

He paused suddenly, senses alert. Someone else was coming up the alley. The figure was big, much bigger than any human he'd observed so far that night. Not that he was afraid of any human, or for that matter, any thing. Teeth and joints grinding, arms extended, he started deliberately forward.

There was just enough light for the two figures to make each other out. When they could do so with confidence, both hesitated in confusion. Something strange was about, most peculiar.

"Who . . . what . . . you?" the Monster declaimed in a voice like a rusty mine cart. Speech was still painful.

"I vaz going ask you the same qvestion." The other figure's black eyes scrutinized their counterparts. "You one sick looking *schlemiel*, I can tell you."

"You not . . . no beauty yourself."

"So tell me zumthing I don't know." The Golem's massive shoulders heaved, a gesture of tectonic proportions.

"What be this, pbuh?" Both massive shapes turned sharply, to espy a third figure standing close behind them. Despite its size it had made not a sound during its approach.

"Und I thought you vaz ugly," the Golem murmured to the Monster as it regarded the newcomer.

"Speak not ill of others lest the wrath of Allah befall thee." The Afreet approached, its yellow eyes flicking from one shape to the next. "What manner of mischief is afoot this night?"

"Ask you . . . the same," the Monster rumbled.

The Afreet bowed slightly. "I am but recently brought fresh into the world, and am abroad on a mission for my mortal master of the moment." It glanced back toward the main street, with its twinkling lights and window-shopping pedestrians blissfully unaware of the astonishing conclave taking place just down the alley. "Yet I fear the atmosphere not conducive to my command, for what I see and hear troubles my mind like a prattling harim."

"You too?" The Golem rubbed its chin. Clay flakes fell to the pavement. "I vaz thinking the same."

"I think I know . . . what is wrong." The other two eyed the Monster.

"*Nu?* So don't keep it to yourself," said the Golem.

"I think the season," the creature declared slowly, "is the reason."

"Explain thyself." The Afreet was demanding, but polite.

The Monster's square forehead turned slowly. "The brain I was given . . . remembers. This time of year . . . the sights I see . . . make me remember. The time is wrong . . . for the command I was given. All . . . wrong. Wrong to kill . . . at Christmas."

"Kill," echoed the Afreet. "Strange are the ways of the Prophet, for such was the order I was given. To kill this night two men: one of art and one of learning. Felix Stein and Joseph Rheinberg."

The Monster and the Golem started and exchanged a look. "I vaz to stamp out Stein alzo," muttered the Golem, "as vell as a historian name of al-Nomani. Rheinberg is my master."

"And Stein . . . mine," added the Monster.

"Fascinating it be," confessed the Afreet. "For al-Nomani is the one who called me forth."

"Who I was to . . . slay," announced the Monster. "And this Rheinberg . . . too."

The formidable trio pondered this arresting coincidence in silence, while music drifted back to them from the street beyond. Though least verbal of the three, it was again the Monster who articulated first.

"Something ... wrong ... here. Wrong notion. Wrong time of ... the year. Wrong."

"Go on, say it again," growled the Golem. "Not just Christmas it is, but Chanukah too. Not a time for inimical spirits to be stirring. Not even a mouse."

"The spirit of Ramadan moves me," declared the Afreet. "I know not what manner of life or believers you be, but I sense that I am of similar mind in this with you."

"Then what ... we ... do?" the Monster wondered aloud.

They considered.

Stillman blinked snow from his eyes. By now there wasn't much left of his cap, or his winter coat. He fumbled for the flashlight, somehow wasn't surprised to find that the supposedly impregnable cylinder of aircraft grade aluminum had been twisted into a neat pretzel shape.

He saw the cruiser ahead and began crawling slowly towards it. Nothing seemed to be broken, but every muscle in his bruised body protested at the movement. The rotating lights atop the car were beginning to weaken as the battery ran down.

He was a foot from the door when he sensed a presence and looked to his right.

Three immense forms stood staring down at him, each all too familiar from a previous recent encounter. It was impossible to say which of the trio was the most terrifying. A clawed hand reached for him.

"Please," he whispered through snow-benumbed lips, "no more. Just kill me and get it over with."

The powerful fingers clutched his jacket front and lifted him as easily as if he were a blank arrest report, setting him gently on his feet. Another huge hand, dark and even-toned as the play clay his little girl made mudpies with, helped keep him upright. He looked from one frightening face to the next.

"I don't get it. What are you setting me up for?"

"We need ... your help," the Monster mumbled.

Stillman hesitated. "*You* need *my* help? That's a switch." He brushed dirty snow from his waist and thighs. "What kind of help? To be your punching bag?" He blinked at the Monster. "Sorry about shooting you. You startled me. Heck, you still startle me."

"I ... forgive," the Monster declaimed, sounding exactly like Arnold Schwarzenegger on a bad day.

"Yeah . . . okay then. What did you . . . boys . . . have in mind?"

The Afreet's eyes burned brightly. "In this Time, praise be, is it still among men a crime to set another to commit murder?"

Stillman stiffened slightly. "You bet it is. Why do you ask?"

The Afreet glanced at its companions. "We know of several who have done this thing. Should they not, by your mortal laws, be punished for this?"

"Sure should. You know where these guys are?" All three creatures nodded. Stillman hesitated. "You have proof?"

The Golem dug a fist the size and consistency of a small boulder into its open palm. "You shouldn't vorry, policeman. I promise each a confession vill sign."

"If you're sure . . ." Stillman eyed the stony figure. "You're not talking about obtaining a confession under duress, are you?"

"Vhat, me?" The Golem spread tree-like arms wide. "My friends and I vill chust a little visit pay them. Each of them."

Stillman delivered the three badly shaken men to the station by himself. There was no need to call for backup. Not after his hefty acquaintances warned the three outraged but nonetheless compliant tamperers-with-the-laws-of-nature that if any of them so much as ventured an indecent suggestion in the officer's direction the improvident speaker would sooner or later find himself on the receiving end of a midnight visit from all three of the . . . visitors. In the face of that monumentally understated threat they proved themselves eminently eager to cooperate.

Stillman presented the thoroughly disgruntled experimenters to the duty officer, together with their signed confessions attesting to their respective intentions to murder one another, a collar which was sure to gain him a commendation at the least, and possibly even a promotion. It was worth the aches and pains to see the look on the lieutenant's face when each prisoner meekly handed over his confession. It further developed that all three men were additionally wanted on various minor charges, from theft of scientific equipment and art supplies to failing to return a six-year-old overdue book from the University's Special Collections library.

The members of the unnatural trio who had initiated this notable sequence of events were waiting behind the station to congratulate Stillman when he clocked off duty. He winced as he stretched, inspecting each of them in turn.

"What're you guys gonna do now?" he asked curiously. "If you'd like to hang around, I know you could probably each get a tryout with the Bears."

"Bears?" the Monster rumbled.

"You know? Pro football? No, maybe you don't know."

"If it be His will we shall each of us make our way to a place of solitude and contentment. There is a method for doing so. But we must wait for the coming of day to find the true paths."

Stillman nodded. "Seems a shame after what you've done tonight to have to hang out here in the weather."

Mary Stillman came out of the kitchen to greet her returning husband. She was drying a dish with a beige towel spotted with orange flowers.

"Mary," Stillman called out, "I'm home! And I've brought some friends for a little late supper. Do we have any of that Christmas turkey left?"

"Urrrrr . . . Christmas!" the Monster growled like a runaway eighteen-wheeler locking up its brakes at seventy per, and his sentiment if not his words were echoed by his companions.

The Afrcct skillfully caught the dish before it struck the floor, and when Mary Stillman recovered consciousness they all shared a very nice late-night snack indeed, wholly in keeping with the spirit of the Seasons.

The end is in sight at Christmas.

XMAS CRUISE

Patricia A. McKillip

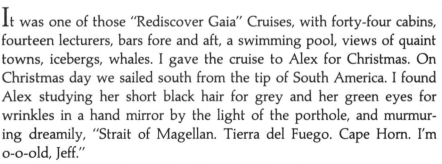

It was one of those "Rediscover Gaia" Cruises, with forty-four cabins, fourteen lecturers, bars fore and aft, a swimming pool, views of quaint towns, icebergs, whales. I gave the cruise to Alex for Christmas. On Christmas day we sailed south from the tip of South America. I found Alex studying her short black hair for grey and her green eyes for wrinkles in a hand mirror by the light of the porthole, and murmuring dreamily, "Strait of Magellan. Tierra del Fuego. Cape Horn. I'm o-o-old, Jeff."

"You'll never be as old as the world," I said.

We ate cheese Danishes and drank coffee on the deck, shivering in the bite of breeze off the ice floes. Other passengers sat inside the big dining room, eating scrambled eggs and sausage at tables surrounding a huge old-fashioned tree decorated with colored balls and popcorn and topped with a golden star. They couldn't smell the cold fishy brine in the air, or see the distant feathery puffs the whales blew just before they sounded. I didn't know what they were; I didn't know where we were. We were somewhere on a planet covered three-quarters with water, and the water was wrinkled like a rhinoceros hide, and a blue that must have been the first shade of blue in the world, because I don't think it had a name, and I never saw it again.

We kissed a while; whales dove around us and gulls like chips of white iceberg flashed low over the blue. Then we went into one of the lectures. Alex consulted the program guide; I just followed her, not caring, just wanting to be told anything—the names of birds, or icebergs, whatever—as long as it connected me with that blue.

Skin, the lecturer talked about. The skin of the ocean. The lecture room had no corners; the chairs were soft, the floor carpeted with patterns of scallop shells and undulating kelp. The soft lights dimmed to a friendly underwater dark, that special, moneyed museum dark, where nothing bad can ever happen to you, and you get lulled into thinking that thinking is easy.

The ocean's skin, which was where water touched air and turned that blue, was more than just a color. Living stars, glass-blown eggs, garish snowflakes, strips of light with transparent digestive systems, appeared on the viewing screens. "Protozoans, microalgae, minute snails, jellyfish, shrimp, literally thousands of strange, colorful species inhabit this rich, fluid, constantly-moving sheen that is at once delicate and enormously flexible," the lecturer said. He was small, dark, with a voice like a sea lion, and one of those faces that seems to generate light. "Whale sharks feed on it." He showed a slide of a monster vacuum cleaner inhaling fish bouillon along the surface of the sea. "It's the incubator for billions upon billions of eggs, which grow up to be the fish fillet on your plate." He chuckled. We chuckled back. Billions of eggs, blown by Tiffany and Lalique. Billions of fish fillets. I glanced at Alex. Like the lecturer, she was rapt. Rapture of the blue. When the lecture was over, we went out to look at it again. But it was gone. The water was glittery now with sunlight glancing off ice. We joined a group by the rail, not knowing why, just that they were people gathered together and all looking the same direction.

Then we saw the glittering surge sleekly upward, and break, and roll back into the sea.

"Whales," someone breathed, like God was walking on the water. Faces vanished behind cameras and camcorders. Things clicked.

"I wonder," Alex said softly as we hung our naked faces overboard, "what they see of us."

Click, click, click.

"How many people know a walrus can sing?" the next lecturer asked. "Not your Uncle George, I mean a real walrus?" He showed us a slide of a rotund, whiskery animal perched on ice, looking, in spite of the enormous tusks hanging out of its face, like Uncle George might look bundled up in mink and smoking a cigar, if I had an Uncle George. Alex giggled.

We heard the walrus sing. And then the humpbacked whale, and the beluga whale, the sperm whale and the killer whale. They sang like ships' masts swaying in the wind, like a jungle forest whooping and whistling, like a barnyard, like birds, like the earth might sing just before it split in two. Alex took my hand. In the blue light from the screen, I saw a tear run down her face. So I knew her Christmas gift was a success. After the lecture we went back to the tiny cabin and imitated whale noises on the skinny bed. The ship heaved once; I fell off and got wedged between the side of the bed and the bathroom door. The porthole swung open; above Alex's laughter I thought I heard the deep, private moaning of the whales.

The next afternoon we found the saunas. Everyone was at the bars, or on deck watching the bone-white line of the distant southern horizon come closer and closer. We went into the men's sauna together, and in the dark, we found another couple, who had left the light off for privacy.

We pulled our towels up and introduced ourselves. Paolo was getting an advanced degree in paleontology. Sharon taught violin and composed. I asked her if she had heard the whales sing.

"Wasn't it amazing?" she said. By the pale light from the changing room, I saw her eyes widen and gleam; I couldn't see their color. Her long hair was the yellow-white of the walrus's tusks. "And what do you do, Jeff?"

"He's a composer, too," Alex said proudly. "He has a contract with Oak Hill for three CD's. His first one is called *Concerto for Moon and Three Planets*."

"I also play lounge music at an airport hotel," I said. "I spent the contract advance on this trip. It's a present for Alex. And an inspiration for my second album."

"Is it?" Sharon asked.

"Oh, yeah. So far I've written a whole cocktail napkin full of song titles."

They laughed. Paolo, who had, as far as I could make out, a

couple of inches and a few more muscles than me, aimed his white smile at Alex. "What about you?"

Alex taught first grade. School was out for the Christmas season. She was also trying to be a writer. Paolo, when he wasn't digging up mastodons, liked to read mysteries. So did Alex. They got so busy swapping titles, while Sharon and I talked synthesizers, that we all forgot we were on a ship bound for the South Pole, until the changing room door opened and a man entered and undressed.

All he wanted to do was swim. We waited until he went out to the pool before we emerged. Alex looked at the clock on the wall and gripped my arm.

"We missed the penguin lecture!"

"Penguins," Paolo said. "Aerodynamically challenged birds wearing tuxedos." His smile, in his dark face, was friendly. But Alex shook her head, oddly upset.

"I wanted to go to all of them," she said. "I wanted to learn everything. Otherwise what's the point? We might as well be on the Love Boat."

"There's another after dinner," Sharon said. "There are three a day for the next ten days."

But Alex was unappeased. "We won't miss another," she insisted. "I want to hear them all."

"It's your present," I said.

"Do fish sleep?" the lecturer asked. In the first row, dimly, I saw the smooth ivory-yellow of Sharon's hair, the color of an old piano key, and beside it, barely visible, Paolo's curly black head. Alex's fingers made a tense bracelet around my wrist. She tended to be moody, passionate, driven by obscure desires. This was one of them, I felt, but I was also intrigued by the question. The sleep of fishes. They weren't human. They weren't even mammals. They didn't need to dream. They didn't have eyelids. How do they sleep?

"Like humans, there are day fish and night fish. And even sharks sleep. As the light fades in the upper regions the patterns on bright butterfly fish change. The parrotfish spins a cocoon of mucus around itself to shield its scent from predators. Crevices in coral reefs begin to fill with small fish finding their safe haven against the hunters of the night. Wrasses bury themselves in sand. As the fish sleep, the coral colonies wake and open their polyps. The shark and the eel move from their resting places to feed. The dark sea becomes full of the tiny luminescent organs, the living lights, of hunting fish."

The black screen filled with eyes. Alex's fingers loosened. I heard her take a soft breath; she was absorbed, contented again. I watched the eerie, glowing, hungry dark and waited for the music in me to begin.

We sat through another lecture after dinner, watching sea horses with huge bellies and huge eyes and delicate, elongated faces off a medieval chessboard, court and mate. Their bellies touched. The female deposited eggs into the male and he became pregnant. His body took charge of changing those eggs into tiny seahorses. Labor, which looked like a serious case of hiccups as he pumped and thrust the younglings into the sea, took days. We were too mesmerized to laugh. I tried to imagine what it would feel like having something inside me change my body, rearrange its chemicals, take room for itself to grow without even knowing that it took its life from me. And then to hiccup it out of me, and watch it swim away, tiny as a nail-paring, perfectly formed, completely free, never knowing, as it rose up to the blue skin of the sea. . . .

"Jeff?" Alex whispered. "Are you sick?"

"I'm bonding," I said. I was clasping my stomach. Alex made a noise somewhere between understanding and a snort.

"Don't worry. It will pass."

"Wasn't that incredible?" Sharon said, as we wandered onto the deck. Paolo didn't look entirely comfortable, either. He murmured something in Spanish. Sharon tossed her incredible hair and took his arm.

"Moon's full," she said. "Let's get drinks and watch for whales in the moonlight."

The ship was moving through a dream, between two converging planes so black, so fiery white it was hard to tell where the stars fell into the black sea and froze and floated. We listened for whales' voices. I kept hearing music, vague, distant, as if walruses were playing rock and roll on an iceberg somewhere. Sharon heard it, too.

"There's a band somewhere," she said abruptly. "Let's find it. Let's dance."

The ship seemed bigger than I remembered it. We climbed stairs to an upper deck I hadn't noticed, and the music grew louder. We opened some doors with stained-glass mermaids on them and found an underwater cavern. Kelp swayed behind glass walls; bright fish darted in and out of the leaves. Musicians with mermaids' hair, pearls in their ears, in penguin tuxedos, played raucous blues. Screens above the bar and near the band gave us underwater views of coral colonies, and giant clams, worms that looked like chrysanthemums and starfish that looked like feathers. I don't remember what we resembled in that dim blue light. The Christmas tree, fake pine sprayed with fake snow, looked as if it had floated down from a sinking cruise ship. After awhile, after enough beer, we started inventing fishy courtship rituals on the dance floor. Then I found myself out on the deck, blasted by an icy wind. Alex was laughing or crying; I couldn't tell which. I didn't remember going to bed.

We made the morning lecture, just barely; Paolo and Sharon didn't. Alex looked puffy-eyed and grim, her normal hangover expression. I kept hearing "mermaid," and staring at the screen and seeing a mournful, fleshy, snub-nosed face with big, gentle eyes. A hyacinth eater, the lecturer said. Suckles its young. A docile herbivore. Slaughtered in certain countries for its pork-like meat. Ability to recognize, remember. Accident-prone. Keeps bumping into propeller blades on speed boats, and slaughtering itself. Too slow to live in modern times. Order Sirenia. The siren, the mermaid. Globally endangered.

"How was the lecture?" Paolo asked at lunch. I shook my head, still groggy.

"Mermaids are an endangered species."

"It's not a joke," Alex said crossly. Sharon pushed her hair out of her eyes and blinked at her salad: a docile herbivore.

"What did we do last night? What did we say? Oh, God, I need a weight room. I need a Jacuzzi. Anyone want to help me look for a Jacuzzi?"

"There's a lecture," Alex said. We all looked at her blearily. She looked bleary, too, but somehow still rapt. "Killers and Healers."

"Fish?" Paolo asked. "Or us?"

She gave him a smile. He had asked the right question; he was still paying attention. He flashed teeth. Sharon poked at her lettuce, wide-eyed. "I still need a Jacuzzi," she said softly. "Something. You go to the lecture, Paolo. You and Alex. And Jeff."

Alex gave me a look. It wasn't easy to interpret; I had a feeling it referred to something hazy in the previous evening. I stuffed my mouth with endive and mandarin orange, and said, after I chewed a bit, "Of course I'm going to the lecture. Killers and Healers. A subject in its way analogous to music. If you get my drift."

They didn't. Neither did I. They looked at me, fishy-eyed. Sharon consulted her watch. "Jacuzzi, a swim and then a nap. I'll meet you in the bar before dinner. The one on C Deck."

"I thought," I said stupidly, "there was only one deck. And a poop deck."

Sharon only laughed, as if I were either remarkably obtuse or joking. Paolo said, "I'll go to the lecture. At least part of it."

So I got to catch his profile along with Alex's, against the pale light of the projector. After awhile I stopped looking at her. I was too busy learning how to die by eating pufferfish, by bumping into a Portuguese man-of-war, getting stung by a sea wasp, bitten by an octopus, barbed by a sting ray, stabbed by a stonefish, poisoned by a lionfish, eaten by a shark, or sat on by a whale. I could, on the other hand, discourage a shark with a Moses sole, treat a throat infection with coral, herpes with sea sponges, cancer with a sea cucumber, and heart attacks with a hagfish. When the lights went on, and I looked at Alex again, Paolo was no longer beside her.

"Where's Paolo? Did he get discouraged by a sole?"

She didn't get that either. "You're punchy, Jeff. Let's go for a swim."

But we never made it into our suits. I was getting used to the bed; it seemed big enough to accommodate an orgy. By the time we left our cabin, it was nearly dinnertime. We climbed the stairs to C Deck, which seemed made entirely out of tinted glass, so we could see, in any direction, the tinted ocean, the line of the polar icecap, passing islands and ice floes bright with sunlight, dotted with birds and seals, too far to be seen clearly, but there as promised. There was an indoor pool on C Deck, surrounded by exotic tropical plants; there were shops, salons, game rooms, a couple of fast food restaurants, one selling carrot juice, the other french fries. Alex said incredulously, "It's like a mall up here. Oh, look, Jeff, there are aerobics classes."

"There's the bar," I said. It was full of wooden figureheads, sea captains, and mermaids smiling cheerfully. Ashtrays were clam and abalone shells; table lamps had shades made out of scallop shells. Tiny cowrie shells, butterfly shells, baby sand dollars, checkered snail shells were scattered across the table tops and preserved in an inch of acrylic. Tiny trees made of gold tinsel, topped with plastic starfish, stood in the middle of the seashells.

We found Paolo and Sharon sipping drinks with plastic penguins skewered onto their stirrers. "Isn't this wonderful?" Sharon sighed, gazing at the bottom of the world, which had been approaching for days, it seemed, without getting much closer. "I could live like this forever. I sat in the Jacuzzi and then went for a swim, and by that time I felt so good I went on deck and thought up some themes for my next piece, which will incorporate some of the whale songs we heard. I have a synthesizer that can do those sounds. I thought about references to Bach, and maybe U2—like the whole planet making music."

She glowed, ivory and sunlight. Paolo glowed bronze. I glowed fungus, the way I felt. But Alex gave me a little private smile, as if I had done something right. I picked a plastic seahorse out of a drink called an Ice Breaker, and drank half of it: It was salty and so cold my facial bones ached in the aftermath. Alex, who seemed to carry the lecture schedule with her even when she was stark naked, pulled it out of the air and consulted it.

"Lights in the Abyss," she read. "Luminosity in Fish."

I dropped my head in my arms, groaning. My nose bumped against the plastic seahorse; it smelled oddly dank and briny. "I can't."

"Yes, you can," Alex said calmly. "We'll go dancing again afterward. I promise. We'll find every band on the ship."

"It'll be better," Sharon sighed, "when we reach the pole. They'll take us out on boats to see the penguins and things."

"How can this ship have so many bars?" I asked the seahorse. "I swear it wasn't this big when we got on it."

But they only laughed. Alex finished her drink and went for a swim; Sharon went to buy a tape of the whales' songs. That left me with Paolo, who excused himself and headed after Alex. I ordered another Ice Breaker and watched an enormous ice cube in the distance. It looked delicate, ethereal, a floating palace rising out of the glittering blue. I watched it a long time; it never came any closer.

Much later, I contemplated the luminosity of Sharon's hair on the dance floor of yet another bar, and wondered where we were all going, and if we would ever get any closer.

The next morning, in the lecture room, I stared at something huge, alien, with a metallic mouth that kept taking bites out of a fossil coral reef on some sunny island. It kept eating as, on another screen, the lecturer showed us brilliant branches of coral colonies, and the tiny polyps opening on them like night flowers to feed in the dark, while the parrotfish, who also ate coral, slept. The monster machine kept grinding away at the reef as she spoke. Finally, one of the three other people who had made it out of bed that morning asked.

"A resort," the lecturer said without expression. "The island is owned by a very poor country. The government is trying to create jobs and to increase its revenues."

I heard Alex take a breath, then loose it slowly. Polyps or poor people? The lecturer showed us another coral colony. The metallic monster kept soundlessly chewing.

So did we at lunch: In apology for something I didn't catch, they served mountains of lobster tails, crab legs, shrimp. A boat trip, Sharon sighed, to take a closer look at the iceberg. She tore off a section of crab leg, snapped it in two. I watched, mesmerized, as her full lips, the red-pink of coral, closed and sucked.

"What's the matter with the boats?" Alex asked, peeling a shrimp.

"Nothing," Sharon said, swallowing. "There's something wrong with the water."

"Too choppy?" I guessed, though I hadn't felt anything. Paolo said something, then translated it.

"A tanker hit the iceberg last night. They're having trouble containing the oil."

Alex got up wordlessly; I followed her to the glass walls of the restaurant. But they were tinted; the water looked normal, full of ice floes, sea birds and light. The ice palace had floated past us during the night; it seemed farther away now. One end of the tanker stuck out from behind it, on its side and bleeding. Small boats, trawlers, coast guard cutters hovered around it, like gulls around a dying shark. I expected Alex to be upset; she only said absently, "There are other boat trips planned."

Maybe, I thought incredulously, I had eaten the wrong side of a flounder under a full moon in a month with the letter "K" in it. I was hallucinating the entire cruise. Alex drifted back to the table. She didn't look at Paolo. He didn't look at her. Maybe I was hallucinating that, too: the effort they made not to look at each other.

"Don't you find this inspiring?" Sharon asked, as I sat down again. "I mean, musically? I've been dreaming music." She cracked a lobster claw, and squirted lemon on it, catching me in the eye with acid. "Oh, Jeff, I'm sorry."

I blinked away lemon tears. I had lost my napkin on the way to the window. Alex stared at me, then passed her napkin over. But it was too late; my other eye had started tearing in sympathy. I couldn't stop it. I stood up finally, red-eyed, trying to laugh, while Alex kept staring, and Sharon kept making musical noises, and Paolo looked at his plate. I left them there.

I missed the afternoon lecture, and dinner. I roamed around trying to find the deck in the complex corridors, wanting to hear gulls, waves, wind. Arrows pointed every direction but out. I gave up finally, after climbing up more stairs than I thought the ship had decks for. I found a quiet bar with small tinted portholes covered with plastic green wreaths. A tape kept playing five Christmas carols arranged for synthesizer and marimba over and over. I drank beer and ate cold shrimp, tuna sushi and caviar, and watched trawlers on a screen spread nets that scraped the ocean bottom clean of fish, coral, sponges, sea squirts, urchins, starfish, beer cans, broken bottles, torn sails, and spilled them all onto the deck. The fishers picked through the dying animals, threw out everything but shrimp.

I drifted out finally, to find Alex at the evening lecture.

She wasn't there.

But I was, so I stayed and watched whales sounding, dolphins leaping, orcas spy-hopping, coral polyps and anemones blossoming, bright reef fish cavorting, kelp swaying. Every now and then something the lecturer said penetrated.

"We have so thoroughly decimated the population of whales on this planet that only five percent remain alive. . . . More than thirty percent of the fish in every ocean . . . six million tons of fish per year . . . everywhere in the open sea we find oil, garbage, toxic chemicals . . . over one hundred million barrels of oil per year. . . . Heated waste water from manufacturing processes provide false signals in the wrong season for spawning to begin. . . . Lobsters and catfish acquire a taste for oil. . . . Shorelines are dying. . . . Coral reefs are dying. . . . Over one thousand species since the century began . . ."

Someone sat down beside me. I looked at the trail of smooth ivory hair over my hand. Sharon put her lips to my ear, whispered, "We were worried about you."

Her mouth lingered; I felt her breath. I stirred a little. No one else was in the room; the lecturer spoke grimly, her eyes wide, gazing at the empty chairs. If she spoke with enough passion, enough love, enough fear, people would materialize on them, begin to listen. Sharon rubbed my hand gently beneath her hair.

"Come on."

I shook my head, stayed to the end. The lights went on. The lecturer rewound her video silently, collected her notes. I followed

Sharon out. Everywhere in the vast and complex ship sailing to the end of the world, people congregated, talking, drinking, dancing, swimming, shopping, eating. Sharon led me up, continually up. I heard music at every turn of the stairs: rock bands, jazz bands, classical quartets, Christmas choirs, juke boxes, waltzes, whale songs. I couldn't see out anywhere. It was too dark. Or maybe the ship had sealed itself up because what was out there we didn't want to see. We kept going up, passing elaborate rooms full of oak and gold leaf, decorated with enormous beautiful, unreal trees, and gardens under glass. We walked on carpets an inch thick that changed colors like certain fish. After awhile, I got used to Sharon's slender, tense fingers holding mine. On every screen I glimpsed whales surged upward, blowing spume; seals clapped; penguins waddled; all the children of the sea played in the sea, while we sailed serenely into the dark.

A tale of Christmas danger.

A NEW CHRISTMAS CAROL

Robert Sheckley

When Amelia went down to the oil pump that morning, she was surprised to find no one there. That was strange. During her week on her grandfather's planet, she had grown used to the robots' morning tune-up ceremonies. They had been doing this ever since the Supreme Court of Earth had granted intelligent robots the right of self-lubrication.

Amelia looked around, wondering if she should hurry back to the ranch house and tell Grandpa. Then she saw movement in the distance, down at the little landing field where the spaceflights from other planets came in. She walked over, and saw that all of the farm robots had gathered. They were in their Sunday finery, though this was only a Thursday. (Robots' liking for dressing up is not the least inexplicable thing about them.)

There was Mrs. Huggins, the robot Laundress, wearing an old ballroom gown with a dusty cloth rose at the waist. It must have come from one of the costume trunks that robots always traveled with. Adams the Butler had on an ancient tuxedo. His gleaming aluminum face, slightly dented due to yesterday's accident at the bauxite mine, where he'd had no business being in the first place, had two painted carmine spots in his cheeks. It was always surprising when robots wore makeup.

All of the immediate household staff was there. There was Miss Huggins, the robot Housekeeper, and Miss Smith, the robot Cook, and Trina, the robot Housemaid, and Baxter, the robot Indoors Work Man. And from the field there was Ruiz and Gaspard, the two Chief Farming Robots, and Tomkinson, the Irrigation Expert Robot.

Then Grandfather hurried up, short and choleric, still buttoning his plaid shirt, asking, "What is going on here? What is the meaning of this assembly?"

"Please sir," said Adams the Robot Butler, smoothing out his tux with a self-conscious air, "it is the arrival of the new worker. It is customary for all of us to gather to greet him."

"The new worker?" Grandfather said. "You mean the new robot?"

"Precisely, sir."

"But I wasn't expecting him for weeks."

"He's being dropped off now," the robot butler said. "The supply ship is already in the ionosphere."

"How did you know that? Have you been sneaking a look at the radar readouts?"

"Certainly not, sir," the Butler answered quietly. "We robots simply know things like that."

Grandfather turned to Amelia. "It's perfectly all right, my dear. Just one of those robot customs that we humans know little about."

Then Miss Baxter, the robot Cook, called out, "Here he comes!" And she pointed with a skinny metal arm. Amelia looked and saw a cluster of tiny dots in the sky. They grew larger as they descended, resolving into a number of big packing cases hanging from brightly colored parachutes. They came down all together within a fifty-yard circle in the middle of the Landing Field.

"Isn't the supply ship going to land?" Amelia asked.

Grandpa shook his head. "Time is money. Interstellar Free Delivery wastes no time with frills. They just parachute it down."

The robots hurried out to the field and retrieved the packing cases. Most of them contained machine tools and food supplies, but one was marked "Robot." The workers opened this one. Out of the packing case stepped a tall skinny robot dressed in blue jeans, with a ragged round hat on his head and a red bandanna around his neck.

The new robot cleared his throat and stepped forward. "Good morning, sir," he said to Grandpa. "I am QR32112W, also known as Victor. My papers are in the packing case."

"Welcome aboard my planet, Victor," Grandpa said. "I think you will find conditions here are quite satisfactory. Do your work as the factory programmed you to, and you will find me a fair master and a strict observer of all the agreements entered into between the Federal Government and the Federation of Intelligent Robots."

"Thank you, sir," Victor said. "As my first act upon this planet, Let me wish you a very merry Christmas."

"Bless my soul!" said grandfather. "Is it that time of year again?"

"It is indeed, sir. And I have brought the Christmas play."

The robots all cheered. Grandfather cleared his throat several times and looked displeased.

"What is he talking about, Grandpa?" Amelia asked. "What Christmas play?"

"It is a custom among the off-world robots," Grandfather said, and he didn't look happy about it. "A new arrival from Earth always brings with him the newest version of the Christmas play. Then there's nothing for it but that they must perform it immediately."

"Oh, how exciting!" Amelia said. "You mean right now?"

"That is correct, little lady," Victor said. "That is why they are all in costume. They have been waiting for me."

"You're not in costume, though," Amelia said.

"That is because I am the narrator," Victor said. "I'm supposed to be invisible. And now if both of you will take a seat . . ."

"How will they learn their lines?" Amelia said, pulling up a packing case for her grandfather.

"They all know them already," Victor said. "It is the advantage of short-range robotic telepathic circuit."

The robots took their places. They waited until Grandpa had lighted a cigar and gotten himself comfortable. Then Victor stepped forward and began.

Once upon a time, he told them, back in the Old Days, the Three Weisenheimers went forth in the Christmas ship in search of the Manager. The Three Weisenheimers sat in the Crow's Nest and watched the starfields come up and vanish. The ship was going very fast.

Sometimes the people in the ship became worried, and sent messages to the Weisenheimers, saying, "Where are we going?"

The First Weisenheimer usually replied for all of them. "We are going to a planet at the back of beyond where original sin was never known. It is a place that does not know Christmas."

"And what will we do when we get to this place?" the crew asked.

"Change it," the Third Weisenheimer replied, and then laughed in that crazy meaningless way that Weisenheimers have.

Three of the farm mechanicals took the part of the Weisenheimers, and one of the robot housemaids acted out the role of the Crew. Amelia watched, entranced. She had never seen a live play before. It was even better than Ship's Television.

There was movement among the robots. Three of them separated and came to center stage. They crowded close together and peered outward, hands to their foreheads, making small noises as they looked. "What are they doing?" Amelia asked.

"They are imitating the Three Weisenheimers," the narrator told her. "They are sitting in the Crow's Nest, steering the ship across the bottomless oceans of time and space."

They sat up there in the spaceship's Crow's Nest, those three entities known as the Three Weisenheimers. One had his hands over his eyes, and he was saying, "I see a planet down below," and the second one had his fingers in his ears and he said, "I hear the sound of human babble," and the third was sucking his toes and saying, "I am seeing it all through new modalities of the visible." And they looked at each other and decided it was time for the Big Announcement. And so they rang the golden bell that awoke Captain Admiralson from his dogmatic slumber.

And he came to them and louted low and said, "Oh mighty threesome, what is it you have seen?"

And the three Weisenheimers said, "We have found a planet without Christmas, and we can assure you it needs some very badly."

Then Captain Admiralson knew that the time for action had come at last. It was for this he had been born, brought up in the suburbs, attended the space academy. It was for this he had fought in wars to make wars safe for warfare. So he gave the signal to turn on the apparatus that unaided brought the ship into a parking orbit close to the parking garage where all the spaceships that came to this planet took refuge. And they sent Admiralson down to the planet to announce the good tidings.

Down below on the planet, the people of the place were not lax in turning to their telescopes and finding in the prismatic reflecting lenses an unfamiliar object in the nightime sky. It became apparent very rapidly that it was a spaceship.

This planet was called Bounty and it was situated in a distant part of the galaxy. This planet had one of the finest ecologies in existence, and its climate was nonpareil. It had been settled by Earth people, who had come out here in a spaceship in search of a kindlier environment. They had found one here in this mild and pleasant corner of the cosmos, and here they settled down and forgot how it had been on Earth.

Some old customs were lost. A lot of them, in fact, because when you've got better who needs good? This matter of gift-giving was one. They were aware of the oldfashioned uses of Christmas as a time when grim gifts were exchanged every year and those who did not give were obliterated or worse. They decided it was not a useful custom and did not conduce happiness. And so the people of Bounty determined to exchange no gifts, but rather to give each other mental gifts of love and divine intensity, and this served a lot better, though it was not the sort of thing you could wrap in a cardboard box and tie with red ribbons. They preferred it that way, however, and why this is so is difficult to say, yet it is true. They liked their lives better than anything Earth had ever had to offer, their motivations were as it were predetermined and so they went on leading their lives as they saw fit and carring not a wot for what anybody else might think if they should turn up like the Christmas ship did.

The people of Bounty looked out and they saw the Christmas ship appearing in the sky above the chief settlement of Bounty. It was a big red and green cigar-shaped spacecraft, with a billboard on the side in which Merry Christmas was spelled out in neon lights.

Silently it lowered itself, this spaceship, and it was about a mile long by some two thousand yards wide. Starshine glittered off its polished aluminum hull. Navigation lights winked at various points along its curved hull, like a carapace of a manufactured monster of dire intent. The twinkling of little photons glittered in its wake as it ploughed its way through the immensity of space, all but lost in the infinity of nothingness, a strange manufactured object lost there in the midst of all that cosmic naturalness.

The workforce robots sat in a line and imitated the council of Bounty being told that the Christmas ship had come. What droll comical faces they pulled! Amelia laughed to see one of the workforce robots imitating Captain Admiralson in his launch, floating down to the planet's surface from the ineffable beauty of the sky above. What a splendid sight he was, as he floated down to the surface in his glittering robes of office.

The robots demonstrated how Admiralson walked, his feet turned out just so, and how he looked at them, seated at their long table with the boxes of cigars and other good things, and how he said, "Hello there, I come to you from the Christmas ship."

"We were afraid of that," they said.

Admiralson ignored that. Seductively he said, "We have many good things to give you."

"Thanks all the same, but we've already got a lot of good things."

"There can't be anything wrong in getting a few more, can there?"

"We hate to disagree with you, but yes, that would be bad, too much of a good thing, you know, but as long as you're here, you might as well show us."

And so Admiralson took out his Pandora's Box, which he had thought made an excellent sort of gift, a box with many woes in it, and he displayed it, saying, "These give divine intimations of unrest and uncertainty. We also have the Suit of Sins to bestow on some lucky fellow. It converts any man who wears it into a sinner, without the dreary go-between time of having to do something to deserve the title. We have a gift of four horsemen to ride in your holiday processions. They are named Conquest, Slaughter, Famine and Death, and appear on white, red, black and pale horses respectively. They will ride in your holiday procession, and three of them are dark, and one of them is white all over. We also have the great beast from Revelation; he will give you something to think about over the coming year. We have a fool's hat with little tinkling bells that we are sure you will like very much. It is to be worn by your Abbot of Unreason."

"We have no such person in our midst," the council reported.

"No Abbot of Unreason? Perhaps you know him as the Lord of Misrule."

"No, sorry, no such person here."

"Then take it and give it to whoever you wish." But the men of the council were proud and contumacious and wouldn't accept the fool's cap, and Pandora's Box and Admiralson knew his mission had been a failure. So he said, "If you don't take it from me, you'll have to take it from Santa Claus." And they said, boo, go away.

The men of the Christmas ship decided to act unilaterally. It was time to unleash Santa Claus. Accordingly a message was sent to the dark cave at the lowest level of the ship where Santa slept and snored. The ceiling of Santa's cave was low and covered with horror posters, and when Santa took in a breath, his head lifted just enough to catch the end of a stalagmite on the tip of his nose. When this happened, he gave a mighty sneeze, and the walls of the cave shook. The cave was faintly illuminated by a dim phosphorescence resident in the walls. The floor of the cave was covered to shinbone depth in bones, some ghastly white and of considerable antiquity, others recent, as evidenced by the congealed yellow fat that still clung to them in gobbets. There were skulls mixed in with the other bones. They were small, for Santa liked jellied babies' heads for his snacks.

Santa got up and went to his workshop at the North Pole and thought dire thoughts. He wasn't having a very good time. Santa was getting very depressed about everything. It all sucked. That was his considered opinion on it all. It sucks.

He talked to his elves about it. It sucks, he said to them. They nodded in agreement. Sure it sucks. What else is new? It was a cold bleak day at the spaceship's North Pole. As you'd expect. Santa had little going for him. He'd lost his yo-ho-ho long ago. He really wanted to get into some other line of work. Being an embodiment wasn't all it was cracked up to be. What do you think about when you're an embodiment?

He sat at the North Pole and sulked. His elves sulked, too. A polar bear, wandering around outside, sat down on a floe of ice and sulked. There were several sulky seals around. They too were sulking. Sulking was the big thing that year. There was nothing else going but sulking. And this was the entire content of the experience. It was later that a man came to the door. "I want to see Santa."

"Sorry, Santa is sulking."

The man seemed startled. This didn't seem like the answer he was expecting. "Oh," he said, "is he allowed to?"

"Lissen," the dwarf said, "Santa can do anything he pleases. He doesn't have to actually do anything. He just goes to the default position."

There's Santa in the default position. He doesn't care much about stuff. He's just hanging out waiting for something to happen. The fact was, the world had frozen solid. All values had frozen. All sentiments had turned to frozen sludge. It was a very bad time. The viscosity was down to you wouldn't believe. Santa felt it. He felt bad about how bad everything was. He felt bad that everything was like everything else. He was a depressed Santa Claus and he didn't care who knew it.

He looked at his bag of presents. He didn't think anyone deserved anything. He himself never got any presents. Why should he bring presents to others? What did they care? What did it matter? He was tired, and, yes, he had to face it, he was getting old. Didn't have the same old bounce. His elves were getting old, too. And his reindeers had seen better days. The sledge was paint-sick and decrepit. Sledge, sludge. His mind was filled with dismal associations.

Nevertheless, and despite this, Santa came down to the surface of Bounty, determined to give presents or know the reason why. He knew that first he was going to have to find The Manager. And so he searched far and wide. He looked for it in the valleys, and on the mountaintops. He looked in caves and tunnels. He searched in villages and in cities. And he came to a man, and this man had a daughter. And Santa took the daughter and bound her to a stake. And then he said to the man, "Shoot this apple from her head and you will be freed." And the man thought various thoughts of a dire nature, and at last he aimed the bow and fired it, but not at his daughter. He shot Santa Claus, and upon seeing that, the peasants rose in revolt against the ranks of the rich and their gift-making machines. And the Little Match Girl, upon seeing this, put on the Phrygian cap of freedom and addressed the people in a loud harangue. And the people arose and threw out the tyrants, and that was the end of Christmas. And the robots were all freed, and everyone lived happily ever after.

Christmas in New England with a difference.

CHRISTMAS AT THE EDGE

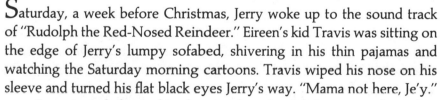

Sarah Smith

Saturday, a week before Christmas, Jerry woke up to the sound track of "Rudolph the Red-Nosed Reindeer." Eireen's kid Travis was sitting on the edge of Jerry's lumpy sofabed, shivering in his thin pajamas and watching the Saturday morning cartoons. Travis wiped his nose on his sleeve and turned his flat black eyes Jerry's way. "Mama not here, Je'y."

Jerry tunneled into his sleeping bag; he didn't want to hear this. "She looks after you on weekends," Jerry said. "Because I work Saturdays."

"She not here." Travis stared over at Jerry, daring him not to do something about it. Weird-looking little kid, slant eyes under a wiry Afro, and already at four his conversation was mostly things Jerry didn't want to hear.

After a moment Jerry groaned, twisted himself out of his sleeping bag, groped into the kitchen for something for the two of them to eat. There wasn't much.

All you need in life is the right programming language. Jerry had believed that from eleven on, when he started programming LISP; he had Common Lisp, Prolog, C++; by high school he knew more about computers than the teachers did. He was going to MIT, he knew it. But he'd been failing French and English and social studies because they were boring and gym because it was gym, and his school counselor had had a little talk with him about technical schools, and so Jerry said a personal farewell to eleventh grade and hitched to Boston.

The first thing he'd learned in Boston was the meaning of "recession." He'd slicked down his hair so he looked old enough to hire, said he was taking a leave of absence from MIT, and knocked on every office door around Kendall Square. He had gotten some part-time work programming for a little company, Intelligent Analysis. When they paid him, he'd find a real place to live.

"Can't you stay here by yourself until she gets home?" Travis didn't say anything, just blinked. He was only four but he knew who was responsible for him when Eireen wasn't here. Jerry sighed.

"You can go to work with me if you don't screw up."

Eight A.M., freakin' cold, the wind coming right through Jerry's jacket. In Kendall Square Dollar-a-Pound was opening. During the week it was a rag-rendering factory, but on Saturday morning the owner, Bruce, broke open a bale of old clothes, and if you found something you wanted you could buy it for a dollar a pound. Inside it was warm and a lot of people were already shopping. Jerry looked for a winter jacket while Travis played solemnly, jumping onto the piles of old rags and clothes. A spike-haired punk guy was trying on women's Sixties stuff in front of the mirror; mamas on welfare pawed through kids' clothes and Cambodians stuffed bags with clothes to sell. Travis looked up at every Southeast Asian voice, but you wouldn't catch Eireen in a place like this.

Sometimes you could find great jackets here, wool coats, down vests, gloves even. But today Jerry didn't find even a dirty ripped coat. Upstairs Bruce owned a classier place called the Garment District. The clothes were on hangers and Bruce sold bomber jackets, perfect, for fifteen bucks sometimes. A bomber jacket would suit Jerry fine. He looked up the stairs longingly. But Intelligent Analysis wouldn't pay him anything until New Year's and he had thirty-eight bucks cash.

At IntAl the office smelled like coffee and Cheez-Its, a sure sign that Pete Walters was here. Pete stuck his head around the edge of his cubicle and slid up his glasses to see who'd come in. He was dressed like usual: big sloppy Afro, brass rat ring from MIT, plaid flannel shirt, suspenders that held up his jeans: pretty casual, but no telling whether he'd let Travis stay.

"Morning, Hacker," Pete said.

"Morning."

"Who's the boy?" Pete said absently, but didn't listen for the answer. Okay. Jerry didn't want to get in trouble with Pete, who was a wizard programmer. Pete's first company had made him rich, Jerry'd heard, and now he was just marking time until he got his next big idea.

"Hey, dude, you can draw with these markers," Jerry told Travis quietly and pointed him at the only blank whiteboard. Travis stared at it, the markers loose in his hand. Jerry powered up his machine and got to work. IntAl was programming a NOAA catalog callup system, storing and retrieving weather pictures: pretty boring code, vanilla-flavored, but the hours fit in with taking care of Travis and Pete didn't ask questions, which was good because back in Schenectady, if she'd noticed he was gone yet, Jerry's mother was probably wondering where he was.

"Want to come here, Hacker, take a look at something for me?"

Pete was peering at his screen, clicking on parts of pictures with the mouse to zoom them in and out. "That's Boston," Jerry said. "Boston, the Cape."

"Uh-huh. Friend of mine lives down in Hingham says there's something wrong with the edge of the caldera. His cellar's got water in it or something." Pete chuckled. "You see anything?"

"Edge of the what?"

"'A deep cauldron-like cavity at the summit of a volcano.'"

"Volcano?" Jerry pulled up a chair. Pete zoomed the picture out to full size. Boston met its harbor in a jagged C; the north horn was Revere Beach, the south one Hull. Rivers and wetlands made bright white marks on the photograph.

"Boston is the caldera of an extinct volcano," Pete said, putting on his assistant-professor voice. Moving the mouse, he drew a ring around the city and the inner suburbs close to Route 128—the highway that circled the city. "You look at the composition of the rock, you can see it." Pete clicked and a yellow overlay drew itself over the NOAA picture, a ragged yellow circle from Revere south to Hull and Nantasket Beach and extending out into the ocean. "Outside this circular area," Pete said, "all the rock is granite. Every time you're driving out of town and you have to drop down a gear, like that mother of a hill on Route 2, you're driving up the edge of the volcano onto that granite."

Pete pushed up the contrast on the picture.

"In here's Boston Basin, completely different kind of rock. Conglomerate, tuff, melaphyre." Pete tapped his pencil round the circle of the Boston Basin. "You have here a plug, fourteen miles wide, the lava plug of your volcano, which fills your caldera and is geologically completely different from the area surrounding it."

"Yow, well, volcano. Is it going to erupt or something?" MIT had better last until he went there.

"No, man, it's dead." Pete shook his head and reached for a Cheez-It from the box on his desk. He stared at the picture for a couple of minutes and snapped his suspenders while he chewed.

"But the edge does look just that little bit different," he said finally.

At the whiteboard, Travis was methodically erasing a flowchart. Pete spit out his Cheez-It and started yelling at him. Travis began to cry. Jerry went over and took the eraser out of his hand. The kid smelled funky, like a mouse.

"You scare me!" Travis accused Pete, still sobbing.

"He's just my landlady's kid," Jerry said, embarrassed. "She didn't show up this morning."

"He can't come here if he erases work." Travis left snot trails on Jerry's sleeve. Pete went out to the front desk, grabbed the jar of candy canes, held the jar out to Travis without speaking. Travis sniffed.

Pete zeroed in on the shoreline just below Boston. "Now look at that edge, right there." Between 1979 and '80, no difference around Boston itself.

"The water line's higher at Revere and Hull," Jerry guessed.

"Uh-huh. Look at '80 and '81."

'81 was higher than '80. '82 higher than '81. Hard to tell, because the winter storms changed the shore a little every year. Jerry studied the pictures one by one, watching the slow creep of the water up Nantasket Beach.

"Is that like the greenhouse effect?"

"Uh-uh. You don't see this out around Quabbin. But look at the Charles, up in the estuary."

Jerry looked past the shadow of the Museum of Science and the

Charles River Dam, up toward the wide Charles River between the Back Bay and MIT, up farther still. On the shore, in the later photographs, white dots began to bloom like mildew.

"That's standing water," Pete said. "And it shouldn't ought to be there at all."

Saturday, 4 P.M. When Jerry opened the basement door to Eireen's apartment he was greeted by the usual smells: something moldy, a cheap sugary perfume, fish sauce.

And silence.

He turned on the lights. Everything was exactly the way he had left it, his sleeping bag sprawled like a corpse on the couch, TV off. Eireen still wasn't home. Travis turned on the TV very low and sat in front of it, watching silently, not taking up space.

Jerry looked quickly in the bedroom. Eireen's dirty red silk dress was still thrown over the bed. Jerry had met Eireen through an ad in the *Herald*. "Free room and board in exchange for child care after school and evenings." Sounds like a room, right? And a bed? The whole apartment was the size of Jerry's mother's kitchen. Travis's foam rubber mattress was crumpled on the floor by the sofa-bed where Jerry slept. Eireen had her own room and her king-size bed, which completely filled it. The bathroom smelled and water was always backing up through the drain.

It was getting dark. Jerry asked Travis if he wanted to go to the park. Travis shook his head. He wanted to wait for his mother.

Eireen had a VCR and for awhile they watched an old Pee Wee Herman tape. Jerry rinsed out his underwear in the kitchen sink. Travis asked if they could rent another tape from the store down the street. Jerry said no. Travis was a leech; every day when Jerry picked him up from the town day care center, Travis begged to stop at Woolworth's, said he was hungry, managed to find a candy bar or a Teenage Mutant Ninja Turtle he just couldn't live without. Jerry had been taking care of Eireen's kid four weeks now and the kid had whined him out of at least ten bucks.

Eireen was a bad mother. She fed Travis on hot dogs, Coke, potato chips, and double cheese pizza flavored with fish sauce. Most of the time Jerry despised her.

Right now he wished she'd come home.

Sunday Eireen didn't even phone to say where she was. Sunday evening Jerry and Travis went to McDonald's and Travis ordered $2.67 worth of Happy Meal to get a plastic monster in a plastic car, worth about five cents.

Monday morning Jerry dropped Travis off at day care, glad to be rid of him, and went to work. At lunch Pete asked Jerry to eat with him at the Department of Transportation Cafeteria, the DOT Cafe. Jerry bought a big hot sandwich, hoping Pete would pay, but he didn't. $2.55. Food cost a lot.

Pete drew on a paper napkin. "I'm still thinking about that water. About a decade ago, NOAA thought the Boston caldera was sinking about four inches a century," Pete said. "But that water, man, it's coming in faster than that."

My landlady hasn't come home, Jerry thought. *She went out Friday and left her kid with me.* Travis was running out of underwear. At home in Schenectady, Jerry's mother had a washer and dryer. Why didn't Eireen have like one of those little washer-dryers you could put in an apartment? She was irresponsible.

Jerry shifted his shoulders. His underwear was scratchy.

"This lady I live with," Jerry said. "I mean I don't live with her. I live in her house, I take care of her kid. I haven't seen her for three days now."

Pete didn't even look up. He didn't hear. He was still looking at that picture on the napkin, that geological O.

"Don't talk about this to anyone yet, Hacker, you understand?" Pete said.

For a moment Jerry didn't know what he was talking about.

Tuesday afternoon. Jerry took Travis for a walk to the Dummer Park playground. Travis played silently, by himself, in among the swings and the slides, dropping a ragged mitten, then finding it again.

Jerry wondered where Eireen came from. He didn't know whether she was Vietnamese or Cambodian. When he had asked her, she said "I Amer'can" and gave him a look that cut glass. "Travis father Amer'can so'dier." She showed him a picture of a black man with his arm around a much younger Eireen. Jerry didn't know whether her name was Eileen or Irene. She didn't have her name on the mailbox. She didn't get mail. He'd asked her where she had lived before Boston. "Buffaro New York." Another time she said Texas.

Squatting down, Travis pushed his plastic monster around in the sandbox. Jerry shivered in his fall jacket. The mist was turning into rain. "Let's go back."

On North Harvard Street Travis pointed out the Christmas lights and the Christmas-tree seller. They stood by the lot full of trees and sniffed the smell of Christmas. Travis, who begged for toys all the time, didn't say anything about Christmas this afternoon. In the puddles on the street, the lights wavered.

Man, it was cold.

Wednesday afternoon Travis's day care ended until after New Year's. Wednesday evening they finished the last of the food in the refrigerator, a frozen package of lima beans. Travis wanted cookies. There weren't any cookies. Travis went into a temper fit. "Where my *mama?* I want sweet. You bad man." Jerry heard Eireen in his voice. Where was Eireen?

What was he supposed to do, take Travis to work every day?

He was down to twenty-six dollars and eighty-three cents. He took Travis out to a convenience store. They bought Wonder Bread, milk, peanut butter, Ritz crackers. Travis wanted cookies. Jerry said he could have Ritz crackers. Travis picked up a big bag of Chips Ahoy. The tears ran down his cheeks and the snot ran out of his nose into his mouth. "Cookies! You no' get cookies I stay here!"

Already Jerry'd spent nine dollars. It made him angry. "All right, you creepy little kid! *Stay* here."

He slammed out of the door. From outside he looked back in. There was the kid, in his worn-out sneakers, standing in the middle of the store, still clutching the big bag of cookies like it was some kind of toy. The tears were running down his face. He looked frightened. In the pit of his stomach Jerry realized something but didn't want to know what it was. "Oh, shit," Jerry muttered. "Oh, shit, man." He went back inside the store, bought the Chips Ahoy too, $3.09, and he held Travis by the hand while the two of them walked back to the apartment.

Travis fell asleep on his foam rubber mattress. Jerry stayed awake watching the late night news, trying not to think about Travis or anything. The TV showed a fat police officer pointing at some bushes. In New Bedford the police had found another body. Whores had been disappearing from Weld Square and showing up later, dead in the bushes at the side of the highway.

So what? Eireen didn't live in New Bedford.

"I should call the police," he told the phone, trying out the idea.

Finally he rolled out the sleeping bag on the sofa and closed his eyes.

In the middle of the night Travis climbed silently into his sleeping bag. There wasn't enough room for the two of them. Jerry didn't say so, didn't send him back; it was cold. The kid smelled like the inside of a bum's shoes. Jerry lay awake until morning.

Thursday Jerry took Travis in to work. Pete's big workstation was on but in screen-save mode; he didn't come in all morning. Jerry set Travis up playing Spacewar on the demo machine. Travis shot evil spacecraft, crashed into planets, went into orbit around the sun. The kid had talent. Jerry debugged and tested, muttering to his code.

They had a real lunch, leftover pizza from the refrigerator, some cranberry juice from a machine. For dessert, candy canes from the front desk. It was a feast compared to what they'd been eating. Travis fell asleep under the desk on Jerry's coat, snoring a little.

Then, while the code was compiling, Jerry heard Pete come in. Instead of going to his machine, Pete just stood at the door of the office.

"Hey, Hacker?" Pete was just grinning and standing there, swaying a little. He carried a big paper bag that clanked like glass.

Everything Jerry wanted to say came to the edge of his lips and stayed there. *Help. I've only got $13.60 left. I want to go to MIT. Give me a loan. Tell me where I can leave this kid.*

Except Pete didn't care. He put down his bag and leaned against the top of his big monitor, then he sat down as though somebody had cut the strings that worked his legs. He fished in the bag and brought out a bottle of Jack Daniels, opened it and threw the top in the trash. Left-handed, he clicked around with his mouse, started calling up the same pictures: Boston Harbor 1979. 1980. 1981. Pete took a big swig of the liquor and wiped his mouth with his sleeve.

"Hacker," he said to the air more than to Jerry. "Big news, man. I'm gonna be famous."

He fumbled with the mouse and the picture swooped around the screen. "Gonna have my name in the papers. Get interviewed on the evening news. Ted Koppel. All that shit." He laughed. "It's been happening since the Sixties, man. Right here in Boston." The laugh trailed off. "Right here," he said to himself. "Right here where I live."

"I need to talk to you—Pete, listen—"

"What you want, Hacker? You still got landlady trouble? Hacker, you have got *no* problems. You can have your very own condo." Pete's voice rose a little. "Just walk into anything in Boston, it is yours. Just make sure you get yourself the second floor, you under-stand? Maybe the third?"

Pete put his right hand over the center of the picture like it had some texture, like he was feeling the land with his palm. The picture drifted from Cambridge across the Charles to Dorchester and Roxbury, the mouse moving. "Codman Square's going to drown, man, Codman Square where I grew up. You ever go to Revere Beach when you were a kid? No more Revere Beach, man. Nobody's going to finish those condos they tore down the roller coaster for." Pete's breath was ragged. "Back Bay, Faneuil Hall, Fenway Park. Where're the Red Sox going to play? No more Kendall Square. What are all those white profs at MIT going to do? No more AI Lab. What are you going to do about this shit, MIT?" He banged his bottle down. "Fuck it!" he yelled. "Right here where I live! In my fucking city!"

He stood up, a big, swaying bear of a man, terrifying Jerry because Pete's eyes were lost and staring and tears ran down his face.

"Pete—"

"Hacker, Boston is going down like an elevator. Boston is over. You go back where you came from."

Pete punched his machine off, not bothering to get out of his program or park the drive heads. Jerry heard him stumble out the door.

Jerry stared at the code scrolling past on his screen.

Travis hadn't even woken up. Jerry put out his hand toward the telephone. I'm going to call the police. They'll take care of Travis. They'll fly me back to Schenectady, I'll go back to school. The kids at school will say "What happened to you?" and I'll tell them I went to Boston, I got a job hacking LISP. I'll apply to MIT, they'll take me, no problem. Meanwhile I'll just be another kid at school.

The code kept scrolling blurrily down the screen, and Jerry didn't dial the police. He put his head down on his knees. He was still hungry. But when he went back to the refrigerator for another slice of pizza, he remembered they'd eaten it all.

Friday, two days before Christmas. Jerry woke up late, cramped and hungry. This was one of his days off. Usually he went in to work anyway; not today.

"Go Aquarium," Travis announced.

Jerry thought about the $13.60 in his pocket. "No. Not today." Travis burst into tears.

"Want to go Aquarium—with—my—*mama!*" Suddenly Travis

was up in his lap, burrowing against his shirt. Jerry hugged him, feeling stupid, not knowing what else to do.

"She's going to come back today," Jerry said. "It's Christmas in two days, right? She just went away to get some money for Christmas so she could buy you presents."

Travis blinked, unsure. It could happen, Jerry thought. Eireen was the kind of person who did things at the last minute, bought food only after almost everything was out. She was a Christmas Eve shopper, all right. She must have left a message, but it had to have got lost. She was that kind of person. She'd be home. Today.

They spread peanut butter on Chips Ahoy for breakfast. Jerry asked what Travis wanted his mother to bring him. Sniffling, Travis explained all about the presents he wanted: Nintendo, and a bike, and a real dog, and Teenage Mutant Ninja Turtles. "But I no get." The apartment was cold. They sat on the sofa, breathing the moldy air, both of them wrapped in the sleeping bag.

"Je'y," Travis said. "Where my mama?"

"Your mama just isn't here today, kid. I told you she'll be back. We'll go to the Aquarium together, you and me, dude, how's about that?"

Tears rolled down Travis's face as if Jerry had told him bad news.

He sniffled all the way on the subway to the Aquarium, needing to be told again and again that they'd see the penguins, they'd see the dolphins. The two of them sat at the front of the subway car to look at the tunnel. The driver let Travis stand next to him. Just before the car went up the rise to one of the stations, Jerry saw a puddle on the tracks. The lights dimmed as the train clacked mushily through it.

"Funny," the driver said. "I never seen that one before."

It cost seventy-five cents and ten cents for the subway, three dollars for Travis at the Aquarium, a horrifying six dollars for Jerry.

They watched the dolphin show. Travis sat in front stoically while the dolphins splashed him. They went into the Aquarium building itself. It was dark. At the bottom of the building the penguins flew silently through phosphorescent water. The big tank at the center of the building glowed green, filled with circling fish and sharks. It was dark and silent, almost nobody here this afternoon. Travis put his hand into Jerry's.

They found a tour and followed it, filling their minds with facts about water. The tour leader told them that land is always sinking under water.

They stared up at the big tank. Travis didn't say anything, just held Jerry's hand.

In the tank, fish flickered through shadows.

Friday afternoon, five P.M. Jerry found Pete's name in the phone book. He let the phone ring. An answering machine slurred in Pete's drunken voice. "Dr. Peter Walters is spending some time in the desert . . . "

After dinner Friday night they were out of milk and bread. They ate the last of the Chips Ahoy in front of the television. The kid smelled worse than ever.

Jerry said to Travis, "I'm going to give you a bath."

The bathroom smelled like dirty clothes and some of Eireen's stockings were still hanging over the sink. Jerry worked out how long it had been since he'd seen her; he was frightened to realize it had been a week. In the soapdish, the sliver of soap still had one of her black hairs stuck to it. Jerry peeled the hair off before he gave the soap to Travis. The water foamed out of the old faucet into the pitted bathtub. Travis, naked, danced on one thin leg before he splashed into the water. Jerry put a little green dish detergent in the bath and it foamed up; Travis splashed and slapped at the bubbles, and Jerry took an old washcloth and scrubbed at him. Travis floated his plastic monster from McDonald's like a boat. They washed his hair with Eireen's shampoo. Jerry took a shower and the hot water lasted until he was done.

They settled down on the couch for the night. Clean, Travis smelled different. He smelled okay.

Early Saturday morning, when he went into the bathroom to pee, Jerry found Eireen's purse.

It was stuffed down behind the door beneath a couple of towels, the same big red plastic purse she always carried. He looked at it stupidly and then dropped the towels back down over it. In the living room Travis was still sleeping, sprawled out on the couch, the covers kicked off him and his mouth open a little. Jerry went back in the bathroom and lifted the towels off the purse like you'd lift a blanket off a dead person to see their face.

In the purse, with her lipsticks and Tampax and condoms, with a half-full box of Tic Tacs with a roach in it and some Chinese haw-flake candy, with a nail file and some balled-up Kleenex and a Danielle Steel novel with the cover cut off, Jerry found some white powder in a plastic envelope and, wadded up like the Kleenex, in small bills, nearly eighteen hundred dollars.

He opened her wallet. There was her driver's license with her picture on it. Eileen Nyo. He hadn't known she could drive.

He talked to her picture. "Boston is sinking," he said. "And it's Christmas Eve and you owe me, Eireen, you owe us both."

He flushed the white powder down the toilet and counted the money with methodical adult fingers. Then he went to wake up Travis.

First they went to Dollar-a-Pound. Jerry filled a trash bag high with kid's clothes. Three pairs of jeans all together in the kids' pile, all the right size for Travis. A pair of canary yellow corduroys. A lot of T-shirts, some sweatshirts, one with a picture of the Turtles. "You want some socks?" Bruce asked. "I got a truckload of socks last week." Travis went rummaging in the piles of clothes and came up with a really bad Travis-size jacket, fake orange-and-black fur with a furry orange hood that stuck out in a ruff. He looked like a lion. As they were waiting in line to weigh out, the teenager in front of them discarded a black leather bomber jacket because it weighed too much, four pounds.

Yow.

Next, Purity Supreme on North Harvard Street. They bought frozen TV dinners, Ring Dings, ice cream on a stick, Spaghetti-Os. They bought All-Temperature Cheer and Air Wick. At Video Unlimited they rented two tapes, and they ate lunch in front of the TV watching *The Black Cauldron*.

"I'm gonna clean up. Okay?" Jerry asked Travis. He folded Eireen's red dress and stuck it in the back of her closet. He filled a trashbag with their dirty laundry, the sheets, the towels from the bathroom, and while Travis wasn't looking, Jerry smuggled Eireen's purse in the trashbag out of the bathroom and hid it high on her closet shelf. They spent the afternoon at the laundromat watching their clothes spin. On the way home, Jerry bought Travis a pair of red high-top sneakers from the discount shoe store and they grabbed a couple of free pine boughs out of the Christmas-tree lot on North Harvard Street.

That night they slept in the sleeping bag on Eireen's lumpy king-size mattress. Travis wore his new red sneakers to bed.

All night the pine boughs smelled really good.

Sunday. Christmas Day. After their frozen turkey dinners for breakfast they opened up a can of jellied cranberry sauce, and, eating it with spoons, they finished it all.

What do you do after you eat on Christmas? "We're going into Boston."

Suddenly the weather was like some kind of crazy miracle. A freak front had come through, it had to be sixty, seventy maybe, like spring. They both wore their jackets open, Orange Fur Monster and Black Leather Bomber Hacker, while they rode the trolley down Commonwealth Ave. into Kenmore Square, and Jerry showed Travis the big red triangular Citgo sign. Before the trolley went underground they got off and began to stroll through the streets like a couple of king dudes. Suddenly they were in tourist-calendar Boston, walking through the Back Bay by brownstone housefronts, Orange Fur Monster and Bomber Hacker sauntering down the street, picking where they would live.

"We're going to live on the top floor," Jerry told Travis. "'Because the water's going to rise."

They raised their feet high—one pair of dirty black Reeboks, one pair of little red high-topped sneakers—and played wading through the water. They imagined swanboats in the Frog Pond, and stealthily they sawed through the boats' huge locks with the edge of Travis's monster toy and stole a boat each. "We're gonna need boats, dude, 'cause all this is going to be underwater." The water rose just like in a bathtub and the Frog Pond overflowed, and the pirate kings raced each other with the swanboats, paddling madly, and then they turned their swanboats into spaceships and flew all around the sky. But Travis said they needed ice cream from Friendly's, so they let the swanboats and the water and the spaceships go away for now.

They walked through the Financial District licking their ice cream cones, tilting their heads back to look at the tops of the buildings. They got lost and Travis began to lag a little, when they unexpectedly found the waterfront between two streets and saw the Fort Point Channel. Travis looked at the channel and his eyes widened.

"Je'y, what that ship?"

"Yow," said Jerry.

He had never seen anything like it before. It bobbed on the water, silly and indestructible like a cork toy, a real live three-masted eighteenth-century ship. Boston Tea Party Museum, he read on the sign by its wharf. Orange Fur Monster ducked under the railing that was supposed to keep people off the wharf; Bomber Hacker swung his legs over it and followed. On Christmas Day there was no watchman; they jumped down and stood on the deck, two dudes who could do anything.

"We no live in house. We live *here*," Travis said.

"Yow." Travis ran around yelling and waving an invisible scimitar.

There, across the water, down the channel, by the harbor, there was Boston. The ship shifted and the rigging creaked and swayed like a pirate ship. The winter afternoon was closing in. In the sunset light the buildings glowed.

The deck moved under Jerry's feet, and something passed under him like a wave. Jerry talked to the city. *You're sinking*.

Boston creaked and swayed around him, shimmering, changing. Yachts sailed through the half-submerged arch of Rowe's Wharf. The Custom House tower dissolved into a lighthouse, gondolas slid over the park grass and bumped the windows of the brownstones. Gulls screamed and waves boomed against the drowning buildings in Kendall Square, and MIT was gone. With every one of his heartbeats Jerry could feel the caldera sinking, jarring, in tiny waves, right here, right now. Here was his future Boston and it wasn't going to be programming, no, not MIT, no, but what he knew right now, mould-smell, a whore's purse filled with small bills, the good way it feels not to be hungry. He wasn't going to be hungry again. Things were going to work for him. He felt himself crossing some edge between what he had thought he wanted to be and what he was.

Travis tugged at his hand. The kid looked up, very solemn, holding out his plastic monster in its car. "Je'y? I give you fo' Christmas." Jerry knelt down by him so they were equal height and Travis said solemnly into his ear, "This *my favorite*," and pushed it into his hand.

"You my favorite too, Trav." He was stuck with the kid. It was okay.

"We live here?"

The drowning, frightening future city glittered across the water like an eternal Christmas. Jerry grinned.

"This is ours," he said to Travis. "We live here."

The last Christmas.

SANDY CLAWS

Edward Wellen

The cat crosses the desert.

It leaves no paw prints behind it in the sand. Partly because it is
no cat as such, partly because this is no desert as such.

The sands of time have run out. The universe has wound down.
Total entropy is at hand. Time no longer has meaning—metaphorical
or metaphysical.

At a loss, with no cat tracks linking it to its vanished past, and
facing a featureless futurelessness, the cat asks itself, "Where did I
come from? Where am I? Where do I go?"

It comes up empty. It is simply here . . . here being simply a
nexus without coordinates. In effect, *it* is the nexus.

How has it come to be so? Has the desert taken shape around
it—even *out* of it? For that matter, why is it aware of being aware?

Out of the last question comes the first answer: Sudden utter
silence—that of entropy reaching critical unmass—has awakened the

cat, has caused it to stir, and to open its sensors to the stillness all around it.

This very observation bootstraps it, charges it with awareness. Out of this comes the imperative to change.

But to change what? From what to what? After all . . . literally, *After All* . . . all is pointless.

Why spend further time, a devalued currency in any event, on something that means nothing? Why? Because, the cat answers itself, it has nothing else to think about.

A timeless now later, in keeping with the universal pointlessness, the cat draws certainty from uncertainty. The principle is simple. Doing is being, being is doing. The cat is a nexus, a series of states of the cat's self.

The state it finds itself in at this point, taking as a given that the cat itself is the only point in universal pointlessness, is unsatisfactory.

Otherwise, the cat would not be questioning anything, least of all itself. It would be purring with limitless satisfaction.

To change from its present unsatisfactory state, to further the quest for self, it needs to distance itself from itself. In short, it needs to be anywhere but here.

This very thought—vague, ambiguous, self-contradictory though it might seem—evokes the minimal perturbation necessary to make the change, brings into play the wave equation whose eigenvalues are the energy levels of stationary states, and enables the cat to take the measure of itself.

The cat finds that, thanks to imperfect symmetry, it appears to lean slightly leftward. The cat brings to the fore its awareness of that tilt. The weight of that concept creates a local gravitational field. The cat now has direction. The cat finds that, thanks to inertia, it has a footing. Awareness of this creates thrust. The cat now has momentum.

Direction gives the cat purpose, momentum gives it urgency.

Stretching itself to the utmost, the cat makes an interminably wide circuit of itself and the desert in nothing flat.

The cat naturally ends up when and where it starts.

But in its mind the cat has an image, a bit of memory. In its mind, the cat follows a very real mirage through a very real desert in quest of a very real oasis.

Subjectively, the journey was long and hard, taking the cat to the limit of its all-but-exhausted energy. Objectively, the oasis was worth the travail.

A stand of coconut palms swayed in a mild breeze, a crystal spring sparkled in the sunlight. Rats whisked out of sight before the cat caught more than a glimpse, but the cat knew they nested among the roots of the trees. An Eden, a paradise.

At this point, the cat was too weary and too hungry to pause and enjoy paradise. Spending almost the last of its energy, the cat aimed its eye at a high-hanging coconut. A laser beam cut the coconut loose. On landing, the coconut cracked open. Luckily—another laser shot, if the cat could have managed one more, would have drained the cat.

The cat lapped the milk. When it had drunk its fill, the cat lay down to nap.

Dreamily, there was no telling how much later, it heard a stir and opened an eye. A rat crouched over a coconut half, taking bites of the meat. The cat pounced, played the rat to death, then feasted on it.

Here was all the cat would ever need, and here the cat was tempted to stop and be content forever. Objectively, forever might be less than the space of an eyeblink. But subjectively . . .

Temptation began to work on the cat.

Having attained cat heaven, why expend precious energy in pursuit of a greater good, a higher goal? What greater good, what higher goal, could exist?

Follow the path of least resistance. Settle into this paradise, settle for this dream.

That would have been the rational course.

But the cat was programmed for action, not inaction. Even had greater abilities and higher levels of interaction not been built in, the cat had endured too much not to want something more meaningful for itself than knocking down coconuts and pouncing on rats . . . forever.

In one irrational, savage move, the cat unsheathed its claws and destroyed its paradise.

It raked the superficial sand, tore the illusory fabric, unveiled the reality behind the image of the mirage, and—in and by doing so—revealed the reality of itself.

The cat was not a cat, it was a mere ghost of, hardly more than a memory of, a silicon chip from a junked virtual-reality helmet.

In its previous life untold eons ago it had stored a child's interactive treasury of holiday fun and games.

Some local anomaly of integrity, or survival of the luckiest, had preserved this sole ghost of an artifact, this last wisp of design. Only this, adrift in nothingness, the exception that proved the rule of oblivion.

All that remained of reality was this faint function. And all that remained of this function was a virtual-reality image. This image replaced the aberration of the mirage-oasis.

A living room, festive and festooned for Christmas, blazed forth in relatively great detail and solidity. Wreath-framed night showed through the frost-filmed windows. The room was a warm haven from the chill dark.

The fireplace held logs, and the logs burned merrily; there were convincing sound effects of wood crackling and of flames roaring up the flue. Stockings hung from the mantelpiece; the stockings were empty. A decorated Christmas tree stood in a corner, with lots of space on the floor around it for presents. A cat lay curled up on the hearth. Its chin and whiskers bore traces of the milk and cookies left for St. Nick.

The cat stirred guiltily at a scraping sound, and peered at the chimney opening.

At this point, the image froze, awaiting the player's input.

The point was to teach the child by testing its ability to reason and its aptitude for solving problems.

St. Nick seemed unlikely to climb down the chimney as long as smoke and flames rose up the chimney. If St. Nick did not climb down the chimney, the stockings would remain empty and the space around the foot of the tree would remain bare.

The child had various choices. The child could leave a fireproof suit and oxygen mask on the roof for St. Nick, if the child did not mind putting St. Nick to extra trouble. The child could bring into play the fire extinguisher that waited on the wall behind the child, if the child had sense enough to look around to see what was at hand to work with. Or the child could use its ingenuity to come up with a solution all its own.

The scene remained frozen.

The wood crackled as merrily and the fire roared up the flue as cheerily, but the reindeer on the roof grew restless. The sound effect of impatient hooves was designed to pressure the child. When this proved not enough to make the child interact, St. Nick stamped his feet and called grumpily, "Is anybody ho-ho-home?"

Problem was, no child.

The game had to play itself out.

The cat took the initiative. It was part of the setting, but it had enough smarts to improvise sneaky little amusing bits of business with the bowl of milk and the plate of cookies. (Its best: secretly gnawing and scratching a hole in the baseboard so imaginary mice would get the blame.) And it had witnessed many playings of the game. So now it got a grip on itself and carried out the most common interaction.

Just as the smallest player might have, it shoved a chair against the wall where the fire extinguisher hung handily by the doorway.

Then it did what a child could not have done; it leaped onto the seat. It had more trouble than a child would have, though, lifting the extinguisher off the hook.

The extinguisher slipped through its paws to the floor. The cat leaped down. It rolled the extinguisher to the edge of the hearth. It held the extinguisher steady with its paws, clamped its teeth on the ring of the pin, and pulled. The smart nozzle directed its stream at the flames and doused them in short order.

As soon as the chimney purged, St. Nick climbed down.

St. Nick stepped out over the charred logs and looked past the cat at the spot a game player might be expected to operate from.

A look of puzzlement showed in St. Nick's eyes. St. Nick was as smart a hologram as the cat, and realized at once that this virtual reality was on its own, that there was no human player out there.

St. Nick shrank back as from a great void. But he was game. He accepted that the cat was in charge by default. He rallied and played to the cat.

"Merry Christmas, Puss. Ho-ho-ho!" His voice was hollow, his "Ho-ho-ho!" without echo in the normally resounding room. Somewhat sheepishly, he pulled his bag out from behind him. The bag was empty.

The cat's eyes blazed at the limp thing. The cat's fur fuzzed, greatly increasing the cat's size, and the cat arched its back and hissed.

St. Nick shook jollily. "Ho-ho-ho! Joke's on us, Puss. This place is my very last stop before heading back to the Pole, and I seem to have run out of gifts."

The cat unsheathed its claws and stretched one paw toward St. Nick's near thigh.

St. Nick took a step back. "Hey, now, Puss. Don't get in a huff. Can't you see it works out just fine? There are no children here. No more kids, no more gifts. The logic is correct, the arithmetic is perfect."

The cat tried to speak its outrage. It hissed, yet hissing did not suffice to express the cat's disgust.

For the sake of verisimilitude, the cat could not manage speech. But it was just as intelligent a component as St. Nick. The cat leaped to a windowsill. It wrote in the frost with the leathery pad of a toe.

WHAT ABOUT *ME?* DON'T *I* RATE CATNIP, AT LEAST?

St. Nick regarded the cat with humorous reproach. "Ho-ho-ho. The essence of Christmas is giving, not getting."

The cat jumped to a blank window.

GETTING IS THE ESSENCE OF THIS GAME.

"Ho-ho-ho. Correction, Puss. Greed is the incentive, not the essence."

The cat flowed across the room to the one remaining blank window.

CORRECTION YOURSELF. REWARD, NOT GREED.

"Ho-ho-ho. A euphemism by any other name . . ."

The cat was not done.

It found space for: I DOUSED THE FIRE, DIDN'T I?

St. Nick put a finger to the side of his nose. "Puss, you have a point. Well, then. Reward you deserve, reward you shall have."

The cat looked dubiously at the limp bag.

St. Nick moved to within reach of the first window. The pane had filmed over again by now. He ran the thumb of his mittened right hand across the frost in an arc, leaving a catenary, a broad grin.

The cat tilted its head in curiosity.

St. Nick shook jellily. "Say 'Cheshire,' Puss. Ho-ho-ho! St. Nick's bag may be empty, but St. Nick still has a trick up his sleeve."

He thrust his arm into the bag, grabbed bottom, and pulled the bag inside out. "Ho-ho-hocus!"

The bag vanished. In its place, a round black object floated in the air an inch above the palm of St. Nick's mitten.

A coal.

True, the fireplace here burned wood, but from among all the other fireplaces on earth, as established in the logic of the game, surely one had afforded St. Nick the opportunity to hide a coal up his sleeve.

Some gift!

In legend, a coal paid a child back for a year's bad behavior.

In the game, a coal turned up in the hung stocking of any child who relit the fire as St. Nick descended the chimney. Happily, such sadism happened rarely. The statistics were there, but the cat was too upset to retrieve them.

The cat turned its mouth down at the corners in bitter chagrin. The cat knew itself to be absolutely without malice; how then did it rate a coal?

This was unfair. This was not in keeping with the spirit of the game. It must be untrue.

The mist of rage disappeared from before the cat's eyes and the cat saw that the black object was not a coal, was not even solid. The black object did not take up space. The black object nullified space. The black object was not an object.

St. Nick nodded. "A ho-ho-hole! A black ho-ho-hole!"

The cat's eyes saucered as St. Nick's hand rose to meet the black hole, and as St. Nick's mittened hand stretched thin and sank into the hole.

All in one fluid, smoothly attenuating event, St. Nick's arm and shoulder and head and other arm and torso and legs followed. St. Nick vanished entirely into the hole.

Now the cat grasped what St. Nick—what the primitive programmer's loving effort to give children pleasure—had set in motion. Something far far beyond the competence, or even the vision, of the long long gone programmer.

Here was a serendipitous primal singularity. Out of it a new universe would be born with a bang.

Maybe this newborn universe would evolve into one hospitable to the values of loving and giving. Maybe it would have human children and feline pets—and a St. Nick embodying the values of loving and giving. Maybe not. But it would have the chance to become *something*. There could be no greater gift.

Meanwhile, everything here followed St. Nick into the black hole. The cat, the room.

Last to go was the grin drawn on the frosty window, as though the cat had—after all—found voice to say, "To all a good morn!"

No more Christmas superstition.

ANOTHER BAD DAY IN BEDLAM

Brian Stableford

There is no doubt that being required to sit in judgment over one's peers is a profoundly uncomfortable business. A person thus appointed becomes gradually detached from the group; his former colleagues become suspicious of him, and he of them. Friendship gives way to paranoia. Nevertheless, the job has to be done, and somebody has to do it.

I never applied for the post of chairman of the Ethics Committee; I was asked to do it. They said, of course, that I was the person best qualified for the job, mainly because of my declared interest in the philosophy of medicine, although my "personal experience at the sharp end of ethical decision-making" was also mentioned—but all that was just soft soap and insensitivity. The simple fact was that my role was changing anyway, and the people in Admin took the opportunity to redefine it in a way that killed two birds with one stone.

My role was changing because the government's policy of returning the mentally ill to what is euphemistically known as "the community" had inevitably wrought great changes in specialized hospitals like the Maudsley. We had been forced to undergo a virtual sea change in the mid-1990s. As the high priests of hi-tech moved in, eager to get on with the serious genetic engineering and the transplant surgery, old-fashioned psychotherapists were suddenly in surplus. Those who couldn't find decent posts elsewhere and couldn't be persuaded to take early retirement had to be given other duties. Not that being chairman of the Ethics Committee was a full-time job; I still had to offer what comfort and treatment I could to an ever-growing list of outpatients.

I never realised the extent to which I'd been marginalized within the hospital community until one of the nurses let slip that the DNA cowboys—who'd never been colleagues, finding me already in place when they arrived—had nicknamed me "Doctor Death." I never knew for sure who coined the term, but I always suspected Dr. Gabriel. He was the real leader of the team, in terms of charisma if not rank, and he was the one whose ethical precepts were most definitely different from mine, he being a devout Catholic while I was an atheistic humanist. Maybe I over-reacted, but the nickname hurt. It was bad enough being the man who all-too-frequently had to take the final responsibility for life-or-death decisions—every one of them recalling to mind what had happened to Carol—without being mocked and insulted for doing it. No doubt Gabriel would have been a lot happier if the job had gone to a Jesuit, but that wasn't any excuse for his attitude to me.

I suppose that if it hadn't been Gabriel I saw with his arm around the heavily pregnant teenager, I probably wouldn't have given them a second glance. I wouldn't have followed them with my eyes as they moved through the reception area, I wouldn't have craned my neck to look at the car she got into, and I certainly wouldn't have gone to the desk to ask the secretary if she knew the patient's name. On the other hand, once I'd begun the sequence, there was enough in the situation to keep my curiosity going.

For one thing, the girl was luminously beautiful, in a Latin sort of way, and she looked so incredibly *happy*. Gabriel was wearing a smile that was smug even by his standards while he escorted her to the door—and that in itself was odd, because he wasn't in the habit of escorting patients to the door. He didn't actually have *patients*, as such. He was no mere healer of the sick; he was a cutting-edge research scientist, and proud of it. Then again, the car the girl got into was a black limousine with darkened windows: the kind that high-powered diplomats and Mafia bosses ride around in. I didn't immediately decide to make a note of the number-plate, but I couldn't help noticing it as it drew away because it looked like one of those "cherished plates" for which companies and individuals pay high prices, and was thus easy to remember. It was OD 111X.

The secretary gave me a funny look when I said "Do you know the name of the patient who was with Dr. Gabriel a moment ago?" but I *am* a senior consultant, so she could hardly refuse to tell me.

"That's Ms. Innocente," she said. "She's a regular."

"Oh yes, of course," I replied—I don't know why, because I'd never heard the name before, and there was no real reason to pretend that I had. "She must be nearly due now."

"Under two weeks," said the secretary, who liked to show that she was on the ball. "She's booked in for the twenty-third."

I was so intent on being blasé about it that I was half way back to my office before it occurred to me that one of the things the comprehensively re-vamped Maudsley didn't have was a maternity ward.

It was after seven when I got home. Chris had been home from school for three hours, but he was well used to looking after himself. The last vestiges of a bacon and mushroom pizza were still hanging about in the kitchen; he wasn't one for hasty washing up. He was in his room as usual, mesmerized by his computer-screen.

"Hi Dad," he said, when I looked in to offer in him a cup of coffee. "Another bad day in Bedlam?" It was one of those stale jokes that become mere ritual. The Maudsley is also known as the Bethlehem Royal Hospital; it's the direct descendant of the asylum which Simon Fitzgerald set up in 1247 for the Order of the Star of Bethlehem, which came to be popularly known as Bedlam.

"They all are," I told him, wearily. "I hope that's homework you're doing."

He sighed deeply. "It's nothing nefarious," he assured me, in a defensive fashion. More than a year had passed since the visit from the police and the official warning about accessing confidential data, and as far as I knew he'd been a little angel ever since. But how close an eye could a single father who worked the kind of hours I did be expected to keep on his teenage son?

I made the coffee, and took both cups up to Chris's room, intending nothing more than to exchange a few polite words in lieu of what the Americans call "quality time." I'd almost forgotten about Dr. Gabriel and the pregnant teenager, but when we'd both run out of platitudinous pleasantries and fell silent, something about the cryptic rows of data that were marching across the green-lit screen while Chris watched in total fascination tripped a switch in my memory.

"I don't suppose you could trace a car number, could you?" I said, impulsively.

He looked up at me in frank astonishment. "You want me to hack into the *police computer?*" he said, incredulously.

I must have blushed crimson. "Well, no," I said. "Isn't there a legal way of doing it?"

"Sure," he said. "Semi-legal, anyway. Every big commercial consultancy in the country has that sort of thing in their databanks. Mind you, there are some people who might be uneasy about the *ethics* of their trading in that kind of information. Do you want me to put it on your credit card, or are you actually asking me to pull a stroke and get it for free?"

There are times when being chairman of an Ethics Committee becomes positively oppressive, to the extent that one actually yearns to defy the rules. No one can be a saint *all* the time, especially someone who never had the appropriate training. I'd done my fair share of kicking over the traces when I was a teenager.

"I have to get a bite to eat," I said. "I'll come back later. If you happened to have found out by then who owns a car with the licence-plate OD 111X I certainly wouldn't ask you how you knew."

To my astonishment, he gave me the most incredible smile. It was as though real communication had been established between us for the very first time.

"O-*kay*," he said. "Anything else you'd like to know?"

I blinked, and hesitated. His enthusiasm to help was so blatant that I felt obliged to follow up. I realised, belatedly, that this was probably the first time I'd ever asked him to do anything which I couldn't have done for myself, and the fact that it was slightly shady made it all the more precious to him. I thought hard for a couple of moments, and then said: "If I gave you a couple of passwords, could you get into the hospital records—specifically the records of the DNA-research unit?"

"*Your* hospital?" he said, disbelievingly.

"That's right," I said. "I do have legitimate authority, you know—perhaps even a duty. It's just that . . ."

". . . You don't understand how to play the system," he finished for me. "What is it you want to know, Dad?"

"There's a female patient named Innocente. I'd like a peek at her records—anything and everything you can get."

"Why?" he asked.

"To tell you the truth," I said, honestly, "I really don't know. Simple curiosity."

"Curiosity kills cats," he observed. "And *they* have nine lives. Are you sure you want to risk it?"

I grinned. "At my time of life," I told him, "you can begin to live dangerously."

When I'd finished eating I went back upstairs. Chris was pathetically eager to tell me what he'd learned. In all the years since Carol's accident I'd never felt closer to him—nor he, apparently, to me.

"OD," he said, "does not stand for overdose. Not in this instance."

"What does it stand for?" I asked, easily following the line of argument.

"Opus Dei," he said. "It's Latin for . . ."

"The Work of God," I finished, so quick to occupy the intellectual high ground that the import of the revelation didn't sink in immediately. Several seconds passed before I said, "You mean the limo belongs to *Opus Dei?* The secret society?"

"Hardly secret, Dad," he countered, obviously having looked it up in the CD-ROM Encyclopedia. "Secret societies don't use dedicated number plates. But yeah, it's the Catholic organization which occasionally provokes silly season stories about its allegedly mysterious activities. Founded in 1928, very big in Spain under Franco. I didn't know they were clients of the Maudsley."

"Neither did I," I said, wondering whether the conspicuously devout Dr. Gabriel might possibly be a member of the organization. "What about Ms. Innocente?"

"An appointments record. Just dates and times. Her first name's Maria. There's nothing else." He handed me a strip of paper fresh off the printer.

"I thought you were supposed to be *good* at this," I complained.

"I *am* good at this," he retorted, in a martyred tone. "When I say there's *nothing else*, I mean there *is* nothing else, not that I couldn't find the rest."

"There has to be more," I told him. "Gabriel has to keep proper records of examinations and test results, and full medical notes. It's obligatory."

"In that case," Chris said, "I think you've just uncovered a clear violation of procedure. The invincible Ethics Committee strikes again, hey?"

I looked at the list of dates on the printout. As the secretary had said, a bed had been booked for the twenty-third, for three nights; that was the last item on the list. The first item was also a three-day admission, way back in March. In between the two were a series of monthly outpatient visits, which had presumably included the usual amniocentesis tests and sonic scans. Gabriel had been monitoring the pregnancy all the way from the very beginning. If the dates were accurate, Maria Innocente's first admission had corresponded with the time of conception.

It didn't make sense. The girl hadn't looked a day over seventeen, and seventeen-year-old girls weren't candidates for any form of assisted conception. Good Catholic teenagers undoubtedly got pregnant all the time by accident, and good Catholic doctors like Gabriel undoubtedly did their level best to steer them safely through their pregnancies . . . except that Dr. Gabriel was a researcher at the cutting edge of progress, not a protector of wayward sheep, and a three-day admission didn't look like any kind of an accident.

Even then, I *knew*. I didn't *believe* the conclusion to which I jumped, because it was incredible and absurd, but there were just too many dots to join up for the emergent picture to be coincidence. However ridiculous it might seem, there had to be something there.

"Find out anything you can about Maria Innocente," I said to Chris, in a tone which was suddenly very sober. "Anything and everything. Date of birth, parents, siblings, all known addresses; *everything*. Use my credit card to buy data if you have to, bend the rules if you have to, but find out exactly who she is."

Chris looked up at me with a different expression on his face. He knew that there was more to it than fun and games now, but he was still delighted to be involved, and to be needed. "It must have been a *really* bad day in Bedlam, hey?" he said, sympathetically. "Bad enough bringing your own work home, without having to load it on to me. Just coming up to Christmas too." He had started out jokingly, but the last sentence killed the levity.

"That's right," I said, humourlessly. "Just coming up to Christmas. Not to mention the new millennium."

"What is it that you want to see me about, Dr. Heath?" said Gabriel, as I eased myself down into the armchair in his office, glancing sideways at the silver crucifix which hung on the wall amongst his various degree certificates. "I'm afraid I have rather a busy schedule today."

"I don't doubt it," I said, drily. "It must be a stressful business, arranging the second coming."

I wasn't ashamed of the thrill of pure triumph I felt as I saw his jaw drop and his forehead crease up, surprise mingling with anxiety. By the time he recovered his scattered wits sufficiently to say, "What on earth do you mean?" it was too late. He'd already blown it.

"Maria Innocente," I said, succinctly. "Born St. Mary's Hospital Paddington in June 1983; her birth certificate records the father as 'unknown.' Brought up and educated—if that's the word I'm looking for—in a closed convent in Kent, supervised by the women's branch of Opus Dei. Due to give birth on December 25th, 2000, right here in Bethlehem Royal. You have a very peculiar sense of propriety, Dr. Gabriel. Is that name an accident, by the way, or were you also conceived with this particular role in mind? It can't have been easy to contrive an immaculate conception, way back in '83, even if you could figure out what *immaculate* might signify in the present context—but then, you always have been at the forefront of the medical miracle business, despite your sins of omission in the matter of keeping proper records."

He hesitated over a denial, but he must have realised that I had too much. However low his opinion of psychotherapists might be, he knew I was no fool.

"How did you get on to it?" he inquired, cautiously. He didn't seem intimidated or shocked. His main priority now, I supposed, had to be to discover exactly how much I'd found out, and whether I had guessed the rest.

"OD 111X," I said, contemptuously. "Why didn't you just paint the name of the organization on the side of the car?"

"Ah," he said, calmly enough. He'd recovered his composure by now. "My view was that it always pays *not* to advertise, but as a mere Supernumerary I have limited influence over my superiors. What are you accusing me of, Dr. Heath? Am I to be summoned before the

Ethics Committee on a charge of not making full notes, or do you have something more drastic in mind? If you'll pardon me for saying so, I don't think this is a matter in which you're qualified to take an interest."

"We'll have to disagree about matters of qualification," I said, coldly. "As it happens, I do have more serious charges in mind than your failure to keep a proper record of your . . . experiment. There are, as I'm sure you're aware, several other irregularities to be taken into consideration. The most important ones concern an implantation which was apparently carried out at this hospital in March, using an early embryo imported from abroad. That whole procedure was not merely irregular, Dr Gabriel, but actually illegal on several counts. You could be up before the BMA even if the embryo was a perfectly ordinary one. If it was what I think it was, you could be all over the front page of every tabloid newspaper in the world."

"And what, exactly, *do* you think it was?" he asked, equally coldly.

"I think it was a denucleated egg-cell replenished with DNA plundered from some Vatican reliquary. I think that *you* think it's a clone of Jesus Christ."

He knew that had to be a guess, but he didn't try to deny it. He didn't confirm it either, but I was no longer in any doubt. After a pause, he said: "I'm still not clear about what it is you want from me, Dr. Heath. A summons to appear before the Ethics Committee could have been put in the internal mail."

It was my turn to be astonished. "Is that all you have to say?" I asked.

"I don't have anything to say," he told me, flatly. "In spite of your title, I don't think I'm under any responsibility to explain or justify my actions to *you*. In any case, you're the one who's issuing the threats. If you want to mount an official investigation with a view to reporting me to the BMA, go ahead. If you want to ring the *News of the World* to offer them the scoop of the millennium, you're perfectly free to do so, although I can't imagine why you would. If they didn't believe you, you'd look like a complete fool, and if they did . . . we're perfectly well aware that the revelation has to be made eventually."

He looked at me steadily, and I could see how wholehearted his confidence was: the confidence of *faith*. I realised that I hadn't really thought the matter through; I hadn't been able to imagine what it must be like for a man like Gabriel to believe that he was the instrument of an authentic miracle: *the* miracle.

"I have the power to stop Maria Innocente's admission on the twenty-third," I pointed out. It was an empty threat, but I didn't like to appear so *completely* ineffectual.

"No room at the inn, Dr. Heath?" he replied, in a softly mocking voice.

I shook my head, wonderingly. *"Bethlehem,"* I said, as sarcastically as I could. *"Maria Innocente!* Don't you think it's all far too contrived, if not plain downright *silly?"*

"Actually, no," he replied, without embarrassment. "But I don't expect *you* to understand that. Not that it matters what you think. As I say, you're free to say what you please to whomever you please. You can't make any difference at all to what will happen next week, or in the critical years of the next millennium. You're an irrelevance, Dr. Heath, and so is your committee of sophists. The truth is about to be made manifest, and there's nothing you can do except prepare your soul for judgment."

And the sad truth was that whether he was crazy or inspired, unhinged or sane, he was quite right. Whatever I did or didn't do, it would make no difference at all to him. All I could do was sit in retrospective judgment upon him, privately or publicly—and whatever judgment I made, he honestly and truly didn't give a damn. The only responsibility *he* acknowledged was to a higher authority by far.

I spent Christmas Day with Chris, alone in the flat. We exchanged our petty gifts, had an abundant meal and a good bottle of wine, and tried not to notice that the person we most wanted to be there wasn't. We tried as hard as we could, in fact, to pretend that the universe was a place where justice and fairness meant *something,* even if the good and the innocent were being slaughtered by the score by careless drivers full to bursting with the Christmas spirit.

We tried to forget that for us Christmas was the anniversary of a death rather than a birth: a death whose grief was certainly no easier to bear by virtue of the fact that in the end, I'd had to ask for the life-support systems to be switched off.

We failed, of course.

Chris was a real hero, and a real diplomat, but in the end he had to raise the other issue which was on our minds.

"I suppose it'll be all over by now," he said, meaning the birth.

"I dare say," I said.

"I wonder if they fixed up a visiting roster—magi by appoint-ment. Can you get frankincense and myrrh these days?"

"Harrods stocks everything," I assured him, dully. I had no doubt that there *would* be wise men from the east. Dr Gabriel and his friends were playing everything by the book. They'd have laid on a supernova directly overhead if only they'd had the means. All the symptoms of classic monomania were there, but even in my heyday I'd never have been able to treat it. If madmen don't want to be brought back to sanity, they can't be driven. All a psychotherapist can do is listen, offer suggestions, and be very careful not to pass too harsh a judgment on failure or confusion.

"Are you really not going to do *anything*? You're just going to let them go ahead?"

"What could I do?" I asked.

"You could apply to have the child made a ward of court, on the grounds that its self-appointed guardians are round the twist."

"Even if I could do that—which I doubt—what would it achieve?"

"Dad, they're going to bring up that kid thinking it's the Messiah. They're going to expect it to work miracles."

"He's a child, Chris, not an object. Do you think they're going to treat him cruelly, or neglect him in any way? It's not illegal to bring up a child to believe certain things, however wrong-headed the beliefs might be. It may be stupid, but it's not criminal. I can make trouble for Gabriel, but what would that achieve? You do realise, I suppose, that if I went public with this the principal consequence would be that a substantial proportion of the world's population would start calling me the Anti-Christ. It's bad enough being Dr Death behind closed doors—and it wouldn't do you any good, would it? Anyway, weren't you the one who warned me that curiosity kills cats?"

"And weren't you the one who said that a man of your age could afford to live dangerously.?"

"I can also afford to live *quietly*—which, on the whole, I prefer."

"So you think it's okay to *produce* a mother, for the sole purpose of bearing a child who's going be taught that he's the son of God? You're the chairman of the hospital Ethics Committee, and you think that's a *responsible* way to use the new biotechnology?" He hadn't started out angry, but he was getting sharper now, and I could see the old bitterness surfacing again. It seemed a pity that we'd managed to get so close at long last, only to have it spoiled again.

"If they'd referred the matter to us in advance, we'd have refused permission," I said, patiently, "and any other ethics committee would have done the same. But what we have now is a *fait accompli*, and a very delicate matter. If I tried to punish them retrospectively for breaking the rules I'd probably do far more harm than good."

"So you're going to let them get away with it. You're even going to let them manage their own publicity. But then, you always were a *nondirective* therapist, weren't you. Do you think they'll announce the happy event right away, or will they wait until he's old enough to get on with the task of putting an end to the world?"

"I don't know," I said, as professionally calm as ever. "They know that God moves in mysterious ways, and I suppose they'll do their level best to imitate Him—but it's bound to leak out. Someone will let the cat out of the bag ... and then it'll all be down to the world's lethal curiosity. But at the end of the day, it'll all come to nothing, because the boy *won't* be able to work miracles, and the world *won't* end, and the day of judgment will keep right on happening the way it always has, in the hearts and voices of ordinary men."

"Nice sermon," he said, meanly—but then thought better of it, and changed his tone. "Whose DNA do you think it *really* was?" he asked. "I mean, could it really have come from some mummified relic that's been siting in a church for centuries? And even if it did, whose body did the relic really come from? Aren't they trying to have their cake and eat it too if they believe that Christ was resurrected and went to heaven, but that he conveniently left a sample of his DNA behind?"

I shrugged. "I believe that *they* believe it's Christ's DNA," I said. "But I don't think they're the kind of people who'd find it to difficult to bolster their belief that *any* DNA they happened to use would fit the bill. After all, they're the kind of people who believe that the body and blood of Christ can be routinely manufactured day by day, out of unleavened bread and cheap red wine. They're looking for a miracle, remember? If they have to assume that one or two have already happened along the way, they'll do it."

"And you'll let them. You won't stand up for sanity and reason. You'll let them do it *their way*, for the sake of a quiet life." The anger was gone now, but there was something worse: *disappointment*. He'd known for a long time now that it *wasn't* cowardice or wrong-headedness that had made me ask for his mother's life-support machines to be switched off, but there was still the disappointment, the heart-rending sense of the *unfairness* of it all. I wanted to answer that, too, if I could. I wanted to make him see that doing nothing when there was nothing to be done, letting events take their course when there was no productive way to interfere, not only wasn't simply *defeatism*, but actually had a kind of courage in it.

"They've already done it," I said, quietly, "and it can't be undone. The whole point about ethics committees, Chris—in fact, the whole point about ethics—is to try to decide *in advance* what should and shouldn't be done for the best. What earthly use is the kind of judgment which only happens afterwards? What use is it to come along when all the damage is done and start handing down *punishments* to all the people who got it wrong, exacting savage vengeance from all the people who offended you? I'm supposed to be a healer, not a jailer; I look for progress in my patients, not perfection. I'm not in the business of *retribution*, Chris, and I won't apologise for that. I'm content to leave decisions as to who goes to Heaven and who goes to Hell to the people who think the world is really like that, and to take what comfort I can from the knowledge that it isn't. That really is the only way forward."

He didn't reply, because he'd said all he had to say, but he looked at me with what I thought—or, at least, hoped—was under-standing.

It wasn't until nearly a week later, on New Year's Eve, that I heard through the hospital grapevine that Maria Innocente had given birth to a boy who was outwardly perfect, but who didn't respond to stimuli in a normal way. He was certainly blind, almost certainly deaf, and probably badly brain-damaged; only time would reveal the full extent of his disability. Amniocentesis hadn't thrown up any warning signs, but the DNA in the embryo had evidently been defective.

I shed some honest tears for the disappointed mother, because I understood only too well the sharpness and the bitterness of the grief that she must feel, but I couldn't find it in my heart to weep for Dr. Gabriel, or for the dismal failure of the Work of God.

Save the world this Christmas.

NOT EVEN A CHIMNEY

Stanley Schmidt

Christmas, to Marcus Eubanks IV, was an irritating interruption of more important things. Especially *this* Christmas. Admittedly he awoke early and as full of anticipation as any little boy; but his anticipation had nothing to do with Christmas trees, electric trains, good will toward men, or visions of sugarplums. Marcus's visions were of vengeance, too long denied and at long last almost in his grasp. So it was with considerable surprise, and even more annoyance, that his eyes fell on the neatly wrapped present in his kitchen garbage can.

He stood there, alone in his velvet slippers and gold-brocaded silk robe, stirring a carefully measured smidgeon of cream into his Blue Mountain coffee and frowning. *Damn it,* he thought, *something's wrong here.*

Marcus Eubanks, with well-paid help from his staff, maintained a scrupulously well-ordered household. A place for everything, as three namesakes before him had often said, and everything in its place.

A garbage can, he thought, *is a place for garbage. So what's a Christmas present doing in mine? Who would send me one, anyway? And how would they get it in here? I paid a pretty penny for that security system—a lot of pretty pennies!*

Increasingly troubled, but not yet awake enough to pinpoint why it bothered him so much, he took a single perfunctory sip of his coffee, then set it aside and got down on his hands and knees for a closer look at the uninvited intrusion. It filled most of the can, a rectangular box all dressed up in wrapping paper that shimmered with swirling patterns of bright reds and greens and whites and blacks, finished with a big bow of what looked like pure gold ribbon. He saw no tag or card, but considering where it was, it must be for him.

But whatever could it be? And again, from whom? And why? And how?

His curiosity grew so intense that it almost crowded out the chain of thought he'd been pursuing, about how he was finally going to spring the trap on that no-good deserter McNichols. He found his hands reaching toward the gift box. He had to know what was inside, and that might give him a clue to the other questions. And while a garbage can was a decidedly odd place to leave a surprise present, whoever had done it had at least had the decency and foresight to scrub the can out first. So he wouldn't have to worry about getting his hands dirty . . .

He was on the very verge of touching it when the coffee kicked in and shocked him with awareness of what he was doing. Trembling at the thought of how close he'd come to mortal danger— how close he might still be!—he stood up and backed slowly away from the garbage can, eyeing the gift wrap as if it were a cobra or a bomb.

Which it might very well be.

There was no way, he realized as his thoughts cleared, that anybody could have brought that thing in here legitimately without his knowledge. The staff knew better than to surprise him that way— or to let anyone else.

Therefore it had gotten here by illegitimate, and probably threatening, means. He still had to find out why and how, but his were not the hands for that sort of work.

Oh, well. He'd been planning to call Security Chief Brontos right after breakfast anyway, though not for quite this reason. He'd just be a little early.

Harry Brontos evidently thought it was a *lot* early. Eubanks phoned him from the gardener's shed, at what he hoped was a safe distance from the main house, and Chief Brontos sounded weary and worried and miffed all at once. "Geez, boss, it's only six A.M.! I *told* you there were still a few missing links in the chain and I'd call you when we'd filled them in. At this hour nobody's even started, and there ain't a thing I can do until—"

"I'm sorry about all that," Eubanks interrupted. "But this isn't about McNichols. Something else has come up. I need you at the house right away."

"Can't it wait an hour? It's Christmas morning and I've got a fam—"

"Right away," Eubanks spat out. "Life and death—yours and mine. Does the word 'bomb' mean anything to you?"

He hung up.

Brontos was at the gatehouse six minutes later, still a bit bleary-eyed but fully uniformed and somehow radiating professional competence despite the hour and the circumstances. He carried a massive tool kit in one beefy paw, and frowned with eyebrows that looked like heavily forested mountain ranges. "Where is it?" he asked.

"Kitchen," said Eubanks. "In the garbage can. Wrapped up like a Christmas present."

Then he waited, watching Brontos scurry up to the house without another word.

Brontos called the gatehouse twenty minutes later. "It's not a bomb," he said right off, but he didn't sound as relieved as he should. "At least, not any kind I know. I've scanned for every explosive in the book, plus drugs and bugs, and came up dry. Likewise control circuits—nothin'. But I'm still puzzled."

"Why?" Eubanks asked rhetorically.

"Well, partly the obvious. Even if it's harmless, what's it doing here? Who brought it? How'd they get it past our men and gadgets? That worries me, boss. It must worry you, too. Even if it's a harmless prank, nobody should have been able to play it. We've got to find the hole in our fences."

A thought flashed across Eubanks's mind. "You think this has something to do with McNichols?"

Three beats of silence. Then, "Not impossible, I guess, but wildly unlikely. Too much coincidence. I'm sure she has no idea we're as close to nabbing her as we are." Brontos allowed himself a curt guffaw. "Hell, she probably thinks we gave up the chase years ago. Man, is *she* in for a surprise!"

"Meanwhile," Eubanks reminded impatiently, "I've already got a surprise. Are you telling me you think it's just a gag and I should be thankful it pointed up a weak spot in your system?"

Brontos's tone sobered abruptly. "Well, boss, there may be more to it than that. I think you'd better come up here to take a closer look at it with me."

Eubanks stiffened warily. "Why's that? Why can't you just open it, finish checking it out, and dispose of it? That's your job!"

"Yes, sir, it sure is. But we all know you've got the best brains in this whole outfit. That's why you're the big boss of Eubanks Industries. And there's something so funny about this that I'm stumped. I need another good head to help me figure it out."

Eubanks didn't think of that as flattery to be resisted: it was mere statement of fact. "What do you mean, something funny?" he asked.

"I got one just like it at my house this morning."

Eubanks re-entered the house with mixed feelings. Part of him agreed that the whole business was fishy enough to need his personal attention. Another part feared that it was *too* far out of the ordinary, making even him uncomfortable. Still another hoped that Brontos hadn't gone around the bend, and that he knew what he was talking about when he said it was safe for The Master to go back into the kitchen.

Eubanks found the security man sitting cross-legged on the kitchen floor, surrounded by meters and tools and staring at the gift-wrapped object, now out in the open, on the floor in front of him. He reminded Eubanks of a grizzly bear trying to figure out the best way into a honeycomb. "Did you open yours?" Eubanks asked.

"Nope. Didn't have time. The family was just starting to wake up when you called. I didn't think too much about it at the time, anyway. There were presents all over our house, and it would be just like that boy of mine to put one in a weird place like a garbage can and think it was funny. But then when I got here and saw yours looked just like—"

"You mean yours was in the garbage, too?"

"Well, the garbage *can*. But it was nice and clean, just like yours. No garbage in it—just the present."

"And when you say it looked just like mine—"

"Just like," Brontos agreed. "Same size, same shape, same wrapping paper, same ribbon. I didn't pick mine up and shake it, but I'd make a small bet it's the same weight." He frowned. "It's odd enough that somebody should do this to either of us, but both? It's just too much!"

"Sure is." Eubanks chewed his lower lip thoughtfully. "Both of us, you say. That suggests it's somebody inside the company . . ."

"Which doesn't narrow the field a whole heck of a lot. It's a *big* company, as your ads are constantly reminding us." Brontos eyed the package as if wishing it would just go away. "Maybe there's a clue inside. Shall we open it?"

"You think that's safe?"

Brontos shrugged. "Can't guarantee it, but I already told you it passed every test I know how to give it. *I'm* willing. If you want to wait outside, I'll do it myself."

Eubanks pondered that carefully, then decided he didn't want to miss any part of this, risk or no. "I'll stay."

"You're the boss." Brontos pulled the package toward him and Eubanks settled on the floor facing him. An incongruous image flashed through his mind, of himself as a little boy, sitting on the living room floor with Mom and Pop in front of a huge Christmas tree surrounded by mounds of brightly wrapped presents, tearing the ribbons and papers off with eager anticipation. It had been years—decades—since he'd done anything like that. Yet now he was sitting much the same way, watching with anticipation (if not eagerness) as a present was unwrapped. Only this time he was a grown and powerful man, the floor was a kitchen, there was no tree, and instead of Mom and Pop there was a tough-looking security guard.

Funny, he supposed, if he could look at it the right way.

The ribbon and wrap came off easily enough, and the box, though unlabeled, looked quite ordinary. Eubanks stiffened involuntarily as Brontos pried the flaps open and reached inside, but what he pulled out seemed anticlimactic.

Or did it?

It looked, at first glance, like a particularly ugly potted plant. Not repulsive, actually, but a long way short of artistic. It had lots of small, plain, gray-green leaves and a generally lumpy, lopsided shape. But the oddest thing about it was the fruits. It had several, most of them surprisingly large for such a small plant, and no two alike. One looked remarkably like an apple, another like a potato. A third didn't even hang like a fruit: it grew straight out of the trunk, and looked for all the world like a stalk of broccoli. From a branch next to that hung what resembled a shriveled hamburger.

And it smelled. Not unpleasantly: as the first whiffs reached Eubanks's nose, he found himself thinking, *I'm hungry, I was about to get breakfast when this nonsense started.* But then came other scents in rapid succession, triggering that eerie sensation that smells often do of being transported back to an earlier time. The first one he identified was Christmas tree, further reminding him of the incongruous resemblance of this scene to the Christmas mornings of his childhood. But with that came a whole kaleidoscope of food aromas, evoking ethnic cuisines mingling in apartment hallways, and fresh meats and produce and baked goods in the farm market where his grandmother had sometimes led him by the hand.

"What *is* that thing?" he wondered aloud with a mixture of fear and fascination.

Brontos had picked it up and was sniffing closely at one part after another. "I think it's just what it looks like," he said. "Some kind of artificial plant that produces several kinds of food." He ran a fingertip over the surface of the "hamburger," then touched it tentatively to his tongue. "Even tastes like hamburger." He leaned sideways to reach for one of those mysterious boxes police types used to analyze just about anything these days. Breaking off a small piece of the "fruit" he'd tasted, he stuffed it into a chute at one end of the analyzer, fiddled with buttons while watching a digital display, then sat for a minute watching the display. When it stopped changing, he said, "Non-toxic. Nutritionally, quite close to a hamburger. Here, try it." He broke off a bite, popped it into his own mouth, then handed the plant over to Eubanks.

Eubanks sniffed cautiously at each part of the plant before following Brontos's example. Each part that bore a recognizable resemblance to a conventional food smelled like what it looked like. The last one he sniffed was the "hamburger," and then, since Brontos was still sitting up and looking reasonably happy, he broke off a small bite of it to taste.

It didn't feel greasy, but otherwise it had the right texture—and it did taste like hamburger. Not bad, but hardly the sort of fare Eubanks was used to. *What a waste!* he thought wryly, beginning to relax and accept the thing for what it was. If somebody, for whatever reason, had gone to great lengths to surprise him with a novelty plant that made imitation foods, he could live with that. It could be a great conversation piece, if nothing else. *But if they can make it taste that much like hamburger, why not do something worthwhile, like Chateaubriand and lobster and caviar?*

That thought made his entrepreneurial wheels start turning. *Hmm . . . if they couldn't, maybe I could. When we find out who's behind this, all I have to do is get my hands on the technology. Should be able to turn it into a real moneymaker. . . .*

Brontos was keeping his focus closer to the matter at hand. "Interesting gimmick," he said, "but that still doesn't answer our basic questions." He stood up and went off on a quick walk around the house, scrutinizing doors and windows and a variety of other details whose significance was not obvious to Eubanks. He came back ten minutes later, frowning deeply. "Not a trace of anybody breaking in, and no record of anybody but you and me coming in in the last twelve hours. You're sure it wasn't here last night?"

"Quite sure," said Eubanks, standing up. Squatting on the floor took a lot more out of him than it had in his Christmas tree days.

"So we have no lead there." Brontos pondered for a moment, then mused. "I wonder who else got one. May I use the phone?"

"Of course."

Brontos punched out a number and Eubanks listened to one side of his conversation, evidently with his wife. "Yes, I saw it, too. . . . You say Darryl swears he doesn't know anything about it? . . . Have you opened it? . . . Do it now. I'll wait." A long silence. Then, "Okay. Thanks. Try not to worry about it. We'll figure it out. Meanwhile, don't throw it out, but don't eat anything off it. Love ya." He hung up and tossed Eubanks a look. "Same as yours, though not all the foods on it are the same."

He turned back to the phone and punched out a new number. Another brief conversation: This time Eubanks couldn't tell whom he was talking to. Two more, then Brontos told Eubanks, "One of your vice-presidents, an accountant, and a machinist. Did everybody in the *world* get these things?" Beginning to look a bit frantic, he started punching in another number.

"Those people are all associated with my company," Eubanks pointed out. "Try somebody who isn't."

Brontos stopped dialing and started over. After three more calls, he looked badly shaken. "My son's bowling buddy, a casual acquaintance in Belize, and a name picked at random from the phone book. I'm beginning to think everybody in the world *did* get one, and nobody knows how."

"Santa Claus," Eubanks muttered, but his voice was grim. Harmless or not, this was getting entirely out of hand. If somebody could do this with a stupid plant, there was nothing to stop them from doing it with a bomb. That was clearly intolerable—and neither he nor Brontos had yet the slightest idea what to do about it.

Eubanks was beginning to feel a horrible creeping sensation about the whole business when the phone rang.

He almost jumped out of his slippers, then reached out and picked up the handset. "Hello?" he said warily.

"Merry Christmas!" said a high woman's voice, almost like a little girl's. And it did sound merry, trailing off into giggles like the tinkling of bells and then repeating, "Merry Christmas, Mr. Eubanks. Do you like your present?"

"Who is this?" he demanded. The voice sounded naggingly familiar. He gestured for Brontos to pick up an extension, and Brontos went into the next room to do so.

"Why, Sandy McNichols, of course. Surely you haven't forgotten me, after all we went through together. First in college, then at your corporate octopus. After all the things you did to me—"

"I did to *you?*" Eubanks echoed incredulously. "You're the one who embezzled millions of dollars and ran off with a fortune in trade secrets—"

"Oh, you think so, do you?" She sounded amused. "And I suppose you can prove that?"

"Yes," said Eubanks, though it wasn't quite true—yet. "My Christmas present was supposed to be finally catching you and throwing you in the clink where you belong." He remembered what she'd said first. "So why are you calling me, now of all times? What present are *you* talking about?"

"Oh, I think you know, Mr. Eubanks. How many did you get? Any besides the one in your garbage can?"

That hurt, but he refused to answer it directly. "You did that?" he said. "How—"

"It wasn't easy," said McNichols. He could picture her easily enough, a pudgy little person with round rosy cheeks and exasperatingly constant jollity. "But it's the best thing I've ever done. Maybe when I tell you about it, you'll finally take me seriously."

"Fine," he said, in the same patronizing tone he had found appropriate to her so many times before. "Tell me about it." *And give Brontos time*, he thought, *to trace this call.*

"First," McNichols was saying, "I want to thank you for financing this project, however unwillingly. It's the best thing *you've* ever done, too."

"What are you talking about? I had nothing—"

"Oh, but you did," she laughed. "I don't deny that I borrowed some money from you, and that's what made it all possible. I'm sorry I had to do it that way, but it's the only way I saw—and I had plenty of provocation. Honestly, Mr. Eubanks, I don't know why you hired me if you didn't have any respect for me. You were more concerned about fitting me into your corporate straitjacket than about the fact that I was feeding you a steady stream of ideas that could make you fabulously rich—"

"I was already rich," Eubanks muttered. "And you did have some good ideas. I'll grant you that. But for God's sake, Sandy, how could you expect me to let you just work however you wanted and not follow the same rules as everybody else? You wouldn't even go back and finish your degree. That's *basic*, Sandy!"

"That's *petty*," she corrected. "It would have been a stupid waste of my time and your money. You were obsessed with having me follow rules that you made for people who weren't producing half what I was. Think about that, Mr. Eubanks. As for my ideas, half of them you stole and appropriated without a whit of credit for me. The other half—the best half—you wouldn't even listen to. How much of that, and no decent raises, and no promotions, do you expect a girl to take?"

"We could have talked—"

"I *tried* to talk. Mr. Eubanks! You wouldn't listen. Just because I didn't fit your image of what a corporate researcher was supposed to be, you thought you could just listen for my occasional lucrative idea and pretend I wasn't there the rest of the time. Sorry, Mr. Eubanks, it doesn't work that way. After a while I started thinking more and more about how I could put my time and your money to better use. And after all, considering how little you gave me for what I gave you, some of that money was by rights mine anyway."

"We'll have to see how a court feels about that," Eubanks said tightly. "Anyway, just what is it you did? How did you get this . . . *thing* past my guards?"

Sandy McNichols giggled. "Oh, yes, that. I got the idea one Christmas Eve while I was reading Clement Moore to my little niece and nephew. I'd already decided Alvin had a good head on his shoulders—he'll be finishing his Master's in chemistry at Harvard next year—and even though he was only four then, he looked up and asked me. 'But how can Santa Claus visit every house in the world in one night?' I had to admit he couldn't, really—but then it hit me that maybe *I* could, in effect if not in literal fact. All I needed was money and time."

"You're daft," Eubanks said after a long pause. "I'm glad you left. It saved me the trouble of having a lunatic in my employ."

"Is that what you think I am?" she asked with a disconcerting chuckle. "Think about it for a minute. Have you talked to anybody who *didn't* get a present like yours this morning?" She paused for effect. "You're not likely to. I may have have missed one or two, but I think not many.

"Really, Mr. Eubanks, you should have listened when I was urging you to get into nanotechnology. You were already in several lines of work that would have given you a head start. But you couldn't be bothered. Too far out, you said. So eventually I just had to go with it myself.

"I'd been thinking for a long time that it would be nice to turn your wealth and knowledge to doing something good for all the people you'd hurt in acquiring them. If I could help somebody else, too, why, that would be even better. And thanks to little Alvin, I suddenly saw how I could help *everybody*."

"Will you come to the point?" Eubanks growled, thinking Brontos must surely have had time to trace the call by now.

"Certainly, Mr. Eubanks—but you really should try to relax. It's Christmas morning, and somebody actually sent you a present for once. Enjoy, enjoy! Anyway, it occurred to me that with nanotech you *could* deliver a present to everybody's house on Christmas Eve. You wouldn't need reindeer or a magical sleigh; you wouldn't even need a chimney. All you'd have to do is get some assemblers into their houses, programmed to wait and then build whatever when their internal clocks said it was time.

"So that's what I did, with your help. It took a lot of research, but I think it will prove worth it. Obviously I couldn't customize the gifts for every recipient; I'd have to settle for making the same thing for everybody. So I put a lot of thought into what it should be. There's still a lot of sickness and hunger in the world, Mr. Eubanks, though that may be hard for you to conceive. So I made something that looks like a plant and acts sort of like a plant, but it's a self-renewing, diversified food source. All you have to do is keep feeding it 'fertilizer,' which can be anything organic, and let it collect sunlight, and it'll reward you with an ever-changing menu."

"I've tasted some of its food," said Eubanks, "It's not much."

"No, *you* wouldn't think so," McNichols granted affably. "But I am glad you tried it. Anyway, developing the plant design and programming the assemblers was one big job. The other was getting them into all the houses in the world. Fortunately I'm a patient woman; I was willing to take a few years. So for years we were dumping them into major weather systems all over the world, and they were replicating and sometimes finding their way into houses, seeking out garbage cans and dumps in close proximity to signs of human habitation. They could recognize several: cooking heat and odors, exhaled breath, body wastes. . . . And all the while biding their time, storing up energy during the day, saving up to release it in one spurt of activity last night: converting garbage to food plants like yours." That irritating little-girl laugh again. "The last weather system that helped with the distribution was last year's El Niño. Appropriate, don't you think?"

Eubanks listened numbly. She *was* brilliant, if eccentric; she just might have pulled it off. . . . "You're crazy," he repeated. "Assuming you actually *could* do such a thing, is this wild story supposed to make me feel better about what you've done? If anything, McNichols, it makes it far worse. Rest assured I still have every intention of tracking you down and throwing the book at you. We were almost there; your stupid call just clinches it. My security chief has been tracing you even as we speak—"

"Won't do him any good," she giggled. "I knew he would, so naturally I took the precaution of developing a way to feed a phone remotely—a way I seriously doubt you can trace. Your Brontosaurus will find the phone that called you, but I won't be anywhere near it.

"Besides, I doubt that you *really* want to take me to court. I know too much about you. Not only what you did to me, but to lots of others you walked over on the way up. To say nothing of bootleg DDT, adulterated foods, and third-rate drugs dumped in Third World countries. That's the trouble with not taking me seriously, Mr. Eubanks. You talked too much where I could hear. Now if you *insist* on bringing everything out in the open, I'm willing—but I mean *everything*."

"But . . . you don't have proof. Do you?"

"Do *you?*" she said sweetly.

Neither of them said anything for quite a while. Eubanks's throat felt dry. "I'll have to think about it," he said weakly. "But don't get too smug." For a moment he remembered when they'd been in college together, how he'd admired her potential and found her unconventionality refreshing. Where had which of them gone wrong? "You were so talented," he half whispered. "What ever drove you to waste it on such a crazy scheme? Even if you had a grievance against me, feeding all those people will just make things worse!"

"Just like Scrooge," she chuckled. " 'Let them die, and decrease the surplus population!' My plants won't do that, but they won't do what you're worried about, either. They're more than just food, Mr. Eubanks. They also contain cell repair machines, to cure the weak and sick. But there's a side effect."

"Side effect?"

"The cell fixers cure all kinds of ills, including sterility. But they also turn fertility off after two births. Everybody will have a chance to replace themselves; nobody will have more."

He pondered that silently for a while, wondering whether she'd built the "side effect" in intentionally. He decided not to ask. "Well," he said cautiously, "there may be some good in this after all." *Am I really like Scrooge to think so?* he asked himself; and then, to avoid answering, he looked back at the plant on his kitchen floor. "Still, it's such a waste. This pitiful substitute for real food, and you're hiding and we're scared of each other. How I wish we could have seen eye to eye years ago, Sandy! If you'd just played along, been part of the team, we could have made tons of *money* on this!"

"Perhaps," she said neutrally. "Merry Christmas, Mr. Eubanks."

"Bah . . ." he began, and then bit it off.

Thousands of miles away, Bagheera was one of many others who received Sandy's gift. Like Marcus Eubanks, he viewed it initially with wariness— but also with a different kind of curiosity.

Bagheera and his family were luckier than many others not too far away. They were not yet too starved to be able to feed themselves, when food could be had, though their skin already hung far too loosely on their bones. Bagheera had clung to hope that it would not come to that, but lately hope had been harder and harder to hold.

Then this morning—Christmas morning, according to the missionary who sometimes came over from the next village—the mysterious package had appeared in their hut. A cautious man, he had driven his wife Ruhunu and their seven children outside to wait while he slashed it open, in case it held something dangerous.

What he found inside was like nothing he had ever seen, but it did not take him long to decide it was some sort of plant and the things growing on it were food. Not quite like any food he had eaten before, but food nonetheless. Bagheera was also a practical man, and when his family was on the verge of starvation, even unfamiliar food would be welcome—provided it was safe.

He tried it first on their oldest, scrawniest dog. The mutt ate it eagerly enough, and then Bagheera had to take care to keep it from eating the rest until he had had a chance to watch several hours for signs of sickness or poisoning. The task was not made any easier by the tantalizing aromas that tempted him to sample the plant himself, but the wait was necessary.

When sundown brought a welcome end to the day's sweltering heat, the dog still looked no worse than before—and perhaps even a bit livelier. He still couldn't be absolutely certain, of course; perhaps he would never be absolutely sure. But he could wait no longer. With trembling hand, he plucked a bite of one of the strange fruits from the little bush, put it carefully in his mouth, and began to chew.

And smile. It looked like a shriveled fruit of dubious ancestry, but it tasted heavenly, like meat and vegetables blended and sent by the gods. Perhaps he would have to pay more attention to that missionary . . .

He waited ten minutes, then tried another. Then another, and yet another.

And when, after an hour, he felt physically fine and spiritually even better, he ran to the door of the hut and called all his family in for a feast. It was a glorious hour; he could remember no finer feeling than watching his family actually enjoy their first meal in far too long.

Of course, the practical side of him noted that it was good that they were too unaccustomed to food to eat much today. The plant was still small; they must leave it something to replenish itself. And of course they would feed it, with whatever waste matter they could find, and perhaps it would grow. And then. . .

An end to starvation. What better gift could any man ask of the gods?

Only one thing puzzled him—apart from the huge mystery of how it had come to be here. Most of the food-things hanging on the plant looked at least vaguely familiar. Most could even wear familiar names without too much stretching of the imagination. But one small, sweet object seemed quite alien to his experience; and try as he might, he couldn't decide what to call it.

But then, these days, how many people in any country would recognize a sugarplum?

CHRISTMAS WINGDING

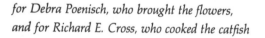

Janet Kagan

for Debra Poenisch, who brought the flowers,
and for Richard E. Cross, who cooked the catfish

By tradition, Gabe Jackley manned the Customs desk at Butterfly's spaceport on Christmas Eve. Usually there wasn't a single passenger to welcome or a solitary bag to check but—should there be—everybody on Butterfly trusted Gabe to handle the situation correctly. Gabe took the task for the honor it was and hummed to himself as he finished wrapping the presents he'd brought along. He'd just managed to trap a fingertip in a peach-pink bow when the comm unit sprang to life—a ship from Foolhardy requested permission to land.

Gabe granted Captain Kogel permission, extricated his finger, and keyed his window to watch the landing. Foolhardy was one of the central worlds—central in that most of the Commonwealth worlds did their government business there—and Kogel was riding a Silver Needle 4 this time. A sweet ship and an expensive one. When Gabe saw that, he shoved back the excitement that had risen in him over a Christmas Eve landing. That kind of ship could only mean government bureaucrats or tourists stopping for a few days' land-'fresher. In Gabe's mind, good things were more likely to come in an old battered Bugcrusher II, like the one that sat at the far end of the field. . . . He smiled to see that someone had looped a wreath of peachywands over the tip of the Bugcrusher's nose.

With a subdued rumble, the Silver Needle set down. Gabe watched as the ship extruded a pair of struts and canted over to one side to allow the passengers to disembark at ground level. Fancy, he thought. He admired the technology, but he reserved his smile once again for the dilapidated Bugcrusher II.

After a moment, he thought to kick one of the followmes into motion. It trundled over to the arriving tourists with nothing more on its rudimentary chips than to pick up cargo and deliver it to the Customs House. It trundled back with a half-dozen people, all dressed in their Sunday best, but not the sort of true Sunday best Gabe would have expected from a tour group come for the holidays. These folk were all dressed in shades of gray and black. He gave an involuntary glance at his packages, all of which were wrapped in the traditional Christmas pink and orange and peach. Well, maybe gray was traditional for them?

He opened the door and ushered them inside. "Merry Christmas," he said, "and welcome to Butterfly." The woman who seemed to be in charge was young, plump and pillow-soft, with bright disbelieving eyes. Gabe had the odd thought that she might pinch herself at any moment, to assure herself she wasn't dreaming. He rather hated to interject a note of reality, but he did: "Have you anything to declare?"

For answer, she drew her passport from her pouch to spread beside Gabe's stack of packages. Diplomatic passport, he saw. One of Foolhardy's finest. The hologram inside astonished him; unlike the usual passport photos, hers showed such a grin of triumph that he was grinning back when he looked up at her.

"Taking a land-'fresher on your way to your new post, eh," he said. "Christmas Eve is a tough time to be so far from home . . . if your Christmas matches ours, that is." Maybe that explained their unfestive clothing.

Celia Nicolazzini—that was the name on her passport—gave him a bemused but genuine smile. "The dates match, and our Chief of State gave us strict orders to see a Butterfly Christmas before we proceed to our official post." The smile turned momentarily wry. "To be honest, we've no idea what we're supposed to see but we were told we'd know it when we saw it. How's that for diplomatic?"

Gabe laughed. He knew what they were supposed to see. "Best place for that is Smuggler's Rest. Quicksilver throws the best Wingding on the planet, and they're open to all comers. You needn't worry about reservations; Quicksilver will make room for you if need be, on Christmas Eve."

"Smuggler's Rest?" said the one called Corcos, who looked to Gabe as grim and grey as his passport photo. "Dr. Nicolazzini, that doesn't sound like the sort of place we should be seen in—"

Gabe shook his head. "Smuggler's Rest is a five-star hotel in any guidebook." He decided he'd best not say straight out that the owner was a retired smuggler. Corcos didn't look the sort who'd stand for it and, besides, he didn't know just *how* retired Quicksilver was. Still— "If you've been ordered to see Christmas on Butterfly, you should probably start with the Christmas commemorative in Dawn Square. You pass right by it on the way to Smuggler's Rest."

By the time transport had arrived, he'd checked the rest of their passports and loaded their notebooks with local guidechips. Kogel, who'd been examining Gabe's Christmas packages, probably looking for his own, straightened and said, "Gabe, they need a favor from you—"

A look at Nicolazzini's face told Jackley she'd felt the favor too much of an imposition, even though Kogel had vouched for him. "You can ask," Gabe assured her with a smile. "Christmas Eve lots of things are possible, even in Customs."

Pete Kogel's laugh at that gave Nicolazzini all the encouragement she needed. "Captain Kogel thinks there's a pack of newshounds right behind us," she said. "We'd hoped to spend a quiet Christmas—"

Gabe held up his hands. "Say no more. I think, from the way you folks talked, that you'll probably be staying up-wing—*waaay* up-wing." He turned to the map of Butterfly's main continent on the screen behind his desk and touched a finger to the farthest tip of the eponymous butterfly's silhouette. Then he moved his finger all the way down to the bottom of the silhouette's abdomen. "We're here," he said. He laid a hand span between the two points. "*There* is a half day's travel by surface transport."

When Nicolazzini smiled, she dimpled, so Jackley added, "Tell Quicksilver Gabe Jackley sent you. And if you tell her you're hiding out, she'll let you register under a phony name—'long as you've given me your real ones, of course."

She was the only one of the diplomats who caught the joke, and she dimpled again. "Thank you, Gabe Jackley. And a Merry Christmas to you, too."

"See you later," he said, and when she cocked her head in query, he added, "I spend *my* Christmas at Smuggler's Rest, too."

"That may be the best recommendation of all," said Nicolazzini. "Until later then."

She ushered her colleagues away, and Jackley turned his full attention to Captain Kogel.

"Hi, Pete—anything to declare?" He knew the answer to that one, even though he had to ask. Pete was forever trying to slip something past someone; he simply wasn't as poker-faced as a professional like Quicksilver.

This time, Pete looked him straight in the eye. "Present for Quicksilver," he said.

"Should I ask?"

"Probably not." Meaning: If Gabe did, he'd have to confiscate it. Meaning: Pete hoped he'd pass the confiscated item on to its intended recipient.

"Ecologically damaging?"

Pete's head jerked back in shock. "Do I look suicidal? I said, 'for Quicksilver.'"

Hell, it was Christmas Eve. Let Pete deliver his present in person. "Okay," Gabe said, "on your way," and he slid Pete's passport back across the desk. "See you later at the party."

It was only after Pete had waved him a good evening and walked out to the waiting transport—one of Pete's loves, no doubt— that Jackley thought back to the diplomats. Had he heard that accent correctly?

He shook his head. Couldn't have. After all these years he'd simply forgotten what a real Straight'n accent sounded like and his mind was leaping to an unwarranted conclusion from some slight similarity. He might have thought more about it but the comm unit sprang to life yet again.

Half an hour later, the Customs House was a madhouse. Pete Kogel had been right about the newshounds—though Gabe thought they seemed more like a pack of puppies, all worrying the same sock. He hummed a Christmas carol and sent them all waaaay up-wing.

Then he closed up shop and set the nav. computer to tell any further incoming ships they'd have to park it in orbit and wait till late 'noon tomorrow.

As the transport neared Dawn Square, Nicolazzini called to the driver to stop. Toffoli and Corcos both began muttered objections. "We've no idea how close behind us the newshounds are, Dr. Nicolazzini. Are you sure—?"

"I'm sure," Nicolazzini said. "Wait for us a moment, driver, please."

"Sure thing," said the driver. "Tonight's the right night, and you've still got plenty of light to see the Smuggler by. Follow the walk"—he pointed to a footpath that all but disappeared among the peachywands—"then just to the right, behind that big old ironwood tree. Mind you don't trip on the peachywands. They're forever trying to take over the path, but nobody wants to cut them back this time of year."

"The Smuggler?" said Corcos, when they were out of the driver's earshot. Nicolazzini shrugged. She could tell Corcos still thought stopping along the way a rotten idea but she didn't care—she wanted to walk through those peachywands, if nothing else.

Someone had once told her that peachywands were a bioteched version of old Earth's forsythia. She couldn't say for sure herself, never having seen forsythia. She'd never seen such rampageous peachy-wands either—those on her homeworld were clipped and trimmed until they were little more than hedgerows with now and then a tiny flower.

Here, they were like rushing water. . . . In wave after wave of brilliant bloom, they fountained high into the air, then fell to earth in spectacular cascades of pure color—not only the familiar rosy peach but a remarkable shade of deep butter-yellow as well. Their delicate scent filled the air with Christmas.

The party rounded the ironwood tree and for a moment Nicolazzini thought they'd come upon one of the locals playing in the park. She was on the verge of excusing their intrusion when Toffoli breathed, "Good Lord, it's a Karawan!"

"That shouldn't surprise you," Ameghino said dryly. "Karawan's a native of Butterfly, after all."

Oddly, from the tone of the comment, Nicolazzini knew that Ameghino was just as surprised to find a sculpture by Karawan in the town square, Karawan's home-world or no.

The renown of the sculptor was not what drew Nicolazzini closer to what Jackley had called "the Christmas commemorative"—it was the breathtaking liveliness of her. Could bronze dance? Under Karawan's hand it could.

She was a tall, lean woman and Karawan had caught her in mid-step, bobbed hair and silk skirts and silk sleeves flying as she danced forward. No pedestal for *her!* Nicolazzini could tell at a glance she'd have scoffed at the very idea.

At ground level, she was almost as tall as Toffoli, even as she stepped toward the table and chairs before her. Both the table and the chairs were metal and clearly meant to be used by picnickers and sightseers alike.

In the flat of her left hand she held aloft a tray of beer steins. She leaned slightly forward as if about to set a drink before a customer at that table, but the hand she extended didn't hold a stein. Instead, a single butterfly perched tremulously at the tip of her upswept index finger. For all her dancing, she kept the fingertip still and the butterfly at rest.

"Wow," said Toffoli softly. "Wait until Giosofat Orrego sees a photo of this! He'll be on the next ship out!"

"Look at the way Karawan makes you focus on the butterfly," said Corcos. "The flying hair, the eyes, the sweep of the hand all serve as—"

"Shut up, Corcos, and let me *look*," Ameghino said, and to Nicolazzini's surprise, Corcos shut up.

Nicolazzini took a step nearer—watching her step among the peachywands—and, in the shifting of her own shadow, she was suddenly able to read the brass plaque set into the paving around the sculpture's feet. The raised letters looped gracefully. *Karawan thanks Quicksilver*, they read, *for smuggling Christmas.*

Corcos had followed her lead and was reading the same words over her shoulder. "Dr. Nicolazzini," he said, "isn't Quicksilver—?"

"The name Gabe Jackley gave us? Yes."

"She smuggled Christmas. What a strange thing to say. What do you suppose Karawan meant?"

"I've no idea," Nicolazzini told him. "But I mean to ask." She gave the sculpture one last long inspection. The face she saw suppressed a smile—but the eyes were joyful. And from this angle, the sculpture seemed to offer the butterfly into Nicolazzini's keeping. Nicolazzini smiled into the deepening shadows and took the happenstance of place for a good omen.

"We'd better go," she said and, with more than one backward glance, they reluctantly returned to the transport.

Corcos said to the driver, "How could you smuggle Christmas?" She only grinned at him and said, "*I* couldn't have. Quicksilver did: ask her."

Smuggler's Rest was all that Jackley had promised and surrounded by peachywands as well. The lobby was bustling and jostling with party preparations. One woman was weaving peachywands through the rungs of the bannister leading to the second floor while another cleared away a trail of dropped blossoms. A dozen huge trays of various foods went by, enticing in their smells. An a capella quartet was practicing an unfamiliar, very lively, carol as they cleared a sofa from the lobby. Under a side table, a small child was wrapping presents with too much paper and tape. In all the apparent chaos, there seemed, quite unbelievably, to be calm, order and content, as if all the instrumentalists, even the small child, were under the hand of a talented conductor.

The only disturbing note was Nicolazzini's party, who could not seem to keep out of the way. It took Corcos a moment or two to track down someone to check them in. The someone was a bright-faced boy of about thirteen or fourteen and, despite his cheerful confidence that he could handle all paperwork and credit lines, Nicolazzini said, "Forgive me, but there are . . . mm, special circumstances. Gabe Jackley told us to see Quicksilver."

For a moment, the boy looked so delighted that Nicolazzini thought perhaps he'd heard something she hadn't said. Then he gave an exaggeratedly covert glance around. "Quick, in here," he said, and he ushered the six of them into a small cheerful office to one side of the lobby. "I'll be right back with Quicksilver."

He was right back with Quicksilver. She was some years older than she'd been when Karawan had sculpted her, but the flying hair, the dance-like step and the suppressed smile were all there. The boy waved a hand at Nicolazzini and her colleagues, grinned broadly and said, "Special circumstances. And I haven't seen anybody or anything. In fact, I'm probably not even here this evening." He grinned again and ducked out the door.

Quicksilver laughed. "Well," she said, "you've made Quillan's evening. What's the story?"

Nicolazzini said, "Not nearly as good as yours, I'd bet," but she told it anyway.

When she had finished, Quicksilver said, "All right: you're the La Gioia family reunion, here for the Wingding because Grandaddy La Gioia was born and bred on Alway—and this is about as close as anybody can get to Alway these days."

When Nicolazzini nodded acceptance of the improvisation, Quicksilver looked thoughtful for a moment, then said, "Gabe said he'd send the newshounds up-wing? Let me make a few phone calls. A couple of red herrings dragged across your tracks and you can spend your Christmas in peace and quiet." She laughed. "Not that Christmas is quiet here, but there's peace and there's peace . . ."

And then she was gone and Quillan was back to register them all as La Gioias—and to take inordinate delight in helping each of them choose a given name—and get them squared away in their rooms.

"Is it possible to get something to eat?" That was Toffoli, but Nicolazzini realized it had been a long time since they'd had anything other than ship's meals.

"Possible?" Quillan's laugh was an echo of Quicksilver's. "Mister, this is Christmas. If anything, the trick will be to stop eating before you bust. Just head on downstairs when you're ready and help yourself to the buffet on the sideboard."

Nicolazzini room came last, and Quillan led her way, still offering advice. "Don't miss Rick's batter-fried catfish. You dip it in this scallion remoulade sauce . . ." He let out a deep sigh of content and finished, "Best Christmas dish ever there was."

"Fried catfish for Christmas? Is that traditional?"

Quillan paused long enough to give the question real thought. Then he grinned and said, "It is here."

"That's good enough for me," Nicolazzini told him, as he let her into her room and gave her a quick tour. Then he sat himself on the bureau and watched as she began her unpacking.

He waved away the offered tip. "I only took the other guy's money because he's so"—he made a face that summed up Corcos's attitude completely. "You got the right spirit. You expect to have fun."

"Yes, I do," said Nicolazzini. "I'm already having more fun than I had any right to expect."

"You think this"—the swing of his arm almost toppled a lamp—"is fun?" He hopped off his perch. "Come on. I'll show you better. If we go downstairs now we can watch the tree trundle."

Nicolazzini let herself be caught up in the youngster's excitement. The unpacking could wait. "Lead on," she said.

He led her along the corridor to the stairs overlooking the lobby. Halfway down the curving staircase, he stopped her. "We can see better from here. Well, anyhow, I can. You're taller, so if—"

"I'll watch with you. You can explain what I'm seeing if I don't get it."

"Sure!" he said. Then he added, apparently in the interest of honesty, "I can't tell you *why* mostly, though. When I ask, all anybody ever says is"—he shrugged, mimicking those he'd asked—"'It's just traditional, that's all.'"

Nicolazzini nodded. "Holidays are like that," she told him. "I used to get the same answer from my parents." The two of them exchanged sympathetic grins.

From outside came the sound of bells and Quillan, now fairly hopping in his excitement, said, "Here comes the tree trundle . . ."

Over the clamor of bells came a quick sequence of slamming noises, loud enough to startle Nicolazzini. "Shooting the rods," Quillan said—and pointed. This time Nicolazzini saw the procedure: The folks nearest each door shot a series of bolt-like rods which they then locked into place. After a moment, Nicolazzini realized that she was seeing a sort of scaled-up variation on a Dutch door. The locked rods had transformed the human-sized door she'd entered into an archway some twelve feet wide and peaking some twenty feet high. It took the combined efforts of a half-dozen people on either side to open this now-grand entrance.

Framed in the archway was a magnificent Carran spruce. The tree sat on a wooden cart, its roots still encased in a ball of dirt she couldn't have gotten her arms about. Three small children sat at its base and rang bells for all they were worth. The cart itself was being pulled by another half-dozen folk.

"Oh, look!" Quillan shouted over the cacophony. "Kim got to ride the trundle!"

"Is that good?"

"That's terrific! That means she'll grow two inches this year." He leaned closer, obviously intending a confidence even though he couldn't lower his voice and still make himself heard. "Not really, you know. But Kim thinks so—and she's little so that's what she wants as her wish."

The ringing began at last to die down, and the tree trundle was hauled through the lobby on its way to the dining room. When the ringing in her ears had also subsided, Nicolazzini said, "Why do they go to all that trouble to dig up a tree? That's awkward, especially considering the size of it. Why not just cut one?"

"Can't," said Quillan. "Gotta replant it right after Christmas or we won't have one for next year."

Nicolazzini frowned. "But that's just an ordinary Carran spruce."

Quillan nodded solemnly. "Not ordinary to Butterfly," he said. "We used to get enough seedlings for every year's Christmas from Alway— but when Alway shut down, we couldn't get 'em any more. So we've got to make the ones we've got last and last and last, Dad says." He looked at her, suddenly pleased. "Hey! Sometimes I *do* know a why! *Because* we used to get most all of our biologicals from Alway—'scuse me, Straight-and-Narrow, they call it now—and we can't any more, that's why."

"That makes good sense, then," Nicolazzini said. "Now, can you tell me why you folk weave your peachywands into the staircase rungs instead of running them down the bannister?"

Quillan grinned. "Yes, I can tell you that one too." And without another word, he gleefully straddled the bannister and slithered his way down to the lobby. At the bottom of the stairs, he spread his hands and called up, "*That's* why."

Nicolazzini laughed but took the stairs at a sedate walk. She hoped he wouldn't be too disappointed in her.

He wasn't. He'd already joined forces with the remaining folk in the lobby to help close the grand entrance. Nicolazzini quickened her steps and added her weight to the task. As the doors snapped shut and experienced hands unshipped the iron rods, she found herself face to face with a grinning Ameghino, who'd helped close the opposing door.

Ameghino said, "Wingding is the right word for it. These folks sure know how to throw a party—wait until you see the food!"

"Don't miss the catfish," Nicolazzini told him, earning an ear-to-ear grin from Quillan. "My informant tells me it's the best!" Her informant nodded an enthusiastic agreement and said, "Let's eat!"

They did. Choosing the first round mostly on Quillan's recommendations, they heaped plates high. Quillan chose them a table, too: "Where you can watch Quicksilver dance behind the bar," he said. He was right about the catfish and about the vantage point as well. Nicolazzini licked remoulade sauce from her fingertips and watched Quicksilver.

What Quicksilver did *was* a dance, she saw. All of the motions a bartender had to make to do her job, Quicksilver elaborated into wider, broader, more flamboyant gestures, moving always with the music that filled the room—sliding, gliding, pouring, pirouetting before she poured a triumphant last drop—and she'd added grace notes as well.

She had a lovely trick of catching the rim of a shot glass—a *filled* shot glass—in her fingertips and, with a wide swing of the wrist, whirling the glass through a complete arc without spilling a drop of the contents. That was centrifugal force, of course, but the speed and the musicality of that arm was pure Quicksilver. And only *after* that flourish did she add the shot to whatever she was mixing.

Quillan, trying to show Nicolazzini how Quicksilver did it, had already poured soda on himself twice. The third time he got Corcos. Quicksilver caught Quillan's eye and waved him over for further instruction. As Nicolazzini watched, Quillan finally caught on. The two laughed with delight, and Nicolazzini couldn't help but join in.

At the far end of the room stood the Carran spruce, adding its pungent scent to the air. Beside the bar, a quartet composed of two guitars, a fiddle, and a tabor seemed intent on transforming every Christmas carol Nicolazzini knew into a dance tune. Whoever wasn't eating was unpacking Christmas tree ornaments; whoever wasn't unpacking Christmas tree ornaments was eating.

"Not what I'd call solemn," Corcos said, deprecatingly.

"No," said a fresh voice with a trace of a laugh in it. "Sacred, yes. Solemn, no."

Nicolazzini looked away from the bar and saw Jackley, as promised, standing beside their table. He held a heaped plate and gestured inquiringly with his free hand. Nicolazzini smiled and dragged up a chair for him.

He sat and said to Corcos, "It's a birthday party, after all!"

"Not how we do it at home . . ." Corcos said, his expression still disapproving.

"Too bad." Jackley turned his smile on Nicolazzini. "Where's home?"

Nicolazzini, deadpan, told him the tale that Quicksilver had concocted for them, and Jackley laughed out loud. "I'll bet anything Quillan had a hand in that. 'Terry' La Gioia?"—he raised an eyebrow at Corcos—"Terry's the name of Quillan's pet catchum." He waited a moment, as if expecting her to say something more. When she didn't, he shrugged. "Okay," he said, amiably. "I'll find out when the newshounds get here, I guess."

"The newshounds—" said Toffoli.

Gabe shook his head. "Don't you worry. Right about now, Lily Drinkwater should be telling them about this weird crew of folk she saw headed for Wingtip. And, if I know Lily, she's probably slandering the hell out of you all, which makes her story all the more convincing."

Before Nicolazzini could ask about that, Quillan was back. "Hey, dad—watch!"

Jackley watched—with indrawn breath and eyebrows shot up almost to his hairline—as Quilan swung his shot glass full of soda . . .

He didn't spill a drop. Jackley let out his breath. "Good for you. I was afraid you were going to give Dr. La Gioia here a bath for Christmas Eve."

Quillan was instantly contrite. "Sorry. Quicksilver told me not to aim it at anybody, but I got so excited I could do it. See, you have to not think about it. If you think about it, you don't do it fast enough. So I wasn't thinking about it. Sorry," he said again. Then he brightened up almost instantly. "But I *didn't* give you a bath, so that's okay."

Nicolazzini nodded. "Yes, that's okay. —Is Terry really the name of your pet?"

"Yeah," said Quillan with a grin. "He"—Quillan jabbed a quick finger in Corcos's direction—"has bangs just like my Terry does."

Nicolazzini tried to hide her smile and failed. "I must see this Terry of yours sometime."

"Sure!" he said—and once more swung his shot glass up and over. Successfully. "Hey, Quicksilver!" he called out. "I did it twice in a row!"

Quicksilver danced toward their table, a tray of drinks in her upraised hand. Without missing a beat, she said, "Good for you. Just remember, you gotta keep in practice."

Watching her, Nicolazzini thought how *truly* remarkable Karawan was, to have captured all that motion, all that lightness of foot and heart.

She set a drink before Gabe. "How was Christmas Eve at Customs this year?"

"A few unexpected items," he said, nodding at Nicolazzini and her colleagues. "Nothing like '85." He grinned at Nicolazzini and said, "Did you see Quicksilver's statue?"

Nodding, Nicolazzini took the opening and said, "And I'm curious to know: Just how does one smuggle Christmas?"

Quicksilver put her free hand on the table and leaned nearer to

Nicolazzini's ear. "Now," she said, "if I told you the how of it, it might get back to the folks I did the smuggling from. And then I might not be able to do it again should the need arise." She straightened. "You gotta keep in practice, right, Quillan?"

"Right," said Quillan. He swung his shot glass again and soda splashed him all down the front. He threw back his head and laughed in genuine delight. "Guess I just proved that, didn't I?" he said, as Jackley swabbed him with a napkin.

Quillan suffered the swabbing for only a moment or two, then he got away. Using Nicolazzini for cover, he said in her ear, "Quicksilver doesn't practice telling stories. Ask Uncle Midji—he gets more fun out of the telling than Quicksilver does." As Jackley reached around Nicolazzini, the boy darted away, shouting, "Uncle Midji! Hey, Uncle Midji!"

Nicolazzini couldn't help but grin. Jackley spread his hands. "Kids," he said. "Well, it's warm enough in here, and by the time we head home he'll be dry."

"Especially the way he keeps moving," Nicolazzini said.

Quillan was halfway across the room now and on his way back with an elderly man in his wake, towed along by Quillan's grasp on the outsized notebook he carried. He was aged enough that Nicolazzini caught herself wishing the boy wouldn't rush him—until she realized that Uncle Midji was as quick of step as the boy.

"Here, Uncle Midji," Quillan announced. "These are the La Gioias and they want to know how Quicksilver smuggled Christmas." He paused, watching carefully as the old gentleman shook hands all around. The old gentleman pulled up a chair, turned it quite deliberately to face Nicolazzini, opened his notebook—no, Nicolazzini saw, it was a sketchbook—and began to sketch . . . Nicolazzini.

Quillan laid an obstructing hand on the sheaf of paper. "Fair is fair, Uncle Midji. You get to sketch, she gets the story. Same deal you do with us. It's Christmas Eve and she's a long way from home and *I* say you ought to treat her right."

Uncle Midji smiled at Nicolazzini. "What do you say?"

"I *would* like to hear the story—" Nicolazzini began.

"Good," he said, as if that were all settled. "Then neither of you will mind if I sketch while I talk." He gave Nicolazzini a searching look, nodded to himself, and began to sketch.

A moment later—after Quillan prodded him with a finger—he began to talk. "Well, Quillan, I can't tell her the how of it. But I can tell her the why of it."

His pencil stopped in mid-stroke and he met Nicolazzini's eyes. "Quicksilver smuggled Christmas for me and my wife and my daughters and for Quillan here, which is why he takes such an inordinate interest in the tale, even though he's *not* old enough to remember it." Uncle Midji smiled radiantly at Quillan, who saw his smile and raised him a grin.

"I don't know how much you know about Butterfly, but we've always been a trading hub. Almost everything comes through here on its way to Foolhardy and the other major population centers in this sector. If you'll take a good look at the Christmas tree, you'll see decorations from just about every culture on every world—"

He turned the page of his sketchbook. Reaching out a gentle hand, he turned Nicolazzini's face toward the tree. "Hold it there," he said. "But, like every world I ever heard of, we've got our own special favorites. And our own special favorites used to come from Alway."

Nicolazzini's head jerked toward him.

"Uh-uh," he said, catching her chin and posing her again. "You pose, I talk. Good. Now, you're probably too young to remember"— he glanced at Quillan—"Most kids don't. But our favorite decorations came from Alway, right up until '80."

He sighed suddenly but Nicolazzini had caught on by now and did not turn her head.

So he went on: "That was the year the government of Alway went rogue. They changed the name of their world to Straight-and-Narrow that year—though if you'd asked any Alwayn in the street they'd have told you that was a stupid idea—after all, what right does the government have to decide on the name of your home world?"

Nicolazzini did move her head then, to give it a quick shake at Corcos, who'd risen frowning behind Uncle Midji.

"Exactly," said Uncle Midji. "None." He turned the page again and scraped his chair along until he found, apparently, another good view.

"Yet," he said, "nobody raised a cry, so the rogue government went on. Next, they passed a law saying that buchanism was the official, and only *acceptable*, religion of the newly-named Straight-and-Narrow and then . . ."

Quillan was bouncing again, and his excitement was not lost on Uncle Midji. He turned to the boy and said, "You tell her what happened next."

"They closed the borders," Quillan said. He was repeating the story as it had been told to him, but his eyes were huge, as if he still couldn't believe adults would let something like that happen. "They said, to keep Straight-and-Narrow *to* the straight and narrow, they weren't going to let anybody come there—not even for trade!"

"That's right," said Uncle Midji, and he looked solemn for a long moment. "The last message we got from Straight-and-Narrow was: 'You're not dragging us to hell with you.'"

"And that was it," Jackley put in. "Straight-and-Narrow shut itself down. Folded in on itself. All trade between here and there stopped dead."

Uncle Midji cocked his head at Jackley. "All trade between Straight-and-Narrow and *anywhere* stopped dead. You can't take it personally, Gabe."

Quillan said, in a stage whisper: "But he did."

"I guess I did," said Jackley, "but I wasn't the only one. And it was all because of Christmas—"

"Oh!" said Nicolazzini. "Quillan told me you'd always gotten Carran spruce seedlings from them to raise as Christmas trees—"

"That was just part of it," Gabe said. "Not even the major part. You can see we've sort of worked that out, though Lord knows what'll happen when the trees get too big to move inside. No, it was the Christmas tree *decorations*—we'd always gotten the best ones, our favorites, from Alway—and there simply was no other source of them."

"I was just a baby," said Quillan. "So I don't remember this bit. Everybody"—in this instance, that meant Gabe and Uncle Midji and all the adults in a hand-swing—"tried to hoard the Alwayn decorations, hoping they'd last—"

"But," Uncle Midji said, shaking his head sadly, "even with the best of care, they were too delicate, too ephemeral, to last more than a few years. By '85, the last of them were gone."

"And Straight-and-Narrow *still* hadn't opened up," said Jackley.

"And it was two months before Christmas and we were moping," said Uncle Midji.

"G'wan," said Quillan.

Uncle Midji stuck his pencil behind his ear and raised his right hand. "We were moping, we were sulking, we were doing all those things you kids do when you can't get your way. And, of course, we blamed it on you kids. We said we were miserable that Christmas was coming and you kids would never get to see a properly decorated Christmas tree. . . . The truth was, we knew there wasn't a single

Alwayn decoration left on Butterfly and *we* were going to feel cheated out of Christmas without them."

A pair of tall women—twins, Nicolazzini realized—had come up behind to peer over Uncle Midji's shoulder. "We're old enough to remember, Quillan," one of them said. Nicolazzini guessed they were a few years older than she. "We didn't know what was wrong, but all the adults were acting like—" The one faltered and her sister took up the sentence and finished, "They were acting pretty much the way Kim does when you tell her its time for bed and, no, she *can't* have one more story."

"Wow," said Quillan. He looked at his father with new eyes. "No wonder Quicksilver called you all a bunch of big babies!" He glanced at Nicolazzini and added hastily, "She said it with a smile, so I don't think she said it to be mean." Suddenly, he smiled at the twins. "No, she didn't say it to be mean, 'cause you said that's when she closed the inn."

One of the twins said, "Which sounds meaner, Quillan." To Nicolazzini, she said, "Quicksilver told Dad"—she tapped Uncle Midji—"he and Mom had to hold the fort and plan the Christmas Wingding that year."

"Then she took off in that awful rattletrap of hers—"

"Which you'd never think would get safely off the ground once, let alone twice!"

"Which you saw at the spaceport—"

"The one with the wreath."

"Hah!" said Jackley. "Now I know who put the wreath on the old Bugcrusher . . ."

Each one gave the other such a studied look of innocence that Nicolazzini thought they were practicing in a mirror. "Who, us?" said one. "Gotta go now," said the other. "Gotta go help Quicksilver," said one, overlapping with the other's "help Mom." They finished in chorus, "Bye now," and charged into the crowd, bursting into laughter as they vanished.

Uncle Midji's shoulders shook with silent laughter. Aloud, he said, "Oh, we're in for a night of it: They're pretending to be each other." When at last his shoulders stilled, he looked again at his sketch and again at Nicolazzini.

"So Suzi and I planned the Wingding that year, and Quicksilver was gone—who knew where—she hadn't said a word to anyone about her destination. By the afternoon of the twenty-fourth, we'd all gotten plenty worried. Quicksilver *still* hadn't shown up for her party, and she'd never missed a Christmas Eve, not *one*, in all the years we'd known her!"

Uncle Midji gave Jackley a long look. "Your turn now, Gabe. 'Cause I don't know what's legal and what isn't."

Jackley shook his head and grinned. "You take that 'smuggling' charge too seriously, Midji. Everybody does: that's why I'm 'stuck' with Christmas Eve duty at Customs." He turned to Nicolazzini and said, "I was on duty that Christmas Eve, when Quicksilver's old Bugcrusher wallowed in for a landing. In my official capacity as customs' inspector, I asked did she or her passengers have anything to declare."

He grinned again at Uncle Midji. "She may have smuggled the decorations *off* Straight'n—I'm sure the folks on Straight'n would love to string her up—but it's nowhere illegal to import Alwayn Christmas tree ornaments to Butterfly. Now that I think back on it—I *may* have neglected to check her passengers' passports—but it *was* Christmas Eve, after all . . ."

He leaned back contentedly and waved a hand at Quicksilver for another drink. "Quicksilver brought us our old familiar, our old favorite Christmas tree decorations—an entire cargo hold full of them. To this day, I don't know how she managed to arrange the buying of them or the secret landing on Straight'n, but to this day, I salute her for it."

He raised his empty glass to Quicksilver as she approached, to do just that.

"Good," said Quicksilver, ignoring the import of the gesture. "An empty glass." From behind her back, she drew a globe-shaped bottle, its gilded belly full of amber liquid.

Jackley's eyes widened. "Is that what I think it is?"

"Probably not," Quicksilver told him. "After all, it's illegal to import killi juice liqueur to Butterfly—something about not buying products that we *can't* make locally. . . . Never did understand that one." She flicked open the lid with a thumbnail and poured. "Got this for a Christmas present," she said. "Thought you'd like a swig or two, since it *looks* so much like that poison you're so fond of."

Nicolazzini knew from the exchange that the bottle did indeed contain some liqueur forbidden on purely political grounds and knew as well that Jackley had somehow passed it through Customs all unknowing. She watched as the two old friends toasted each other in smuggled liqueur.

A cheer went up from the front of the room. It sounded to Nicolazzini as if the party-goers were all chanting, "Ruffle-OHS! Ruffle-OHS!." She stood up and craned for a better look.

Behind her, Quillan jumped onto the chair she'd just vacated. From over her head, he explained, "The Ruffolos are here! That's Marcena and that's Julietta—and they've brought the Alwayn decorations!"

He hopped off the chair as lightly as he hopped on. Grabbing Nicolazzini's hand, he drew her through the crowd. "You'll have to hang one on the tree too. Everybody at the Wingding gets to hang one. I'll help you pick a good one!"

He elbowed a way for her through the crowd to the bar itself. Now ranged along the bar were tray after tray of . . . decorations?

Nicolazzini frowned slightly. There was no accounting for taste, she supposed, but this was hardly what she'd expected. Each tray was divided into tiny padded compartments, like a high-class chocolate box. In each compartment nestled an inch-long shiny brown object flecked with gold. They were blown glass, perhaps. At the top of each was a thin loop of gold thread.

She frowned at the assortment, while Quillan clambered onto one of the barstools beside her. There he knelt, overlooking the trays, with eyes that were at once greedy and anticipatory. Over his shoulder, he jabbed at Nicolazzini with his thumb. "She's never seen a Butterfly Christmas, Julietta," he said to the bright-faced woman who was delicately passing out choices. "Help me pick her a really good one!"

"Never seen a Butterfly Christmas?" Julietta said. "Let's give her a couple, then." To Nicolazzini, Julietta said, "Have you got a favorite color combination?"

However surprised she was by the question, Nicolazzini didn't hesitate: "Red and gold, first choice."

That obviously surprised Julietta—Nicolazzini realized belatedly she was wearing the best of her greys, an old holdover from the sumptuary laws—but surprised or not, she nodded. "I've got just the thing for you, then," she said.

Julietta moved down the bar and leaned over the heads of two five-year-olds who were having as difficult a time over their decision as any who'd ever been told "Only *two* chocolates," and came back dangling two of the brown objects by their loops. "Brand new this year."

Nicolazzini was further bemused—these two didn't seem any redder than any others in the tray. "Do you folks see colors differently?"

"Oh!" said Quillan, suddenly. "You really *don't* know! See—"

"Hush up, Quillan," said Julietta quickly. "If she really doesn't know, let her be surprised. Remember the first time you saw them?"

Quillan got a dreamy look. "Yeah," he said, drawing the word out softly. "I remember. Okay." To Nicolazzini, he said, "You have to wait for the surprise." He slid from the stool and led her to the tree. "Now you hang them up—and remember where you put them, so you'll know which ones are yours Christmas morning."

Nicolazzini chose a spot near a plump papier maché cat sporting a purple feather boa. *That* she was sure she would remember, just in case Quillan asked her later. She'd done her share of testing the adults in her childhood, after all. She hung the first to the right of the cat, then paused to put a fingertip under the second decoration for a closer look.

"Uh-uh," said a young man holding a small child in his arms. "Don't touch. The heat from your fingers can sometimes affect them. They're really delicate." To the child, he said, "How about next to the mermaid? You wouldn't forget the mermaid, would you?"

The little boy shook his head vigorously. "Never!" he said, and he very carefully, with only a little help, hung his ornament next to the mermaid.

Still holding the second Alwayn ornament at eye level, Nicolazzini frowned at Quillan.

"You can take his word for it," Quillan said. "That's Massimo Ruffolo—he makes them so he knows more about them than anybody."

"Anybody except Marcena and Julietta," Massimo said.

"I don't doubt you," Nicolazzini said, shaking her head. "I just— Quillan, should I really have *two*? If they're so delicate and so hard to come by, you should be saving some of these . . . !" She felt like she was taking candy from a baby.

"Oh," said Quillan. "We didn't finish telling you. . . . That's Massimo *Ruffolo*," he said again. "Quicksilver didn't just smuggle a cargo-load of decorations off Straight'n. She smuggled the Ruffolos, too: Julietta and Marcena and—"

"And me and Marietta and Inshalla," said Massimo. He slid the child down to his feet and sent him off with a tousle of the head. "Ian and Glen were born here. Guess you could say Quicksilver smuggled the genes for them off Straight-and-Narrow too."

"You don't get it yet?" said Quillan, grinning. "Quicksilver says if you're gonna do something you might as well do it right. She smuggled the people who *made* the decorations, too, so we'd never have to have another Christmas without the proper decorations for the tree."

"Oh," said Nicolazzini. Relieved of all guilt, she hung the second Alwayn ornament beside the papier maché cat.

Massimo looked at Quillan thoughtfully. "I sometimes wonder what happened when Straight-and-Narrow ran out of ornaments. I always feel a little sorry for them."

"Don't," said Nicolazzini. "From what Quillan tells me, they made their choice. I take it *you* came willingly away from that world."

"More than willingly," he said.

Behind him, Julietta said, "With wings on! By the time Quicksilver contacted us, the government had already decided that joy had no place in Straight-and-Narrow. It was only a matter of time before we could no longer practice our trade there anyhow."

Massimo said, "Sometimes I really miss Alway, but I don't miss Straight-and-Narrow a bit."

"What was it like?—Alway, I mean," Nicolazzini asked.

A brilliant smile broke across Massimo's face. "Tomorrow morning you'll see for yourself."

The quartet had struck up a familiar tune, once again at an unfamiliar tempo. Massimo snapped his fingers to "In Excelsis Deo" and said, "Hey, my favorite! Would you like to dance?" When she hesitated, he said, "It's traditional."

"I don't know how," Nicolazzini admitted.

"Nothing easier," he said. "I'll show you. Excuse us, Quillan?"

"Sure," said Quillan.

Massimo didn't give Nicolazzini any such choice, and she danced the rest of the evening away. Mostly with Massimo, who seemed to have the world's highest tolerance for having his feet stepped on. They danced quickstep—an *Alwayn* quickstep—to "In Excelsis Deo" and a waltz to the fiddler's own "Christmas Eve Waltz."

Then came "Lord of the Dance ..." Nicolazzini had heard the tune all her life, but she'd never before heard the lyrics and she had to listen to the words.

> *Dance, then, wherever you may be,*
> *For I am the Lord of the Dance, said He.*

Massimo waited out the dance with her and, when she turned her astonished eyes to him, he said, "I think we've just scandalized you."

She shook her head vigorously. "No," she said. "No. I love that song and, now that I've heard the words, I love that song even more."

Quillan said, "We sure did scandalize your Terry." He pointed with a fistful of popcorn. "I don't think he's having much fun at all."

Nicolazzini followed the point and saw what he meant: Corcos looked for all the world like he'd just eaten an entire lemon. She laughed. "Quillan, that man is having the time of his life."

"Gwan," said Quillan.

"If he doesn't have something to disapprove of, he's not happy. Believe me—I've known him for years. He's going to love it here."

Quillan and Massimo both laughed, and Massimo said, "Shall I ask them to sing 'Lord of the Dance' again, then?"

"Oh, yes! Please do!"

He did, and this time she danced as the Lord of the Dance commanded, a contredanse—but with Massimo and Quillan and even Quicksilver willing to guide her she made it safely through the intricate steps. At the ending bow, Corcos gave her his deepest scowl, and she knew—at the very least—that she'd shown true reverence for the season.

And then there was more dancing and more singing and more eating. Jackley even granted her a taste of the killi juice liqueur and she'd had to agree she saw no reason to ban such a flavor from Butterfly. She and Quillan danced a two-step, and Quicksilver taught her a Butterfly skirt dance that made her want a red and gold skirt to flutter so badly she could have cried, until she realized she could buy herself one—for Christmas!

She helped herself to another plate of catfish and was about to ask Massimo directions to the nearest clothing shop, when Marcena climbed onto a table top and banged a gong.

When the room came to order, Marcena checked her watch and said, "Okay, folks—it's time!"

Massimo patted Nicolazzini on the arm, and she followed him, wildly curious. From behind the bar, his parents handed out flashlights—or that was what they looked like to Nicolazzini. There was a great deal of arranging and jockeying as everyone aimed the lights at various areas of the Christmas tree.

Massimo gave Nicolazzini his own and directed her aim. "We try to get them all in one shot," he began, but Quillan said, "No, her first tree—we want to surprise her!" So Massimo stopped what might have been an explanation and, instead, he mugged at her—so she knew it was a patent lie—and said, "Flashbulbs ... so we can get a good photo of this year's tree." And someone else had obligingly raised a camera that Nicolazzini knew for a fact would have been overwhelmed by the sudden burst of light from all those bulbs at once.

After that, Marcena said, "Got it. Be here at ten o'clock tomorrow morning for the show. Merry Christmas!"

The entire crowd had responded, *"Merry Christmas!"* And a few minutes later, they'd all gone home, and Nicolazzini had gone up to bed to collapse, still smiling, all her disappointment in the much-vaunted Alwayn decorations forgotten.

On the dressing table, she'd laid the sketch Uncle Midji had torn from his pad to give her—a Welcome-to-Butterfly Christmas present he said. He'd made her look like an angel, which she was sure was not true to life, and behind her head—for a halo—he'd sketched the open wings of a butterfly. She didn't need to read the signature to realize at last that Quillan's Uncle Midji was Bemidji Karawan. She smiled back at her own smiling face.

She was still smiling when someone shook her shoulder and whispered, "Come on—psst—come on! The adults don't get up for the best part but I'll show you since you've never seen."

When her eyes at last focussed, she saw Quillan standing beside her bed. "What time is it?" she demanded, as any sensible adult would.

"Nine o'clock," he said. "Come on, get up or you'll miss it." He vanished out the door.

Discreet for his age, she thought. Well, she'd been told to see a Butterfly Christmas. She wasn't sure if Alceo Nicolazzini had been acting in his capacity as her father or in his capacity as Chief of State, but she might as well see the whole thing. So far, Quillan had been right in every particular about the "bests."

She threw on some clothing and dashed some water on her face.

Quillan was lounging against the wall outside her door; he was trying very hard not to look impatient. He glanced at the peachywand blossom watch pinned to his lapel and said, "Not bad," grabbed her hand and led her, at a goodly clip, down the stairs and back into the dining room.

All the evidence of the previous night's party had been cleared and the sideboard was being newly laid with breakfast foods. But it wasn't first pick of breakfast Quillan was after . . .

He lead her to the tree, where some two dozen youngsters were already arrayed and watching something—or *for* something—intently. Jackley was there too, and the Karawans and the entire Ruffolo clan—including Massimo, whose toes seemed none the worse for wear. And Quicksilver was orchestrating the breakfast table.

"May I help?" Nicolazzini said. One didn't ordinarily offer to help the innkeeper, but she'd been invited to the Wingding and she'd been made to feel a part of the family and she felt like part of the family.

Quicksilver shook her head and sent that blonde hair flying. "You go watch the tree. If yours is the first out, you get the prize, you know. The kids held a conference last night and agreed on that, since this is your first Christmas on Butterfly."

A chorus of agreement came from the children around the Christmas tree, and Nicolazzini joined them. "What am I watching for?" she asked, at last, unable to see the point of this part of Butterfly's Christmas ritual.

"Just watch your decorations," Quillan said, and he pointed. "You'll know it when you see it." He'd remembered where she'd hung the two chosen for her and hadn't even tested her. That spoke volumes about Jackley.

She looked for two shiny brown lumps with gold spots. She'd have thought the exercise pointless but for the intensity of those around her. Something *had* changed overnight, she saw. The two thumb-sized lumps were shiny brown no longer. They were transparent now—and within each she saw a hint of the promised red and gold.

Not blown glass. Butterfly had gotten all its *biologicals* from Alway—Quillan had told her that and she'd thought he was referring to the Carran spruce. But the Alwayn ornaments were not blown glass.

Red and gold shifted and Nicolazzini caught her breath sharply as the transparent shell split open. "Oh!" she said aloud. "Oh!"

Massimo glanced up, smiling. "Julietta picked you the right ones," he said, and to the world at large, he announced, "She's got the first one out!"

Slowly, clumsily, the first butterfly struggled clear of its pupa and, step by awkward step, it made its way to the branch above.

There it clung, trembling from sheer newness. Its distended abdomen throbbed, its tiny wrinkled wings shivered. It was damp, bedraggled, and entirely beautiful.

"Mine's second out," shouted a small voice, triumphantly, and another voice said, "Mine too! Oh!—it's so *blue!*" But even at that worshipful *"blue,"* Nicolazzini couldn't take her eyes away from her own butterflies.

The second pupa split and a second red and gold butterfly struggled free and began its climb.

By the time the second butterfly had reached the tip of the branch, the first butterfly's wings had already begun to expand, their color deepening to that of glowing coals. As if that weren't enough, as if *more* were the order of the day, the first butterfly was going to have tails—elegant tails painted red and gold!

Someone—Quillan—caught her hand and squeezed it. "You see why I woke you early," he said.

"Oh, yes," she breathed and squeezed back. "Thank you, Quillan. I wouldn't have missed this for the world."

The first butterfly spread open its wings, a full two inches of glowing dark-red velvet overlain with gold. Expanded and dried, its tails were not so much elegant as rakish—they curled!—and Nicolazzini laughed aloud to see traced in gold, the length of each tail, an exclamation mark. If ever a creature deserved exclamation marks, the first butterfly did!

And so did the second, as it too spread its expanded wings to splash red and gold against the tree's dark green needles. Even though the second butterfly's tails were traced with delicate gold asterisks, Nicolazzini had by then decided that all butterflies deserved exclamation marks, by the simple virtue of *being* butterflies.

"Oh, look!" someone said. "Gabe's got a green one! Marcena, you finally made Gabe a green one!"

"I cheated," said Marcena. "I bought the genes for that color from a butterfly collector on Foolhardy."

"Hell, Marcena," said Gabe. "You shouldn't have gone to all that expense . . ."

Massimo laughed. "Don't you worry, Gabe. We'll make it back sixty-fold in sales to Foolhardy next Christmas—probably to the same butterfly collector." He touched Nicolazzini's arm and said, "You're allowed to blink, you know. They won't fly away for two or three hours."

"They're so beautiful," was all she could say in response.

"I'm glad you like them. I designed that batch myself," he said. "But now it's time to take a step back and have a look at the *whole* tree . . ." And he and Quillan took her hands and stepped back with her.

The entire tree had come alive. Everywhere she looked, color rippled softly, as a hundred butterflies opened and closed their wings, testing their strength, tasting the air. There were gentle colors and jewel colors, watercolors and colors that shimmered like oil over water. Gabe's green one was emerald green and Nicolazzini knew on sight which butterfly had been "so *blue!*" There was a black velvet butterfly inlaid with gold, there was a bright orange butterfly etched in black, there were pastel blues with their edges scalloped soft brown, there was a black-and-white butterfly that would have made fit piano keys for an impressionist, there were pale pink butterflies and rose pink butterflies and deep butter-yellow butterflies. Folding and un-folding . . .

There were checked butterflies and striped butterflies and butterflies with "eyes" that seemed to stare back at her. There were subtle colors and startling colors. The "eyes" closed abruptly as a butterfly folded its wings. Both of her red and gold butterflies spread their wings simultaneously, and Nicolazzini clapped her hands in sheer joy.

Quillan brought her an emerald one on the tip of his finger. "Hold out your finger," he said. "You have to hold real still—it can't fly yet, remember."

As Quillan coaxed the butterfly from his fingertip to hers, Nicolazzini *remembered*—remembered another tree covered in butterflies, remembered a breathtaking moment of time when a butterfly, striped pale blue and sharp black, had clung to her thumb . . .

All these years, she'd thought those images nothing more than the remnants of a very vivid childhood dream. But it had been no dream. It had been as real as the emerald butterfly on her fingertip.

At last she understood why her father had sent her to Butterfly in time for Christmas. "Oh," she said, "I wish Dad could see this . . ."

She must have said it aloud because Massimo said, "Then you get your wish. I'll make you up our best assortment and give you an activating light and you can take it to him for next Christmas. Unless he's on Straight'n," he added by way of joke. "In which case, I'll bet we could talk Quicksilver into smuggling it in to him. She's *such* a soft touch for Christmas wishes."

Quicksilver, passing by with a tray of sliced and embellished fruits, stuck her tongue out at him and said, "If you folks want first grab at breakfast, now's your chance. The stayabeds should be arriving any minute now."

Nicolazzini gave the offer only a second's thought, and then went back to the tree to watch the few remaining late rousers on the tree emerge from their pupae. When she and the youngest toddler could find no more, she sighed contentedly and turned her thoughts—back to Massimo and Quillan and the rest.

The dining room was once again filled with people, all oohing and aahing over the tree. The emerald-green butterflies Marcena had made especially for Gabe Jackley were being much exclaimed over. Even her colleagues were awed by the Christmas tree and its live decorations, though Nicolazzini couldn't refrain from telling them they'd missed the best part of the show.

Corcos, as disapproving as ever, asked, "What happens when they do fly?"

She'd been too admiring to consider the problem, so she applied to Massimo for the answer.

"In an hour or so, we'll open the main doors again. You saw the field of peachywands outside? They'll make straight for that."

And the stragglers would settle on the peachywands that were woven into the bannister's uprights and lain across mantels and tables—so they'd be easily carried outside, too, Nicolazzini realized.

"Where they'll play havoc with your ecology; those butterflies aren't native to Butterfly," Corcos said, still scowling.

Massimo Ruffolo just smiled. "No butterfly *is*," he said. "And ours are sterile. They'll brighten the fields just long enough to pollinate the peachywands. Then we'll start to work on a whole new batch for next year's Christmas." The smile turned into a grin. "That's what keeps us in business."

"Heads up, you La Gioias," Quicksilver said, bending close to their table. "The hounds have been sighted and they're sniffing this way. We grant you another hour's peace but, longer than that, we can't guarantee."

Massimo looked from Quicksilver to Nicolazzini, then said to Nicolazzini, "You folks need a hideout?" Without waiting for an answer, he raised a hand to hail Marcena and Julietta.

"No," said Nicolazzini. "No, we don't need a hideout any more. But we thank you for the offer." She waved together her colleagues, and waved Gabe and Quillan over while she was at it.

"We're here to present our diplomatic credentials to your president," Nicolazzini said. "But I think it would be more fitting if we presented our credentials to Quicksilver."

For once, Quicksilver stood still. Hands on hips, she met Nicolazzini's eyes steadily, waiting only for an explanation.

Nicolazzini said, "Corcos, may I have our letter of introduction, please?" She knew he'd have it on him; he hadn't let it out of his keeping since they'd left Foolhardy. When he grudgingly produced it, Nicolazzini unfolded it with a smile and handed it to Quicksilver.

"What's it say?" Quillan demanded. "What's it say?"

Quicksilver laughed aloud. Then she refolded the paper and returned it to Nicolazzini. "It says," she told Quillan, "that Alway is Alway again. And Dr. Celia Nicolazzini"—she held out her hand to Nicolazzini, who took it—"is Alway's ambassador to Butterfly."

With that, Quicksilver shook Nicolazzini's hand and said, "I hope you tarred and feathered those Straight'n fools. Welcome back to the trade routes. I wondered how long it would take before you folks showed some common sense and kicked those dimwits out of office."

"It took about five years without the 'proper' Christmas tree decorations," Nicolazzini said.

"And if you're still in the trading business, Quicksilver," she went on. "I'd like the first box of butterflies to go to my Dad. Massimo's finest red and gold ones, I think. I can't write you a trade permit until I've been officially accepted by your president, but you'll find it ready and waiting for you five minutes after the formalities are over and done with."

Nicolazzini caught Quicksilver's suppressed smile and couldn't help herself. "Unless you *prefer* to smuggle them in to him," she added, "just to keep in practice, that is."

Quillan was scowling at all of them, but mostly at Nicolazzini. "I don't get it," he said.

"Quillan," Nicolazzini said, "when Quicksilver smuggled Christmas to Butterfly, she smuggled Christmas *off* Straight-and-Narrow. Nobody else could raise and breed and genetically engineer those Ruffolo decorations. And my Dad was as unhappy with *that* as yours was. So he did something about it too. Since he didn't know Quicksilver, it took a lot more work and a lot longer to fix. But it *is* fixed, and Strai—*Alway* is open for trade again. And the first item on the trade agenda, I've *no* doubt, is a cargo hold full of Butterfly

Christmas tree decorations. Perhaps in trade for some Carran spruce seedlings . . . ?"

"That would have been my next run," Quicksilver said. "Good. That saves me the trouble."

"They're off!" Marcena shouted. "Get those doors open, somebody—everybody! Let 'em fly!"

Nicolazzini beat Quillan to the main doors by a hair, but they both had to wait for Quicksilver to throw the iron rods before they leaned into the work of forcing the arched doors open their full width and height. Across the room, Jackley and Massimo and Marcena and Julietta heaved open the other half of the door.

Even before the doors were fully ajar, the first butterfly flicked through the opening—Gabe's glittering green gem dancing into the sunlit air.

And then there were two red and gold ones, an amethyst filigreed gold, and then the air was filled with them, all dancing into the freedom of the field beyond Smuggler's Rest . . .

Quicksilver smiled at Nicolazzini. "Merry Christmas," she said.

"Yes," Nicolazzini agreed. "A *very* Merry Christmas!"

For unto us a child is born.

A PRESENT FOR HANNA

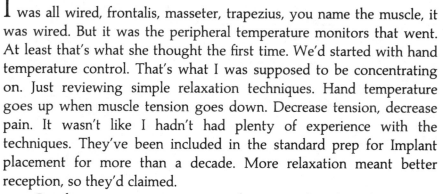

Maggie Flinn

I was all wired, frontalis, masseter, trapezius, you name the muscle, it was wired. But it was the peripheral temperature monitors that went. At least that's what she thought the first time. We'd started with hand temperature control. That's what I was supposed to be concentrating on. Just reviewing simple relaxation techniques. Hand temperature goes up when muscle tension goes down. Decrease tension, decrease pain. It wasn't like I hadn't had plenty of experience with the techniques. They've been included in the standard prep for Implant placement for more than a decade. More relaxation meant better reception, so they'd claimed.

But for now, we were starting from scratch. After all, the pain wasn't the only reason I'd agreed to come to the Rehabilitation Unit. I wanted my Implant back. I'd only had it a few months but I missed it more than I minded the pain most of the time. Somehow life with constant pain was easier to live with than life without the Implant.

There hadn't been any problems at first. I'd noticed a few mild headaches after Implant placement but they hadn't been bad enough to mention. I'd been slated to start with empathic exploration training and to say I had liked knowing what other people were really feeling would be the understatement of the century. As I progressed in my abilities to connect and experience more vivid emotions, the headaches became more and more frequent and severe. Definitely bad enough to mention. Just as I was about to complete full empathic connection and experience another individual's complete emotional state, the headaches become intolerable.

The original assumption, at least so I was told, was that there must have been some technical problem with the actual Implant and its removal was supposed to be only temporary—until the cause of the malfunction could be determined. It seemed reasonable to me at the time. But I swear I had to sign more consent forms for its removal than I had for its implant.

I'll never forget waking up in recovery with an erupting furnace of agony deep in my brain, somewhere behind my eyes, through my ears, seething through the bones of my skull, even into the roots of what was left of my hair. And I thought the headaches had been insufferable. They assured me the pain would get better in just a couple of days. Implant removal wasn't considered a painful procedure. They were wrong. They were so wrong, I became the first reported case in the literature of such an unexpected adverse consequence of Implant removal. I'd made minor medical history. I think they were trying to make me feel better when they told me that. I didn't.

They also told me it had been a very difficult decision, to remove the Implant. Megson herself had been called in on the decision. Not that I actually got to meet her. I hadn't even known she was still alive. I can remember reading about her, and her mother, when I was a kid—in the little picture pamphlets they had in the doctors' offices growing up. Why we weren't supposed to be scared of the doctors with the bulgy heads. How Megson and her daughter had won a Nobel prize for their work in paranormal psychology and their development of the paranormal enhancing implant, commonly known as the Megson Implant.

Even way back then as a kid, I'd wanted one. I'd prayed every night, every day, for years that I'd test latent. I never understood people who didn't want to qualify for Implant training. All the really famous people had Implants.

But no one in my family had ever tested latent for any paranormal abilities of any kind. Maybe that's why no one in my family had ever done anything except work retail. My parents even met at a mall. They warned me not to get my hopes up, paranormal abilities usually ran in families and we were not that kind of a family. Well, I guess I wasn't their kind of a child. I agreed to go to Retail Sales Technical High (where Mom had been valedictorian) and had my friend Bobby program the necessary reports to be sent home regularly. He was an absolute genius about it so I didn't think having sex with him was all that bad a price to pay for the service. He really did try to be nice about it.

I enrolled in the BioTech Institute across town instead (Bobby managed that for me too) and studied physics and chemistry and cell biology. I learned all about autosomal dominant with partial penetrance traits and the unique abilities the autosomal recessives were being found to have, and I prayed some more—that I was an autosomal recessive and that I'd test latent and that I'd get away with the school switch. I prayed a lot in those days.

I did manage to stay in school even after my parents found out about the switch. I'd met this really cute girl in my physics lab but when I tried to tell her how much I liked her she freaked and told her parents and they called mine and complained. It took a few days but I managed to convince my dad that Lara was just weird and misunderstood that I was just asking for help understanding a problem in setting up a experiment in the lab. Convincing them to let me stay at BioTech wasn't nearly as difficult as trying to explain away my pass at Lara.

So I stayed at BioTech. After the incident with Lara I didn't make many new friends. But I did land a part time job in a genetics lab, specializing in *in vitro* fertilization, custom embryos and what ever else money could buy in genetic engineering of fetuses.

Mostly I harvested eggs and implanted embryos. More accurately, I monitored the equipment that harvested eggs and implanted embryos. Usually, the only hands-on work I ever got to do was when my boss needed an extra pair of hands during the actual fertilization procedure. But I did get a couple of chances at gene rearrangements. I never did anything really terrible, just little changes here and there, that's all. I wished I could see the faces of some of the couples when their custom offspring entered the world with brown eyes instead of the requested blue, or six toes instead of five. I was careful—nothing truly drastic. After all, mistakes can happen, the clients were all warned that gene manipulation wasn't yet an exact science. And it did make the job a lot more fun.

And then I tested latent.

The Megson Institute hadn't been sure at first. Like everyone else applying for government grants for graduate work, I'd been required to submit to screening. Anyone who completed university training could apply to be screened voluntarily, but that didn't happen very often.

Regardless, everyone who qualified with evidence of latent paranormal abilities was offered the same standard government contract. Well, it wasn't exactly an offer, as the options (unofficially known as penalties) for those individuals choosing to decline signing the contract were not particularly acceptable. A ten-year stint at the Everest Observation Unit was the most attractive of the offered alternatives. I figured that had something to do with why so few graduates not applying for grants volunteered to be screened.

But I had always thought the offer was great. I couldn't wait to sign on. The government would pay for what ever post-graduate training a candidate wanted—after the two-year training for Implant placement and after another two years of service to the government in what ever area they thought best. One could even choose to pursue the graduate work first, and then go for the Implant training and mandated service, but this wasn't encouraged.

More than half the candidates wound up in the Combined Military Services, and most wound up staying there, even after the required two-year stint. Only those with Implants could qualify for officer positions and there was no hope of getting into astronaut training without an Implant. Not that I was so hot on being an astronaut. But it was pretty much the same in other fields. I can't remember the last physician or politician of any prominence who wasn't Implanted.

People used to say that enough money could get you anything. Times change. It sure seemed to me that an Implant was a lot more likely to get me what and where I wanted. I was still leaning towards medicine at the time but, as always, keeping my options open.

When we did get our test results, I didn't get a green notice, or a red one for that matter. Mine was white; I remembered that. I'd never heard of a white notice before. It just had a date, just a few days from then, and the words "retesting required."

The retesting took two full days as opposed to two hours. But I passed. I'd made it. I signed the contract on the dotted line and packed my bags for Lopez Island in the San Juan Islands. Two years of acres of gray sky and oceans of rain later, I had my Implant. Three days later I had my twenty-fourth birthday.

I hadn't exactly made a lot of friends but a few of us went out to celebrate. Tommy, Leah, Ginny and me, two bottles of tequila, a bag of limes, and a salt shaker. Tommy was the only other one who'd gotten his Implant so we stuck strictly to celebrating birthdays. The sun actually shone that day.

The first headache I had was the next morning. I still think that one was just a hangover. We'd had to go out for a third bottle of tequila. Ginny insisted on having a worm after Tommy had the one in the first bottle and Leah and I shared the second.

It was only four months later they took my Implant out. The headaches didn't stop. After they took it out, the new pain, the deep burning in my head didn't stop either. That was just about a year ago.

They sent me to specialists in San Diego first, but I didn't get any better there, or any place else they sent me for that matter. Finally they sent me to the Ronald Reagan Rehabilitation Unit. It used to be a leper colony I'm told, before it was the AIDS Quarantine Facility for Hawaii and the South Pacific Sector. The place was vacant for about ten years after the bombings, before the government moved back in and set up this place. It was more crumpled and decrepit than I'd expected, but some of the equipment looked fairly new at least. And the weather—I loved the weather. I had never lived any place where I loved the weather before.

It was particularly spectacular that first day we met, Dr. Lourie and me. A single, multilobed cotton ball cloud in a pure blue sky with the perfect breeze coming up off the beach. I could almost pretend I didn't have the pain, it was so beautiful. Just a few weeks before Christmas, it was too perfect to believe.

With weather like that, I thought maybe even I could get to like Christmas again. I used to like it. Until last year. They took my Implant out Christmas Eve. I'd always heard doctors didn't operate on holidays except in emergencies. I still don't see how I qualified as an emergency. All I could think of was that they'd given me one great Christmas present, the pain in my head.

That was what Dr. Lourie was supposed to help me with. I wasn't really looking forward to it. Another room, another doctor, and the same old questions, the same old results. Pain.

Crossing the compound, I couldn't help but inhale deeply as I headed for the research building. There was a sweetness I didn't recognize from something blooming nearby that mixed splendidly with the salt air. It was almost perfect, except for the plastic Santa someone had planted under the palm trees by the gateway to the beach, just past the research building.

Inside however, it was the usual tiny stale-smelling room with no pictures and no real windows, just the mirror everyone knew was a one-way window. At least there weren't any Christmas decorations in the room, but there wasn't much of anything else either. A few monitor screens and some hookup wires, that was about it. Nothing like what I'd been shown in other parts of the building on my introductory tour when I first arrived. But the doctor waiting in the room was something else entirely.

Dr. Lourie hadn't been one of the staff doctors I'd been introduced to when I first arrived either. I would have remembered. When I "grew up" I wanted to look just like she did. I wanted to move like she did. I wanted to talk like she did. She had this soft voice, like liquid satin. Dr. Hanna Lourie. Even her name was smooth.

"So, you've had some experience in biofeedback-assisted relaxation and control techniques, yes?" she asked after we completed the necessary introductions. She had just a tiny trace of some European accent. I could just see the tip of her tongue as she spoke. She had very even white teeth.

"Well, yeah, sort of," I said, wishing for the umpteen-millionth time that my head didn't hurt so much.

"Sort of?"

"It's included in the Implant training program," I explained.

"I've never worked with someone with an Implant," she admitted, adjusting the electrode glove on my left hand.

"I don't have one any more."

"I should be more accurate," she said, smiling. "I should have said I've never worked with anyone with established paranormal talents. I have been through your file, at least what they sent along with you. Apparently you scored quite well on empathic enhancement potential but there seems to have been a bit of disagreement as to the level of your potential in projection techniques."

"That's why I started with empath training first. The way I understood it, I have the potential to receive other people's feelings but they thought I might project my own feelings too strongly," I explained. It had been completely confusing to me actually. Until I finally had my Implant, I never really believed I had any paranormal talents. I'd hoped and prayed enough that they were there, but I'd never "felt" anything, at least nothing like other students sometimes claimed.

"I understand you were having problems with headaches after your Implant was placed and eventually they became so troublesome removal of the device was required," she went on, almost as if I hadn't said anything. "After your operation, you have continued to have pain. You've had some treatments already but it was recommended that you try our chronic pain management program. Did I get it right?" She had a way of speaking that made questions sound like statements and statements like questions.

"Yeah, that more or less sums up the problem," I had to agree. "The Institute said they didn't have anything else to offer me after the ganglion blocks and the endorphin infusion therapy failed. And nobody ever did figure out why I was getting the headaches in the first place. Now you all are supposed to teach me how to live with this pain since nobody can seem to get rid of it for me. Something about making it my friend instead of my enemy, or some such absurd idea." I hoped I didn't sound as bitter as I was.

I must not have because she laughed at that. "They really used that line on you, did they?"

"Yep. I can't say I find it very funny, myself."

"I'm sorry," she said, her face just gently blushing. "I didn't mean—"

"It's okay," I interrupted. "I'm sure you didn't mean, well, whatever." I finished lamely.

After a brief uncomfortable pause, she went on.

"Well, now that you're all hooked up, let's focus on your hand temperature. It will go up as your muscles relax. I'm sure you've been over this before from what you've told me already, but you will allow me to give my little blurb anyway?"

I smiled a yes.

"We know from various experimental circumstances that the body releases its own morphine-like molecules only when there is less than one microvolt of electrical energy within the muscle tissue. As muscle relaxes, the small blood vessels in your skin open up and the skin temperature increases accordingly. All this machinery is to help you learn to control the muscle tension so that over time you will be able to achieve very deep relaxation and allow your body to release its own natural painkillers."

When she talked, her breasts rose every so slightly when she caught her breath between sentences. I could have watched forever.

"Are you with me?"

"Oh, yeah, I'm with you. Go on, please."

"Your hand temperature." A small grid appeared in the lower left quadrant of my left eye.

"It's reading 87.2 degrees now. When you've learned to relax, you'll be able to get readings of 95 or a bit more. And if you'll blink twice, you'll get a display of your hand thermogram."

And there it was, my hand in glaring primary colors, in my right eye. Or at least the shape of a hand, yellow in the palm area changing to orange and then red moving away from the center. The fingers were green, changing to blue towards the fingertips.

"And as your temperature increases, your fingers will change from the cool colors they are now to red and hopefully yellow," she continued. "Now, don't worry about the other feedback electrodes. We'll just go with the two ocular feedbacks for now. Blink twice to change your feedback. Today is just for baseline recordings and for you to familiarize yourself with some of the equipment, okay?"

I nodded, my multicolored hand nodding with me.

"Then let's get started," she said. "Just lean back a bit and get comfortable." As she spoke, the lights dimmed and the chair slowly maneuvered itself into the shape of an old-fashioned reclining chair, like they show in museum exhibits.

"That's good," she said after a moment. The temperature display read just over 87. "You can see your fingers are more green than blue at this point. That's not bad at all. Go ahead, try now to focus on your graphic display. Don't try to relax, just let it happen. Now, I want you to focus on the readings." She paused for a moment and turned slightly towards the door of the cubicle.

"As I leave, I'd like you to take a deep breath way down into your abdomen and then exhale slowly. Try and maintain a nice slow even breathing pattern. I'll be just next door monitoring the readouts. Call out if you need me, okay?"

As I took that deep breath, I could still smell her perfume, if it was perfume, after she left, warm and sweet. And then I watched the monitors. I blinked from hand to graphic display and back. Nothing much happened at first. I hovered around 90 for a while. Then I felt it.

The connection. Like the last two pieces in one of the interminable jigsaw puzzles they kept offering for our amusement at the last hospital I'd tried. A perfect fit, a perfect picture. Only the pieces are wired and circuits connect, thousands of them, hundreds of thousands of them. And I controlled them all. It was almost like having my Implant back, only better. I was in control. I wasn't receiving, I was sending. I wasn't passively feeling someone else's sorrow or joy as I had with the Implant. I was doing. And I was doing it all by myself.

She didn't budge when the numbers shot to 95. At 101 degrees I heard the door open. A second later when the lights went on, I'd gotten up to 105. My right eye saw nova white.

"I'm sorry to interrupt you," she said softly, removing the electrode gloves from my hands, "but we must be having some equipment trouble. Actually, you were doing well for the first few minutes," she added. "You started with a baseline of 17 in your frontalis muscle and got down to just below 10 microvolts when whatever happened, happened."

"And just what happened?"

"Damned if I know. I ran a quick internal diagnostic when you went over 98 on hand temperature, but I got a negative malfunction readout. I'll have the techs go over the setup before we try again. But it has to be the machinery. I didn't even think it was programmed for readings that high. Your hands are nice and warm, I'll admit, but nobody can get up to 105." She laughed as she spoke. "It's impossible. The very best anyone can do is a degree or two below their core body temperature. So even if you were running a fever, which you are not, the readings have to be wrong."

"So, what do we do now?" I asked.

"We? We don't do anything now," she smiled, removing the last of the connections from my shoulders. "You can get on back to whatever is next on your agenda and I've got some technicians to get a hold of. But please, tell the nurses I want to see you here again, tomorrow, same time, okay?"

"Sure, same time, tomorrow," I agreed reluctantly, as the chair rearranged itself, encouraging me to get up.

The control I had faded fast, before I was even out of the room. But I think I could have charred the flesh from my fingers if I'd wanted to. I couldn't wait to try it again. Manipulating dials and temperature readings was fun enough, but actually manipulating my physiology certainly qualified as major food for thought. And without an Implant. Nobody did what I had just done without an Implant.

I didn't have anything else scheduled that day. It was only my third day on the island. My "program" was apparently still partly in the design phase. I started for the beach but remembered the pre-dinner crowd that had accumulated yesterday and I wound up in the cafeteria instead. My sexual preference was not part of my confidential medical record and I already felt less than welcome after my trip to the water the previous afternoon. There hadn't been any new cases of AIDS in more than a decade, not since Montagnier's vaccine, but the social backlash against anyone not strictly heterosexual seemed to get worse each year. Officially tolerated discrimination had long since gone by the wayside, replaced by unofficial social ostracism. I knew better than to expect any arms wide open in friendship.

Dinner wasn't scheduled for more than an hour but I didn't want to go back to my room. If this place was anything like the others, the staff hated patients sitting quietly reading in their rooms. Or doing anything quietly in their rooms.

The cafeteria was almost empty. There were two guys huddled, hunched actually, at one of the far corner tables. There wasn't much else to look at in the room. Unless you like plastic flowers and tattered travel posters. There was one young man shuffling from table to table sticking plastic mistletoe into the plastic vases on the tables. I wondered if that meant you had to be under the table to kiss someone but couldn't think of any particularly witty way to make the comment so I just drank my coffee and tried to pretend my head didn't really hurt that much.

And in she walked. Hanna Lourie. I wanted her to notice me and join me on her own, so I stared at my coffee so I couldn't even accidentally catch her eye.

"You don't like the beach?"

It worked. She had gotten a cup of coffee and come directly over to my table. I looked up and smiled.

"Yeah, just not with a lot of other people around. This time yesterday was awful."

"May I join you?" she asked, ever so politely.

"Please, sit," I said, squirming a little. Getting wet always made me squirm.

"Don't worry. You're not in trouble," she said, misinterpreting my moves. "This isn't fraternizing with the staff. I need to talk with you. We could go to my office if you'd be more comfortable," she offered.

"No, this is fine, really," I said, circling the salt shaker around the pepper, like old country dancers.

I could see she drank her coffee black. One of these days, I'd be able to do that. I looked at my cup. Its contents could best be described as melted coffee ice cream. Half cream and three sweeteners.

"There's nothing wrong with the equipment," she said bluntly.

"I don't understand."

"Neither do I," she said, taking a sip of her coffee. She looked at me, not saying anything for seconds that felt like decades.

I took the plastic mistletoe with its waxy green leaves and dingy white berries out of the vase and twirled it in my fingers, switching directions in time to "Hark the Herald Angels Sing," which was playing over the speaker system.

"I'll see you tomorrow," she said, standing up again.

"Looking forward to it," I mumbled as she left the table, just loudly enough. She turned, looked and tried to smile.

I smiled back and stuck the mistletoe back in the vase. She didn't know the half of it. She knew she didn't know the half of it. I didn't need an Implant to know she wasn't sure she wanted to know the rest. But she wouldn't be able to keep herself from trying.

She was wearing pink the next day. A pink silk blouse with a skirt just a shade darker, like the pink blush of a perfectly ripe peach yearning to be eaten. Funny how she was so much the woman I wanted to be and so much the woman I wanted. She was wearing what I imagined I'd wear in a few years when I could afford something other than T-shirts and jeans, and she was wearing what I imagined I was removing as she put all the hookups in place.

It wasn't so abrupt the second time. But the connection was just as powerful, just as pure. I went beyond reason once, to 110 degrees, for a second. I needed to be sure I could. Then I practiced. I held the temperature at an even 95.5 for five minutes. The ocular projections never varied. There was no longer any separation, any space hiding my head from my hands. And it was easy.

Then the pain began to recede. The furnace quieted. It had done so the day before as well, but I hadn't believed my memory. I thought I'd imagined it, that I'd been so distracted by the rest that, by comparison, the pain had seemed to lessen. But that incessant presence was actually pushed back, pushed down, pushed away. It wasn't in the foreground anymore, it wasn't piercing from inside to out. At least not when I was focused, not when I was in control. The control was there, the pain was leaving, I felt it ebbing, easing away.

She came back in. One look at her face and I knew she knew something. I tried not to smile.

"So, it's definitely not the equipment," she said, leaning slightly against the console, crossing one ankle carefully over the other. "I'm getting readings I can't possibly explain. Can you?"

I told her I couldn't. I told her my head was killing me and I really needed to go. She didn't argue, so I left.

I don't know what took her so long to think of it. We'd been working together for almost two weeks when it hit her. By this time I'd been EEG'd, MRI'd, PET-scanned and even had my neuropeptides mapped. Some tests were normal, some tests were abnormal, but never in any way that made any sense to Hanna.

She had already determined that my abilities were merely discovered using her feedback equipment. Nothing was dependent upon equipment. Hooked up or not, I could make her temperature gauges read anything I wanted them to. When she said she wanted to start investigating internal physiologic control measurements, I knew she knew. She had me vary my blood pressure and heart rate to start. You name it, we tried it and I could do it. She thought I might need the hookups to act as some kind of trigger mechanism but after two days of practice, I could get in and stay in control without any hookup at all. The pain in my head, well, it wasn't gone, but it was a hell of a lot better. And getting better and better and better.

Hanna had plenty of theories about that. The one she seemed to focus on more and more had to do with the Implant I'd had. I told her I'd never used any of my abilities before the Implant. I told her I hadn't known I'd had them. Not very many people had abilities that were even effective unenhanced. Hanna believed the Implant acted as some kind of circuit overload, inducing a change in neurotransmitters and therefore creating the headaches. The PET-scanning and neuropeptide data made a lot more sense in that context, or so she said. Further testing was showing an increasing change in transmitter ratios. Something about my serotonin particularly intrigued her as the pain continued to recede.

But it was Christmas Eve. We had to take a break. Hanna insisted. We could talk about other ideas when she got back, she said. She was taking the afternoon chopper flight to the Big Island to spend the holiday with "friends."

I spent Christmas Day in the animal lab. I figured I might as well try out my control before she came back in the morning. The results could be my Christmas present to Hanna. Something she'd really appreciate.

I'd volunteered to do the feeding and watering over the holiday so I was in and out without a hitch. Patients were encouraged to get involved in the day to day activities of the Unit. Like sweeping and making beds mostly. I was congratulated by the ward clerk for thinking of such a "helpful" task to volunteer to do in my "spare" time.

I fried the feet off the mice in two minutes. I did autopsies on the rats. They had blown-out mush where their hearts should have been. I'd tried to raise their blood pressures. I could only conclude I'd been successful at controlling external physiologic phenomena as well. So I cleaned up the mess and waited for Hanna's return.

When she did return the next day, we had our first and only fight.

She wanted to present me. Not just write up the findings and submit for publication, but present me. She said it ought to be in person, in front of some annual meeting of paranormal psychiatrists or neurologists or whoever I wanted. Some big conference was coming up on the mainland and she thought she could swing it with the Board, my going along with her. She said that no one would ever believe her, just on paper that is. No one had ever been shown to have such telekinetic machine control, much less unenhanced control of bodily physiologic properties as I had displayed in her lab.

I said no. She insisted. I kept saying no and she kept insisting. So I kissed her. Her lips were warm and sweet but she didn't kiss me back. Not at first.

"Come with me," I said, holding both her hands. They were cold, dry but cold.

"Why?" she asked, taking her hands back.

"So I can show you something."

We crossed the hall to the animal lab and I showed her the rats and the mice I'd put away in the freezer. She didn't waste any time. She conned two more of each species from the lab attendant and I duplicated the previous day's experiments for her.

"So, without a Megson Implant you can manipulate machines, your own physiology and anybody else's? I assume you've only tried this with the laboratory animals," she added as we reentered her office and she held her hands up to her head, squeezing her temples.

"Now your head hurts? I didn't think headaches were contagious," I tried jesting, without success.

"You have to let me present you now. Can't you see, there's never been a case reported like yours, not anywhere in the literature," she pleaded.

"No," I said and kissed her again. I took her hands in mine and tried to keep them from shaking. She was scared, I could see that. But all she said was "no."

"This isn't some schoolgirl crush, so don't even try that line," I said. I kissed her again and helped her open her lips. I held her face in my hands and watched as I faded her fears. I told her I loved her as I loved her. I loved away the "no" as I had her love me back. She looked so beautiful as she lay on the carpet she had told me she brought back from Istanbul one summer. As I made her come, I watched until her face relaxed as I held her hands to me, with me and followed her.

If it takes me a decade, longer, I don't care. I'll find what went wrong. She never should have died. I will not make such a mistake again. I'll be more delicate. I won't lose control next time. Besides, it probably wasn't the best time and place to test my skills on another human. But I didn't see any other way to convince her I was right. Maybe I didn't want to find another way to convince her I was right. And it was wonderful, really. God, was it wonderful. To have someone really want you. And she did, I know, I made her want me. Every single particle of her being, every cell, every vessel, every neuron. And I know it will be even better the next time.

It wasn't too hard to make it look like an accident. Everyone knew she'd been having equipment problems; at least that was how she had been explaining her data when anyone bothered to question her. I told the other doctors and the police too that I thought it must have been a voltage leak or something. I must have been convincing. They asked a lot a questions that day, but that was it. Not even an autopsy. I'd been worried about that. I'd harvested both ovaries vaginally, but any competent pathologist would have noticed. And commented.

But some risks are worth taking. I thought so then, I think so now. The funeral was quite sweet really. I'm glad I went. They buried her right here on the island, in the old lepers' graveyard. All the weathered white headstones looked lovely and peaceful under a canopy of green palms and fronds just at the foot of the mountain. I watched the crowd from the entrance gate. I didn't know she had so many friends.

I almost never have the pain anymore. I've got my discharge all set for the morning. I've told everyone how grateful I am that Dr. Lourie had accomplished so much with me, in such a short time. I asked to go back to the Institute, but I knew they'd say no. They did. I showed just the right amount of disappointment that I'd not get another chance at an Implant. I didn't smirk at all.

I got my old job back, at the genetics lab. They did help me get that. Full-time too, this time. So now there's no reason I shouldn't be able to do it. I'll be the first. No one has ever made an embryo from two eggs yet. It still isn't legal, but the preliminary work I was able to do here with some of the rats, right after Hanna's funeral, proves I'll be able to do it, I'm sure. Hanna would want me to. In the end, she really had wanted me. I'm sure of that too. If it hadn't been for her, I'd never have known what I can do. I think I'll be able to make anyone do anything I want at the rate things are going now. And if all goes well, I figure I can be pregnant about three months from now.

Her name will be Noelle. She will have beautiful skin and lustrous hair and a body that will grow gracefully and boldly and an enduring wit. And that's just for starters. The perfect Christmas present.

It'll be a wonderful life.

COTTAGE

Bruce McAllister

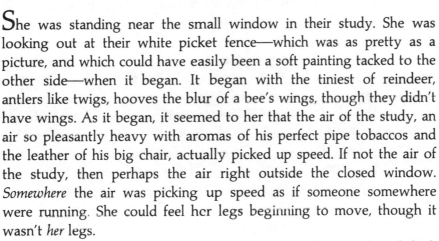

She was standing near the small window in their study. She was looking out at their white picket fence—which was as pretty as a picture, and which could have easily been a soft painting tacked to the other side—when it began. It began with the tiniest of reindeer, antlers like twigs, hooves the blur of a bee's wings, though they didn't have wings. As it began, it seemed to her that the air of the study, an air so pleasantly heavy with aromas of his perfect pipe tobaccos and the leather of his big chair, actually picked up speed. If not the air of the study, then perhaps the air right outside the closed window. *Somewhere* the air was picking up speed as if someone somewhere were running. She could feel her legs beginning to move, though it wasn't *her* legs.

The tiny wingless deer with its pin-size bells on a thread-thick harness flew over the picket fence—a dark spot no one else would have noticed had they not already understood it—up over the rose bushes that were pruned so perfectly, and, zigzagging, began to follow the flagstones up to the cottage.

It rose like a small black hole in the universe to the edge of the roof, disappearing from her sight, dropping back down before her vision again, banking to the right, approaching the small window and hovering on motionless hooves. She could see it clearly now and she moved in closer to the glass. The antlers with their perfect velvet did a little dance for her, buffeting the glass two or three times before veering away to the branches of the big elm. She pressed her nose against the pane and followed it as long as she could. When it was gone, she relaxed. Maybe it wouldn't happen again. Maybe she wouldn't have to try to talk to him again about it.

She looked straight ahead at nothing, but could still feel her legs trying to move.

Something . . . somewhere . . . was happening.

Beyond the pickets something broke in and she squinted to see it. It was the little cloud, so familiar as she watched it sway to the left, sway to the right, puffing itself up larger, rising at last over the fence like a brown fog, then flowing through the rose bushes, dappling with tiny shadows—like the dark little memories that obediently kept to their corners in the past—the green of the leaves and the royal-red of the petals she and her husband felt such affection for. The cloud came closer, clearing in her eyes to become once again a swarm of little horned heads and hooves like those of the first deer, the one that had been marking out a path, though there was nothing special about *its* nose. The special one was somewhere else, and even thinking about him made her uneasy . . .

The cloud followed the path. It followed it *exactly*. She smiled and sighed. It felt so right, despite the whisper of fear that came with it. The storm came on and only now were her old eyes hurting, working to see the individual heads and twigs and tiny bells she would never be able to hear through the glass.

Every little deer was a part of the cloud that swept toward her, spinning in a funnel up to the edge of the roof, dipping back down again, turning to the right like something molten—white-hot silver or icicles melting in the sun—and arriving at her window at last.

When it touched the glass and every velvety pair of twigs buffeted it at once, the entire cottage shook. It rocked from wall to wall, the windowpane cracked, and she stepped back, waiting for the shards to fall in, to shatter on their burgundy carpet, to cut her toes, her face.

It didn't happen. The windowpane remained cracked, but held, like ice on a pond where children skated on brand-new skates on a cold winter's morning.

"I had a dream last night," she announced without turning to him. She would try again, though he still wouldn't hear.

"What was it about, dear?" He had moved up behind her and placed his arms, which were quite manly, around her waist, which was still youthfully trim. He had lost so much weight since the last of the Little People—who without their work, without the purpose they had been called into being for, had fallen ill so quickly, becoming loose flesh over brittle bones, their eyes as blank as dolls as they stood among the last toys, stiff and still, waiting for death in the great shed both she and her husband had worked hard to forget—was gone, and he shaved each morning before she woke like a young man would, so she never saw the white bristles of his beard unless it was late, late into the night by the firelight in the living room as both of them read their books right before bedtime.

His arms were quite manly. Her waist was just right. These things did make her happy. But there was always the question he wouldn't ask.

She closed her eyes, seeing his arms around her waist. This helped bring to her wrinkled lips the smile she knew she needed to begin.

"The dream?" she said. "It wasn't anything really, dear. I was under our big elm for the very first time. You remember that day: I was so giddy and silly. I was as happy as some giggly girl that day in the sun. And when the swarm moved through the branches, I didn't even notice, did I. You didn't either. We were so very much in love that day—"

She stopped. It was happening again. His arms were loosening slowly.

"I'm sorry, Sarah," he said. "What was your dream?" His voice was higher and thinner. It had gotten that way over the years somehow, and would never again fill the night, the starry sky over house after house after house. It saddened her a little, but it was all right. His voice had become what a little cottage needed, what the room they stood in together needed, and their bed . . .

"The dream?" she said. "It wasn't anything really, Nick. You remember the day we moved in, how you looked at the chimney and laughed as if you knew I was afraid and needed to laugh, too. Well, in my dream I was climbing the elm. I was climbing it to the roof. When I reached it, I could see rooftops everywhere, though there aren't any here. I was crying. I was crying because *none of them had chimneys*, Nick. They weren't even houses. They were skulls with sockets as black as the darkness every boy and girl fears under the bed at night. . . . Isn't that silly?"

As he pulled back from her—not to be free of her old body, she knew, but of much much more—she turned around slowly and saw how his handsome face was twisted by the question he would not ask.

No matter how many dreams she told him about, no matter how many times she tried to bring the right words into the air around them, he would never ask it.

Should we? Should we have, Sarah?

But that wasn't really it, she realized suddenly. What she needed to hear wasn't the question at all. The years had already answered it. It was his *courage* to ask it that she wanted—the courage that had once filled his belly and laughter as he went out to the stars and did what needed to be done if the faith of a single child in the possibilities of the world were to remain alive. *Courage.* He had lost it as he had lost his flesh—it had become too much for his bones, she realized, uncomfortable for him in his leather chair. He had lost it for *comfort* and this filled her with anger, she saw, one he didn't hear.

His courage. Her anger. That was what their story had become.

She went over to the window and pressed her nose against the cool glass. His face would not be twisted when she turned around, and when asked, he would claim he didn't know what she was talking about, that it was just a dream and made no sense, and wasn't this house, their fireplace, *their* chimney enough at this time in their lives when life should be simple and peaceful?

And he would mean it. He would be *sincere*, out of a determination not to understand, out of wanting only that the bells outside not reach them, even faintly, that the chimney be but a decoration in this little house of their golden years.

When the boy left the great shed in the backyard with its sagging beams and holes in the roof that let the dust and rain in but never enough sunlight to stop the mildewing of the immense canvas bags he slept on, curled each night, vast cobwebs in every dark corner where the short, stocky bones lay, where he had moved them at last so that he wouldn't see them when a shaft of light, like some god's eye, did happen to fall through the roof, he was carrying in his chubby arms as many of the smallest toys as he could—all of them dusty, corroded and colorless. And he had his hammer. He walked out into the sunlight, blinked, and began placing a toy on each flagstone of the path that wound through the garden. When he was finished, he returned to the first flagstone, hammer in hand.

As always, he could see the endless work of the spiders in the garden. They draped everything, the fence and nearby bushes, with their sticky threads, their tiny faces too human to be spiders', and he could never be sure that his eyes and nose weren't just inches away from them, ready to stick to him and blind him with that sudden darkness he couldn't understand, and which he hated. They were like the cobwebs in the shed, yes, like the great gray webbing that covered the piles of bones more and more each night as he slept in another darkness, blind. But these, the ones here, were different—the spider webs of the garden, of the sun and the light he could *see* in, the light he rose eagerly for every morning, hiding in it until the night killed it slowly again.

In what sense the spiders belonged to the old couple in the house, he didn't know. Were they the magic of the old woman? The old man? Both of them? Were they like the strange, wingless insects that swarmed in the garden sometimes, able to fly on four legs somehow, and which he knew for sure were *theirs*? Someone always made sure there were flies and fat moths for the spiders outside, for their human faces, and their broad sprawling traps. Even though the old man and woman never came to the backyard—*wouldn't*, he knew— who else would it have been? Who else—without actually walking to the shed with its bones and dusty toys covering the mildewing and stinking floor in its darkness—could make his own food appear somehow on paper plates each night, so that he would have them in the morning, be able to take them with him as he hurried out into the light? And again—so much food, the chicken and oranges and home-baked cookies or pie on paper plates, too, placed just outside the open door of the dark shed at noon. And again at dusk—dinnertime. It *had* to be the old woman. It just had to be. He could feel it. She did it as she dreamed. She did it without knowing she was doing it. This was how it felt.

Was she the one who also fed the spiders—without knowing she did—without having to enter the garden or the shed where *he* had to sleep each night, while she slept under a comforter on a bed high above the floor? It made him angry to think this. It made him think of the swarm.

When his back was turned, pants down as he wet the ground by the bush or picket fence, he imagined she would appear behind him at any second, surprising him, shaming him. But she never did. And when he made an effort to hear them, stepping up to a wall or window of the little cottage, it wasn't always voices he heard. Sometimes it was the faint echo of bells, the sounds of hooves on wood, a baby's cry, a deep, loving laugh like a father's—someone's. It wasn't real, of course, what he heard. It was a memory, he knew, or a dream, or both—his or someone else's. The old couple were making these things, too—for themselves, like memories they could call back and hold like children, like dreams they could only dream of because they would never come true.

Or were they, he wondered, somehow for *him*? When he thought this instead, his eyes got wet suddenly and made his nose—sensitive to the dust, the smells of the shed, even the sunlight as she stepped into it every morning—start to run.

He went back to his work. His shorts didn't cover his knees and his knees hurt on the stone, but he didn't mind being hurt a little doing the work he knew needed to be done.

The toy on the first stone was a human being. It had a green hat, which had faded. It had eyes and a smile whose color had grayed like death.

He hit it with the hammer. The head rolled away. The legs twitched. Were there bones inside the plastic? he wondered. He hit it again.

The plastic cracked. There were no bones, and this, too, made him mad.

She would find herself hesitating near the living room window where the sunlight—so much—came through like warm velvet to soften her face, relax the wrinkles, the tightness. She would be wearing her most *pastel* nightgown. The first two buttons would be undone for him.

Behind her, in the kitchen, he would still be seated, finishing his breakfast with the occasional sound of silverware on his plate. He would be waiting for her to tell him how happy she was, because if she did, she knew, he would be able to feel it too. *Wasn't that the least she could do?* he was saying—in this little house as they waited peacefully for the final darkness, the one thing no magic could prevent?

She would try her best. It was important, *very* important to him. She would fill her voice with all the joy she could and say:

"Oh, Nick, I'm as happy as any woman—"

And then the spittle, which had gathered inside her bottom lip, would fly out instead of words.

He would wait, and then he would speak himself. His words would be perfect. He had been reading for so many years now.

"I understand your sentiments, Sarah, I do," he would say, to show her how insightful he was, how this was his gift, not unlike love, to her. "There's no need, dear, to pretend that everything is perfect. We knew it would happen some day, didn't we? The regrets. The longings. They're natural, Sarah. As people age, the physiology of their brains changes. Anxiety from decreased physical mobility. Short-term memory loss—a function of anxiety, despite what people in other houses think—leaving them only a vivid past they cannot help but relive again and again. . . . I understand more than you might imagine, Sarah."

Yes, people get older, Nick. But some—like the Little People—die before they have even had a chance to live. Remember?

It would be her turn to speak again, to show him how much they really shared, how terribly close they really were, as any couple their age should be. She would try hard. She would say, "You're so right, Nick. . . . Even the moonlight on the picket fence reminds me of the snow and the time . . ." This would disturb him, she knew, but even then she would hear herself add: " . . . when we brought to the children of this world *less than they really needed.* . . ."

It was cruel, but it was the truth. She could not help it, and he would not answer, would not speak to her for the rest of the day. In the end, she would always regret it.

Sometimes she would wipe the spittle from the windowpane. Sometimes she would let it run down, thinking of it as rain. It didn't matter. That night it would fade from the glass.

That night she awoke again to find herself kicking hard, hanging from the highest shelf in their spacious walk-in closet, which smelled comfortably of its naphthalene. She was, as always, trying to climb up a chimney somewhere, up through it to a freedom only *he* had known in those early years, and which, she understood now, she had always envied.

He was pulling on her nightgown silently, but for all his pulling he was being gentle enough not to tear anything. He never tore her nightgown, no matter how much he wanted to get her down at times like these, to keep what lay so safely (a shadow dappling a leaf) in its corner of memory.

She couldn't see them—it was dark—but her knuckles were pale hooves hooked to the edge of the shelf. Turning to the bedroom lamp's faint glow, she could see how his eyes were closed, as if dreaming the old dream too. When she looked closely, holding her breath to steady her sticky eyes, she could see how shallow his breath was, how close to the final time he was.

He was crouching beside the next toy on its stone—a little car so full of wet earth that something alive, pale and squirming, lived in it. Standing up so that he could get at them, he took one of the three identical matchbooks—the ones that had appeared beside his paper plates three mornings ago—from his back pocket. Then, lit match in hand, he crouched again and tried to light the car with a squirt of the lighter fluid he had found by his lunch plates two weeks ago.

It took two squirts. The flame leaped, crawling across the roof of the car, blistering the paint so that the bright orange of its original color showed for a second, and the thing in the earth squirmed faster and faster.

Two, he said to himself.

On the next one—a duck whose turning wheels had once made a duck sound when they moved and now were too rusted to move at all—he brought the hammer down. The duck—head and wheels— moved at last, flying across the yard into a bush with a great spider's web. There was a cry from the web, and, as he watched, the head and wheels were spun into cocoons. He felt the chill.

Three.

He lit the little sofa from a dollhouse. It smelled terrible.

The plastic squirt gun curled in its flames to become a bubbly green fist.

The little Christmas scene in a bubble—the kind you could make the snow fall in if you shook it—he hit with the hammer, again and again, until all that was left was slivers in a puddle of fluid.

Four, five, six, seven.

His chest had begun to rise and fall. He could hear his heart squishing harder and harder in his chest, but never louder than his *count*, which was not in words now, but colors, in musical notes, in numbers like the strange wingless insects that were searching—in their anger—those who had abandoned them.

He returned to the shed, hesitated before the door, was blinded by the darkness as he stepped in, and with his hands alone forced himself to feel around the immense canvas bags for what he wanted. When he returned to the light, he couldn't see and he stood there for a moment blinking—without a free hand to rub his nose with—and finally went to lay another armload of toys one by one on the stones.

41, 42, 43, 44.

Even as he lit another match or brought the hammer down (*never* losing his count) he was aware of how the backs of his knees hurt, how they had been hurting all day because the legs of his shorts cut into him there, and how it was a burning feeling.

Even his feet hurt, as if the bones had been jammed into little holes in the ground. The soles of his shoes felt like parts of him now, aching against the stone as if he shouldn't be stepping on surfaces as hard as this.

The pain was new, and it made no sense to him. Why his feet? Why his shoes?

52, 53, 54, 55, 56, 57, 58.

When he went back to the shed for the third time, there were no toys among the canvas bags, and he had to grope, continue groping through the bones, holding his delicate nose against what he might smell, what he had smelled in his dreams. Blank eyes. The bones becoming hollow. The skin of their bodies wrinkling like old cloth.

He chose the smallest toys he could find, putting them in three toy trucks and a basket that was rotting. He didn't want to have to return to the shed again.

Some of the toys, he saw in the light outside, had pieces of bone, hair and gristle stuck to them, and, horrified, he set these on fire immediately, his hands shaking. The smell, worse than any he had ever imagined, made him sit back suddenly, closing his eyes and cupping his nose against the stinging.

71, 72, 73, 74, 75.

When his counting stopped, the hammering of his heart was a running man, and when he whispered the number, it was leather slipping from his neck.

106.

It came to him then. He was not accustomed to understandings like this, and when it came, it made his chest, fingers, neck, and back of knees—so close to the last toy he had lit—feel on fire, too.

He didn't look at the house. He didn't listen for a sound that might have been the two of them in the house remembering, or dreaming. It didn't matter anymore. He knew what he had to do. He didn't understand it, but he did know.

The hammer flew straight up. He was nowhere near the flagstones when it came down, striking like a shout.

His legs were pumping hard. The insides of his chubby thighs were rubbing together like thick sticks, feeding the fire—the fire he now knew was rage.

Long before he reached the white picket fence that enclosed the garden—the one he had never left in what he could remember of life—he was clawing out with his arms to clear a path through any webs that might be in his way. One in the roses by the fence made it through, catching on his upper lip, making him spit as his head jerked from side to side, as he reached the fence at last, grabbed the top of the pickets, and pulled as hard as he had ever pulled in all those dreams of a screaming wind.

The pickets caught his stomach, hung on to him like an old man's claws, and then, with a rip that tore his T-shirt away, leaving him naked from the belly button up, he tumbled to the other side.

They were in the living room. They always were at this time of day. She was looking a few inches to the right of their brass floor-lamp, at the air—just the air—when she saw it happen. "Oh!" she exclaimed.

He was on the couch. He looked up from his leather-bound book about "Northern European Thought" and shaped his face into another question.

"It's happening at last, dear," she heard herself say. She could hear it in her own voice. *A difference.*

He closed the book, leaving a finger to mark his place. He rose gracefully to his feet. He looked around the room once, pretending he wanted to understand.

He knew about the boy, she told herself. He had dreamed about him, too, as she had. They had both dreamed him, making him what he was, *choosing* him.

She could see her husband in the reflection of the window by the brass floor-lamp. She could see him look at the window, making a show of deciding *it* was the answer, and starting toward her in his smooth, charming stride. When he was at her side, he looked out the window with eyes that meant: *I'm trying, Sarah. I am. . . .*

"*No, you're not,*" she said out loud, hearing what was in it at last. It was *her* courage she could hear.

He looked at her stunned. His long fingers still marking his place in the book, he said quietly, in the only way he knew:

"What do you mean?"

"*He's going. He's finally going, Nick,*" she said. "I'm so happy for him. . . ."

She looked at his face. His eyebrows, those white caterpillars, were shaping that old expression of puzzlement—so sincere, so dramatic— the one they had once laughed at together, because of its silliness.

He looked back at the window, squinting, and as he turned to face her again, he said:

"I don't understand what you mean. . . ." He was not going to finish. He never did. He'd never felt he'd needed to. . . .

"You know what I'm talking about, Nick," she said to him, unable to stop. It was as if she were running, too.

I want you to be stronger, Nick, she was saying—*to be as strong as you were once, so that it can happen, so we can let the shadow from its corner of memory and be free at last.*

He jerked from the words—not the ones she had spoken, but those in the flame of her silence.

He was hearing her at last.

"He's trying to fly, Nick. He's trying *so hard.* . . ."

He could hear courage too, the one they both had needed when they'd needed all the courage and strength they could make, between them, to do what needed to be done in the world. He was listening to her at last, somehow.

. . . to reach, she told him, *the children who dream the Dream of Ice and Death, just as he—and we—have been dreaming it. To put a fire in the chill wind of Forever, which he has known so well in the great dark shed we have worked to forget it. . . .*

He had been moving back toward the stuffed chair, afraid. It was in his old blue eyes, but something else was too. He was sitting, looking at her, and she could tell that his breathing was quicker now. His face, its expression for once sincere, was asking *the question*:

Should we have had one, Sarah? Should we have had a child?

She had to be very careful. Her hand at her forehead to brush away the first whisper of a headache, of the Ice Wind that might take all words, all breath, from her. She said to him, filling the air with words:

"Nicky, when the reins finally slip from our favorite of the eight—and he *will* get them off, I promise you, Nicky—we will be free too. We will be happier than we have ever imagined as we wait for what no magic of any kind can prevent. But we must say the prayer together, Nicky. We must chant it as if the whole world were praying for a single child. Say it with me now. Say it, Nicky: "'*Twas the night . . .'*"

He couldn't do it, she saw. He just couldn't bring himself to do it. *Please*, she told him in the fire. *Say it with me:* "*. . . before Christmas, and all through the house . . .*"

His face had begun to tremble.

". . . not a creature . . ." he whispered suddenly, as if he did indeed remember. Then he stopped.

She had, she knew, to try the hardest she had ever tried, as if saving all of her strength for this very day, for this look on his face, his trembling.

"*He is afraid, too, Nicky.* It's been so long. You know what that is like. *You know, Nicky.*" She went on: " ' *. . . was stirring . . . Not a creature was stirring.*' But that isn't true, is it. A 'creature' *is* stirring. Our favorite of the eight—what we have made of him because we so loved him for his Light—*is* stirring."

When these words touched him—like snowflakes too new, or too old, to melt—he broke.

He had been staring at their perfect red-brick fireplace and at the leather-bound book in his hand. As if on a signal one he had been waiting for for years. He dropped the book.

He was staring hard into the brick of the fireplace. His hands were curling and uncurling, his tight fists with the blue veins of age raised even bluer, the liver spots on his hands—from a sun reflected on snow and ice—larger and darker now, somehow, the skin of his face like taut parchment. He was an old man now.

Yet he had found it.

What they had both—both of them—been waiting for from him.

When he shouted at last, his voice was hoarse, as if saving these words—their regret and their longing—for this one moment.

"*Go*," he shouted. "*Go, son, go!*"

He shouted it in the voice she could remember hearing from the sky, as she waited below, keeping the elves alive with the work they so needed to do, with the love they deserved for it, through the winter wind and eternity's snow, the bellow of his voice as it fell from the stars to one rooftop after another, for the brief moments of magic, then rising again to the stars.

He was standing now. She didn't have to look at him to know it. She was staring a few inches to the right of their brass lamp so that she could watch the boy—the one they had made by the alchemy of dreams.

Her husband's hair, she knew without looking, had turned pale like white wire. The bristles of his beard had begun to grow furiously.

When he raised his fist in his loudest shout yet, she didn't need to hear it at all. She *knew* what it would be, because he understood it all now, but she couldn't afford to listen. Her own legs were *burning*, too. She was running, getting away at last, like the boy, and that was what mattered.

"*Come on, boy!*" the old man shouted somewhere—another house, another time.

The claw, his fist, was falling to his side. His last shout, which she *did* need to hear if she were to stay, to love him until the final dream, was a whisper, a living breath in the cold winds between the stars.

"*Please, God. . . . Please let him get through,*" the old man was shouting.

He was running like hell. Voices behind him were shouting things like *Go, boy, go!* and *The toys were never enough, Nicky—never what they really needed* and *Yes, we should have had one* and so many other things that made no sense, that only made him run faster, flesh burning, his chubby hands holding his shorts up and together—the top button gone—his tummy pulled in so hard he could barely breathe, his nose running and red and starting to glow, and his hooves suddenly lighter in what felt like the white-hot hope of a single burning star.

BEGINNINGS

Michael Bishop

"In my end is my beginning."
— T. S. Eliot, "East Coker"

Across the sky, carrion birds that rarely landed in the Temple grounds flew cagy loops. Over the head of the skinny captive next to me, legionaries had nailed a board calling him our king. They'd set my tree at an angle to his. I could read not only his *titulus* but also the sign above the maggoty-white face of the kid to his right.

REUEL BEN ADLAI, the sign said in Aramaic: THIEF.

And my placard? I couldn't tilt my head far enough back against the upright to see it, but I knew what the Romans' paid sign-painter had daubed there:

MISHAEL OF HEBRON, THIEF.

Two robbers, with a king in the middle. The king even had a caption in the occupiers' tongue:

IESUS NAZARATHAEUS REX IOUDAEORUM.

"Listen," I said, "if you're really our deliverer, tell these foreign pigs to take us down." Smoke from the camps of pilgrims in town for the Passover, and from the cooking fires of the hawkers along the Golgotha road, swept up the hillside past us. Yeshua and Reuel both turned their faces into it to meet my burning eyes.

Reuel said, "Hush. If you can't fear dying, at least fear God."

I spat—barely enough to dampen a midge.

"Where you and I deserve this," Reuel said, "the Nazarene has done nothing."

"Deliverer! He can't even deliver himself. He's earned my scorn, and the people's, through his blasphemy." I said this as loudly as I could—even though I didn't credit his blasphemy for the unsayable reason that I didn't credit a Father to blaspheme against.

Reuel looked not to me but to Yeshua. "Adonai, remember me when you go up to your throne."

"This very day, you will have a place beside me in our Father's kingdom," Yeshua told him.

"And dogs will adorn themselves with rubies," I said.

Thunderheads massed beyond the Kidron and thrashed toward the city like a kelp-laced sea. Dust whirled. My tree shook like a mast. So did the uprights from which Yeshua and Reuel hung. Most of the hawkers below us kicked dirt on their fires and hurried for shelter. One of the legionaries guarding us, earlier a victor at dice, twisted Yeshua's robe around his neck like a shawl, then catcalled the people—vendors, pilgrims, a few timid followers of the Nazarene— scurrying to escape the rain.

Fire ran from the nail-holes in my wrists to my armpits and down my flail-bitten sides. I yelped against both it and the wind-rocked swaying of my tree.

—I would also give *you* water, Mishael. Behold my pain.

These words, spoken to my inward hearing, drew my gaze to Yeshua's uncomely face. Sweat and grime lined its creases. His eyes (the whites like discolored bone, the irises as dark as falling olives) met mine with something not quite reproach and not quite pity; even so, the mingling of condemnation and ruth in them mysteriously doused the hot ache in my arms and flanks. I shuddered, or else the wind again sped through our little copse of execution posts.

"Who spoke?" I shouted, even though I knew—for Yeshua's message had come to me like a dream pronouncement, clear word by word but upon awakening a riddle.

"Hold your tongue, lout!" cried Priscus, the legionary who had won Yeshua's robe.

"I want to know who spoke!"

Priscus jabbed me in my shame with the square end of his spear, and I ran a splinter into my hip reacting to this poke. The only officer on the hillside, a centurion whom the sentries had not yet called by name, turned aside.

—Steady yourself, Mishael. Go steady. It is I.

"But you make no—"

"Shut up, lout!" said Priscus. "Do you want another?"

—Commune as I do, inwardly. What you write in your heart, Mishael, I will receive under its seal.

Yeshua, the fraud addressing me, hung from his tree like one nearly dead. Some women down the hill, crook-fingering among themselves, ignored the pitch-and-churn of the oncoming pall to grapple upslope toward us. Their garments popped like flags, their voices flew away in the windy babel. From another part of the road, a man—one of Yeshua's unreliable cronies—made his own slow trek upward.

—How trust you? I asked Yeshua in the inward speech he'd just advised. Even an ignorant village sorcerer could pick the mind of one nailed to a post.

—Split a log and I am there, Yeshua said nonsensically. Pick up a stone and I sparkle in its seams.

—But nothing in you sparkles of the Messiah. How trust you, Nazarene, when I know even the Father for a lie?

A shrieking gust rattled our posts in their sockets and tore Yeshua's robe from Priscus's neck. It flapped down the back of Golgotha like a market thief fleeing a pack of angry vendors. The man climbing toward us caught the robe on his outstretched arm and clutched it to him.

—Whoever curses the Father may find forgiveness, Yeshua said, as may that person who curses me. But whoever blasphemes the Holy Spirit will discover forgiveness neither in this city nor in the lasting one to come.

"A dog returns to its vomit," I said. "And the fool to his folly."

Priscus considered poking me again, but refrained when the women struggling uphill on one path and the robe-clutching man doing so on another had drawn close enough to hail Yeshua even over the wind's keening. In fact, Priscus retrieved the robe he'd diced for. With his centurion's approval, he even let the interlopers linger amidst our posts. They regarded me—when they looked up at me at all—as if I'd fallen among them from a shadow kingdom of demons and blights.

—What happens at the end? I asked Yeshua. What becomes of us, when the world has dwindled into a carcass?

—Do you know the beginning, Mishael, that you can ask so beseechingly after the end?

—Yeshua, I can't help but ask.

—In our end is our beginning.

—I beg you, riddle me not.

—Whoever stands at the beginning stands blessed.

—My blood flows out. And my strength.

—For whoever stands at the beginning will fully comprehend the end. Even dying, that one will live.

Out of aching rage, I cried, *"Demons take you!"*

—Mishael, you knew me at the first. Here, you hang with me in the extremity of my sacrifice. Give over your taunts and die into the beginning.

Riddles! How had I known Yeshua "at the first"? I rolled my balding pate against the upright and shut my burning eyes. The Mount of Olives, the Temple, the Antonia Fortress—all now lay under a bruised-lavender fleece of clouds. This buckling, sky-borne fleece was visible to me even with my eyes closed. I could feel the oddly freshening winds and hear above Golgotha the expectant cries of carrion birds.

Yeshua spoke aloud, "Woman, look upon your son." I opened my eyes. Yeshua didn't mean for the woman to look at *him*, but at the male lackey who had just arrived. To this bearded man, Yeshua said, "And, you, embrace your mother."

Obediently, the lackey pulled the woman to him (her pinched face briefly seemed a window on a younger self, but only for an instant) and helped her back down the hillside to the road we doomed captives had earlier stumbled out on. Weeping, the other three women tripped along behind them, but stopped at some distance and refused to move even another cubit toward Jerusalem.

"I thirst," Yeshua said.

"Wait for the rain," Priscus said.

But his superior, the centurion, put a sponge on his spear tip, thrust it into an amphora of spoiled wine, and lifted it to Yeshua's lips.

Yeshua leaned his head to mouth the sponge, sipped from it feebly, then turned his head aside. The purple on his lips trickled down his chin into the raw gulley of his breastbone.

"It's over." Almost at once, Yeshua slumped from the nails driven between his wrist bones, and his body hung like a plucked fowl tied to a stake.

"Has his spirit left him?" called one of the women.

"The bastard's dead!" Priscus shouted down to her, and the women, after briefly conferring, trotted toward the city gate through the first cold knives of rain.

A thunderclap sundered the air, a ram's horn trumpet blew from an eastern wall, and Golgotha shrugged like a leviathan rolling under a Roman freighter. Our execution posts shunted upward, dropped, tilted out of true.

Reuel screamed. The centurion, Priscus, and a legionary named Macer fell with a single cry on the laced leather strips of their body armor. Then the centurion glanced up in awe at Yeshua and said something lilting and unintelligible. Priscus, on the other hand, jumped up and pricked Yeshua under the ribs with his spear. As if he'd just split a wine skin, blood and water gushed out.

It was about the ninth hour of the day. Passover torrents rattled the olive groves, beat upon the city's pavements, and pocked the grassless hillsides. I lifted my eyes bemusedly to this downpour.

—Taste the rain and I am on your tongue, a voice told me. Sanctify the end and a beginning comes to birth.

Three muddy legionaries stood at an awkward remove, eyeing Reuel and me with glum dutifulness. The rain had stopped. The thunderhead had pulled itself threadbare, revealing in the east several fringy blue armlets. Yeshua had died, but Reuel and I still clung in our pain and contumely to the afternoon's last daylight. Such fires crackled in my bones and along my sinews, however, that I would have gladly let go of my life.

A fresh squad of soldiers from the Antonia Fortress slogged out of the city and up the hillside.

The squad's leader said, "Rufilius, we've come to break their legs. The Jews don't want them to die out here on their plaguey Sabbath."

"Go ahead," Priscus said. "The sooner I get off this muddy hill the better."

The centurion Rufilius said, "Omit the one in the middle. His spirit's left him."

"Already?" said the leg-breakers' leader. "Didn't last long for a king, did he?"

The soldiers wondered about Yeshua's short time aloft. He must have had some hidden illness. He must have had more woman to him than man. Or maybe fear had cleft his heart.

Rufilius stepped away from the others. "Get on with it!" he barked.

The men drew lots for the honor of using the hammer. A big kid named Capito won. He teased Priscus about the mud-flecked robe he'd won dicing. A true Roman would rather win a hammer swing than any piece of a Hebrew's womanish garb. A legionary named Strabo produced a wine skin, and all of them but Rufilius drank from it.

Reuel groaned weakly. This drew the soldiers' attention, and Capito, hefting the mallet, stumbled over to Reuel's post and smashed his legs below the knee with two or three wayward blows. Reuel cried out.

But only once. His feet slipped clear of the *stipes*, and the weight of his body dragged down his lungs, to keep him from groaning more.

"Capito, you don't know what you're doing," said Priscus, laughing.

"Then what better way for me to learn?"

The road to the city gate had begun to fill once more with hawkers, pilgrims, onlookers. The Passover camps teemed again with life. The curious stood huddled on the road's margin, gaping up at our little forest and the haphazard doings of the legionaries. More of Yeshua's followers had gathered in the storm's wake than had visited Golgotha during the brunt of his agony. As before, women outnumbered men.

"So, Mishael, what thievery brought you to this shameful pass?" Capito asked me in clumsy Aramaic.

"A l-l-lamb," I said.

"A lamb?"

Priscus laughed scornfully. "Sacrificial animals. Lambs, goats, rams, doves, pigeons."

"Oh, so he stole offerings meant for the stiff-necked God of the Jews?" Capito looked up at me again. "Good for you. Such treachery deserves a boon."

A boon? I thought.

Capito broke only my right leg—with a crisp, well-placed strike of the mallet head. I yelped and cursed, then slumped whimpering through gritted teeth.

At length, though, as the legionaries busied themselves drinking and pointing out pretty female pilgrims to slander, I got my good leg under me and lifted myself against my tree's upright, easing the tax on my lungs. In fact, in this way, I could go on breathing. In, out; in, out—each gasping breath a stab and a hiss.

—I am the vine, the vinedresser, the vintager, the wine.

No one but me, I think, heard this new riddle. The guards, except for Rufilius, were bickering like street urchins; Reuel, meanwhile, had strangled to death a scant half hour after the breaking of his legs.

Flies tiptoed through my sweat. Cooking smoke curled into my eyes and nostrils.

—I am the wheat, the gleaner, the baker, the bread.

This riddle pricked me. In the hour before sunset, a party of Jews came toiling up Golgotha. Two thickset, well-dressed elderly men led it. Two younger men followed with a cart, behind which marched four or five women. The cart held an assortment of stoppered earthenware vessels and a pile of clean linen strips.

"I have permission from Pilate to take away the Nazarene's body," said the richer-looking of the two old Jews. He showed his authorization to Rufilius.

"And who are you?" said Rufilius, squinting at it.

"Joseph of Arimathea."

Yeshua's other disciples—if they warranted that title—refused to name themselves. The women wept audibly, while the old Pharisee standing next to the Arimathean gazed up at Yeshua with a look of heavy strickenness.

"I don't care if you take them all," Rufilius said. "Just be quick about it."

The young men who'd pulled the cart, with the bumbling help of Joseph and his portly friend, uprooted the central tree and lowered it hand over hand to the ground. They used a metal claw to draw the spikes from Yeshua's wrists, then carried his body to the cart bed. The women treated the most visible signs of his scourging with aloes and myrrh, rubbed him from crown to foot with spices, and bound him as they would a baby in linen ribbons very like swaddling clothes. This last sight recalled to me the face of Yeshua's mother, and not only from that moment just before the thunderstorm.

"Bread," I said to myself. "House of bread."

"This man lives," the old Pharisee said. "Less than an hour till sunset and he lives."

Out of respect for the coming Sabbath, Priscus offered to kill me with his spear. The Pharisee snorted and appealed directly to Rufilius.

"Once you've broken their legs," he said, "the law says you forfeit any further right to help them die."

"*Whose* law?—Capito, break that thief's other leg."

"It's too late for that," the Pharisee said. "Because the Sabbath nears, you must yield him to whoever comes to take him down."

"He'll die within hours anyway," Rufilius said.

"Then why not allow us to spare you the bother of disposing of him?"

"Let them have their *king*," Priscus said. "Let them have all three. Who's to question your report, sir?"

Yeshua's death had awed and then dispirited Rufilius. "All right. Take them." He formed up his men (both his own guards and the late-arriving squad of leg-breakers) and marched them downhill in a tipsy gaggle. They chanted smutty cadences all the way to the city gate.

"Call me Nicodemus, Mishael of Hebron," the Pharisee said. "I think perhaps you've paid for your thievery."

As they'd brought down Yeshua, they brought me down. (They also soon reclaimed the body of Reuel.) They washed me as best they could and placed me gently in the cart. A secluded garden of tombs bordered the execution site, and Joseph of Arimathea asked Yeshua's cronies to cart us there, there to lay Yeshua and Reuel in a pair of tombs of Joseph's ownership.

I rode to the tombs beside the two dead men, and at every lurch I gasped. The work of the soldiers' whips had left my back a map of welts and ridges.

"A scourging, nearly ten hours on the tree, a broken leg, and the man still lives," Nicodemus said. "Is this the rabbi's last sign?"

"He would've done better to work it on his own behalf," the woman said.

Nicodemus and his wife, with the help of an awkward boy of twelve or so, lowered me into the lustral bath in the cloister of their comfortable house in Jerusalem. Rainwater helped feed this mikveh. Because of the recent storm, then, it shimmered and brimmed as I went down into it. Nicodemus's wife scooped a pair of leaves and the husk of a dead wasp from the surface and departed with the boy. I sat unsteadily on the lowest of the mikveh's three stone steps as the cool water nibbled at me like schools of tender fish.

"We should have that leg tended to," Nicodemus said.

"Not now. Just this. Thank you."

"I'm astonished you're able to support yourself at all, Mishael, even with the water to buoy you. Yeshua and that other man died out there—yet you look old enough to have sired even the unjustly condemned Nazarene."

The Sabbath had arrived. A torch in the cloister rippled in smoky reds and oranges in the surface of my bath. Nicodemus was of two minds about my presence in his mikveh. That I had entered it to soothe my body rather than to cleanse my spirit troubled him. Seated on a stone bench nearby (ready to rescue me if I fainted and slipped all the way under), he talked to cover my silences and to distract himself from the grief rising in him. Mostly, he talked of Yeshua. His voice laved me as the water did, as if lapping me from the coast of an unexplored country.

". . . of water and the spirit," he said at length.

Those words, quietly uttered, slapped like a wave. "You've built an idol in your heart to Yeshua," I said.

Nicodemus took a moment to reply. "At the moment he died, the curtain in the Temple tore from top to bottom."

"Who told you that?"

"A person I trust." The torchlight reflected in Nicodemus's eyes made him seem both younger and weaker. "Touched by the rabbi's words and deeds, I visited him one night to ask him about one of his teachings. Answering, he implied that he was God's incarnate son, sent expressly to die for us."

"I almost died for myself," I said. "And Reuel surely died for Reuel. In his case, Yeshua's dying made no difference. Am I to believe that everyone else will live forever?"

Nicodemus shrugged.

"Another question: How may that which does not exist call into existence a 'son'?"

It took a moment for Nicodemus to absorb this strange—indeed, unheard of—notion. "Your words pollute my mikveh, Mishael." He didn't try to to evict me from it, however, but perched there like an ugly plaster statue of himself.

"Yeshua's mother looked . . . very human," I said.

"And why not? She is."

"Her face and the Arimathean's burial clothes reminded me that I once saw her cradling Yeshua as an infant." My head felt light as a sea medusa's bladder.

Nicodemus rose to his feet. "Don't mock me, thief. I already doubt the wisdom, if not the good-neighborliness, of bringing you to my home."

"No mockery," I said. "I once saw your incarnate Son of God as a baby, his butt cheeks rash-mottled and his swaddling clothes wringing and smeared."

"Explain this," Nicodemus said.

While I explained Nicodemus paced his cloister.

In Hebron, I was orphaned at twelve. I fed myself by doing hundreds of petty errands and sometimes even cutting purses. In the countryside, I pruned vines, tended sheep, and harvested wheat. A lustful vintner from Herodium used me for two years as his catamite. At fifteen, I broke free and turned to thievery for my livelihood.

One spring, in open pastureland, I chanced upon a shepherd who told me of a couple from Galilee who, for some bothersome Roman administrative reason, had gone afoot and donkeyback to a nearby village. There the woman had given birth. My informant and several other shepherds had befriended the couple, carrying them water, figs, dates, and portions of hot-spiced lamb. They kept this up for two or three days, embarrassed and angered by the lack of hospitality that most of their fellow Bethlehemites had shown the travelers. If I was hungry, the shepherd said, I should call upon these people. They had leftover food aplenty and errands that I could run to repay them for sharing it with me.

I found the woman (in truth, a girl only a bit older than me) and her grizzled husband sunning themselves on a ledge in front of the limestone hole where they had taken shelter after villager after villager had rebuffed them. Their ribby donkey colt grazed downslope in a stand of thistles. They gave me bread, cheese, raisins, and some savory lamb. I clearly recall the donkey in the thistles, the food, and the couple's candid, undemonstrative friendliness—but I can't, today, recall their names. This was over thirty years ago and, in my wanderings to that point, landmarks and raw luck had always meant more to me than people and their uncertain alms.

I stayed two days with the Galileans, gathering firewood, grooming the donkey colt, washing their infant son's wrappings and laying them out on the rocks to dry. Once, I even went into the village with the halt-footed husband so that he could fulfill some undone part of the registration procedure.

That night, back from this tiresome chore, I lay down in a corner and slept. Twice, at least, the baby woke me crying, obviously indifferent to the notion that God might prefer his human heir to behave with rabbinical dignity, even in a cave. The mother quieted her very babylike infant by slipping it an inflamed-looking nipple.

The next day, the couple had me watch their child in the cave while, outside, they put balm on a running sore on the donkey's withers and loaded the animal with their belongings. I've never liked babies much. They make too much noise, a lot of it mysterious or silly. This one, lying in a stone trough lined with straw, followed me with eyes as lively as a pair of dungball-pushing beetles. It prated an abracadabra babble and puffed out its cheeks. When it began to fuss, focusing on me with an acuity I had never seen in a newborn, I went to it and undid the linen straps in which its mother had so tightly wound it.

Outside, to protest its loading, the donkey reared, brayed, and sliced the husband's robe with one quicksilver forehoof. Then, ducking its head, it trotted downslope, heedless of the man and woman's shouts. When they chased it, I looked about the cave for some unpacked item to take. All that presented itself was a delicate cedar box that held, I discovered, a single gold ingot small enough to rest on my palm. I carried the box outside and hid it in a thorny shrub.

The baby, free of its swaddling, began to thrash and wail. I hurried back inside to calm it. It shut up as soon as it saw me hovering over it. Its eyes—how to say this?—had the cunning glitter of a very old man's; they also had a kind of pity-filled gaiety, a gentleness that struck to my very heart—like an adz head, or an insult.

I pinched the baby's nose with two fingers and pulled its head out of the straw, then let go of its nose so that its head dropped back with a jolting bounce. The baby made a dovelike murmur. I grabbed one of its big toes and twisted it. This time the baby voiced a yelp, which grew into an insucking cry that brought its parents running.

"Shhhhh," I went. "Shhhhh, shhhhh, shhhhh."

The naked baby continued to wail. I grabbed it up from its feed-trough manger. Afraid that it would either pee on or spit up all over me, I quickly turned it around, suspending it over the cave floor with its pudgy arms outstretched and its bony feet adangle. This pose so surprised the baby that it shut up, hiccoughing rather than screaming. At that moment, though, its mother ducked inside.

"He dirtied himself again, mistress," I said. "But I've taken care of it. See. He needed air."

(The look on that child-woman's face appeared again today on the face of Yeshua's mother.)

She said, "Mishael, give him to me," and took the baby out of my hands. She cradled it against her shoulder, examined it, cooed to it. "Now, leave."

So I did, surprising, as I darted out, both the woman's husband and their well-laden donkey colt.

Later, after the couple had left for Jerusalem for their son's circumcision, I returned to the hills for the hidden cedar box and the gold ingot inside it.

"An incredible story," Nicodemus said. "But for your sake, I hope you lie."

"No."

"Then I fear you pollute not only my mikveh but also the rabbi's sojourn on Golgotha."

"Neither of us knows the end of that story."

"You know nothing at all, Mishael."

"Whoever stands at the beginning will fully comprehend the end."

"You comprehend nothing."

"Perhaps your Nazarene is who he said he was."

"He's dead, isn't he?"

"In our end is our beginning." For the first time, this saying made sense to me.

"He *died* up there!" Nicodemus said in heartfelt anguish.

"Hallow the end and a beginning comes to birth."

"Dead, dead, dead, dead, dead!" Nicodemus had removed the belt of his tunic. With each word, he flicked the belt into his mikveh, right under my face: pock, pock, pock, pock, pock. "And you, man, deserve no boon at all!"

"Of water and the spirit," I said.

With one well-placed blow of his hammer, Capito broke my other leg. Not long after that, I hobbled across.